Praise for
State of Decay

"Knapp's intense debut is a high-adrenaline thriller that takes the familiar zombie story down a radically new path. . . . [His] writing is sharp and his fast and furious plot twists keep the pages turning. . . . Fans of zombie fiction and readers looking for a good thrill will find it here." —*Publishers Weekly*

"Will appeal to readers who like Jonathan Maberry's zombie thriller *Patient Zero*, and fans of gritty SF author Richard K. Morgan (*Altered Carbon*) will enjoy it as well. Highly recommended." —*Library Journal*

ALSO BY JAMES KNAPP

STATE OF DECAY

THE SILENT ARMY

JAMES KNAPP

A ROC BOOK

ROC

Published by New American Library, a division of
Penguin Group (USA) Inc., 375 Hudson Street,
New York, New York 10014, USA
Penguin Group (Canada), 90 Eglinton Avenue East, Suite 700, Toronto,
Ontario M4P 2Y3, Canada (a division of Pearson Penguin Canada Inc.)
Penguin Books Ltd., 80 Strand, London WC2R 0RL, England
Penguin Ireland, 25 St. Stephen's Green, Dublin 2,
Ireland (a division of Penguin Books Ltd.)
Penguin Group (Australia), 250 Camberwell Road, Camberwell, Victoria 3124,
Australia (a division of Pearson Australia Group Pty. Ltd.)
Penguin Books India Pvt. Ltd., 11 Community Centre, Panchsheel Park,
New Delhi - 110 017, India
Penguin Group (NZ), 67 Apollo Drive, Rosedale, North Shore 0632,
New Zealand (a division of Pearson New Zealand Ltd.)
Penguin Books (South Africa) (Pty.) Ltd., 24 Sturdee Avenue,
Rosebank, Johannesburg 2196, South Africa

Penguin Books Ltd., Registered Offices:
80 Strand, London WC2R 0RL, England

First published by Roc, an imprint of New American Library,
a division of Penguin Group (USA) Inc.

First Printing, October 2010
10 9 8 7 6 5 4 3 2 1

For Kim

ACKNOWLEDGMENTS

Big credit to my test readers, editor, and copyeditor, who help me be the best I can.

Also, to the mouse who lived in my wall and wouldn't stop chewing the woodwork. You kept me awake and made me write. I'm sorry one of my cats ate you.

1

Smolder

Nico Wachalowski — Royal Plaza Hotel

Some things you never forget. For me, the thing I couldn't leave alone was the way Faye looked at me just before the panel slammed shut between us. I remembered the fire raging behind her when I took her by the arm. When she pushed me away, her hand was cold. The big revivor shoved me back, and when the panel started to close, she looked me in the eye. I was sure an automaton couldn't have looked at me like that. It was the last time I ever saw her.

"Revivors aren't people," someone had once said to me. "Remember that."

"I know what they are," I had answered.

But I didn't.

Everything should have been different. If I couldn't save her, I should have at least put her to rest. I never should have done what I did. The Leichenesser would have destroyed her body, but I'd removed the capsule myself. The soldiers didn't get her either. When I had my chance to put an end to it, I couldn't. I put her right into the hands of Samuel Fawkes.

The rain was beating down, streaking diagonally across the glow of the one remaining streetlight. The hotel across the street was dark. It hadn't been occupied in years and no one had come or gone for hours, but it wasn't empty. The satellite confirmed it was tapping power off the grid, and had identified multiple heat signatures inside. Someone was there.

A message from the SWAT leader came in over my JZ implant. The words floated in front of the fogged windshield.

They're inside. We're just waiting on confirmation.

Things stayed quiet after the attacks, at first. For a week or two, revivors were news again, and images of their reanimated corpses stalking the streets alongside the National Guard circulated day and night. The questions the government didn't want anyone asking got asked again as people looked at the images and wondered what signing up for revivor status really meant. The footage of the walking-dead soldiers so close up disturbed them, and for a while they wondered, Was avoiding third-tier status while keeping out of the grinder really worth becoming one of them? There were protests and debates and investigations, until public opinion tired of the whole thing and the buzz moved out to the fringe, where it was mostly forgotten. It wasn't until two months ago that, out of nowhere, a bomb went off at the Concrete Falls recruitment center, where they did most of the city's Posthumous Service signups. Despite the initial backlash against revivors, the facility was turning bigger numbers than ever. The economy tanked, and holdouts were lining up to trade their third-tier status for second. A spike in PS recruits put numbers at a five-year high. Concrete Falls had supplied the military with greater numbers of revivors than anywhere else in the country, but not anymore. No one claimed responsibility.

It had been a dead end until the group moved again. Information trolled off the communications networks suggested another high-profile strike was being organized, and this time we caught it early. No target had been confirmed, but both the seller and the buyer were involved in the previous bombing—I was sure of it. A shipment of heavy explosives had been smuggled into the country, to Royal Plaza, where it was about to change hands. There was a lot of pressure to put a name, any name, to the Concrete Falls attack, and to bring the people in.

My old friend and tech man, Sean Pu, was the one who tracked them down. The two of us went way back, having served together in the grind. He'd saved my life back then, and two times since. He had a big interest in the case, and for some reason he didn't want me on it. Something had him nervous and although he never said anything, another agent, Mike Vesco, was brought in to take point. I was being edged out completely, until wiretaps uncovered illegal revivors at the site.

Sean had saved my life three times, but two years ago things had become more complicated; Sean turned out to be something other than what I thought he was, something he'd hidden very well. I always thought he was my right-hand man, but it turned out I was wrong, and it was the other way around. I was his right hand, and he used me as a fist that he sometimes struck hard with. The fact that he kept up that lie for so long didn't jibe with what I knew about him. I hadn't decided yet where we stood.

Whatever his reasons, he wanted me kept out of this one, but impounding revivors on UAC soil still fell into my jurisdiction. After Fawkes's attack, no one wanted revivors in the city. If he decided to keep me involved, it was because he thought he could control me. I wondered how much longer that would last.

A helicopter floated between the buildings high overhead. The hotel was being monitored from the air, and the scanner had isolated twelve voices inside.

This is Vesco. We have confirmation. The shipment and the buyer are both on-site. At least six revivors are confirmed inside as well.

Roger that.

Move into position, I told them.

I pushed open the door and stepped out into the rain. Sticking to the shadows, I headed toward the building.

Wait for my signal.

The building's layout was projected via my implant back onto my retinas so that it glowed softly against the dark alleyway. I pinpointed the revivor signatures, and placed them over the map. Most of them were on the first floor.

Up ahead, under a rusted fire escape, a fire exit led inside. I flashed my badge at the scanner there, issuing a federal override and suppressing any alarm they had rigged. A light on its plastic housing flickered and turned green. When the bolt snapped, I drew my gun and went inside.

I pulled the door shut, blocking the sound of the rain behind it. Inside it was dark. I adjusted my visual filter to let in more light and looked around.

I'm in.

There was a swinging door ahead of me, and I pushed it open into an old kitchen area. Thermal signatures from rats scattered when I stepped through, and disappeared into the walls. The short-order line was covered in grease and dust, with spiderwebs stretched between stray pots and pans that still hung over it. Brown water had collected in one corner near a crack in the wall.

They're working out of the large, highlighted area, Sean said. *I'm still trying to pinpoint the shipment.*

Understood.

The area he referred to might have been a restaurant or bar at one time. Corridors headed off in four directions from there, three of them flanked by small hotel rooms. Five of those rooms had a revivor signature inside.

Opening the kitchen door a crack, I used a backscatter filter to peer into the walls on the other side. There were two cameras hidden behind the tiles there, one watching the kitchen and one watching a corridor to the left.

I've got some security here. Visuals will be offline for a minute.

Roger.

The baffle screen would disrupt the cameras, but also my internal recording buffer. They'd send someone to check out the disturbance, but I didn't need long.

I slipped past the camera and headed down the corridor. There were a few rooms on the south side of the area. Two of the rooms had revivor signatures present.

I'm past the cameras and heading into the room on the right. You see it?

I have you.

I listened at the door but didn't hear anyone inside. Sticking close to the wall, I reached out and tried the knob. It was locked.

Give me an override on the door.

Done.

I showed my badge to the scanner and the bolt clicked. No one inside moved or spoke. Using the back-scatter, I looked through the door. No one was waiting on the other side.

I pushed open the door and slipped through. There were more cameras mounted in the ceiling but they were turned away, watching the bed.

We're picking up some activity in there. How long, Wachalowski?

Not long.

The hotel room was lit by simulated candlelight. As soon as I was inside, I caught a blast of perfume and damp air. There was a water stain on the far wall where a strip of wallpaper had been torn away. The bed was made and the blankets turned down. The revivor signature was coming from the bathroom.

Moving into the room, I noticed something under the bed.

Hold on.

Across from the foot of the bed I saw the revivor through the open bathroom door. It was standing in the dark with its back to me, looking into the mirror over the sink. It was female, with stick-thin legs and a pair of sheer briefs hanging from a flat behind. It wore a wig the color of bubblegum.

I got down on one knee and looked under the bed. In the shadows, I saw a pair of bare feet, toes down.

"She put her there," the revivor said from the bathroom. When I looked, it still had its back to me.

I grabbed the ankles, and the skin was cold. Keeping out of range of the cameras, I dragged a second female revivor out from under the bed. It didn't have a signature.

"Who did?" I asked. In the bathroom, the revivor just kept staring in the mirror. I left the body and moved in behind it.

SWAT, get ready to move on my mark.

Roger.

I came within a foot of it, until I saw its eyes reflected back in the mirror. It had a pair of large, bare breasts thrust out in front of it with the characteristic dark gray nipples and black veins tracing the curves. Underneath them, ribs stood out, and down the middle of its back, I could see the knobs of its spine. When I leaned in, I caught a whiff of decomposition underneath heavy perfume. Wherever the thing was made, it was a botch job. The inhibitors were failing, and the body was beginning to rot.

"Who put the revivor under there?" I asked.

"She did."

I blinked hard, deactivating the JZI. For a few seconds, I'd be completely offline. The revivor looked at me in the mirror, and met my eye.

"Am I for you?" it asked. I spun it around so it was facing me. I took a photograph from inside my jacket and held it in front of its face.

"Have you seen this woman?" I asked it.

"It's a revivor."

"I know that. Have you seen her?"

"No."

"Do you know the name Faye Dasalia?"

The factory fire where I'd last seen her burned for three months straight. When it finally died down to the point where it could be scrubbed, there was nothing left. There was no way to know if Faye or any of the other revivors had come out of there intact, or where they'd gone if they had.

It looked up from the picture, focusing on me again. "I don't know that name."

I blinked and the JZI reinitialized. Before it could say anything else, I touched the scanner to the back of its neck and squeezed the contact, firing a wire filament up into the spine. It made contact with the primary revivor's node, and the body went rigid for a second before it went limp. I caught it as it started to fall.

Sean, Vesco, I have a connection.

You dropped. What happened?

That was Vesco. He'd been keeping an eye on me, a little too closely. Someone had their hooks in him.

Repeat: you dropped. What happened?

Cut the chatter and wait for my signal.

The revivor felt cold through my wet shirt. Hoisting it up, I eased it back into the bathtub.

The data miner started boring through the security they'd installed on it. A central command was being used to control them, which meant they needed an open connection to each revivor. A centralized hub like that, in the hands of an amateur, could allow access to all their systems if you made a direct connection with one of the revivor nodes. I was counting on that.

On the edge of my peripheral vision I could see audio waves piped in from the eye in the sky. The analyzer was pulling out three voices spiking over the haze of conversation. They were coming from the basement level, where a second group of revivors were located.

The miner drilled down and opened a channel. Using the JZI, I joined the revivor network.

Node count: eleven.

Five upstairs. The rest had moved to the basement. The link went green, and I tapped into the central node.

They'd put plenty of security on all the typical channels, but sure enough, the revivor spokes were wide open.

I'm in.

Moving in now.

I started pulling the files. Less than ten seconds later, I heard a boom that vibrated through the floor. The audio being monitored spiked, and I heard shouting as footsteps tromped down the hallway. The last of the files came through, and I broke the connection to the revivor.

The door opened and a man came through, pointing an automatic pistol. I fired twice and he pitched back, his gun clattering across the floor.

"This way!" someone yelled from outside.

I picked up the pistol and handed it to a SWAT officer as I stepped back out into the hallway. Several more of them had men under armed guard.

"This is a raid! Get on the ground now!"

Down the hall, uniformed men were holding rifles on three guys. Two were in sports jackets and the last was in his underwear, holding a balled-up bedsheet to his chest. Mike Vesco waded through the mess, holding up his badge.

"Drop it and get down!"

"Step away from the—"

A high-pitched hiss blasted through the air back in what used to be the hotel lounge. Behind the bar a white light flared up as smoke blew through the seams of a computer chassis.

"Get an extinguisher over there, goddamn it!"

Watch those exits.

Down a side hall, hotel room doors were hanging open as SWAT cleared the rooms. Through one of the

doorways I saw an overweight, middle-aged man standing naked with his hands up. A revivor was bound on the
floor next to the bed, gagged and handcuffed.

Do we have a lock on the shipment?

Negative.

In the next room down was the only guy who hadn't
gotten caught with his pants down. He was an Asian
man, dressed to the nines, with an expensive watch and
long, thick hair. He was sitting on the edge of the bed,
unconcerned. There was no revivor with him.

Who is this guy? I asked Sean.

He's not involved.

How do you know that, Sean? Who is he?

No one. Come on, leave the pervs for Vesco.

When I scanned his face, I found him in the system.
His name was Hiro Takanawa, and he was as rich as he
looked. It looked like it wasn't the first time he'd been
caught paying for time with a revivor.

"Where'd the revivor go?" I asked him.

He shrugged. "I don't see one here," he said. "Do
you?"

I didn't. I shoved open the bathroom door and looked
in, but it was empty.

SWAT, how many revivors are accounted for?

*We got four, plus the two defunct in the room where
you found them.*

I checked the remaining signatures. There were six
more beneath the floor somewhere, down on the basement level. Six up here, and six below. One was already
defunct when I got there, so that put the node count at
eleven. That was all of them.

"Which one was with you?" I said to Takanawa. He
just shrugged.

"Understood," Vesco said into his radio. He turned

to Takanawa. "All right, you. Get out of here. Sorry, Wachalowski, that comes straight from the top. Let him go."

Takanawa stood up and walked calmly toward the door. He gave me a wave over his shoulder as he headed out the door.

Sean, who is that guy?

He's no one, Nico. Leave it alone.

The particle analyzer's picked up the chemical signature, Vesco said. *The explosive materials are nearby.*

Takanawa headed down the hallway, hands in his pockets and a cigarette already in his mouth. He left a thin trail of smoke as he turned the corner.

In spite of whatever else he might be into, I trusted Sean; I'd known him too long and watched him put his life on the line too many times not to. He'd earned a certain amount of faith from me, but he knew more than he was saying. He knew who Takanawa was, and he knew why he'd been released. I suspected he might know Takanawa personally.

On a hunch, I followed him. Moving away from the crowd, I hung back and followed the heat traces left behind by his footsteps. They led down a dark corridor to an emergency stairwell.

Vesco, I'm heading down to deal with the remaining six revivors.

Roger that.

Have SWAT just keep the others together for now.

A metal door slammed down below, and I eased the door open and slipped through after Takanawa. The stairs took me down a dark, musty corridor. More rats scrambled as I came through, and I pushed the light filter up until everything turned black and white. The sounds of the raid faded behind me, then were gone altogether.

Up ahead there was a stairwell door. His handprint was cooling on the handle.

Got it, Vesco said. *We've secured the explosives. Bomb squad, prepare for transport.*

Nico, I'll move a team downstairs. Wait for them. That was Sean.

I pushed open the door and started down the stairwell. It was pitch-black, but on the landing below I could see the other side of the door was lit. Just then, the audio spiked as someone shouted on the other side. Six revivor signatures glowed on the scanner.

Nico—

I cut the connection. As I went through the door, I heard voices from down the long, cinderblock corridor. The far end opened into a storage area that was lit with floodlights. Chain-link enclosures were assembled there, each one with a naked revivor sitting in it. Each revivor was shackled with a collar that was chained to the fence.

"... want to think about getting out of here," I heard Takanawa say.

A woman's voice answered, "I didn't expect to see you so soon."

"They're here."

The thermal footprints I was following skipped for a second. A few steps later, the glitch happened again as more rats scurried down the hall.

"Leave them alone," the woman said up ahead.

Around the corner, I saw Takanawa standing in front of a good-looking woman in an expensive suit. There was a metal briefcase on a desk next to her, lying open. Inside I saw a series of boxes, each the size of a brick, nestled in a bed of black packing foam. One of the slots was empty, and Takanawa held the box in his hand.

"Hard to believe they're so small," he said.

"Put it back, and get out of here already."

He slipped the box in his jacket pocket instead. She made a face and reached over, slamming the case shut.

"What about you?" he asked. "Aren't you coming?"

"Shortly. Go."

He shrugged and stepped out of view. A service door began to grind open.

Keeping low, I moved in as the door began rattling shut again. When I looked around the corner, I saw Takanawa's expensive shoes just before the door came down. A green light on the wall turned red as the lock engaged.

"There you are," a man said from somewhere off to my right, his voice echoing in the open space. Three sets of footsteps were approaching the woman. She crossed her arms and leaned back on the desk, waiting.

"Yes, here I am."

Two men in suits came into view, tailed by a big revivor.

"The fucking Feds are here," one of them said. "You wouldn't know anything about that, would you?"

She drew a pistol from inside her jacket fast enough to surprise both men. The first shot caught the man who'd just spoken in the face, and his head jerked back. The next hit the other man in the side. He staggered, and managed to draw his gun as she shot him a second time.

I crossed in front of the chain-link cages, my weapon drawn.

"Federal agent!"

"What the fuck are you doing?" the bleeding man grunted to the revivor that was with him. "Kill her!"

He went down on the floor next to his friend. The

big revivor stepped over them, toward the woman. It reached out and grabbed a fistful of her shirt as she shot it three times in the chest. Her heels came up off the floor as it hauled her forward, then slammed her back down on the desk.

It grabbed her head in its hands and leaned in, baring its teeth. I fired a shot into its temple and it jumped back, letting her go. It swung one arm at the open air, black blood squirting from the hole as I put a second shot through its open mouth.

It gagged, black specks spraying from between its teeth, then fell onto its back. Its signature warbled, then blinked out.

The woman sat on the edge of the desk, wincing as she looked over at me. She still held her gun in one hand, pointed down at the floor.

"Who are you?" she asked.

The other revivors had started shaking their cages, trying to get out. The closest one had its face pushed into the chain-link, fingers straining through the holes as it ground its teeth.

"FBI."

"You with Sean?" she asked.

"Slide the gun over."

She did. I stopped it with my foot, then picked it up.

"Put your hands up."

She nodded, cracking her back and wincing again as she lifted her hands up over her head.

Scanning her, I didn't see any hidden weapons. She wasn't wired and didn't have any physical augmentations. Her face didn't match anything in the databases.

"What's your name?" I asked her.

"Jan Holst. Can I put my hands down?"

"What is that?" I asked her, nodding at the briefcase. She frowned, but didn't answer.

"Open it," I said.

She turned and keyed in the combination to the case, then lifted it open and stepped away. I looked inside, and a warning appeared in the JZI.

Radiation detected.

The particles were coming from the case. I looked through one of the bricks and saw it contained a metal capsule. Inside the shell were wires and components, tightly packed around a radioactive core. There were eleven devices inside.

"What are those?"

She sighed, crossing her arms. I closed the case and contacted the SWAT leader.

I found the rest of the revivors. Six total. One is down. Good.

I found something down here. I think it's what we're looking for.

We've secured the shipment, Wachalowski.

I don't think so. I'm looking at eleven nuclear devices. The suspect who was just released, Takanawa, may have a twelfth. We need to lock down this area now.

There was a pause on the other end of the connection that went on longer than it should have. I opened an emergency channel back to Assistant Director Noakes, and sent down an alert.

Agent Wachalowski, what's going on down there? he responded. I recorded the image and radiation signature of the case and transmitted it to him.

The buyers were here to pick up nuclear weapons. They're handheld, and at least one of them is moving. We need this whole block contained right now.

A terrorist alert went out and began branching down to response teams.

Understood. They're mobilizing now. Find that missing weapon.

"Are you the buyer?" I asked the woman. She didn't answer.

Just then a revivor spoke connection opened. I looked around for the source but couldn't find it. The signal hadn't come from any of the revivors in the cages.

Someone just opened a connection to a revivor band down here. Any missing from upstairs?

Negative.

It was close. Too close to be from upstairs.

I've got a stray down here somewhere.

"How did you know—" the woman started to ask but I held up my hand. She frowned.

I tapped into the signal, listening. The source was close by, somewhere in the room. I did a slow sweep, looking into the dark. No revivor's signature was showing up, but it had to be there.

I moved past the cages to the edge of the lit area and scanned into the shadows. There was nothing there.

. . . eral agent here.

The partial message came across the connection. It was a fragment of a text communication.

. . . should I abort?

No. Upgr . . . forget the target . . . the case.

. . . about the . . .

Kill her.

The revivors began shaking the cages harder. Something had them riled up. I couldn't hear anything over the racket.

"Shut up!" the woman snapped. "Just shut—"

Her voice cut out. I looked back at her and she was

clutching her throat. Her eyes were wide, and blood had started leaking from in between her fingers. The big revivor was still on its back. I didn't see anyone near her.

Vesco, one of the prime suspects is down. I need an EMT here, now.

I ran to her as she took her hands away. Her palms were covered in blood. Her face turned white as blood poured from a gash in her throat, and she slid down the desk, onto the floor.

"Hold on," I told her, easing her onto her back. "Help is coming." Her eyes lost focus. Her mouth moved, but she couldn't speak.

The revivor connection cut out. I heard the flutter of fabric next to me, and the case on the desk flickered, then disappeared.

Shit.

The nukes are moving. The target is cloaked. Coordinate with local authorities and initiate a lockdown in a three-block radius.

Leading with the gun, I scanned the room. There were no heat signatures, no heartbeat—nothing.

It's a revivor. . . . There was no revivor signature either, though. It was keeping itself well hidden.

I scanned for radiation. It was faint, but I found a concentration of particles a few feet away. They were clustered around an object floating at chest height.

The case. The Light Warping field could bend visible light, but not radiation. The pattern swayed back and forth slightly. The revivor connection opened again.

. . . about the agent?

. . . ut don't ki—

But—

Don't kill him.

I reestablished the link with Sean.

Wachalowski, what the hell—

Sean, show me all the ways in and out of here.

The case appeared on the concrete floor and I heard something heavy shift its weight. I took a step toward it, and a cold hand clamped down on the back of my neck, hard. It pulled me back onto my heels as another hand grabbed my wrist, slamming my gun hand into a support column. I caught a glimpse of the woman's face, flecked with blood, as I was dragged away from her.

Nico, what's happening? Vesco said. I could hear footsteps pounding down the hall in my direction.

Something connected hard with my cheek and I was spun around. One leg went out from under me, and I went facedown on the concrete. When I tried to get up, a boot landed between my shoulder blades and my chest slammed into the floor under it, forcing the wind out of me.

I need backup down here, now. Where the hell was SWAT?

The boot lifted and I heaved myself onto my hands and knees, firing a back kick blindly into something solid. Heavy footsteps staggered back and I swung around, pointing my gun.

Before I could pull the trigger, a sharp pain stabbed into the side of my neck and the strength went out of me. My arms got heavy and fell to my sides. The gun slipped out of my hand and clunked onto the floor. Toxin warnings flashed as I staggered and started to fall.

Smooth material brushed my face as someone darted past me. The case disappeared again, leaving only the radiation signature. The cluster of particles moved away quickly, fading away to nothing as they moved out of range.

It's doubling back the way I came in. Intercept it.

I went down on my knees, shaking. One of my internal stim packets popped as the JZI tried to cut through the fog. My stomach churned, and I had pins and needles in my legs as the feeling came back. I manually popped two more.

That did the trick. Everything got brighter. My heart pounded as oxygen and adrenaline flooded my bloodstream. I picked my gun back up and pushed myself to my feet, the room spinning around me.

The revivor had gone back down the corridor, but it had too much of a head start. If it left through the closest exit, then it would come out near the loading dock. I made for the freight entrance instead and slapped my palm on the button.

The stim wouldn't last long, but if I didn't beat him down there, it wouldn't matter anyway. The door began to rise on its track and I ducked through the gap, my muscles starting to tighten. It was getting hard to breathe. A cold gust of wind and rain hit me as I crossed the dock and slipped on the steps. People stopped on the sidewalk a few feet away from me and stared. Sirens had begun to wail, and I saw red-and-blue lights flash down the length of the street.

The map put me on the western side of the building. If the revivor made a run for it, it would be through the alley out back. Rain pummeled me as I tacked left past a pile of trash and between the buildings. Water was running down in a stream from a clogged gutter up ahead, and I headed toward it, looking for signs of the radiation signature. It was getting harder to move. The side of the building was veering away. I shook my head, trying to focus. Something splashed in a puddle near a pile of trash bags. I stood there, trying to keep my balance, and watched it.

Where is it?

Every time I took a breath, my chest got tighter. Looking back and forth down the alley, I didn't see anything.

It's gone. I missed it.

I watched the rain stream down from the gutter, splashing into a puddle formed around a crack in the pavement. The stims weren't working anymore. My arms and legs started to get heavy again.

I'm going to need a medic, Sean.

There was no answer. I was still staring at the water kicking up droplets when I realized the words never appeared in the HUD. I hadn't sent the message. The coupling to the JZI had dropped.

Sean?

The air blurred in front of me. The water was streaming in slow motion, and for just a second I saw it stop about five or six feet above the ground. Water sprayed off something I couldn't see; then it continued like it never happened.

Sean?

Something moved next to the pile of trash bags; then a dark shape flew toward me. A large plastic bag hit me and tore open, scattering garbage as I heard feet hit the pavement, running for the street.

"Stop!"

I couldn't get a bead on it. I lunged and felt cloth under my hand. I grabbed a fistful of it, but it slipped through my fingers as the footsteps moved away. My chest burned. When I took a step, my leg crumpled under me and I went down on the wet pavement.

From the blacktop, I could see the crowds of people moving down the sidewalk. Wind blew sheets of rain across the street as I watched them pass. One of them glanced over at me, but kept walking.

Everything was going blurry. The blind spot floating in front of my eyes started blooming, getting bigger until everything began to go dark.

The revivor had gotten away. Along with the one Takanawa had taken, twelve nuclear devices had just left the hotel and disappeared into the city.

Zoe Ott—Outside Empire Apartment Complex

I'd been sitting on the bench, watching it rain for, like, an hour, and even with an umbrella, it was pretty miserable. The slicker kept me mostly dry, but it was cold enough that I could see my breath coming out through my nose. I figured I'd probably end up getting sick. I don't know why I didn't just go home.

Everything had changed, back when I first met Nico. I still don't remember a lot of it, since I had been drinking nonstop then, but I know at some point I had gotten sucked into whatever he was involved in, and I almost got killed. A lot of it was a blur, but I remembered a revivor came into my house and dragged me away. My downstairs neighbor almost died trying to save me. Nico brought that woman—the one from my dreams—back to life, and she almost killed him. I think I might have actually killed someone myself.

After, when the FBI questioned me, I told them I didn't know anything. I made them believe me, and I went home. It seemed like a long time ago.

Nico kind of took me under his wing after that. He started bringing me to help with interrogations at the FBI, which, in a weird way, was kind of how we first met. No one knew how I got my results. They just knew I did. I got cleaned up, sort of, and got semiregular work there. I moved with Karen downstairs, and we got to be good friends. The roommate thing was doomed to fail, though, and I was back upstairs in four months. The drinking just got to her after a while, and she never said it, but I think the visions did too.

"I'm so stupid. . . ." I muttered, watching the rain fall.

The rain was supposed to go all week, I'd heard. It was so dark and gray all the time that most places kept their lights on even during the day. It was the most depressing time of year, and it was the first time I'd tried to face it when I wasn't drunk. So far, I'd hated every minute of it.

Something hissed next to me on the bench, and when I turned to look, I saw a woman sitting beside me. She was hunched over with her hair covering her face, and her coat was black and burned. When the rain hit her body, it sizzled, and smoke drifted off her. The ends of her sleeves still smoldered. She wasn't real.

They never were.

She didn't look at me. After a minute, she looked up at the apartment building across the street, and I saw her face was scalded and covered in soot. The rain that fell on her face turned black, streaming down her neck. She looked sick and in pain.

"Why?" she whispered.

A line of cars went by, almost splashing me. The last one in the row rolled to a stop and I saw it was a police car. When I looked back at the bench, I was alone again.

Great.

I waited to see if it would just drive off, but it didn't. The window went down and an officer with a square face and a mustache looked out at me. He waved for me to come over.

There was no point in trying to ignore him. I got up

and went over to the car. Warm air drifted out through the window, and I could smell his cologne when I leaned over.

"Evening, ma'am," he said.

"Hi."

"Hell of a night, huh?"

"I guess."

"Security camera has you watching that building for over an hour," he said. "You want to tell me why that is?"

"A friend lives there."

"A friend?"

"Yeah."

"If you know someone who lives there, why are you out here in the rain?"

"He didn't come home."

"Was your friend expecting you?"

He wasn't, but I didn't want to say that. I felt my face getting red. The cop sighed. He looked like he felt sorry for me.

"Okay," he said. "What's your friend's name?"

"Nico."

"Last name?"

"Wachalowski," I said. "Agent Nico Wachalowski."

He raised his eyebrows, and I could tell he didn't believe me.

"Hold on." He leaned back into the car and I saw the computer screen light up his face. He fiddled with it for a while and said something into his radio.

I looked back at the apartment building. His window was still dark. He said if I ever needed to talk to him I could, and I just needed to talk to him. I should have left when I saw he wasn't there, but I figured I'd wait a few minutes, and then, somewhere along the line, it turned into longer than that. I didn't even think about the security cameras. If he saw a recording of me standing out there, he'd think I was some kind of stalker or something.

The cop leaned over again. The expression on his face was a little different.

"How do you know Agent Wachalowski?" he asked.

"I work with him sometimes."

"Doing what?"

"It's classified."

He looked tired. "Lady—"

"I really do work with him sometimes. Look," I said, fishing out my contractor's badge. It had my picture on it. He looked between the picture and me for a minute.

"Look, ma'am, it's late. Other people live here besides just your friend, and I can't have you just hanging around watching the place from across the street because then I have to check it out. You get me?"

I shrugged.

"If you don't clear out, I'm going to have to come back and ask him about it directly. Is that going to be okay with you?"

My face got even hotter. He got that pity look again.

"Ma'am, come on. It's raining out—"

I focused on him and everything got bright around me. The raindrops looked crisp and sharp, like little pieces of ice, as they dripped off the edge of the umbrella between us. The lights came up around his head and I eased them back, smoothing them down until they were all a calm, deep blue.

"Sleep," I told him. His eyelids drooped.

"Can you hear me?" I asked. He nodded, barely moving his head.

"Did anyone call this in or did security just see me on the camera?"

"Just the camera."

"Go back and tell whoever sent you that you checked it out and it was nothing. It was just a woman waiting for her friend, but she got tired of waiting and left. Understand?"

"I understand."

"You have better things to do than check out stuff like this. You should get back to doing real police work."

He nodded. "Yeah."

The colors faded and the light dimmed back down again. The cop looked out of it for a second and then his eyes cleared. He picked up his radio and spoke into it.

"This is car seven-oh-one."

"Go ahead, car seven-oh-one."

"She checks out. It's nothing."

"Copy that." He switched off.

"Be careful out there," I told him. He nodded.

"You too, ma'am."

The window went back up and he drove away. I watched him go until his taillights got lost with all the rest; then I figured I'd better get going. At that point, it seemed like it would be worse if Nico actually did come home and found me.

I made my way back to the subway entrance, and the closer I got, the more crowded it got. A few blocks away I saw the first dealer, or maybe prostitute. There was more and more neon until between the cars and traffic lights and signs, it was nothing but squiggles of bright color. It took the edge off the rain, but there were too many people. I found the stairs and made my way down into the tunnel.

Once I was through the turnstile I started to smell

food and coffee. I followed a row of stands selling anything and everything, and headed for the platform. The whole area smelled like a mixture of meat, bread, and spices. Places like those stayed open all night.

The next row of stands sold drinks, with all the same variety: one sold beer, the next one sold absinthe, the next whiskey. One sold sake. I slowed down and stopped for a minute.

Stopping something you've done forever is hard, especially something like drinking. Even if you take away the shakes and the sweating and just the physical need to do it, there's still this other part that's almost harder to let go. It's hard not to do what you've always done. I couldn't remember a time I lived in the city when I passed by a row of those stands and didn't have a drink. Even if I was already drunk and even if I had a bottle in my hand, I always stopped. I just always did. Now I had to just walk by, and so far I'd managed, but every time I did, I wondered how much longer I'd make it.

Why weren't you home? I thought.

I wondered where he was and what he was doing. I wondered if he knew that I thought about him, or if I was just invisible to him like I was to everyone else. I wondered if he'd met someone, and if that wasn't why he had drifted off like he had lately.

The sake stand was run by an old Asian guy who kept a little TV mounted in back of the little bar. He filled the little ceramic glasses in front of the people sitting there, steam rising off the tops of each one while the TV flickered. I could smell it from where I was standing.

The nights were too long now. I stayed in my apartment as long as I could, but I couldn't sleep. I wanted to go down and bug Karen but she'd gotten back together with that asshole and I could hear her down there with him.

I stared at the big ceramic jug in front of the Asian man, and the steam coming out of its spout. I wanted to talk to Nico. I wanted . . .

A hand touched my shoulder and I jumped. When I turned, I saw a woman, about my size with straight black hair and bright blue eyes. She was wearing a red rain poncho with a wool hat, and around her neck was the tattoo of a snake. It went all the way around, until it swallowed its own tail. Its red eye stared from over her jugular.

She pinched my shoulder and my arm locked up as she turned me around so we were face-to-face. One second she wasn't there and the next she was, right up in front of me. She was looking right at me.

Without thinking, I focused on her and everything went bright, but only for a second. In that second, I saw the colors come up around her and something else, a band of white that circled her head like a halo. As soon as I saw it, it was gone. The lights went back to normal and it was just her, standing there staring right into my eyes. Her lips curled just a little bit.

My breath caught in my throat. I'd first seen a halo like that after I got kidnapped. I'd seen it down in the cages, where there were others like me. This weird woman was like me.

"Don't be afraid," she said. "I just wanted to say hello."

Her hand moved away from my shoulder and my arm came unstuck. I looked around to see if anyone else thought what was happening was weird, but no one was paying any attention to us. When I looked back at her she was still staring at me.

"Who are you?" I asked.

"I'm Penny," she said. She had this calm, quiet voice that was a little creepy.

"What do you want?"

"Just planting a seed," she said. "I'm going to be your friend soon."

I felt like I was falling all of a sudden, and stumbled a little. She reached out and steadied me. I felt dizzy for a second, and she held my arm until it passed. Then, before I could say anything else, she winked at me and walked away. She merged with the rest of the crowd, and then was gone around the corner.

Was she was real? No one else seemed like they even saw her.

I guessed it didn't matter. Real or not, she was gone. When I looked back at the sake stand, a news lady was on TV, standing outside next to a broken concrete wall with rebar sticking out. Blood was splashed on it and by her feet were what looked like bodies, missing their heads and arms.

"*. . . nightmare in the ghetto of Juba, where scenes like this one are becoming all too common . . .*"

The war. The grinder, some people called it. They were on the other side of the planet. It looked hot over there. It was a hot, dirty place where lots of people died.

I looked back at the sake, but all of a sudden I just wanted to get home. The whole trip had been a bust, and I was really starting to hope Nico never found out I'd been there.

Part of me still thought he might warm up to me. I think there was a part of me that really believed it, but there was another part of me that always knew it wasn't going to happen. Even if I was prettier or sexier or just had more of whatever it was he was into, it probably wouldn't have made a difference in the end. He was still hung up on a dead girl.

I should have just accepted that. If I had, I could have saved myself a world of hurt.

Calliope Flax—Metro Center Station

On the train, in a car full of dregs and drunks, was the first time I felt like I was home. After two years in the grinder, it was kind of hard to believe.

"... in other news, the last appeal for the controversial 'Five-Percent Bill,' which would have allowed offshore UAC company sites to pad up to five percent of their workforce with revivor laborers, was shot down today in a move that was not unexpected, with the note that if the companies are to remain UAC based, then UAC law will apply in this case. Key members of the corporate conglomerate who pushed for the bill were quick to assign blame."

My left hand tingled. It tingled all the time, and it was always cold, like the blood was cut off. I made a fist and cracked my eyes open, head to the glass. It was dark out there. The TV feed hung in front of my eyes like a ghost. Since I made corporal and got the implant, I had TV twenty-four/seven; the UAC dream.

They cut from the news bitch, and some fat asshole with white hair popped up.

"We were supposed to have Heinlein Industries' support," the fat, white-haired asshole said.

"Even Heinlein Industries is bound by UAC law, Mr. Hargraves."

"This whole thing was a sham! This was going to bring big business to them, and they knew it. They were one hundred percent on board with it, but what do they have *to worry about now? With that massive decommission forced down our throats, they've got a military contract sitting in their laps like this world has never seen!"*

"Are you saying Heinlein was—"

"I'm not saying anything! This isn't over!"

"According to the UAC Supreme Court, it is over, Mr. Hargraves."

I shut it off and closed my eyes. The "massive decommission" had geared up while I was over there. Someone got it into their head to scrap every revivor that was stored before a certain date. They said they were obsolete even though they weren't, and someone up top was pushing it hard. Disposal was a piece of shit work we all got stuck with at some point. I never thought about Heinlein, and how much they'd get paid to replace the ones we threw out. Some shit never changed.

"Next stop, Brockton–Stark Street Station," a voice crackled over the speaker. I stood up and hung my bag on my shoulder while I held the rail. In front of me, pasted over about fifty other notices, was a pink piece of paper with smeared black print that said TIER TWO IS A LIE.

In some ways, it was like I never left. Two years gone, and it was more of the same; people pissed about tiers, revivors, and the grind. Most people were still tier two, and they still screamed the most. They never shut up about the grind, even though they saw it only on TV. The grind wasn't like they thought. It wasn't like anyone thought. The only part anyone got right was how bloody it was.

My unit got dropped in a place called Yambio, or what was left of it. Next to it, Bullrich was fucking heaven. They wanted the place locked down—why, I had no clue. The fuckers that lived there were cut off, and to feed them took more than they had. The ones with the drugs had cash and guns. The rest just had guns. Yambio was a war zone that didn't know or give a shit about the rest of the grind, never mind the world.

I did my time in a ghetto called Juba. The folks that lived there spent most of their time trying to eat and not get killed. Every night there was a gunfight, and it felt like every day when the sun came up, we pulled bodies off the street. In two years, the body count got a little lower, and that was about it. That's what I had to show for my two years—that, and losing the fastest pound I ever lost.

Still, to the guys that had to live there, fewer bodies on the street was a big deal. Getting killed out of no-where was their every-fucking-day. Any one of the bod-ies you found facedown in an alley, stinking and covered with flies, was somebody to someone. Some extra feet on the ground were a real big deal for them.

"Now arriving at Brockton–Stark Street Station."

The bell went off, and I cracked my back. That was my stop. I did my part for Juba. I lost my hand, saved a life, and bunked next to five filthy jacks for almost two years. That was enough.

The station was mostly empty when I got off. I'd been on the red-eye all night, and the sun was still down. A few sad sacks stood staring at the tracks. Some got on and a few got off with me. Mostly it was bums, and not many of them. I looked around for my ride, but didn't see him.

Figures.

When I shipped out, the guys from the fight club moved my shit to storage for me. I signed up for four years on the Army's tit, but after the hand, they sent me home and I was on my own. My old place had been a shit hole, but at least it was a place to land; it was long gone now, and I had to live somewhere. Some group called Second Chance stepped up to help out. They got me set up with a new place while I was still in the med center. It wasn't far out of Bullrich, but far enough. They said a rep would meet me at the station when I got back, but so far . . .

Meeting: EMET Corporal Calliope Flax.

The words popped up on my HUD. That was the guy.

I took a step off the platform, and someone stepped out in front of me. It was some spooky chick with a red poncho and a wool cap. Her blue eyes were smeared with black makeup.

"What's your problem?" I asked her.

"I want to tell you something," she said. I felt kind of dizzy for a second.

"So tell me."

"Come closer," she said. She waved me in with one hand, and I leaned forward.

As soon as I did, she got on her toes and whispered right in my ear. I didn't catch what she said because of the noise, but right then I got dizzy like before, but worse. I swayed, and she put her hands on my shoulders and squeezed.

You will remember Zoe Ott.

I got a weird flash. There were guns, fire, and smoke, but it wasn't Juba. It was before. It was cold and dark. I was heading down, deeper and deeper. I had no clue where I was. All I knew was someone was calling me. Someone needed me.

She pulled back and the flash stopped. She gave my shoulders one last squeeze.

"Jeez, you're ripped," she said. The dizzy spell passed.

"Beat it, you fucking nut job," I said, but the little bitch was already walking away.

Meeting: EMET Corporal Calliope Flax.

The words came up again, then faded out. I tried to place the weird memory, but I couldn't. It was snowing, I thought. Nico was there. When I turned to look for the little weirdo, she was gone.

Meeting: EMET Corporal Calliope Flax.

I shook it off, and followed the strays off the platform. The station was like the land of the dead. One guy stood out, though—an old black dude in a long coat and a hat with a brim. He was parked on a bench next to a bum with shaky hands and a big scar on his face. He talked, and the hobo nodded.

Look up, I said.

The old guy raised his head. With the hat out of the way, I saw there were a lot of miles on his face and his kinks had gone gray. There was a Second Chance pin on his collar. When he saw me, he smiled.

"Excuse me for one moment," he said to the bum, who dug at his scar with a yellow fingernail. It looked like someone had cut him a long time ago.

"Corporal Flax?" the old man asked as he got up, and held out his hand.

"Cal," I said. His skin was like leather and his grip was strong.

"Cal it is," he said. "I'm Leon Buckster. I'm with Second Chance."

He gave the bum a pat on the arm, then gave him his card.

"You go ahead and call that number," he said. "Or just come down, and I'll get you set up."

"Just like that?" the bum growled.

"We can get you to the minimum requirements. After that, we can get you a whole new level of help. Understand me?"

The guy nodded.

"I have to go now," Buckster said. "Don't lose that number. Take that first step. It'll get easier after that, I promise."

The bum stared at the card. Buckster turned back to me. "Thought maybe you weren't showing," he said. "Shall we?"

"Sure."

We left, and when I looked back at the bum, he was still looking at the card.

"What was that?" I asked.

"Recruiting."

"You recruit bums?"

"Indigent," he said. "Or homeless. Don't call them bums. We don't recruit them for ourselves; we help get them rehabilitated enough to qualify for Posthumous Service."

"You talk bums into getting wired?"

"PS is an automatic upgrade to tier-two citizenship. At tier two they have access to better aid, better facilities. We can get all kinds of help for them we can't manage for a tier three."

"They're okay with that?"

"Did that guy look like he had anything to lose? The homeless are quickly becoming the largest percentage of posthumous servers, above even your educated service-duckers."

"If you say so."

"We recruit quite a few from Bullrich. I grew up there."

"Yeah, well, no offense, but fuck Bullrich."

"Give it a few years. You may feel differently," he said.

"You serve?"

"Yes, ma'am."

It was hard to guess how old he was, but old. Had this shit been going on that long?

"I've got a car outside," he said. "Come on, I'll take you where you want to go."

"Thanks."

I followed him out. Up on the street it was pouring out, but it was home, and it was good to see. Neon was lit up all over, and no matter where you looked, there was a TV screen. It looked great.

We headed to the pickup entrance, then down three flights to the lot. He walked up to a piece-of-shit microbus and pulled the driver's-side door up.

"You can put your pack in the back."

He leaned inside and popped the trunk. I stowed my pack and climbed in next to him.

"Where to?" he asked.

I fired the address of the storage place to him over the JZI as he backed out and started up the steep ramp toward street level.

"Actually, we were contacted by an old associate of yours by the name of Eddie, from the old Porco Rojo. He provided a bunch of muscle who helped move your things to your new place. It's all in boxes, but it's waiting for you. All you have to do is move in."

"Oh," I said. I wasn't expecting that. "There, then, I guess. Thanks."

"You got it."

He flashed his ticket at the scanner, then pushed his way out onto the main street.

"How long were you in for?" I asked him.

"Six years. You?"

"Signed up for four. Got two."

"Wounded?"

"Yes, sir."

"You don't have to call me sir."

"Habit."

"What happened, if you don't mind my asking?"

I took the glove off my left hand and held it up so he could see. He looked over, and I thought he'd make a face, but he didn't.

"I'll be damned."

I was glad to have it, don't get me wrong, but I hated the thing. The new hand was a good match. The skin was about the right color, but it had that gray look and the dark veins stood out.

"It's revivor tech," he said.

"Watch the road. Yeah."

"I heard they were doing that."

"You heard right."

"It beats a prosthetic, trust me."

I looked over at him.

"Left leg," he said. "Below the knee. Even with the nerve interface, it's not the same. You have full feeling? Full strength? Full range of motion?"

"Yeah." The dead hand was stronger, actually. It could crank twenty PSI more than my right hand, which was my good one. The one thing it didn't have was body heat.

"You were an EMET Corporal . . . What was it like leading a team of revivors?" he asked.

No one ever asked that before. It was kind of a tough one.

"Quiet," I said. It was the first thing I thought.

"Quiet?"

Every outfit used them to fill out the ranks, but there was still a chain of command, and the ones on top had pulses. The EMET rank went to grunts who were two things: good with revivors, and bad with people. I'd never seen a jack in the flesh until I went over, but it turned out I had a knack for messing with their heads. I drove them through my JZI, and it was fun—at first.

When I got good at it, though, they moved me so I could specialize, and I found out most of the grunts picked for that honor had screws loose. When I got my last upgrade and hit EMET, I was glad to get out of there and far away from the rest of them. When you were put in charge of those things, they were your squad. You ate, shit, and bunked in front of them. They were with you twenty-four/seven, and they never talked.

I didn't say that to Buckster.

"Driving jacks was easy," I said instead.

"Jacks?" I shrugged.

"That's what we called them."

"Why was it easy?"

They were easy because they never talked. They never ate, shit, or slept; they just always had your back, day or night. When the command spoke was lit, they did what you wanted. When it was off, they watched, and waited for it to come back on.

"They do what they're told," I said.

"My men always—"

"It's not the same. They get imprinted. You could use them for target practice, as long as the spoke is lit."

"Ever worry the command spoke would drop or the imprint would fail? That you'd lose control of them?" Buckster asked.

"Only every day."

"That must be nerve-racking."

"It isn't. The controls don't fail. You could shove a bomb up their assholes and point them at a schoolyard; they don't care. They'll do it."

It was nerve-racking at first. I slept the first few months with one hand on my gun, but after a while I got to like the quiet. You spend enough time with five guys, even jacks, and you get used to them. You get used to the smell of them and they way they act. Each one is a little different, but they're all wired to you, like extensions of yourself. In a weird way, I missed it. I missed my extra eyes and ears.

"You really do that?" Buckster asked.

"No, man," I said. "Revivors don't have assholes."

He didn't talk for a while. He just drove.

"They didn't have that many revivors in the field when I served," he said when he piped up again. "I think they're relied on too much these days."

"Then why you pushing bums into jack service?"

"Homeless," he said. "The military won't take them on active duty if they've got physical or mental problems; with revivors filling out the ranks, they don't need to. If you've got issues like that, the best you can do is tier two, because if you're just going to get reanimated, it doesn't matter. What are they supposed to do?"

"You got me."

"Besides, it beats being dead."

"It is being dead."

"They still have the memories and experiences they had when they were alive. They have consciousness, of a sort."

"Yeah, well, trust me. It ain't the same."

He shrugged. "What are you going to do now that you're back?"

I'd thought about that some, but not much. At first I

thought I'd hit the fights for extra cash, but Eddie said my left hand counted as an augment, and it disqualified me from the ring. There were back-alley bouts that pit man on revivor, but those weren't strictly legal, and I knew better than to go bare-knuckles with a goddamned jack.

"I heard you guys got a job program?" I asked.

"We do," he said. "Come by and we'll get you signed up. It won't be a dream job, but we've got a lot of contacts. I can't promise a time frame, but I'll set you up with something."

I watched the rain come down until we got to the place. It didn't look half bad. It was a long walk from Bullrich.

"Here we are," he said, handing me a set of keys. "You're on the tenth floor, unit 3B. You sure you don't need any help?"

"I'm sure. Thanks."

He popped the trunk, and I lifted the door open.

"Hey, Leon," I said. "Thanks. For everything. I mean it."

"It's why we're here."

The rain was blowing into the car. I went to get out and he stopped me.

"Can I give you one piece of advice?"

"Shoot."

"Stop wearing the glove now," he said, "before you get used to it. You were wounded in service to your country. Don't hide your scars."

"I'll think about it."

"You're tier one now; you can do better than what we can offer, but you've got to do the legwork. You got any contacts, use them."

"I know one guy."

"Ex-soldier?"

"Yeah."

"Good. You have my card. Call me if you need any-thing, or just feel like talking. Take care, Cal."

I got out and got my pack, and he pulled away. The rain was worse by then, so I hustled in through the gate. At the door I fished out my ID and held it up.

"Flax, Calliope. First Class," the door said, and the light turned green. I wouldn't admit it, but it felt good to hear that.

I pushed the door open and went inside. It was warm in there, and it looked clean. I took the elevator up to the tenth floor, then hauled my bag to my new unit. There was a note taped to the door.

Welcome back.

I pulled it down and stuffed it in my pocket. I put the key to the scanner, then pushed open the door and took my first step into my new place.

There wasn't much, but all my shit was there, in a pile. The room looked like a prison cell, but it was big and it was clean.

I dropped my bag and kicked the door shut behind me, then walked up to the biggest pile of boxes. There was note on the top box.

> *The storage fuckheads let us take all your shit,*
> *so I guess you're lucky it was us and not a bunch*
> *of goddamned thieves. Welcome back.*
> *   —Eddie*

There'd be no more fights for me; I was off the roster, and I'd never go pro. The note was pretty much good-bye.

"Fucker."

I think it was the one nice thing the asshole ever did. It didn't make me happy, exactly, but it did make me smile.

It made me feel like I was home.

Nico Wachalowski — Mercy Greaves Medical Center

A long, deep unconsciousness brought me back to the grind, like it often did. I'd stopped trying to make sense of it or make peace with it a long time ago, but it had a way of creeping back in when I didn't expect it. While someone, usually Sean, worked to put my body back together, my mind turned those memories over and over like a puzzle still missing a piece.

"Sean?" I said, but I couldn't hear myself through the ringing in my ears. My head was still spinning from the concussion grenade, and the stars wheeled by above me as I was dragged through the dirt on my back. Someone had me by one of my ankles and was pulling me behind them. When I lifted my head, I saw three men.

Two flanked the one who had me, and I saw a flash of light as the one on the left glanced back. All of them were naked, and all of them had skin that was starting to wrinkle and pock.

I reached for my gun, but it wasn't there. My knife was gone too. I struggled, and yellow eyes turned back to stare at me from above. I tried to kick free, but one of them grabbed my other leg. They dragged me out of the brush onto damp, soft soil. I heard the creak of wood, and then I was being pulled downward.

I craned my neck back to see the mouth of a tunnel getting smaller behind me, the earth swallowing the sounds of screams and gunfire. Dirt went up the back of my shirt and I could feel insects scrambling against my bare skin.

They'd dragged me into an abandoned underground supply dump, with dirt walls reinforced by wood planks. An electric light hung from an extension cord, and it still glowed weakly. They pulled me into the middle of the floor, then let me go.

There were bones down there. Whoever deployed the revivors left them out there to eat whatever they could find. I could see a human rib cage in the dirt a few feet away, picked clean.

Revivors came back with what they called a cognitive disconnect. They didn't exhibit human emotion, and they couldn't recognize it in others. They didn't understand fear or pain. Their old moralities and taboos were gone. They only knew their wants. If I wanted to get out of there alive, I had to act, but I couldn't move even when one of them crouched down next to me. The look in its eyes made me think of an animal staring at fire. There was a primal fascination there, with something it didn't understand.

The others surrounded me. Fingers slipped in between the buttons of my shirt and tore it open. A string of cold saliva touched my neck.

Move. You have to move.

I didn't, though, not until the first set of teeth bit down. Pain bored into my shoulder as the thing's wet, grimy hair brushed my neck and face. I heard the crunch and I screamed. By the time it raised its head and I saw a chunk of my own flesh clenched in its teeth, the next one had already crowded in and bit down where the blood was pumping out. They were eating me. They were eating me alive.

You have to move.

I pushed against them, but the space was too tight. I had no leverage, and they were too heavy. A knee bashed into my ear; then a thumb went into my left eye. I tried to twist my head, but they had me pinned.

The pressure on my eye built up until I felt something cold slip into the socket. Warmth gushed down my cheek, into my ear. With the eye I had left, I saw one of them pulling a big strip of skin away. In the dim light, I could make out the chest hairs sprouting from it.

I'm going to die, I thought. Everything went black for a second; then I heard a faint voice.

I'm going to—

"Wachalowski!" The voice was Sean's, coming from back up the tunnel. He'd found me somehow. The fingers and teeth that had borne down on me were gone.

"Wachalowski!"

I turned my head and looked across the dirt floor. With nothing but darkness on the left side, I saw blood and many footprints. I could still hear them nearby, but they'd left me. I tried to lift my head, so I could see. . . .

I opened my eyes. I was lying on my back in bed and I could hear a vitals monitor somewhere behind me. Normally if I hit trouble in the field and needed attention, I'd end up back at the tech center with Sean, but that wasn't where I was now.

Looking around as best I could, I saw someone in the room with me. A man in an overcoat sat at a console to one side of me, watching information scroll by, his face turned away. According to my JZI, it was well after visiting hours.

"I take it you're not my doctor," I said. My voice was hoarse.

The man looked over at me and smiled weakly. He

was middle-aged with wavy hair that had grayed at the temples. I'd seen that face before.

"I know you," I said.

"Bob MacReady," he said. "Welcome back to the land of the living."

MacReady worked for Heinlein Industries, the UAC's largest government contractor and sole controller of revivor technology. It had been largely based on technology discovered by Samuel Fawkes. When my investigation two years ago pointed me at Heinlein, he'd provided a lot of information to me. I couldn't prove it, but I was sure he also had a hand in transferring Faye's newly processed body to me too.

"How did you get in here?"

"Money talks," he said. "How are you feeling?"

"Like I got hit by a train. What happened?" The last thing I remembered was lying next to the curb.

"From what I can tell from your records, you were injected with some kind of custom tetrodotoxin variant," MacReady said. "It causes paralysis even in very small doses. It's not easy to get."

"It was a revivor," I told him.

"Our revivors can be outfitted with injectors capable of administering a payload like that at short range," he said. "Usually they're loaded with something a little more deadly, and cheaper, than that."

I checked the FBI logs; Vesco and SWAT had arrested the survivors at the hotel, and all the revivors at the site had been impounded. No one had found the man, Takanawa, though, and no one had managed to intercept the cloaked revivor. Wherever it came from, it got away carrying eleven tactical nukes. Each one was about the size of a cell phone, and could take down a skyscraper.

I checked my buffers, but the information I'd pulled from the computers at the hotel was gone.

With some difficulty, I sat up and faced MacReady. The only light was from the glow of the monitor, but I could see he had aged visibly in the last two years. He looked tired.

"I assume this isn't a social visit," I said. "Why did you come here? Are you here representing Heinlein Industries?"

"No," he said, "but I am here to talk to you about one of our former employees, Samuel Fawkes."

Fawkes was officially dead, and even his revivor was considered destroyed, at least on record. Two years back he had orchestrated the largest terrorist attack ever executed on UAC soil. From an unknown, remote location, contained inside a metal stasis crate, he had managed to infiltrate Heinlein Industries. With the help of revivors smuggled into the country, he was able to kill hundreds of people and cause millions of dollars' worth of damage.

He'd done it, so he claimed, because of information he uncovered while employed at Heinlein. It was there that he learned of the existence of people like Zoe Ott and Sean Pu.

"What about him?" I asked.

"We believe he is still operating."

"You believe he is, or you know he is?"

"I believe he is," he said.

"Why?"

"No one was able to trace it, but some weeks ago, his identifier was picked up, attached to a long-distance communication."

"If that's true, then why didn't you report it?"

"I only just became aware of it, and I'm reporting it now, to you," he said. "It wasn't reported previously because I assume the recipient of the communication doesn't want anyone to know."

"Who was he talking to?"

"I don't know that either, I'm afraid. But I'm telling you—Samuel Fawkes is still out there and he's still operating. The events of two years ago are not over."

I nodded. I'd known Fawkes was never found, but he hadn't tried to communicate with me since. I had been starting to hope he'd been uncrated and destroyed in the field, but never really believed it. He'd made his intentions clear the last time we'd spoken.

"How much do you know about his motivations back then?" I asked.

"Very little I could verify," he said. "I know he infiltrated Heinlein's systems, and used it to gain access to the information he'd amassed on Zhang's Syndrome back when he'd been alive. I also know he used our systems to analyze huge amounts of recorded brain-wave data."

"Did you study the Zhang's Syndrome data?"

"That data has since been classified, and, I believe, destroyed."

"Destroyed? Whatever else Fawkes might be, that information—"

"That information painted a picture no one inside Heinlein Industries is anxious to see come to light. A long-term study, with hard data, suggesting hidden memories that can only be accessed once a person has crossed over and become a revivor? A shadow government that is controlling the minds of the rest of us without anyone knowing? Can you imagine the media storm that would result if that ever came to light? No matter how crazy it is, it would spread like wildfire and would never go away."

"So, you think Fawkes was insane?"

"Fawkes is clearly very intelligent, and he's clearly very determined, but how would you frame it? From the information I have, I can deduce only that Fawkes coordinated the attacks as a means of fighting this shadow he obviously believes exists."

"Is there any chance he's right?" I asked. MacReady watched me evenly.

"His data appears very conclusive," he said, "but there are other possible explanations. Fawkes didn't pursue them. He followed his paranoia down the rabbit hole."

"Could he still have been right?"

MacReady sighed. "You can always make a case for these things," he said. "Not long after the events of two years ago, a new law was passed. It ensured that revivor consciousness would revert to pre–generation seven levels—basically removing some of the higher functions to make them more obedient but less self-sufficient. Now all revivor models of Fawkes's generation or lower are being scrapped and replaced. One could look at those things and see how it might fit into Fawkes's thinking."

I couldn't tell if he believed it or not. In the light of the monitor, his face was hard to read, and maybe he wasn't even sure what he believed himself.

"Do you have concrete proof of Fawkes's communication?" I asked.

"No. You'll have to trust me on that, but it worries me, and that's part of why I'm here. It was one thing to have Fawkes infiltrate Heinlein's systems and access our data without anyone's knowledge . . . it's another for someone inside Heinlein to be willingly communicating with him. Before, he controlled revivors that he'd smuggled into the country to do what he needed done, but if he's making allies inside the city who are human . . ."

He didn't have to finish. That would mean Fawkes had managed to get people, regular flesh-and-blood legal citizens, to buy into his conspiracy theory and help him. That would give him a much, much wider reach. Maybe even wide enough to try to acquire weapons like the ones uncovered at Royal Plaza.

"Does Heinlein know you're here?" I asked.

"No," he said, "and they can't. I don't know who on the inside might be compromised. I won't communicate with you over the wire for the time being, until I know, but I'll try to help you if I learn more."

"Thanks, MacReady. Looks like I owe you again. Be careful."

"And you, Agent."

He got up and headed for the door, stopping to turn back before he left. Silhouetted in the light from the hallway outside, he looked like a shadow himself.

"Even if he was right about Zhang's Syndrome," he said, "I would be very cautious of Samuel Fawkes."

He left, and when he closed the door, the only light left was the soft glow from the vitals monitor. I began to fall back into sleep.

I could almost have dreamed him.

2

Whispers

Nico Wachalowski — Mercy Greaves Medical Center

Outstanding message: Pu, Sean.

The words lit up in the dark behind my eyelids. I brought the time up next to them and saw it was morning.

Opening my eyes, I found myself looking at a foam-tiled ceiling. A fluorescent light flickered off to my left.

The hospital.

The vitals monitor wasn't beeping anymore, and my strength had returned, for the most part. I stretched. My muscles felt stiff, but I could move.

Outstanding message: Pu, Sean.

The message had come in on the channel we used to use back in the service, during silent operations. He'd never used it since. None of us had.

The message was sent at a little past three in the morning. It was flagged as an emergency transmission. I opened it.

31 03 76 11 52 57 81 1

That was it—just a list of numbers, with no accompanying text or voice.

It could have been a glitch, but it didn't look like it. Whatever the numbers were, he meant to send them to me. I put in a call to him on the JZI, but he was offline.

I closed my eyes again and brought up the footage from the night before. The data I pulled during the raid had been removed, but I still had the visual recording up to the point I'd entered the basement. I skipped through, marking off key sections.

In a window, I watched as I tailed Takanawa down the stairwell. The view moved slowly in the darkness, letting him stay well ahead. His thermal signature trailed across the floor, and I followed it. Smaller signatures scurried here and there as a group of rats were startled. The marks intermingled for a second, and something flickered.

I stopped the recording. I remembered the distortion, but at the time I thought it was a trick of the light; I didn't expect to see it show up on the recording. Going back, I slowed it down for a better look. The patterns from his footsteps were steady; then the rats scattered. I saw the flicker again. The glow from the footsteps disappeared for a second, then came back.

I checked again to be sure. Something blocked them out temporarily, moving right to left. Something crossed in front of them. Something I couldn't see had been sticking to the right wall. It startled the rats, and when it did, it crossed over to the left, causing a skip in the patterns.

The Light Warping field. It would bend visible light, but not the radiation signature from the case, and not thermal radiation either. Whoever took the case wasn't already in the basement, waiting. I hadn't been the only one following Takanawa.

I cut back to when SWAT first broke in on him. He was sitting on the edge of the bed, still dressed. Unlike the others who'd been caught, he was alone. There was no revivor with him.

"Where'd the revivor go?" I asked him.

He shrugged. *"I don't see one here. Do you?"*

Bringing up the SWAT report from the raid, I cycled down the inventory of revivors that had been impounded. There were twelve total: the eleven active ones, plus the defunct one I'd found under the bed.

"She put her there." The revivor I found in the bathroom had said that when I discovered the body.

"Who did? Who put the revivor under there?"

"She did."

The revivor specified "she," but it seemed unlikely Holst had done it, and no other women were found in the hotel. The only females at the site were revivors.

It hit me then. I hadn't seen a revivor in the room with Takanawa, but maybe there had been one there. The revivor under the LW cloak could have been female; I never actually saw it. Sean told me Holst and Takanawa were there to intercept the weapons, but the original buyer might have already had an operative inside. A revivor from the outside could have deactivated the pleasure model and taken its place, stowing it under the bed of another room.

That could have put the operative in the room with Takanawa. It had an LW suit and used it to disappear when the raid began. When we let him go, it followed him, hoping he would lead it to the case before it left the hotel.

No. Upgr . . . forget the target . . . the case.

. . . about the . . .

Kill her.

Forget the target. Get the case. "Target" might have referred to Takanawa. "Kill her" must have referred to Holst.

Sean had said she was being treated here at Mercy Greaves. I brought up the inpatient records for the hospital.

HOLST, JAN—she was there, in another wing. Her condition had been upgraded from critical to stable, but the damage to her larynx was severe. She couldn't swallow and was being fed intravenously, but, amazingly, her attacker had missed both jugulars. I checked her records to see if she was wired for Posthumous Service. She wasn't.

"Mr. Wachalowski?"

I opened my eyes. The doctor had come in. I packed the recording away.

"Good morning, Doctor."

"Good morning to you, Agent," he said. "But I don't think you should be accessing those records. Is Miss Holst classified as a terrorist?"

"She's a person of interest in an ongoing investigation. Under the current alert status, I have authorization," I said. His face said that he already knew this, but disagreed.

"Can I convince you to stop the records access, at least until you've checked out?"

I nodded. "How is she?"

"Miss Holst is in stable condition, as you now know," he said. "She is shaken, but except for her voice box, she'll make a full recovery. The rest will require more specialized attention, but although she won't sing, I think she'll speak again before it's over."

"That's good news. Is she well enough for a visitor?"

"She's not well enough for an interrogation."

"She's stable, though?"

The doctor nodded.

"Thank you. Am I clear to go?" I asked.

"There is no trace of the substance left in your bloodstream, and there appears to be no long-term damage. Aside from that, you have some lumps, but nothing serious."

"Thanks."

When he was gone, I checked in at the FBI, but Sean hadn't checked in. I tried his cell, but there was no answer.

31 03 76 11 52 57 81 1

The numbers floated there in front of me. Something was wrong.

I put in a call to Assistant Director Noakes. He picked up immediately.

Wachalowski, you're awake. Good.

Noakes, where is Sean Pu?

I don't know. In the field, I think. Why?

Did he log out?

Hold on. He went idle for several seconds. *No. What's this about?*

Maybe nothing. I'm trying to track him down.

Are you checking out of the hospital today?

Yes.

Then get down here. Looks like we got another survivor from the raid last night.

Who?

Your gunshot victim in the basement—son of a bitch lived. The medics are clearing him now, and then Vesco's going to take a crack at him.

I want to bring someone in on that, I said. He knew I meant Zoe. I waited to see if he'd argue, but he didn't.

Then you'd better hurry.

Understood. I'm on my way. Noakes cut the connection.

I sat in the hospital bed, thinking for a moment longer. Zoe could help me get information I might not otherwise get access to. She might be able to help me in more ways than one.

I made the call. Her voice mail picked up.

"Zoe, this is Nico. I need your help," I said. Then, after a second: "Keep this one under your hat. I'll meet you at the Federal Building."

I hung up, and began to get dressed.

Zoe Ott—Pleasantview Apartments / FBI Home Office

I opened my eyes, and the first thing I saw was her. I was sitting in a folding chair, angled away from a gray conference table, and that woman, that dead woman, was standing in front of me. The concrete wall behind her was painted green.

"It's you," I said.

The first two buttons of her blouse were undone, and I could see she still had the big scar there, right in the middle of her chest. She was wearing a wig—a straight, black, shoulder-length deal—and her eyes glowed a little as they stared out from under the straight bangs.

A big boom came from somewhere above us but it was muted, like we were deep underground. The overhead light flickered, and dust sifted down from the ceiling. It had been a while since I'd fallen asleep and ended up in the green room. I'd been hoping that dream was over for good.

"God, just kill me . . ." I said.

"You don't die here. You die in a tower."

"I hate you."

"I know."

I was more lucid these days, and I tried to make a point of looking around when I got stuck in a vision. The room looked the same as it always did, more or less; the table was there, and the chair, along with the three hanging lights at the far end. The electric switch box was mounted on the wall next to the metal door, and the steel panel that hid the handset was next to that. Something was a little different, though. Had the switchbox and door been on the opposite wall last time?

The boom came again, and more dust sifted down from the ceiling. Something flickered then, a red band of laser light that reminded me of a bar scanner. It shone through the dust from behind me, but when I turned around, it was gone. I couldn't see where it had come from.

"I came to tell you something," she said.

"Good," I said, still distracted by the laser. I'd never seen that before. "Start by telling me what this place is."

She just stared and didn't answer.

"Where are we? Where is this place? What's with the explosions? What's happening up there?"

"I came to tell you something," she said again.

"I know you're real," I said. "I've seen you in the real world. . . . Is that who I'm talking to now? Or are you just who I picture when the information comes?"

She didn't answer, and I could see she wasn't going to. I shook my head.

"Fine. Just . . . say what you came to say."

"The city is going to burn."

I shrugged. "Yeah. I've seen it. I saw it years ago. Did you come to tell me something I already know? What do you want me to do about it?"

"The day will come when everything will fall on you. The fate of everything will be in your hands."

I smiled and shook my head. It was almost funny. Not quite, but almost.

"Then the fate of everything is in big trouble," I said.

"That's true."

She turned and threw the big electrical switch on the wall. A buzzing sound came from the ceiling and three lights snapped on at the far end of the room. Two people were standing there, not moving, one under the left light and one under the right light. The spot under the middle light was empty.

The person on the left was Nico. The person on the right I recognized too. She was there that night in the factory.

"This one could be your salvation," she said, pointing at Nico. The number 3 was pressed into his forehead in black ink.

"What happened to him?" I asked, moving closer. That scar of his usually covered a big patch on the right side of his chest and right shoulder, but now it was just on his chest. Before it got to the shoulder it stopped in a neat line, like it had been painted over or something. The other half was just gone. Everything on the other side, the shoulder and arm, were the wrong color. Unlike the rest of him, his shoulder and arm were pale and gray. They were the same color as the dead woman.

"Your chance of successfully navigating this relationship is sixty percent," she said. When I looked at her, she was staring at him, but I couldn't tell what she was thinking. After a minute, she pointed to the woman.

"This one is a destroyer. She will cause you to lose something very dear," she said.

She was a mean, muscle-bound woman with a bent

nose and black lipstick. She had the number 2 inked on her forehead.

I got a flash, then, from that place with the cages and the dead men, the place where they tried to study us. There were other people there, people like me, all locked up, and the dead men forced us to do things. . . . When I thought it was all over, a small woman appeared to me and told me something . . . something important. She showed me how to take control of a woman I'd never met; this woman with the mean face and the broken tooth. I brought her down there to me, and she saved my life.

"What will she make me lose? Why?"

"Your chance of successfully navigating this relationship is ten percent."

"Lose what? What does she have against me?"

Another boom went off overhead, making the light fixtures sway and shadows play over the walls.

"Goddamn it. What is that noise?" I asked.

"Some people are more susceptible than others," she said, ignoring me. She was still pointing at the woman.

"I know."

When I looked closer at the muscle-bound figure, I saw her left hand was a pale gray, just like Nico's arm. It triggered a flash of memory.

"She was there that night. I've seen her here before too," I said to myself. A lot of what happened two years ago, I never really got clear on. The shakes were hitting me really bad by then, and everything was happening at once. I remembered a woman peeking through a hole from the cell next to mine. I remembered being hooked up to a bunch of electrodes, and then ending up in the green room. . . .

"I called her," I said, remembering. "I could sense her, and I called her, and she came."

I remembered her shooting the lock to my cage and pulling me out.

"She rescued me."

The dead woman nodded. "She may save your life a second time."

"What about the middle spot?" I asked, but as soon as I said it, it came back to me. We'd had this conversation before.

"The middle spot is where—"

"You stand," I said.

"We will meet two more times, before this is all over," she said. "Your chances of successful navigation are, respectively, one hundred and zero percent."

"Can those be changed?" I asked her. "If I can pass or fail, can the percents be changed? Can I change them?"

She wasn't listening, though. She moved away, back toward the table, and flipped the switch back down. The lights over Nico and the other one went dark.

"You said I die in a tower. Can that be changed?"

"You die in a tall tower."

With the lights out, I saw something flickering through the glass window in the room's door. I got on my toes and looked out into a dimly lit hallway, where a bunch of people were sitting, leaning against the walls. They were all looking at the floor, their clothes and skin burned black. Orange and red spots glowed under the ash on their coats and boots. One, a woman, looked up, her face covered in soot. Her skin was cracked and raw. She mouthed something, but I couldn't hear her.

"What do you want from me?" I asked the dead woman. Three men in uniform stepped into view down the hall and started tromping past them, toward the door, dragging a scrawny, dirty man in handcuffs between them.

"It's too late for us," the dead woman said, "but not for you."

I turned, forgetting about the people in the hallway. "What?"

"He still needs you. He will call to you again," she said.

"What do you mean, 'It's too late for us'?" I asked.

"Should he fail, it will fall to you."

"Wait!"

The metal door opened, and dust swirled in from the hallway. The uniformed men shoved the one in handcuffs toward the far wall where the three lights were.

"This is a mistake . . ." I heard him whisper.

Behind them, I caught a glimpse of a woman, a skinny woman about my height, with her hair in a bun, but she was in shadow.

"Who are—"

She turned her head to look back over her shoulder, and when she did, I could just make out some kind of tattoo that circled her scrawny neck. There was a ring-shaped scar there, where her jugular stuck out. Against the dim light behind her, her profile had a big, beaklike nose. . . .

I woke with a start and my eyes opened. The green room and everyone in it were gone. Something was beeping.

"Damn it," I whispered.

I was on the monorail, leaning against the window. The car was packed, and there were bodies all around me, damp from the rain and murmuring on cell phones or getting work in during the commute. A fat man in an overcoat formed a barrier to my left, leaving me in my own little world as I watched rain streak across the plastic and the city sprawl by outside. In the distance, the CMC Tower rose like a giant needle out of the fog.

The beeping sound came again, and I realized it was my phone reminding me to take my medication. The fat man glanced at me as I fished out my cell and shut off the alarm.

Mornings were when I still got the strongest urge. I thought it would be at night, but it wasn't. It was when I first woke up, then for the rest of the morning. I held my hand out of view of the guy next to me and watched it for a minute. The fingers shook, just a little, not like before. I still missed it, though. I kept waiting for the day to come when I stopped missing it, but it never seemed to come.

I reached into my coat pocket and found one of the pill tabs. I pushed the chewable tablet through the foil and into my palm, and then popped it in my mouth. They were minty, but had a real bitter aftertaste. When I swallowed, it left a medicine taste on my tongue. That was one. I was supposed to take them three times a day.

The medication helped, that was for sure. Nico got me on a program, which I pretty much agreed to try only because he said I couldn't come back to the FBI until I did. I didn't think it would work, but whatever was in the tablets, it took the edge right off. When I woke up in the morning, I didn't feel sick until I could get a drink. My hands stopped shaking so much, and I could go longer and longer without needing one. I still wanted it, but that sick feeling, and all the shaking and sweating and heart pounding, stopped. I hadn't thrown up in almost six months.

I snorted. There was something to be proud of; a whole six months without ending up facedown in the toilet. In return, all I had to put up with was no appetite and hideous cramps.

The city is going to burn.

I hadn't had that particular vision in a while, and I didn't miss it. In general, the visions hadn't been nearly as vivid since I stopped drinking, so there was that too in the plus column.

The problem was that the chemicals took only the physical edge off. They couldn't change the fact that being sober was horrible.

My phone vibrated in my hand—a text from Karen, my downstairs neighbor. I opened the chat portal and read her message:

Missed you this morning.

I typed back a response: *Sorry, had to run. Work needed me early.*

That was partly true. I was supposed to meet Nico and he did have something he wanted me to do, but I didn't even know what that was yet. I could have stopped by, but I'd kind of been avoiding her in the morning because I knew Ted was back. Her eyes had that look they got whenever her on-again, off-again asshole boyfriend was back on again. She didn't want to say it because she knew I'd be pissed, and she was right.

Want to meet for lunch? She asked.

Sure.

We made a point of getting together to do that at least once a week, but that had tapered off a little too. Ted didn't like me, and so he didn't like her hanging around with me.

Sorry I've been MIA, she said.

I sighed, and decided to cut to the chase. *I know he's back.*

She went idle for a long time.

You don't have to say anything. I know.

He's a complete jerk.

You don't understand.

She had that right. Whatever she saw in that guy, I totally did not understand. Whatever it was, though, she was really stuck on him. She actually got mad when I insulted him.

It's none of my business, I said. There wasn't anything I could do, not really. From the sound of it down there, at least she was seeing some action, which was more than I could say for myself.

Let's not talk about that, she said.

Fine.

Meet in Federal Square at noon?

Noon.

She signed off. I put my phone away and looked back out the window.

Ted is bad news. I should just make her dump him. I'd thought about that, but honestly, I was a little afraid of what he might do if she did. I could make him dump her instead, but then she might know I had something to do with that, and she'd never forgive me for it.

I could make her forget, though. . . .

I'd thought that before too, but I wasn't ready to do that. Not yet.

The train stopped at the Federal Square station and I followed the rest of the bodies out into the rain, then down off the platform. It was a cold, windy walk to the Federal Building, and by the time I got there, my jacket was soaked. In the smoked glass at the entrance, I saw my hair had frizzed.

When I went through the guard post, I was surprised to see Nico across the lobby. He stepped out of the elevator and started crossing the big seal imprinted in the marble floor, heading for the front entrance. I was supposed to be meeting him there, but he had his coat on. He was leaving.

He almost blew right past me before he saw me, and I didn't need any special ability to know he'd already forgotten our meeting.

"Zoe," he said. I sensed something from him, something that came off him like a high-pitched whine.

I focused on him, and the room grew brighter as a swirl of colors phased in over the crowd of heads moving through the lobby. I concentrated, letting the rest fade into the background while bringing Nico's forward. There were red and orange there, arcing and spiking under a shell of calm. Something was wrong.

I couldn't control Nico anymore. . . . Two years back something happened to him, and I never found out what, but it left a sort of hole in him. When I focused on him, I could still see his colors and I could still read them, but that was all. When I tried to push him or change those colors, it didn't work. He tricked me a couple times when he knew it was coming, but he couldn't hide everything, at least not from me. When I really burrowed down, it was like behind the moving lights there was a dark hole, and if I pushed too hard, I would push through into nothing but darkness. No matter what I tried or how gently I approached him, I always ended up in that dark spot where I couldn't change anything.

It didn't work on him anymore, but he could tell when I was trying to do it. He raised his eyebrows and I backed off, letting the colors disappear and the light go back to normal. I got a good look at his face for the first time, then. He looked like he'd been in a fight.

"What happened?" I asked.

"It's a long story, Zoe, and I'm sorry, but I've got to run. I need you to do me a favor while I'm gone."

Whenever Nico said "favor" he really meant he

wanted me to use my ability on someone. He usually wanted to keep that quiet. I was getting annoyed.

"Yeah, I kept it 'under my hat,' just like you said. What kind of favor?"

"We uncovered something in a raid last night," he said. "Something big."

"What favor?" I asked again, raising my voice a little.

"There were two surviving witnesses," he said. "I need you to talk to both of them—"

"Two?" There went my lunch date with Karen.

"The first one is happening now," he said. "You'll need to get up there. We've got a suspect shot in a raid who's about to be questioned. He could know something vital to—"

"Now?"

"Yes. Vesco and the others know you might be coming, so just go in—"

"You're not going to be there?" The whole thing was starting to stress me out. Vesco hated me; he thought I was a joke. They all thought I was a joke. Nico always kept the rest of them off me, and even then sometimes I was so nervous I could barely do anything. Working for him at the FBI was his idea in the first place. Now he was just ditching me?

"Zoe, please," he said, pulling me aside. "This is very important. I had meant to be with you, but I think a friend of mine is in trouble and I have to check it out. Please do this for me."

I could tell something was really bothering him. He didn't say who the friend was or what kind of trouble he was in, but something was really bothering him.

"Fine," I said.

"Thank you. They're upstairs now. Here."

He handed me a folded piece of paper with a series of questions on it. He usually did that, so I could include them in my "notes" and it didn't look like he was telling me what to ask once we got inside. To me, though, they had started to look like grocery lists, things I was supposed to pick up for him and bring back.

I didn't say that. I just folded the paper in my hands.

"The second part might be trickier," he said, "but get it if you can."

"Fine."

"I have to go."

"Fine."

I watched his mind shift gears as he walked past me and out through the glass door. He shielded himself from the rain as a gust of wind made his overcoat flap around him.

I checked the paper he'd given me and got the name of the interrogation room, then took the elevator up.

It was true; they were expecting me, sort of. I could hear Vesco talking as I approached the doorway, and a couple other people inside with him.

". . . that creepy redhead," I heard him say. Someone chuckled.

"I don't know why Noakes allows this shit," someone else said. "There's more to that story, I'll bet."

"You think Wachalowski hits that?" Vesco asked, and two men laughed. My face got hot.

"Can it, you two," I heard a woman's voice say. And then I was through the door, and everyone shut up.

There were three people in the room, and through a one-way glass panel I could see a fourth sitting in the interrogation room. Vesco was there, a smirk still on his obnoxious face, and some other guy I'd never seen who had to be the one who laughed.

The third person was a round-faced Asian woman with short, straight hair. Like the two men, she wore a dark suit and even wore a tie that somehow looked right on her. Before the other two could say anything, she stepped forward and offered her hand.

"My name is Alice Hsieh," she said, as I shook the offered hand briefly. "Agent Wachalowski said you might be joining us. This is Agent Ves—"

"I know who he is." Heat was coming up from under my collar. I knew my face was totally red. I felt completely humiliated.

"Then if you'll join us in the—"

"I'll talk to him alone," I said. I'd just interrupted her twice, but I didn't care. Vesco got ready to say something, and I swore—right then I swore—that if he started in on me, I'd make him shut up, no matter who saw.

I didn't have to, though. The woman, Alice, made him shut up instead.

"That will be fine," she said.

"Like hell," Vesco said. Alice didn't raise her voice, but her eyes turned serious.

"Are you contradicting me?" she asked. The look on Vesco's face, and his friend's face, left no question as to who in the room was in charge. He was angry, but he pressed his lips together.

"No, ma'am," he said. Alice turned back to me.

"You're on."

I walked past Vesco, and took some satisfaction in the anger I could sense coming off him. The interrogation room was cold, like they usually kept it, and a man sat in a wheelchair across the table from me, almost shivering. I took out my notebook, and smoothed the paper Nico had given me over the open page, keeping it out of view.

"Who are you?" the man asked. His face was sweaty, in spite of his slight shiver. He had a tube under his nose, and a few more stuck out from inside his robe. According to Nico's notes, his name was Franco Reese, and he'd been shot in the side not even twenty-four hours earlier.

"Never mind who I am," I said. "I'm going to ask you some questions."

"I'm not saying anything without my—"

His voice trailed off as the room brightened around me, and the colors appeared around his head. Over the past two years, I'd gotten better at doing what I did. I didn't have to get close anymore or tell him to go to sleep. Most people didn't even need to be totally under for me to get them to tell me what I wanted to know, and it was less obvious that way.

"Just take it easy, Mr. Reese," I said.

I eased the colors back into a cold, calm blue, and watched his face relax.

"I just have a few questions. Will you cooperate?"

"Sure," he breathed, settling back into the wheelchair.

I risked a glance back toward the glass panel that separated the rooms. It was a one-way mirror, so I couldn't actually see the people on the other side, but I could sense them to the point that I knew where they were standing. Vesco and his friend were together, back toward the far wall. The woman, Alice, was standing directly in front of the glass, watching me. Her mind was calm and interested, but not suspicious. I looked back to Nico's list.

"Did you smuggle in the twelve devices?" I asked. The paper didn't say what kind of devices they were.

"Yes."

"Was Holst your original contact?"

"No," he said, "but the guy who set up the deal and the one who did the pickup were supposed to be two different people. I knew that."

"So you were expecting Holst?"

"I didn't know who I was expecting. The guy who set it up supplied a cipher. The pickup man provided the key. They also had the money. Everything was in order."

"So nothing seemed strange about the deal?"

Reese's brow twitched. "One thing," he said.

"Tell me."

"The buyer wanted the revivors too. The two that came to make the pickup didn't say anything about that."

"No?"

"No. That blond bitch, especially. She looked put off by the whole thing. Next thing I know, the goddamn Feds are busting down the doors, so I figured it was a sting; the bitch and her pervert friend were undercover. I go downstairs to take care of her, and she starts shooting."

"You didn't see where the case ended up?"

That actually seemed to excite him a little. An electric white began to course under the cool blue that surrounded him.

"I thought you had it," he said. He didn't know.

"Did the buyer say what the targets were?" I asked.

"Just that they were big."

"Big?"

"At least three large-scale urban targets," he said. It took me a minute to realize what it was that he was saying.

"They're going to blow something up?" I asked.

"What the hell else do you do with a nu—"

"The nature of the case's contents is classified," a voice snapped over the intercom, loud enough to cut the man off, but it was too late. I knew what he was going to say. He had a weird look on his face, a sort of excitement in his eyes, even despite being under. Whatever was going to happen, he wanted it to happen.

The city is going to burn. That's what the dead woman said. Was this what she meant?

"Okay," I said weakly. My heart had started to pound. "That's all."

"You can't stop it now," he said. "Change is coming, and you can't—"

"Shut up," I said, and he did.

I looked at the bottom of the paper Nico had given me, and it seemed to be turning in a slow circle in front of me. There were a few more questions he wanted asked that I was not expecting. Normally I think I would have chickened out, but I was still reeling from what I'd heard. I barely thought about it when I called back into the next room.

"Agent Vesco, can you come in here for a second?" I called back. "The rest of you can go if you want. I'm done with him for now."

The door opened and Vesco came in. He looked at me like I was an idiot.

"He's lying, Ott," he said. "If interrogation was that easy, anyone could do it. That case is worth millions; he knows where it is. They would have had a route set up to carry it back underground in the event they got busted."

"He's not lying."

"So you ask him a question, and just accept the first thing that comes out of his mouth? He's a black market–arms dealer sitting inside the Federal Building; he'll say whatever he—"

"He's not lying. Shut up," I said, and he did. His face

went slack, but not too slack. I was careful not to push him too hard.

"Come closer," I said. "Sit down next to me." He did, and I leaned closer, to whisper in his ear.

"Did you know Holst and Takanawa would be in the hotel?" I asked. He whispered the answer in my ear.

"Yes."

"What were you told?"

"Not to process them. To let them leave with the case, and then report that it was never at the site. To keep Wachalowski out of it."

"Who told you that?" I asked. He paused.

"I don't remember."

"Why did you agree to go along with that?"

"I . . . don't remember."

He wasn't lying. He couldn't be, not to me.

"That's all," I said, and let him go. I folded the paper and stuffed it in my pocket. Vesco blinked and looked confused for a second before he got up and walked out without saying another word.

Jerk, I thought. The door closed behind him. I could sense his presence as he passed by the one-way mirror, and back out into the hall. His friend had already gone, but the other presence, the woman named Alice Hsieh, was still there. She was still standing near the glass, watching me. Her mind was still calm and curious.

Without looking back at the mirror, I focused on her. I was going to make her leave too, before I called the guard back in to take the suspect away. When I concentrated on her, though, and began to push, something gently pushed me back. Around the cool and curious glow of her consciousness, I saw a thin, white halo appear, so faint it was almost invisible.

Then I really did turn and look, and I could feel her

looking back. That faint halo showed up on only one kind of person.

Alice Hsieh was like me.

Calliope Flax—FBI Home Office

I tried Wachalowski one more time on my cell across the street from the Federal Building and let it ring. I'd called him a few times, but he wasn't picking up. I picked the phone up at a convenience store, and I was supposed to be gone another two years so it wasn't a total ditch, but I was sick of getting his voice mail.

". . . Special Agent Nico Wachalowski. Leave a mes—"

I hung up. After a minute, I crossed the street.

The last time I had a run-in with the Feds, it wasn't exactly a win. They screwed me on a reward I had coming, doped me, grilled me all night, then kicked me to the curb. The place still made me a little edgy.

A camera followed me up the steps, and drones in suits watched from a gate just past the door. I walked up to it and flashed my ID card.

"Flax, Calliope," the door said. "First Class. Violations including: assault, illegal possession of a weapon, public drunkenness, and speeding place you as security risk: medium-high."

Some asshole going by looked over. The door kept talking.

"Records show a recent return from military service," it said. "Honorable discharge at rank EMET Corporal. Awarded commendations: Bronze Star, and Purple Heart. Welcome back, EMET Corporal Flax."

"Just open."

The door clicked, and I pulled it open and went in. The

place looked part military and part corporate jerk-off, full of suits with guns and big wallets. The lobby was decked out, and the floor had a big, fancy seal on it. There were flags and spy cams on every wall, and a big metal detector and X-ray up front. I took off my jacket and dropped it on the belt while the bald guy behind it watched.

"Welcome back, Corporal. Step through, please."

I went through, and after he checked me out, he gave the coat back.

"You meeting someone?" he asked.

"Agent Wachalowski."

"He expecting you?"

"He said look him up when I got back," I said.

"Sign in, please."

I signed the log, and he gave me a badge to wear.

"Elevator's that way. He's on the fifth floor."

The lift was full of suits, and on the way up I did a sweep with the JZI. I found a ton of nodes, so a lot of the goons there were ex-military. One of them could have been Wachalowski, but I hadn't actually talked to him on the JZI yet, so I didn't have his ID. When the car hit five, I got out and headed down the hall to find someone to ask.

Halfway down, an old guy eyed me and moved in. He was my height and blocky, but soft in the middle. His face wasn't soft, though, and one of his eyes was a fake. I could tell right off he was in charge.

"Can I help you?" he asked.

"Yes, sir. I'm here to see Agent Wachalowski. Do you know where I can find him?"

"What's your name?"

"Cal Flax."

Orange light flashed in the darks of his eyes, and I picked up an intrusion on my JZI. Some message popped up about me being inside a federal facility, and my security dropped. He scanned all my systems, top to bottom. The guy was heavily wired.

"EMET Corporal Calliope Flax," he said. "Aka Fang, aka Hayvan." That last one made him grin a mean grin. "The Beast?"

The guys in my platoon called me Fang because of the missing tooth. Hayvan was what the punks in Juba called me, after I started patrolling with the jacks.

"Yes, sir." He was reading something on his JZI, I could tell. As he did, his face changed. Some of the hard-ass went out of him. I used a backscatter filter on him while I waited, and he let me. Under the muscle and flab he had some armor plating, muscle and joint work, and some ugly chunks of scar tissue.

After a minute he held out his hand, and I shook it. His big hand gripped like a vise.

"I'm Assistant Director Henry Noakes," he said. "Agent Wachalowski is in the field, but he'll want to see you."

"If you say so." I was half thinking he might backpedal when he saw me on his front doorstep.

"He dropped your name a couple times," he said. "He'll want to see you. Hold on."

Orange light flickered in his eyes again. A few seconds later, a call came in. It was from Wachalowski.

"Thanks," I said. He nodded.

Call accepted.

Calliope, he said.

Cal.

I didn't expect you back so soon.

Two guys in suits came around the corner. One looked over his shoulder, then back at his buddy as they passed, and I caught the G-man's name.

". . . Wachalowski find her anyway?" he said.

"You got me."

Neither did I.

I'm glad you came by; I was hoping you would when you got back.

It was an honorable discharge.

I don't doubt it. Is Assistant Director Noakes still standing there?

Yeah. The guy's hard-core. He's wired up the ass.

That might be the one place he isn't wired. Can we meet later?

Sure.

Name the spot. I'll find it.

The Pit? It's in Bullrich.

Got it. I'll get in touch as soon as I'm out of the field. We'll meet there.

Right then a scrawny chick in a raincoat came around the corner, tailing the two suits that just passed. She was short and built like a stick with a big beak nose. Her hair was red and she was pale as a ghost. She looked down at the floor when she walked. When I got a good look at her face, it hit me like a brick.

You will remember Zoe Ott.

I got that weird flash again. I was underground. It was cold and dark. I could hear gunfire. Someone was chasing me. I pushed past a sheet of plastic and down a long hall to a room filled with cages. . . .

Gotta go.

I cut the line.

"You got any other business here?" Noakes asked.

The stick with the red hair went by us. When she did, she looked up at me, then back at the floor.

"No," I said. "Thanks again."

"Welcome back."

She was heading for the elevators, and I went after her. When the car showed up, I followed her in.

In the reflection off the brass, I saw her check me out. I knew her. She was down in that cold, dark place two years ago.

How the fuck did I just forget her?

I set the JZI recording, and got a good look at her face. I didn't know why she was there, but it was a good a time as any to get some answers. The numbers ticked off on the LCD as the car headed down, and I went for the emergency stop button.

I didn't do it, though. Something stopped me and I just stood there. When the doors opened, she scooted out and made a beeline for the front door. I stepped out, but I didn't follow her. I just stood there.

"Elevator trouble?" some guy in a suit said.

"How the fuck should I know?" I said. He gave me a look and made a point of clipping my shoulder when he passed, but I still just stood there. Why the fuck did I just let her go?

I killed the JZI recording. At least I had a face to go by, and if she was there two years ago, then Wachalowski must know who she was. I bumped to the start of the footage and let it run so I could see her face again.

In a window I watched the footage play. The feed showed the shiny brass doors of the elevator, and I could see my own reflection in it. She was standing to my left. I got some good frames of her face, but that was it. Then I heard myself talk.

"Hey," I said to her. She didn't look up.

"Hey."

I froze it. I stood there and stared at the image in the window. In it, I was looking down at her beak profile and she had her eyes on the floor. I hadn't said anything to her; I knew I hadn't. The whole thing happened less than a minute ago.

I leaned against the wall next to the door and let it keep running.

"Where do I know you from?" I asked her.

She shrugged. *"You don't."*

I hit the emergency stop and the car bucked as the bell rang and kept ringing. She jumped and looked up at me.

"What are you doing?" she squawked.

"Who are you?" I asked.

"What?"

"Goddamn it, I know you," I said. *"You were down in that fucking pit. I went in after—"*

I remembered then. Last time I'd seen her, she was on the other side of a cage door. Everything was burning. People were shooting. I looked through the glass, and saw a stream of fire reflect off it. I went down there to get her. Somehow I knew her.

She knew me too; I could see it in her eyes. She knew me.

"You're wrong. I—"

I stepped in on her and she stepped back, against the wall. She looked scared as I stuck my finger in her face.

"Don't lie," I said. *"Tell me who—"*

Her eyes changed then. The black parts got big, until the green part was almost gone. My voice stopped cold and I just looked at her.

"Sleep," she said. Nothing happened for a few seconds; then she leaned close.

She looked scared before, but not now. In the recording, she looked at me like a bug under a magnifying glass. It happened just like that, like someone flipped a switch.

"Can you hear me?" she asked.

"Yes," my voice said.

"You don't know me. You have the wrong person. Whoever you think I am and whatever you think is going on, you're wrong. Understand?"

"Yes."

"I'm going to tell you to unstick the elevator, and when I do, you're going to forget this whole thing. Whatever you planned to do, you decided not to do it. We don't know each other. Got it?"

"Got it."

"I've got stuff I have to do during my lunch; don't follow me. Now unstick the elevator."

I watched my hand reach out and hit the button again. The bell stopped and the elevator kept going. We both just stood there the rest of the time. She left, and I stayed behind.

What the fuck?

I went back to a freeze-frame of that ugly face staring up at me, eyes gone black.

Who the fuck are you?

At the front door, I hit up the guard.

"Do you know who that was?"

"Who?"

"The stick. The one with the red hair."

"Oh, her," he said. "Name's Zoe Ott."

"Who is she?"

"Don't know. Some contractor."

"That's it?"

"She drinks, I think."

"Zoe Ott, huh?"

"Yes, ma'am."

"Thanks."

When I got outside, she was long gone. I had a name

and a face, though. Ten minutes and twenty bucks later, I had more than that.

> Name: Zoe Alia Ott.   Sex: Female.
> Hair: Red.   Eyes: Green.
> Parents: Harold Llewellyn Ott (deceased), Nichole Alia Donovan Ott (deceased).
> Citizenship tier: Three. Served: No. PH: No.
> Criminal Record: (7) counts of public drunkenness.
> Employment: Self/Other. None. Awarded monthly compensation in work-related death of Harold Llewellyn Ott. Currently contracts for Federal Bureau of Investigation in undisclosed capacity.

I brought up her picture again, staring up at me in the elevator. It was like she just erased my goddamned memory. How the hell had she done that?

There was more info on her, but mostly stuff I didn't care about. I skimmed through until I found the one thing I did care about.

> Last Known Residence: Pleasantview Apartments, apartment #613.

Zoe Ott—Mercy Greaves Medical Center

The second part of Nico's little favor took me halfway across town, a tidbit of information he'd completely forgotten to mention when he was blowing me off. I had to call Karen to bail on lunch, but I was all the way to the hospital and she still hadn't picked up. A sign outside said I couldn't have my phone on once I went in, so I'd been waiting in the rain for ten minutes before I finally got her on the line. I was going to be late.

"You have to cancel," she said.

"I'm sorry, Karen. Really."

"Don't sweat it," she said. "It's just lunch; we'll go tomorrow or something."

"It's just something came up. Nico's got me doing this thing, except it's not at the Federal Building. It's off somewhere else across town, so I had to go right over there."

"That's good, though, right? You get paid by the hour, don't you?"

"I guess."

"Then what's the problem?"

"I don't know. It feels like he's using me sometimes."

"Zoe, it's work you get paid to do," she said. "He's not using you. He's contracting you."

"I guess."

"He does that because you get results. Plus you're working with him. That's one of the best ways to get to know someone."

She had a way of making things seem better than they probably were. I guessed what she said might be true, but I was still ticked off.

"He ditched me today. I'm doing this totally on my own."

"He trusts you," she said. "He knows you can come through on your own."

"Maybe."

"Here's what you do; instead of us going to lunch tomorrow, you take him to lunch tomorrow instead."

"I can't do that."

"Zoe, it's been, like, two years. You're never going to get him if you don't even try."

My face got hot when she said that. It was easy for her to say. Guys stared at her all the time; they never looked at me that way. It wasn't the same.

"It wouldn't work anyway," I said. "He's hung up on someone else, I think."

"You always say that. You always say 'That wouldn't work anyway.' You're just afraid to try."

"Look, if you're so smart about guys, then how come you're still hooked up with that loser?"

"He has a name," she said, clipped. "We're not talking about that right now."

"Yeah, I know. You always say that. He's bad news, Karen. I know he's bad news."

She didn't say anything for a minute.

"Just . . . go do whatever you have to do," she said. She sounded pissed.

"Fine."

"I'll talk to you later." She hung up.

I shut my phone off like the sign said. First I was late getting into work; then those jerks made fun of me when my back was turned. I had to miss my lunch, and now Karen was pissed at me. Plus that woman . . .

This one is a destroyer. She will cause you to lose something very dear. . . .

She was in the green room. In the elevator I thought she was going to punch me. How did she remember me? Back then, I made her forget. How did she remember?

Shaking off my umbrella, I closed it and went inside, where a bunch of people were sitting like they'd been waiting there forever. A big, round woman in a flowered shirt sat behind the main desk.

"Can I help you?"

"I'm here to see Jan Holst," I said.

"Visiting hours resume at one," she said. "You can have a seat and wait if you like, or you can come back."

"I'm not here to visit. I'm here to do an interview."

"Interview?"

The room got brighter, and I stared at her until her fat face went slack.

"Just tell me where her room is."

"Sixth floor. Room 6E7."

"Go back to what you were doing and never mind me."

I stopped pushing her, and she looked back to the computer screen.

Alone in the elevator, I hit the button for the sixth floor. The inside of the door was mirrored, and in it I looked like a drowned rat. My hair was frizzed and tangled, and my face was blotchy. My ears were bright red.

As the car went up, I thought about that woman back at the FBI, Alice Hsieh. She had the same abilities I did—I was sure of it. For the first time, it occurred to me that if I noticed her, she must have noticed me too. If that was true, she must have known how I got the information out of the guy in the wheelchair. She must have seen too when I got the information out of Vesco, but she didn't try to stop it or ask me about it after. She just left, and never said anything about it at all.

"You think Wachalowski hits that?"

The memory wormed its way in, pushing the other stuff out. Vesco joked about Nico having sex with me. Then he and his friend laughed about it. Nico being interested in me physically was actually a joke in the office. It was something to laugh about.

My reflection got blurry, and I wiped my eyes. Any second the elevator door was going to open and I'd be standing there crying. I took a deep breath, but my reflection stayed blurry. I blinked hard a couple times and rubbed them, but it didn't go away. It was like I was looking through a haze or something, or like heat was rippling the air. The elevator floor creaked and I turned, but nothing was there. When I looked back, my reflection was normal again.

Shit. Not here.

When I saw things, it happened out of nowhere and it didn't matter where I was. I couldn't afford some kind of episode in the middle of a hospital, when I was supposed to be doing an interview. I took a few deep breaths and tried to calm down. The antsy feeling I got up and down my spine when I really wanted to drink was kicking in big time. The last thing I needed was some kind of panic attack. . . .

The bell dinged and the doors opened up. No one was waiting for the car on the other side. I smoothed down my hair and wiped my eyes one more time, then stepped out. The door clunked behind me, then slid shut.

I found the right room and went inside, where a man in a white lab coat stood next to a hospital bed. I peeked past him to see the woman who was lying there. There was a bandage across the front of her neck, covered in gauze tape. After a minute, she noticed me and looked past the man in the coat. When she did, he looked over.

"Can I help you?"

"I'm here to see Jan Holst."

"Who are you?"

"I'm Zoe Ott."

"You're with the FBI?" He said it like he couldn't believe it.

"Yes."

I fished my contractor's badge out and held it up so he could see it.

"Okay," he said. He turned to the woman. "Are you sure you're up to this?"

She nodded, still looking at me. She looked pretty beat-up, but she smiled, just a little.

"You'll have to leave," I told him. He frowned, and I felt a little surge of anger come from him.

"Look, Miss Ott," he said. "This wom—"

He stopped in midsentence as I concentrated and the room got bright. As the colors drained away from everything except the light around his head, out of the corner of my eye I saw the woman's smile get a little bigger. I pushed back the spike of red light that had been forming until it disappeared back into the blue.

"I need privacy," I told him. "If anything happens, I'll get you."

He nodded. In the doorway, he looked back at her one more time, then left, closing the door behind him. The lights went back to normal. When I turned and looked at her, she was still smiling. There was a chair in the room and I pulled it over next to the bed and sat down.

"How are you doing?" I asked. She shook her head, and pointed to the bandage over her throat.

"Sorry, right."

Nico told me about that in the phone message. I had to sign out an electronic tablet. I took it out of my purse and turned it on, making the little gray screen light up. She held out her hand and I gave it to her.

"Does it hurt?" I asked. She shook her head, then tapped on the little keyboard and angled the screen so I could see.

I'll be okay.

"Good."

What did you want to ask me, Agent Ott?

"Miss Ott. I just work for them sometimes."

Digging in my coat pocket, I found the list of questions I was supposed to ask and pulled it out. Smoothing the paper, I looked at the first question.

Where is Hiro Takanawa?

I focused in on her so I could put her under, and she closed her eyes. When the aura appeared over her head, though, I saw that thin, white halo. The swirl of color behind it stayed calm when I tried to change them, and couldn't. She opened her eyes and smiled as she met mine.

My heart was beating faster. Nico's questions sat forgotten in my hand.

She tapped on the tablet's keyboard.

You can see.

"Yes." She could see me, too.

We've contacted you more than once. Why don't you respond?

That was true. I'd gotten several notes and a few weird phone calls. I knew they were interested in me. The weird little woman that appeared after the revivor took me and wired me to their machine told me they were interested in me.

I didn't have a good answer for her. I just shrugged.

Aren't you even a little bit curious?

"I've just . . . been avoiding it, I guess."

Why?

My words got caught up in my throat, but then I started to relax a little. For a second, it actually felt like I'd taken a big shot of ouzo. I felt the tension inside me loosen.

"Because I was scared," I said.

Scared of what?

"Nico doesn't trust you . . . I thought he'd be mad . . . I was worried he might be right, maybe, or that . . . I wouldn't be special?" I said. The words were flowing like I was drunk. "That I wouldn't be any good, and I'd be as bad at this as I am . . ."

I trailed off, and she smiled again.

You are special, and there's no reason to be scared. We would welcome you, and I know how lonely it feels to think you're alone.

My throat burned and I felt tears in my eyes again. She was right, in a way. It seemed like I'd gotten to the point where I was doing everything right, or the way I was supposed to do them anyway. I was trying to be like everyone else, to go to bed sober and wake up and go to work and make friends, but it wasn't working. Even though I knew more people now than I ever had, I was lonely. Karen acted like it was the drinking that made her kick me out, but it wasn't. It was part of it, but it was the other stuff she couldn't stand. My ability, and the dreams, and all the things she thought were so cool at first; they started to scare her.

The people around you don't understand you, Jan typed. *They can't.*

I shrugged as her fingers moved over the screen.

You need to understand what it is you can do—how to do it and when to use it. Let us show you.

"Maybe," I said.

These people and the way they treat you make you sad, but these people, the ones who aren't like you, what they think doesn't matter. They don't deserve to hold this power over you—

"Stop."

She deleted the message. She didn't look disappointed or mad or anything. She just stopped typing.

Nico didn't trust them; that was the thing. Sometimes, the way he talked, it was like he thought that all those people that got killed back then deserved what they got. Sometimes, the way he talked, I wondered if maybe he didn't trust me either, and I really wanted him to. I wanted him to believe in me. I wanted him to know that whatever side he was on, I was on it too.

"I'm sorry," I said.

It's okay.

I looked back at the paper Nico gave me, the one with the questions, but I knew I wouldn't ask them. I crumpled it and shoved it in my pocket.

"Is the city really going to burn?" I asked. Her eyes got very serious.

Yes.

"Why? How?"

Meet with us and you'll get your answer.

As I read the words, a bad feeling came over me. I started feeling really dizzy, so bad it made me sick to my stomach a little.

"I can't . . ."

If you don't, she'll be forced to—

I practically jumped out of my skin as a loud popping noise went off right near my head. At the same exact time, one of her eyes blew up. It just blew apart and caved in, leaving a big red hole behind. Her whole body jerked on the bed, and the eye she had left rolled in the socket, looking off at a weird angle.

The tablet slipped out of her hand and clattered onto the floor. She slumped back onto the pillow, and the machine she was hooked up to was beeping over and over. Someone was shouting from down the hall. A puff of smoke was rising from a spot in front of the bed.

I was still trying to figure out what the heck just happened when the IV rack next to the bed shook all by itself, then tipped over and crashed onto the floor. When I looked over, I saw the air ripple there, just for a second. For just a second, I saw a guy standing there. He was bald, and his skin was gray. His eyes glowed a dull yellowish color, and for that quick flash, they were staring right at me. He moved, and I saw a gun in his hand before the air flickered again, and he was gone.

What just happened?

The doctor came through the doorway. He looked from the woman on the bed to me. The look on his face snapped me out of it.

"What happened?" he asked. When I concentrated on her, just the barest blue light appeared, like a pilot light, and then even that flickered out. The vitals monitor started droning a steady beep, and the doctor's eyes widened.

"Jesus, what did you do?"

Other people started filling up the room, pushing me out of the way. I grabbed the tablet and backed away.

"What the hell did you do?" the doctor demanded.

"Nothing, I . . ."

"Call the police!" someone yelled. The doctor reached for me and I focused on him, stopping him before he could grab me.

"Leave me alone," I told him. His eyelids drooped, and his hand began to lower back by his side.

"Leave me alone."

I slipped out the door and ran.

Nico Wachalowski—Sigil Veranda Apartments, Apartment #901

Mist gave way to a short squall of snow as I inched

down the street. The strip of sky above the buildings had turned dull gray. Sean's place was on the other side of town, and by the time I got there, the commuters were in full swing. Traffic had piled up in front and behind. People trudged along the sidewalks on either side with their collars turned up and their heads down. I nosed past a group of people waiting impatiently at the curb, crept down the side street, then took a concrete ramp into the garage below.

According to the apartment's security logs, Sean got in late the night before. The timing suggested he'd gone straight home after we spoke. That put three hours or so between when he arrived home and when he sent the message. Another two had passed since then, and he never showed up at work. He was in trouble.

Heading up the front entrance, I checked the logs for visitors. There had been a handful, but none were signed in by him. Cameras didn't record anyone who was unaccounted for, coming or going.

Inside I took the express elevator up, and then made my way to Sean's unit. I gave the door a knock, but no one answered. I knocked again.

"Sean, open up."

Using the backscatter to scan through the door, I could make out his coat on a rack. Next to that, I could see his shoes. Nothing moved in the gray space behind them.

"Sean, if you're there, open up."

I listened for a minute, but didn't hear anything. I took my badge from my pocket and put a call in to Noakes.

Noakes, I'm at Sean's apartment, and I need a silent entry. I also need a warrant related to possible crime in progress.

Done and done, Agent.

He stayed on the line while I held my badge to the

door scanner and the bolt released, suppressing any voice or electronic response. When I pushed open the door, I saw that the apartment was dark. I went inside and closed the door behind me.

Through the thermal filter I could make out faint traces of footsteps, but none of them had been recent. None approached the door. No one had come or gone for hours.

Creeping into the main hall, I drew my gun and adjusted my visuals to let in more light. Nothing looked disturbed. The apartment was completely quiet.

"Sean?"

No one answered. The thermal signatures were very faint, but got stronger through the living area. He had sat on the sofa for a while, and there was an empty glass on a marble-topped end table. Fresher footsteps headed toward the bedroom. I followed them in.

The bed was still made, but I could make out a warm spot in the middle, as if he had lain there on top of the covers at some point. I recorded the image, then followed the footsteps through a door and into the master bath.

In the bathroom, he'd stood in front of the sink. There were drops of brown liquid on the porcelain and bunches of tissues in the trash, stained with something black, maybe ink. There was a thermal handprint on the toilet lid.

Lifting it up, I looked in and saw the water was stained pink. A wad of tissue was clogging the bowl, and floating above it was a wrinkled white orb that trailed red tissue.

Noakes, are you getting this?

I zoomed in on the eye. It looked like it had been cut out. The iris was clouded and scarred.

I got it. Is it his?

Checking . . .

I tried to scan the retina, but it was too damaged. Something had scorched it.

Kneeling in front of the sink, I fished through the trash. Under the tissues was a small, glass bottle with a dropper. It was unmarked, but had a sharp, chemical smell.

What is it?

I'm not sure. Hold on.

Back in the bedroom, I noticed some scoring on the frame next to the bathroom doorknob, and pinprick burn marks on the carpet. When I zoomed in on the latch, I saw the metal bolt had been burned through. Someone cut their way in to get to him.

Someone broke in.

I'm sending a forensics team over, Noakes said. *Keep me informed.*

Roger that.

He closed the connection.

Rain drummed against a window next to the bed. I switched to the backscatter and searched the room, looking for anything that might have gotten left behind. When I scanned across the floor, I found a safe concealed under an area rug next to the bed.

Moving the rug aside, I raised the panel to find it fitted with an electronic lock. I remembered Sean's message.

31 03 76 11 52 57 81 1

I keyed the sequence into the safe's keypad, and a moment later I felt a thump through the floor as the bolts retracted. Whatever he was trying to tell me, whatever he wanted me to know, it was inside.

I turned the arm and pulled open the heavy door. The only thing inside was a small recording device. A yellow LED flashed on one side of it.

It looked like the recorder was receiving from a wireless source, or at least it had been. I tapped into the recording buffer, and a window came up in my field of vision, displaying a test code. The recording came from a camera eye, a version of a JZ implant's optics, or a revivor's eye. News peddlers and paparazzi used them. The eyes had a recording buffer, but they could also transmit to an external recorder.

Sean had one implanted, then. The eye would be inferior to the recorder he already had, but whatever it recorded wouldn't end up in the JZI buffer. The only reason for him to do that was so that he could record things without anyone at the FBI seeing them.

I played the recording. There was no sound, just a streaming image from Sean's point of view. He was standing in the bathroom, looking into the mirror in front of the sink. I knew the expression I saw on his face; he was in trouble at the time the recording was made.

He looked into his own eyes in the mirror, giving the illusion he was looking out at me. He reached up with an erasable marker and began writing on the mirror in black ink.

I know we can't influence you anymore.

I don't know why.

He wiped the message away with a tissue. He dropped it in the trash next to the sink and wrote again.

I'm sorry.

He frowned, and his eyes looked sad as he added:

I tried to protect you.

He wiped the mirror clean, then looked back through the bathroom doorway like he heard something. After a second, he turned back to the mirror again. He held the marker up to it, and began to write again as a light flickered somewhere behind him.

Motoko Ai believes you are an important element. She's been looking for you. She will contact you soon. Be careful; she lies.

Motoko Ai . . . I didn't know that name. He wiped the mirror clean, and began writing more quickly, glancing back through the doorway again. Sparks were spitting out from the seam next to the knob of the bedroom door. A cutter was being used to slice through the bolt.

Fawkes has the nukes. He was the buyer. The same buyer was behind the first attack. Fawkes was behind the bombing of Concrete Falls.

He underlined the last part, then stopped writing and turned around as the bedroom door opened and a figure stepped through the smoke. He pulled the bathroom door shut and locked himself inside. Just before it closed, I caught a glimpse of a pale face moving toward him. It was only for a second, but the soft glow behind the eyes was unmistakable. As he turned back to the sink, I saw sparks begin to fly from the door seam as the cutter began making its way through.

Sean turned back to the mirror and started to scrawl one last message:

Second Chance—

Light flashed behind him and he stopped, throwing the marker aside. He opened the medicine cabinet and I watched him remove the small brown glass bottle I found in the trash. The camera looked up at the ceiling as he held the dropper over it. A fat drop swelled at the tip, then fell and the image immediately warped. A second later, it went blank. From the look of it, whoever came for him removed the eye, but was too late. He'd destroyed it.

The mirror above the sink was wiped clean. Either

he'd done it after he destroyed the camera, or the intruder had.

Fawkes was behind the bombing of Concrete Falls.

It wasn't some kind of terrorist protest, then. If it was true and Fawkes was behind it, he wouldn't have staged a strike like that without a very specific reason. If Sean hadn't taken the chance to say what that was, then he either didn't have time or didn't know.

I rewound the footage, looking for the revivor's face. The recording was hectic, but he managed to pick up a few frames' worth anyway. The skin was Caucasian but definitely revivor, with its characteristic gray tinge. It had a complete lack of hair. Follicle dissolution was usually associated with assembly-line revivors. I cleaned up the image, canceling out the motion blur. When I did, I stopped cold.

Faye.

In the image, she was stalking through the smoke, toward the door. Her eyes stared dispassionately but with purpose. She was still out there, and for whatever reason, she had come for him.

I took the recording chip from the unit in the floor safe and slipped it in my pocket. At least for the time being, no one else knew about it. I meant to keep it that way.

She hadn't been lost in the fire. I'd hoped to track her down one day, but the circumstances couldn't have been much worse. Sean wasn't just a federal agent; he was more than that. In another circle, one I wasn't allowed to ever see into, he was something else entirely.

If it got out who had taken him, it was going to mean trouble, and not just for her.

3

Rise

Faye Dasalia—Alto Do Mundo

I sat in a wooden chair and I waited. A man in the next room spoke on his cell phone, his voice easy and certain. Somehow I felt sure he was speaking to her ... that physically frail woman with the oversized head and the fishlike face; the woman he answered to, both his leader and master.

His suite was inside the Alto Do Mundo. The third largest structure inside the city, it housed much of the elite. In life I had seen it only from afar, watching it from the rail that took me to work. Once I investigated a murder there. Part of me had always envied those inside, even then.

His apartment suite was big and very cold. It conveyed his privilege and power to all, no matter where they might look. The design he'd chosen was minimalist, open rooms integrating high-end appliances and electronics, where each line and edge was arranged perfectly. I admired what he'd done, the oasis of order that he'd fashioned away from the chaos of the streets below. My eyes followed the room's flow, and I found comfort in it, even though I knew that it would soon be gone. Very soon the man on the phone would be dead. Very soon the Alto Do Mundo itself, and everyone inside it, would exist only as fading memories.

Normally, I'd never have gotten inside, but we were a vice of his, and he'd had me brought in, bypassing security. When I arrived, I found the door was open. In the entryway he'd left a cardboard gift box for me, with a note card. The gift box contained a series of items: an elaborate set of silk lingerie, a black wig, and an array of cosmetics. There was a computer printout, explaining what he wanted.

It should have been humiliating to me, applying makeup to my lips and nipples, cinching in my waist, and pushing up my breasts, then sitting and posing while he took his time. It should have been an affront, but as I sat on the chair, I felt nothing. The truth was that I'd hoped I would feel something. I wanted to feel some sense of humiliation, even excitement, but the reality was that I did not. The closest I came was the wanting itself.

What drove me now were purpose and survival. Not survival in the traditional sense—I'd already lost my life—but my mind was still aware. It knew that it was finite, and that whatever came after was unknown . . . dark and empty and endless.

That unknown was like a void. Beneath my consciousness and my memories, it yawned like a black hole in the depths of space. With each passing second, it pulled me deeper, away from all that I knew. Any second I might fall across that rim, that dark event horizon, and plunge down through the field of my memories to the one thing left that scared me to my core. Life and death were just concepts, but not that endless unknown. That bottom-less void was real.

The man on the phone was speaking Japanese. I tuned my hearing a little as he spoke, and watched the translation scroll at the bottom edge of my periphery:

No. Wherever it came from, it wasn't supposed to be there. I was already out of the building when . . .

The words passed by over the swell of my breasts. I'd been attractive in life, and I'd known that. Men had stared at those breasts, compelled by their curves, but they were just meat now. The blood that moved through them was black and cold. The veins could be covered up with body paint, but the flesh was not alive.

The man who had me brought to him did not care.

. . . knew where I was, it was arranged beforehand. I didn't do anything wrong. . . .

He moved past a doorway, through my line of sight. He wore a gold watch and an expensive suit of which the tones matched my lingerie. He glanced at me, and I captured his image. He was a powerfully featured Asian man, with long hair that was thick and luxurious. His skin was smooth and pampered.

Identity confirmed: Takanawa, Hiro.

He moved out of view and continued speaking. My mind drifted as I watched the words go by.

. . . should be thanking me. I managed to keep one of them. You only really need one. . . .

The field of my memories stirred like embers, a field of lights that were tagged and catalogued. I could access each at will. I saw images of him at the hotel. During the raid, the agents had let him go. He'd left with something of ours.

My memories were now of two different types: those formed before my death and those formed after. A laser line cut between, and it was there that I found my new purpose. Each second that passed, it was a reminder. In my first living memory, I was five, and for a time my memories had been pure. As my life went on, they became fragmented. Bits and pieces were stolen. They were manipulated and sometimes changed. I had been rewired by an unseen force and lived two lives, and not known. Approaching the memory separation between my life and my death, the embers came to contain more lies than truth.

Until my last, when I lay on a sofa and blood pumped out of my chest. I saw the face of the man in front of me, and heard the last words I would hear in my life.

"What a waste."

Too much of my life had been just that: a waste. I'd worked so hard for a shot at moving up, not knowing it was all lies. I'd pushed myself until there was nothing left. I did it because I regretted my choice, and because I was afraid. Once I was dead, I didn't want to come back. I'd have done anything to get out of it, but I never got the chance.

The name of my killer turned out to be Lev—Lev Prutsko, the last of four Slavic recruits brought in for key terror strikes. Samuel Fawkes had bought him through a broker for the price of a new car. He was the closest I had now to a friend.

Fawkes's purpose was Lev's purpose, and now mine: preserve the free will of all humanity. Stop any more people from sharing my fate. It was clear and absolute. An echo from my old mind latched on to it as a justice to be served and also, more secretly, as a distraction from that dark void, below.

Yes. Yes. Good-bye.

Mr. Takanawa stepped through the doorway and

slipped his cell phone into his suit jacket. I sat still and did not breathe as he approached and faced me at arm's length. I couldn't read the expression on his face. Men had stared at me before, but this was unlike anything I recalled. He inspected me like he might a statue, not yet certain what he thought. Only his erection betrayed something more. After a minute or so, he came closer and knelt down in front of me. He moved his face close to mine.

An orange light coursed up each side of his neck, thick, hot lines that branched out before fading. I followed them down below his shirt collar, to the heavy coal that pulsed inside his chest. A thin line appeared in my periphery. It spiked each time his heart beat.

"You're a beautiful woman," he said, so close that I could feel his breath on my face.

Another of them once said those words to me. Later, I'd be told to forget what I'd heard, and I would, like I was told. Every time I heard them it was like the first time, unexpected and welcome.

Nothing stirred inside me when I heard them now. As best I could interpret, he was earnest, but I was not beautiful, nor a woman. I was something different now.

"I said you are beautiful," the man said again, his eyes narrowing a little.

"Thank you."

He looked into my eyes for a bit longer, their soft, moonlit glow reflected on his face.

He likes that, I thought. *It's part of it, for him.*

"May I ask you something?" I said to him softly. His face changed, just a little. It wasn't interaction that he wanted; it was something else, but I was curious.

"One question," he said.

"Why revivors?"

He was known to be suddenly violent, and I was ready for that, but he stayed calm. In answer, he just smiled. He moved so close I saw the glow from my eyes reflected in his own.

His pupils opened to two dark, glassy spots. It happened when they exerted their power. He was trying to control me, I could see. When he failed, I saw fear creep into his eyes. The heat in his chest pulsed faster and harder, and the orange glow up the sides of his neck grew hotter as the veins there became engorged. The line monitoring his heart spiked higher. What he saw scared him, but it was more than that. It was exhilaration.

"There's a darkness inside of you," he said. "All of you. I can't control you or know you, and that . . ."

He reached forward and took my hands in his own. They were dry and very warm. He stood, and pulled me up gently to face him. His eyes went back to normal.

"Come with me," he said, and walked past me. When I turned, I saw him cross toward the bedroom. As I followed, I pulled the wig from my head and let it fall to the floor. Cold air blew across the skin of my bare scalp. When we were inside he turned, frowning as I placed my cold hands on his chest.

"That's wrong," he said. "Put it back on."

I slid my left hand up the side of his neck, running my fingertips through his coarse black hair. He didn't pull away, but was still frowning.

"You heard me," he said. "Do what I sa—"

My hand split along an invisible seam and splayed between the middle and ring finger. His body, so alive, jumped. His eyes darted to the cavity and stared. Fear returned when the blade inside caught the light.

I could have impaled him before he could move, but the blade was not for him. A thin plastic tube shot out from beneath it. The needle locked on the heat inside his neck and plunged into the branching orange band of light.

By the time he slapped his hand over the sting, the tube had reeled back and my arm had snapped shut. He just stared at me, confused.

"What—"

The toxin acted fast and paralyzed him. His arms fell to his sides, and he staggered back. The muscles in his face began to loosen.

I stepped in and supported him as he fell. I reached into his jacket and took the gun, then tossed it onto the bed.

"What . . . are you . . . doing?" he gasped, as I eased him back onto the plush comforter. I recorded and transmitted his vitals. The excitement he'd shown before was gone now. All that was left was his fear.

Subject secured.

Good. Site 1 confirmed secure. Transmitting collection point.

Takanawa could see the gun, out of reach. His eyes locked on to it, but he couldn't move. I watched him try to, and fail, as I sat down on the bedspread next to him. I waited for him to look back up at me.

"Where is the last one?" I asked him. He could still speak, but he tried to shake his head.

"You know what I mean," I said. "We got the other eleven, but you were seen to take one. Where is it?"

". . . don't know," he breathed.

"If it's here," I said, "I will leave with that and nothing else. Do you understand?"

He understood. I could see it in his eyes.

"Where is it?" I asked again.

". . . not here . . ."

I'd search just to be sure, but I believed him. He'd have handed off the device before now. Lev would find out what he knew.

I left the room and changed back into street clothes, then stowed the lingerie and wig in my bag. I looked at myself in the bathroom mirror, and wiped the makeup away.

It had taken time to find myself again, after reanimation. There'd been a disconnect with my reflection, like it was somebody else. At first I thought it was the physical change; the grayish skin tone or dark veins that showed through. As time passed, though, I saw it was something else.

The image in the mirror was someone else; Faye Dasalia had been lost long ago. She had been lost before she was ever killed. All that was left of her existed in me. She'd been revived, in me, when Nico woke me. All that she truly was and ever would be had emerged only in death. I'd only recently made her face my own. The woman from before was not really Faye. My memories formed from across that divide, and they were not corrupted. I was Faye Dasalia, more complete than I ever had been in life.

Beginning transport.

Acknowledged.

I went back into the bedroom where he lay, his chest rising and falling very slowly. He was awake and aware. His eyes bargained with me as I approached him.

"It's time for you to come with me," I said in his ear as I got a grip on him. I pulled the LW suit over us, and lifted up his body. He was frightened, but he didn't need to be.

Whatever answer he'd sought in revivors, he'd understand soon enough.

Nico Wachalowski — The Shit Pit, Bullrich Heights

I approached the place where Calliope suggested we meet, thinking maybe I should have picked the spot myself. The narrow street outside had a row of motorcycles hugging a brick wall under an overpass where everything was covered in graffiti. Heat rose from a metal grate next to the curb, and a patch of fog drifted across a broken sidewalk littered with cigarette butts.

Information request complete.

The results of my dig on Concrete Falls came up as I crossed the street. The miner found a lot of media noise about the bombing, but most of it was commentary. The limited footage of bomber didn't provide a positive identification. That fact alone suggested he'd known where the security cameras were. There were only a few seconds of footage, and even taken from different angles, they could show only so much. The bomber was male. He had dark skin. He appeared to be between thirty and forty. No thermal images or X-rays were taken. It could have been a revivor.

Whoever he was, he'd moved past the recruitment stations and through a door that led into the back offices. When this was noticed, two guards moved to follow, but never reached him.

Given his movements, it was thought that the bomber had specifically targeted the offices where the Heinlein reps were set up. If Sean was right, though, and Fawkes was actually behind the attack, then it wasn't just to make some political point or to hurt Heinlein. It wasn't easy for Fawkes to make a move like that, and it put him at huge risk of being discovered. There had to be a reason for it.

Hey, you showing up or what? Calliope.

I'm here now.

The first time I met Calliope Flax was in a parking garage after a revivor tried to kill her. The last time I'd seen her was after her interrogation, banged up and fuzzy from the dope. She was third tier, a heartbeat away from living on the street. The reward I sent her way for the tip she provided didn't even cover her medical bills, and I knew that without help she was going under. I suggested the service.

Later she disappeared. When I finally tracked her down, I found out she was stationed in Yambio.

I could hear the beat from outside as I approached the front of the place. Pushing through the heavy door, I walked into a dark room full of loud music. It was packed full of tough-looking customers. A few guys looked at me, noting the reflection from the JZI. Word started spreading that a cop just walked in.

I looked around but I didn't see her. Between the darkness, the smoke, and the bodies it was hard to spot anyone.

I'm here. Where are you?

Downstairs.

A set of stairs led to a basement floor where a second bar was set up in front of a bank of video screens. Sitting alone near the top of the steps was a woman who looked out of place. She was well dressed, with a plain wool cap that didn't match the outfit. The only thing she had in common with the other patrons was her tattoo: a snake that ringed her neck, then swallowed its tail. She was sitting at a table without a drink in front of her. She looked bored.

When I started to move past her, she looked up with bright blue eyes and waved for me to come closer. I held up my hand to indicate I was meeting someone else and couldn't stop, and she reached out and took it. The second her cold fingers touched my hand, she zeroed in on a pressure point and sent a jolt up my forearm. She smiled faintly when she saw my surprise, and pulled me gently toward her table.

"I'm Penny," she shouted over the music.

"Can I have my hand back?" She let go and I flexed my fingers.

"You're kind of cute," she said, reaching toward my face. I went to stop her, and she brushed my hand away casually. She touched my cheek, then ran her fingers through my hair.

"Are you always this forward?"

"What's the matter? Are you not used to being touched by a woman?"

The truth was that I wasn't. Not anymore. She seemed satisfied by my lack of an answer, taking her hand away.

"So you're him, huh?"

"Him who?"

Her pupils widened, and I felt dizzy for a second. It passed almost immediately, and her eyes went back to normal.

"You are him. You're Nico Wachalowski," she shouted.

"Okay, you got my attention. Who are you?"

She leaned closer, putting her lips to my ear.

"Someone wants to meet with you," she said.

"You don't say."

"I do say."

"And who would that be?"

"Motoko Ai."

I remembered Sean's words scrawled on the bathroom mirror: *Motoko Ai . . . she will contact you soon.*

"Should I know that name?" I asked.

"She has information you'll be interested in."

"What kind of information?"

"Information about Samuel Fawkes."

If she didn't have my attention before, she had it then. She leaned back, looking satisfied. Her big eyes looked me up and down.

"I guess I can see why she's into you," she said.

"What?"

"Not Ai. She's not interested in stuff like that. I mean Zoe."

"Are you a friend of Zoe's?"

"Sort of. Tell me; are you just completely clueless?"

"What?"

"Because if you are, then open your eyes, and if you aren't, then stop being careless with her."

The whole thing caught me off guard. Before I could answer, she changed the subject again.

"Will you meet with Ai?"

"Where?"

"We'll set it up through Zoe."

"Zoe?"

"She's coming too. Will you come?"

"Yes."

"The events of two years ago were nothing, Mr. Wachalowski. Please be there."

Before I could answer, she hopped off her stool and gave me a wave as she moved off into the crowd.

You get lost or what? Cal.

No. Keep your pants on.

I made my way downstairs and found her standing against the far wall with a big guy on either side of her. She looked like I remembered, with the same cropped hair and the same crooked nose. Somewhere inside me, tension let go; she was in one piece. She was talking to a

black man with a cauliflower ear when she noticed me
and waved. When she smiled, I saw she never replaced
the missing tooth.

What are you drinking? I asked.

You buying?

Sure.

Whiskey. Straight up.

I got the bartender's attention and let him scan my
card. With a glass in each hand, I made my way over to
her. The two guys were gone before I got there.

"Friends of yours?" I asked, handing one over.

"Fight buddies," she said. She took it and drank half
without blinking.

"You get set up okay?"

"Yeah. Guy named Buckster from that group Second
Chance picked me up. They set me up with a place."

Second Chance. Sean had written that on his bathroom mirror, minutes before he disappeared.

"Who set you up?" I asked.

"Second Chance," she said. "They work with vets.
What's the problem? You look like you just shit yourself."

I ran a search on the organization. It was like Cal
said; they were big on fund-raising for vets and charity
work. They ran free clinics in some of the worst neigh-
borhoods. They were also one of the biggest referrers
for Posthumous Service recruits, funneling third-tier
citizens to recruitment centers to get wired. Centers like
Concrete Falls.

"What was your contact's name again?" I asked.

"Leon Buckster. Seriously, what's up?"

I shook my head.

"Probably nothing," I said. "Keep an eye open for me
though, would you?"

"Keep an eye open for what?"

"Anything to do with revivors."

"Hell," she said, "he was trying to get some hobo to wire up when I stepped off the fucking train. I figured he got a kickback or something. Does this have to do with a case?"

"Maybe," I said. "Just keep an eye open. Have you found a job yet?"

"Still working on that."

"Will you go back to the arena?"

Can't.

She held up her left hand so I could see it. Even in the dim light, I could see the black veins standing out.

Sorry, I said. *I didn't know.*

Ugly, huh?

I've seen worse. The hand's not a bad match. Where's the join?

She pulled the sleeve of her jacket up so I could see where the skin changed color. Inside there was a thin filter, a piece of revivor tech that handled the nerve and muscle interaction and kept the living side from attacking the necrotized one. A small circulator ran the revivor blood through the limb. It wasn't a bad job.

How's it working out for you?

She shrugged like it was no big deal, but I could see it was.

Do you get used to it?

Not really.

I did some digging. You made a name for yourself over there.

She shrugged again, like it was no big deal, but, honestly, it was. With no formal education, she'd gone from grunt status to full control over a squad of revivors in less than two years. In that short time, the bandits who ran the area learned to know her by a name they themselves had given her.

I'm impressed, I said.

Yeah?

Yes.

How impressed?

I wasn't sure what she meant. When I didn't answer, she gritted her teeth, then leaned forward and grabbed my lapel. She put her lips near my ear and I could smell the whiskey on her breath.

"I know the score," she said. "A tour buys you a leg up, but that's it. I'm done with the grind and I can't fight anymore, but I didn't lose my hand over there to come back and flip burgers."

She sighed, breath hot on my neck, then leaned back and let go of my coat.

"Before I left, you told me I could be more than I was," she said. "You said if I busted my ass, it could all be mine. You mean that?"

"I did."

The reality was that if she hadn't enlisted, Calliope would have ended up in jail, in a shelter, or on the street. The housing project where she was holed up got shut down while she was gone, and the police had forced everybody out. Some were arrested, and the rest slipped through the cracks. With no education, money, or assets, and sitting at tier three with no way to get any, she would have lost what little she had.

I told myself that when I looked at her hand.

"Well, here I am," she said.

The military had changed her. She looked more in control and more focused. I thought I could help her. I owed her that much. In some ways, I owed her my life.

Ex-military, especially decorated ones, pulled a lot of weight. *I have some contacts. What can you do?*

I'm wired to run revivors—units or groups. I know weapons and intel extraction.

That wasn't bad, actually. It would be easy, even after coming back, for someone like her to end up back where she started. It would be a waste.

How did you like soldiering?

Better than flipping burgers. I raised my eyebrows, and she changed her tone.

I liked it, she said.

There's always private military. Stillwell Corps takes a lot of soldiers on after their tours. It's good pay, access to the latest tech, and some great training.

She thought about that, and I could see the idea take root. She nodded.

That sounds okay, she said.

Let me put out some feelers.

She smiled and nodded again. She punched me in the arm. *Thanks.*

The smile went away and she looked at the floor. Her tongue poked through the gap where her tooth was missing.

Thanks for writing me over there too.

No problem.

You do that because you thought you had to?

At first.

The truth was, I did it because I didn't think anyone else would. Any kind of contact from back home was a big deal over there. I kept the messages short, and wrote three times without hearing back. After that, I stopped. It was months later when, out of the blue, I got a message back from her. After that, it got to be a regular thing. I kept her up on things she asked about, and she told me stories about day-to-day downtime in the middle of a war zone, something I knew well. She never talked about combat or any of the bloodshed I knew she must have seen. I never asked.

Yeah, well, thanks.

I liked hearing from you. It took me back.

I'll bet.

We going to stay friends?

We'll see.

She smiled, eyelids drooping. She was drunk.

You worry about me?

I did, a little.

A call came in as she shook her glass at the bartender across the room.

Incoming call. It was headquarters. I held up one hand while I picked up.

Wachalowski here.

Agent, your victim, Holst, from the raid. She's dead.

I thought she was stable.

She was. Someone assassinated her right there in the hospital.

What?

Your operative was the only one with her when it happened.

What are you saying? Zoe shot her?

I'm not saying anything. I'm just telling you what happened.

Where is Zoe now?

She fled the scene.

That would have been hours ago. If it was true, she had to be losing it by now.

Do not let them bring her in, understand? I'll find her.

I'll do what I can, but—

Don't let them bring her in.

Calliope was looking at me and I noticed her scowl.

"You got somewhere else you got to be?" she asked.

"I'm sorry, official business. Have a few drinks on me. We'll have to catch up later." Her scowl deepened.

Who is Zoe Ott?

That took me by surprise. Cal hadn't seen Zoe since the factory, when she pulled her out of Fawkes's holding pens. She hadn't said anything about it even under direct questioning. I had assumed that Zoe made her forget, though she never admitted to it.

I ran a check on my JZI, and found a brief intrusion. She'd been monitoring the wire for references to Zoe, and when she got a hit she'd snooped at least part of the conversation. I'd underestimated Calliope Flax.

Cal, listening in on FBI communications is a felony— Who is she, Wachalowski?

She was one of the people we recovered from the underground factory when it was infiltrated.

I know that. I was there. I mean, who is she?

What do you mean?

Her mouth parted to show the gap from her missing tooth, and her eyes got serious.

Look, I saw her at the FBI. I know you know what I'm talking about. What is the deal with that spooky little bitch? What did she do to me?

I didn't have a good answer for that. She needed one, I could see, but I didn't have one for her.

Don't tell me you don't know her, she said.

I know her.

Did she make me forget?

If she was asking, then she knew the answer to that. I wasn't sure what Zoe had done to her, exactly, but I knew it was something. Cal needed someone—me—to verify that, but there were more of them out there than just Zoe. That kind of knowledge could be dangerous.

You saved her life. Do you remember going underground?

Parts.

You went down there to get her, I think.

Did she make me forget?

We'll talk about it later.

It's a yes or no question, Wachalowski.

It's not that simple. We'll talk about it later, but for now, don't say anything about it to anyone else.

What?

I mean it. You'll attract the wrong kind of attention. Don't talk about it.

What wrong kind of attention? What the hell is going on?

Look, what happened two years ago . . . it didn't end then. The bombings, the attacks—they're going to get worse. Powerful people are involved in this, and I don't want you getting caught up in it.

And this thing you can't get into, it involves revivors and Second Chance?

I have to go. Forget I said it. I turned to leave but she grabbed my coat.

I want in. Let me in. You can trust me.

I know.

Then trust me. I'll sniff around.

I should have stopped her, but I didn't. The truth was, though, that I needed all the help I could get, and even at the FBI, I wasn't sure who I could count on.

I have to go.

She nodded, but I already didn't like the look in her eye. I had a second opportunity to stop her, and I didn't.

Instead I waved good-bye and began to make my way back through the crowd.

Zoe Ott—Pleasantview Apartments, Apartment #713

I sat on my couch, waiting for the police to come knocking on my door. They were going to blame me for what happened at the hospital; I knew they were. Someone shot that woman, and as far as they knew, I was the only one there. I wasn't, but they weren't going to believe me. No one else saw the other guy or revivor or whatever it was. No one else saw it. They thought I did it. The cops were probably looking for me already.

I should have just stayed there. I didn't have a gun; I couldn't have done it. Now they'd think I just threw it away or hid it or something. Going right home was stupid; it was the first place they'd look. They were probably on their way over already and there I was, just waiting for it to happen.

If they did come, I'd send them away. I'd have to. I could just make them think I didn't have anything to do with it, which I didn't. It wouldn't even be a lie. I'd tell them the truth. A revivor did it. It didn't matter if they believed me. I'd make them believe me.

I wanted a drink. I couldn't calm down, and I just really, really wanted a drink. The pills helped, but right then I didn't care. My heart was still beating too fast and I tried to breathe slower, but I couldn't.

I closed my eyes and squeezed my fists against them. My hands were shaking, and I was sweating. I wanted to scream. Maybe the drinking was killing me before, but I must have been happier than this. I never had to feel like I did almost every day now....

"They took the ship," a voice said. I opened my eyes, and my apartment was gone. I was sitting on a metal floor, painted white. The room I was in was small, and it was dark except for an emergency light mounted on one wall.

There was a man sitting a few feet away. He had long, dirty hair and the start of a beard. His face was pale and his lips were chapped and peeling. His eyes were half shut. He looked like he could barely move.

"Who are you?" I asked him. Behind him, I could see more people huddled against the wall. They all looked like him, or worse.

"They took the ship," he said again. His voice was hoarse. I watched as he lifted a glass jar off the floor and it shook in his hand, like he could barely lift it. Dark yellow liquid sloshed inside, and I realized it was urine. He put the jar to his chapped lips and drank.

I put my hand over my mouth, horrified. His eyes looked apologetic and ashamed.

"We can't go out there," he whispered, "We won't make it. This way is better."

Someone knocked on the door, and I jumped. When I turned, I was back in my apartment. The strange room was gone. The man with the urine was gone. The knock came again.

It was the police. They were here to get me. My heart started thumping as I got up off the couch and stood in the middle of the room, not moving.

"It's not the cops," a woman's voice said from the other side. "Come on, open up!"

I headed over and opened the door. It was that woman, the one from the subway the other night. She had on the same wool hat and the same red poncho. Under one arm she had a big, flat cardboard box that was tied with a bow.

"Oh," I said. "It's you."

"Penny," she said.

"Sorry, I thought . . . I can't get into it. I just . . ."

"The cops won't come here," she said. "Don't worry. It's taken care of."

"Taken care of?"

"They thought about it and realized they made a mistake. Besides, the Feds stepped in and took over."

"But they'll—"

"They'll be looking for the revivor, like they should be. You're off the hook. Forget about it."

The whole thing was weird, but I had to admit, it was a huge weight off my chest.

"You going to let me in?" she asked.

"Um, sure."

I moved out of her way and she walked in, looking around my place. She didn't look like she thought much of what she saw, but she didn't say anything.

"How do you know where I live?" I asked. She shrugged.

"I know a lot about you."

"Have you been following me?"

"A little."

She said it like it wasn't a big deal. Who was she? She stared up at me with her blue eyes that kind of reminded me of Nico's, and I felt a little dizzy for a second.

The phone rang, and my heart jumped. Maybe it was him.

"Never mind that," the woman said. "He'll leave a message. I want to talk to you first."

I got that dizzy feeling again. The phone rang a few more times; then the machine picked up.

"Zoe? It's Nico. I've been trying to re—"

"Who are you?" I asked.

"Ai sent me," she said.

"Who?"

"Ai. I work for her."

"*. . . straightened it out with them. Just stay put for now. Call me as soon as you get . . .*"

She talked to me like we knew each other, like we were old friends. She was like some robot friend in a box that got mailed to my doorstep. It was weird, but I didn't feel funny about letting her in. Something told me I could trust her.

"No offense . . ."

"Penny."

"No offense, Penny, but what do you want?"

"Ai wants to meet with you, and your friend Nico too."

"Who's Ai?" She pronounced it like the letter I.

"You'll recognize her when you see her," she said. "You've seen her before, sort of. She's seen you too."

"Who is she?"

"The most important person you'll ever meet," she said.

"Why does she want to meet with me?"

"You're important too."

"Yeah, right."

There was another knock at the door, and I saw I'd left it just hanging open, which I never did. Karen was standing there in the doorway, looking from Penny to me.

"Oh, sorry," she said. "Am I interrupting?"

"No," I said. I started fumbling for how I was going to introduce the weird girl who'd just showed up and who I didn't even know, but she introduced herself.

"I'm Penny," she said, holding out her hand with a smile. Karen smiled back and shook it.

"Karen."

"It's very nice to meet you, Karen."

"You too."

She looked at both of us for a second.

"Are you two related?"

"No," I said. "No, no. She's . . . from work."

"Oh, you work at the FBI?" Karen asked.

"No."

I saw Karen's smile kind of go down a notch, and she looked confused.

"Actually, I'm with the Lesbian Recruitment Corps," Penny said. "We're—"

"Okay, that's it," I said, cutting her off. I went to usher Karen out so I could get rid of the weirdo, but before I could, Penny's eyes changed. Her pupils opened all the way, and Karen's face relaxed. The confused look that was starting to get mad went away, and she looked totally at ease.

"It doesn't matter what we say," Penny said to me over her shoulder. She thought it was funny.

"I'm a new friend of Zoe's," she said to Karen. "I don't work at the FBI, but she met me through work. That's all you need to know. I'll be a very good influence on her, and I'm no threat at all to your friendship."

"Oh," Karen said.

"I'm pretty too. And funny."

"Come on," I said. "Stop it."

"Well, those things are true," she said, but I thought that might be debatable.

"Let her go."

It wasn't like I'd never done it to her myself, but I wasn't comfortable watching someone else do it to her. Penny didn't argue; she just nodded.

"Forget everything else we said after we met," she told Karen. "It's not important."

"Okay."

Her eyes went back to normal, and Karen snapped out of it.

"Give us a second," I said to Penny. I led Karen back to the front door.

"Sorry," I said. "She won't be long."

"It's okay," she said. "I just wanted to tell you I was sorry about before. You're right about Ted. I shouldn't have snapped at you."

"Don't worry about it. I'm sorry I canceled our lunch date."

She looked over my shoulder, then back at me.

"She's really pretty. She's funny too," she said. I nodded weakly.

"You're not mad?"

"About what?"

"I don't know."

"Because of her?" she said, smiling. "No. We should all go do something together."

I tried to think of an excuse of why we shouldn't do that, but nothing came into my head.

"Dancing," Karen said.

"I don't know about dancing, Karen."

"Too much? Well, something. I'll get out of your hair for now."

She lowered her voice and leaned closer.

"Tell me all about her later."

"I will. So you're not mad? About her or Ted or anything?"

She hugged me. Karen liked to hug, and I wouldn't admit it, but I kind of liked being hugged by her too.

"Yes, I was mad. Friends get mad at each other sometimes," she said in my ear. "I love you."

She pulled away and waved, then slipped out. I stared

at the door. I don't know what made her say that last part. I don't think anyone had said that to me since I was little.

"Sorry about that," Penny said. She actually looked kind of apologetic.

"Just . . . tell me what you want."

"I would like to officially invite you and your friend Nico to meet with Ai at Suehiro 9," she said.

"What's that?"

"A restaurant."

"Why a restaurant?"

"I don't know. It's public. It's exclusive. They have good security. Plus I think she wants to impress you."

"Is it fancy?"

"Totally."

A fancy restaurant didn't sound like anyplace I wanted to go. I didn't have anything to wear to a place like that.

"Don't worry about what to wear," she said, like she read my mind. "She gave me this to give to you."

She handed me the cardboard box with the bow on it.

"Go on. Open it."

I pulled off the bow and took the top off the box. There was some thin paper underneath, and under that was a black dress. There were high-heel shoes in there too. They looked expensive. They looked really expensive.

"It'll fit," she said.

"She's giving this to me?"

"Don't worry so much," Penny said. "It's not a big deal. Come on, she's footing the bill. If you don't go, then I don't get to go."

"That woman," I said, still looking at the dress, "the

one I was with at the hospital. She was with you guys, wasn't she?"

"Yes."

"You know I was with her when she died?"

"Yes. Don't worry about her. It wasn't your job to protect her. She knew what she was getting into."

"Why does your friend want to meet with me and Nico?"

"I don't know," she said, "I just know it's important. She'll explain everything."

"I don't know if Nico will go or not."

"Don't worry about him," she said, waving her hand. "He was easy. He'll go."

"I don't know if he'll want to go with me."

"I'm telling you; he's on the hook."

"Why didn't she just come herself?"

"That's what she's got me for," she said. "Besides, I think she thought you and me would hit it off, maybe become friends."

"Friends?"

"Yeah, friends," she said, holding out her hands. "You don't want to keep all your eggs in one basket. Do you have something against friends?"

"No—"

"Okay, then."

She opened the door and turned to face me in the doorway before she left. She gave me a weird look, and I felt my heart rate slow down a little.

"It's tonight," she said, handing me a card. "Call Nico, and tell him to pick you up. See you there."

She left. I closed the door behind her. After a few seconds, I locked it.

I should go see Karen.

In spite of how strange the visit was, that was the thing I couldn't stop thinking as soon as she left. The way Karen's face looked when she pushed her like that, and the way her whole attitude just changed completely afterward. It didn't seem right somehow.

But you do it all the time, don't you?

Not all the time.

But you do it.

Maybe. I guessed I did. Not as much as before, but I had to admit I did sometimes still, and not just to her. Was that what it was like? If anyone else watched me the way I had just watched them, would they think it was just as wrong?

"Karen's my friend," I said out loud. She was my friend because she wanted to be, not because I made her. Not even I could make someone be my friend. You could make people do a lot of things, but you couldn't make them like you.

In the end I decided not to go down. It seemed weird to show up again right after that. She was happy when she left. I figured I'd leave it at that.

Instead I took the dress the rest of the way out of the package. It looked like it cost a mint. I held it up in front of myself and went into the bathroom to see.

It was gorgeous. It was the nicest thing in my whole apartment.

I picked up my cell and called Nico's number again. I was kind of hoping he wouldn't pick up so I could just leave a message, but he did.

"Wachalowski," he said.

"Um, hi. Nico?"

"Zoe. Did you get my message?"

"Um, not yet."

"It's okay. Look, I made some calls, and I don't think you have to worry about the incident at the hospital."

"No?"

"No. It got dropped."

"Why?"

"I don't know. Someone else must have gotten involved."

"So they're not looking for me?"

"No," he said, "but I don't think this is over."

"Yeah, me neither."

He paused on the other end of the line.

"What's wrong?"

"I kind of have something to ask you."

"Sure."

"I was wondering, if you're not doing anything else, and if you feel like it, if you might want to go out to dinner."

"Are you asking me out to dinner?"

"Not exactly," I said. I was so embarrassed, I could hardly talk. He thought I was calling him to ask him out on a date. If I didn't say something soon, he'd start making excuses why he couldn't go. My throat felt like it was going to close up on me.

"Not exactly?"

"Well, someone wants to meet you . . . us . . . and . . ."

"I understand," he said. "I was told to expect your call. Do you know who she is, Zoe?"

"The one who came here is named Penny. She said the one that wanted to see us both is named Ai, though."

"Do you know that name?"

"No. Do you?"

"No."

"Do you think we should go?"

"I do," he said. He sounded serious. "Where and when?"

I flipped over the card she'd written the time on the back of it.

"Suehiro 9," I said. "At seven."

"That explains the suit," he said, kind of to himself.

"What?"

"Nothing. I'll pick you up at six thirty?"

"You're going to pick me up?"

"Of course."

"Oh. Good. Six thirty sounds good."

"I'll see you then."

I hung up, then flopped down on the couch and let out a deep breath. It felt good. Ten minutes before, everything seemed like it was going wrong and there was no end in sight. Then that weird girl showed up, and just like that I was off the hook with the cops, the woman being dead wasn't my fault, and I was going to a fancy dinner with Nico.

I was a little nervous about the restaurant. I wanted to go out somewhere with Nico, but that wasn't how I pictured it. I was terrible in social situations, but with other people there I wouldn't have to worry about what to say. Those other people would be like me, too. The woman in the hospital asked me if I wasn't curious about them, and it was true that I was. Penny said the person we were meeting was the most important person I'd ever meet. I wondered what that meant. Why were they watching me?

"You're important too."

I held up the dress and looked at it again. I hoped I'd look okay in it.

"You guys have the wrong person," I said to myself. They had to.

I was a lot of things, but important wasn't one of them.

Faye Dasalia—The Healing Hands Clinic

I awoke to darkness and total quiet. The sleep that came before was absolute, and completely devoid of dreams. When thought and sensation began to return, it was like being reborn.

When I was alive, I was always cold and tired. I no longer felt either. My metabolic system was now inert, and nanomachines in my blood did repairs. I didn't need any kind of rest or sleep. Still, I found myself drawn to those rare moments when the darkness was complete, and I let everything go.

Impulses began to fire through my brain, as the implants lit up and formed connections. When my communications node went active, messages began to stream through the darkness.

Update: target obtained: Harris, Erica. Designation yellow.

Update: target obtained: Janai, Ryu. Designation yellow.

Update: target reclassified: Holst, Jan. Upgraded from yellow to red.

Update: target eliminated: Holst, Jan. Designation red.

Update: target reclassified: Ott, Zoe. Upgraded from green to yellow.

Update: target yield within eighty-five percent of target.

The field of memories appeared below them, and for a moment I was floating in space, consciousness and nothing more. They swirled around and through me like hot embers, revealing their contents in quick, bright flashes.

In one, keystrokes whispered under my fingers as I typed quickly into a chat portal at my home computer:

I feel like I should be able to let her go.

You didn't kill her, came the reply.

I know. This shouldn't bother me this much. Not anymore.

Maybe she had something to say, the person on the other end of the chat said. *Something you didn't hear.*

In another, a street woman sat with me in a holding tank, back in my old precinct. She had the look of a late-stage junkie, with rotting teeth and bad skin. Only her eyes betrayed her intelligence, and the burden of a terrible knowledge.

"He doesn't kill them all," she said, her voice low. *"I do."* I didn't know who she was.

Update: New node(s) installed: eleven.

The embers scattered as the message came in. Sensation returned to my fingers and toes, and the low vibration in my chest resumed as my mind and my body reconnected. Once again, I was awake.

"Faye," a man's voice said. I opened my eyes and sallow light seeped in. I was lying on my back, reclining in a large examination chair. He was standing next to me, moonlit eyes glowing softly in the shadows.

"Lev."

My nodes finished their initialization. According to the network chronometer, I'd been down for a long time. I didn't recognize the room I was in. Several other revivors were there with us, their backs against the far wall. They stared at nothing, waiting.

Nearby I heard a snap and a buzzing sound, the closing of an electrical circuit. The buzz turned to a low hum.

"Hold," a soft, synthesized voice said. "Gathering for iteration three-six-one."

The hum continued for a minute or so, then began to rise in pitch. I heard restraints creaking as they were pulled taut.

"Active."

"Why was I down for so long?" I asked. After dropping off Hiro Takanawa, I was sent to a safe house for maintenance. This went beyond maintenance. I scanned my nodes and found a new component. "Why was a new node installed?"

"Fawkes will explain everything."

"It's a second communications array."

"I know."

Bodies were moving nearby. In the gloom to my right was a plastic tent, hung from the ceiling with hooks. Through the clear sheeting I saw figures inside. They moved among rows of metal gurneys there, where bodies writhed and twisted.

"Checking signature," the electronic voice said. A digital readout behind the plastic displayed the total reanimation time. They had gotten it way down.

I sat up slowly and looked around the room. There were ten other revivors there with us, electric eyes jittering in the darkness like they were trapped in a dream. The military kept revivors cut off, unable to communicate directly. Revivor command links were all hub and spoke; we each had a permanent link back to Fawkes, but he allowed, and encouraged, us to sync. When alone, we would set up a common pool and each of us would connect. On our communications band I sensed them, passing embers of memory back and forth as Lev and I sometimes did. They compared information, sometimes hoping to fill in empty fragments, sometimes just out of curiosity. In life I'd feared revivors, though I wouldn't admit it. Now I'd found a strange sense of community in their company and ranks. To be alone with them brought a sense of calm. There was no reason to breathe or blink my eyes. There was no need to make eye contact or touch without an urge to do so. We might never speak, and would never have to. By nature of what we were, we'd shared experiences no human had and no human ever could.

It wasn't necessary for us to speak, but Lev and I liked speaking to each other. Free from our brain chemistry, the act was satisfying, and that was all it ever needed to be.

"I searched," I said, "but it wasn't there."

"I know."

"We'll never get to it now."

"We have the other eleven devices," he said. "Fawkes said they will be enough."

The way he said the words caught my attention. He had recently talked to Fawkes directly.

"He plans to execute soon?" I asked. Lev nodded, his face solemn.

"How soon?"

"Very."

"He's given you the full list of targets, then?" In the shadows, he nodded.

"Alto Do Mundo," he said, which I had already known, "The Central Media Communications Tower, and the UAC TransTech Center."

"That's it?"

"Three low-yield nukes for each site. The remaining two will be contingencies."

The CMC Tower, the TransTech Center, and the Alto Do Mundo . . . they were the largest structures in the city.

The UTTC was the largest in the world. I tried to picture destruction on that scale, that kind of terror unleashed on the city, but it was impossible. I recalled the suicide bombing I'd seen, staring through the storefront window with Nico at all the blood and pain that one bomb had caused. It made something stir inside, something I thought I'd completely forgotten. I thought what I felt was dread.

"When?" I asked. The many eyes jittered, unaware of us.

"Soon."

When I was alive, I'd hunted Lev Prutsko. Or, rather, I'd hunted him and his comrades, thinking they were the same man. The murders they'd committed seemed glamorous to the media machine. I'd begun to see my face on the news bands, each time looking older and more desperate. I'd thought I was just driven, looking for a way out of the second tier, but my obsession had been manufactured. Fawkes's enemies had been pulling my strings, stressing me like an engine ready to fail. In a way, Lev had saved me.

Fawkes went on to kill six hundred of what he'd termed the mutations, but it hadn't been enough. Ai hit back, and destroyed almost everything.

Lev's hand gripped mine and he helped me from the chair. For some reason, he only ever touched me.

"He wanted to speak to you when you woke up," he said.

"Fawkes?"

"Yes."

I hadn't expected that. They were looking hard for him, and he knew it. If Fawkes would risk direct communications, he planned to attack before it would matter.

Incoming message: Fawkes, Samuel.

"What does he want?" I asked.

"I don't know." He wouldn't say any more. He moved to the wall to join the rest of them. A moment later his eyes began to move, tuning into that wave of random jitter and leaving me there, alone.

Incoming message: Fawkes, Samuel. The words flashed in the darkness.

Accepted.

Hello, Faye. How are you feeling?

Better. My blood version has changed.

Yes.

I've also had a secondary communications node installed.

Yes.

I don't recognize the specifications. What is it for?

It's experimental. You'll all receive one. You'll need it soon.

Where did you get them?

They were stolen from Heinlein's supply lines overseas and smuggled back.

Isn't that dangerous?

Yes, but you'll need them to communicate with the others.

Others?

I've nearly gathered the forces we'll need to finish this. You know about the surplus nodes; they will come by sea. The second wave will strike from inside the city.

From inside? How?

They are also experimental. You will use the secondary communication nodes to communicate with them; previous models will be incompatible.

I don't understand.

Hold on. I'm going to bring the new node online to help explain. It may be disorienting at first.

Disorienting how—
Link established.

Information came flooding across the link. At first it seemed like a stream of junk data, but as it piled in the new node's buffers, I realized it wasn't random at all; it was hundreds of individual links. The node sorted through the jumble of circuits, assigning a connection point to each thread. As it did, I understood what those links were.

It's a revivor network. Once I'd gotten over that initial rush, I could view each of the separate connections. It was a revivor band, but not anything like the one that I knew. The data streams were constant but out of sync. Each one was a soft but chaotic trickle that I could sense but couldn't decipher.

Do you hear them? Fawkes asked.

Yes, but I can't understand. What do they mean?

Right now they're still asleep. Maybe they're dreaming. Do you want me to turn it off?

No.

They reminded me of waves at the shore, like hundreds of whispers rising and falling. They were almost as compelling as the void.

They're inside the city? I asked.

Yes, but like the rest, they must remain hidden for now. When the two forces combine, they will be unstoppable.

When will that happen?

The ship is on its way now.

That soon, I thought. *What do you want me to do?*

I have a special task for you. I want you to offer a deal to Nico Wachalowski.

For a moment, I was stunned. His name stirred something inside me, something I couldn't define. I waited for the swirl of embers to calm, for my memories to reorganize themselves. When faced with it, I saw how much I'd loved him. The ache that I'd spent so much time denying was clear enough to me now, though I could no longer actually feel it. I had truly loved this man.

I didn't ask Fawkes why he had chosen me. It was because he thought Nico loved me, too.

What kind of deal do you mean? I asked.

I will explain to you how I want it phrased, he said. *He needs to understand that he can't stop this, but he can minimize it. He will have the power to save many lives, if he will do the right thing.*

You think he'll listen to me?

Yes. He is still looking for you. I think he will listen.

If he agrees, will we hold up our end?

Yes.

Under the tent, a circuit closed with a snap. Restraints were pulled tight as the buzz rose in pitch.

"Hold," the electronic voice said. "Gathering for iteration three-six-two."

And if he doesn't agree? I asked.

Then you will have to kill him.

I nodded, though he wasn't there to see it.

Do you understand, Faye?

I nodded again, by myself, in the dark.

Yes. I understand.

4

Reap

Nico Wachalowski — Suehiro 9

Pleasantview Apartments were ironically named. They weren't the worst I'd seen, but the upkeep was a problem and it had gotten worse over the past two years. Trash was piled up in bags near the main entrance, and with all the rain, you could smell it from the sidewalk. Not for the first time, I wondered why someone with Zoe's abilities would live in a place like this, but then she didn't seem to find anything wrong with it. Her downstairs neighbor, Karen, was a good friend too. That might be a factor now. Karen was better for her, in many ways, than I was.

I approached the front, stepping over a pothole filled with water. As I made my way up the stairs, I checked in with the home office.

Any word yet on Takanawa?

Nothing yet.

We needed to bring him in soon; he was the only concrete link left to the missing case. His apartment was empty, with no sign of it or the device he'd left the hotel with. Travel records indicated he hadn't left the country, at least not legally, but he was nowhere to be found.

The door recognized my ID and let me in when I flashed my badge. The elevator inside was out of order, so I hiked the six flights before I remembered that Zoe had moved back into her old place. She was on the seventh floor now. I still hadn't gotten the full story on that.

Stop being careless with her. The strange woman at the bar, Penny, had said that. Maybe things were moving too fast for Zoe. I was asking a lot of her and being sober was still a struggle; I could see it. Was I being careless with her?

I knocked on the door, and when she answered it, the first thing that struck me was how sad she looked. She was clean and she had some color even, but her eyes looked as sad as ever. When she looked up at me, there were almost tears in them.

"You look nice," I told her. Whoever had picked the little black dress out for her had gotten it right. She'd splurged and had her hair styled. She looked the best I'd ever seen her.

"Thanks," she said, but she didn't look me in the eye when she said it and she didn't smile. "You do too."

The suit they'd sent over for me put anything else I had to shame, and fit almost perfectly. I wasn't familiar with designers, but I got the sense it cost a fortune.

"Are you all set?" I asked. She nodded and managed a smile, but it was gone just as quickly.

On the stairs she had trouble in her heels, so I gave her my arm. When she took it, her face and neck turned red. I held my coat over her while I got her into the car, then went back around and got in next to her.

"You okay?" I asked, pulling back out onto the main street. She nodded, looking at the floor.

"What's wrong?"

"Nothing."

An armored vehicle with military markings passed by the street ahead of us, a floodlight sweeping through the rain. In the distance, a helicopter moved between two buildings.

"Why are there so many cops?" she asked.

"Something happened," I said.

"The briefcase?"

"Yes."

She looked down at the floor and made a face.

"I didn't get anything out of that woman at the hospital," Zoe said. "Sorry."

The photos had been grisly. By the time I got in touch with them, the police had already been called and photographed the scene. Zoe had been captured on the security camera leaving the building, but sometime between then and when I actually arrived at the hospital, someone had gotten to the people involved. The police dropped Zoe as a person of interest and turned the whole thing over to us, with no resistance at all. Someone was watching us.

"Don't worry about that," I said.

"The guy from this morning doesn't know where the case is," she said, "but he did say there were several targets."

I nodded. I'd seen Vesco's report.

"Are they nukes?" she asked in a small voice.

I wasn't supposed to divulge that information, but I nodded. She got quiet.

"Do you want to get out of the city?" I asked her. "After tonight, you could take off for a while."

"Would you come with me?"

"I can't."

Fog blew past the headlights as another helicopter banked down the main drag in the distance. Zoe was quiet for a minute, clutching a little purse in her lap and fiddling with the clasp as I drove.

"I talked to Vesco too, like you wanted," she said.

"And?"

"Someone got to him. They wiped his memory. Alice—"

She stopped short. When I glanced over at her, she looked uncomfortable.

"Alice Hsieh?" I asked. "What about her?"

"Nothing. She was nice. That was all."

Something was bothering her, and not just the threat of public embarrassment. She seemed distracted.

"Sorry you got stuck with me tonight."

"I'm not stuck with you, Zoe. You need to stop—"

"I know—it's your idea of a hot date, hanging out with a skinny, ugly alcoholic."

I opened my mouth, and she cut me off immediately, holding up her hand.

"Don't answer that."

This is going to become a problem.

"It doesn't matter anyway," she said. "You're leaving with her, not with me."

"Leaving with who?"

"She leaves. She leaves in a hurry, and you go after her."

I glanced at her, slouched in the passenger's seat. Sleet began to pepper the windshield.

"Was that something you saw—"

"Just never mind," she said. Despite my occasional prodding, she wouldn't say anything else for the rest of the trip.

When we rolled up in my car, the valet took one look at it and said something into his two-way radio. He looked surprised when he scanned my ID.

"You're expected, Agent Wachalowski," he said. "Business or pleasure?"

I used the backscatter to look into the soft tissue of his eyes and saw the camera implanted there. We were going to end up on the news, assuming he could sell it.

"I'll let you know on the way out," I told him.

I tossed him the key as I guided Zoe away, toward the entrance. In the crowd gathered outside, I picked out at least twenty more concealed cameras looking for celebrities, politicians, or both.

"Who are you with?" a voice shouted from behind. "Hey! Who are you with?" I opened the door and ushered Zoe through.

Inside, Suehiro 9 was more or less what I expected; a place where the wealthy went to enjoy being wealthy. It was the kind of place that third tiers associated with first tiers, but the truth was, I was no more welcome there than they were. When we approached the hostess, she looked us both over, mentally identifying designer labels. She looked like a model.

"Name?" she asked without smiling. She looked at Zoe with so much contempt that it made me angry.

"We're with Motoko Ai," I told her. The name got an immediate reaction. Her face stayed cool but her eyes flashed. She changed her tone immediately.

"Mr. Wachalowski," she said. "This way."

If Ai was trying to impress me, it worked. To orchestrate the meeting on such short notice couldn't have been easy or cheap. The meeting could have happened anywhere, but she chose the most exclusive restaurant in the city. She was trying to influence us, maybe, to wine and dine us, but I wondered if it wasn't something more. I wondered if she wasn't flaunting me specifically, and the agency I worked for, for the eyes that she knew watched her.

When we approached the table, I saw that Penny, the woman who approached me at the bar, was there. I could tell right away that she wasn't a colleague or a chaperone; Penny worked for Ai. It was clear from the way she sat at attention.

Ai herself was very small. I would have thought she was a child, except for her face. Her clothes had to be tailored specially for her, and the jewelry she had on display must have cost a fortune. Her head was large, a little too large for her body, and her thick lips protruded over an overbite, giving her a vaguely fishlike appearance. I realized then that I'd seen that face before. The last time I'd seen it, I'd pulled its image from the camera buffer of a dead man's eye. She'd sent a freelance news reporter to Goicoechea Plaza the night I busted Tai and his smuggling ring, the night it all started.

"Hello," she said, smiling. She had a slight accent, but her diction was perfect and her voice was quite deep, despite her small size. "I am Motoko Ai, and this is one of my associates, Penny Blount."

"Hello," I said. "It's nice to meet you, and thank you for bringing us here."

She waved her hand as if it was no big deal and I saw her small fingers twitch. She kept her eyes on me, but they looked strangely unfocused.

"Please sit," she said. Zoe sat down right away next to Penny, and I took the remaining chair.

"This can't be any small expense," I said.

"I wanted to impress you."

"You have."

"I also wanted this to be formal."

"Wanted what to be formal?"

"Cementing your alliance with me."

She was completely serious. She had an air of power and authority, but also a confidence beyond anything I'd ever seen. It wasn't just arrogance or bravado or even ignorance. She believed what she said. She was certain of it.

A small tremor moved through her hands again. Her head bobbed, and I saw Penny tense up for a second. Was something wrong with her?

"Am I entering into an alliance with you?"

"You both are."

"No offense meant, ma'am, but why would I do that?"

"I've already seen it. You do," she said, and I could see that was all the answer she needed. She didn't know the why. It was irrelevant to her.

Precognition, I thought. Unlike Zoe, who often seemed confused or frightened by the things she saw or thought she saw, Ai seemed completely at ease with it.

"Do the things you see always come true?" I asked her.

"It's not that simple," she said. "There are levels of probability, but once they reach certainty, then yes, they always come true."

Penny fiddled with her cell phone while Zoe looked over a menu. She was flustered to find it was completely in Japanese.

"Don't worry," Ai said. "We won't get to order." Penny looked disappointed when she heard that. Based on some of the dishes I'd seen pass by, I was a little disappointed myself.

"Why not?" I asked.

"Because things are very dangerous right now," she said. "We're being watched."

"Then why come here in the first place?"

"Significant events are tied to this meeting," she said. "It happens here."

"Because you foresaw it?"

"Because I felt like it."

"But if it's dangerous—"

"With the exception of one of us," she said, "I know when everyone at this table dies. The one I'm unsure of outlives the rest. I know that much. None of us dies here."

Ai and Penny both suddenly glanced over at Zoe at the same time. Zoe's pupils had gone wide, but she looked confused. A second later they went back to normal. Penny gave Zoe a little shake of her head. Ai didn't say anything. She just looked back to me.

"I know you know who I am," she said.

"I've heard of you."

Her little body shivered as her pupils, black on dark brown, swelled to fill the irises. I felt a wave of dizziness, far worse than I'd felt with Sean or even Zoe. She was trying to control me.

I let my eyelids droop a little as the dizziness passed. Ai smiled as her eyes went back to normal.

"Don't pretend," she said, waving one tiny hand. "That may have worked on your friend, but not me."

She watched me for a few more seconds, the silence stretching out before she spoke again.

"How long have you been like that?"

"Two years. You're not surprised?"

"Just the opposite. I've been waiting for it. What caused it?"

"Before the assault on the factory, I was injured, and flatlined for several minutes. It happened then."

"I can't influence you," she said. "If I can't, then you truly are shut off from us."

I thought that fact would put her on edge, but instead the edges of her lips curled just barely.

"Do you know you share that immunity with revivors?"

"Yes."

"Who first told you about us?"

"Samuel Fawkes."

She smiled broadly then, having assumed, I thought, that I would lie. She nodded.

"Did he also tell you about me?"

"Not specifically. He told me there's an underground movement of people with abilities like yours."

"And?"

"That this movement has a hierarchy, and that they manipulate society in secret."

"As a means to their own unscrupulous ends?"

"That was the gist of it."

"Well, Agent Wachalowski," she said, "You've heard from Mr. Fawkes. Now I would like you to hear from me, if you don't mind."

"Please."

I glanced over at Zoe. She was staring like she was in a trance.

"Do you have any idea how many people Mr. Fawkes killed two years ago?" Ai asked in a low voice.

"There were a lot of names in his database, but very few deaths were actually reported."

"If they were reported, those names would obviously all be connected. We didn't want that, but believe me— Fawkes was very successful. When the National Guard was deployed and the revivor units went missing, they moved on a large spread of targets. We were not expecting that."

"You didn't foresee it?"

Her large eyes narrowed a little, and the dreamy expression cleared. "We knew he would attack."

"But not the specific form the attack would take?"

"We're not here to talk about that," she sniped. "They went into people's homes and killed men, women, and children alike. Doesn't that matter to you?"

"Yes," I said. "I'm sorry."

I'd seen the names coming off the database Fawkes kept, and I knew he'd kept it accurately. Their bodies were disposed of using Leichenesser, and those who survived had covered it up, but I'd always suspected that hundreds of people had been killed that night.

Something buzzed across the table, and Penny reached into her purse. She removed a second cell phone and snapped it open, looking down at the screen.

Using the backscatter, I peered through the plastic casing of the phone until a fuzzy image of the LCD appeared. From my side the text was backwards, but I captured a piece of it before she moved.

. . . anawa tracked . . . IMO 1092

Takanawa, maybe. IMO stood for International Maritime Organization. The message might have had to do with an incoming shipment. Were they tracking Fawkes's supply lines themselves?

"It's easy sometimes," Ai continued, "to stop seeing your enemy as human. In battle, it can be easy, maybe even convenient, to remove yourself from the human cost your struggle inflicts on your enemy. You understand that."

I nodded.

"Sometimes war necessitates ugly choices, but Mr. Fawkes is not a nation and he is not a soldier. Mr. Fawkes is an individual. Strictly speaking, he is not even a citizen of this country any longer. No matter what his beliefs are, he had no authority or right to do what he did."

"I agree."

"Fawkes is still a threat. We both know what he recently acquired, and we both know he'll use them."

"Miss Motoko, if you have specific information—"

"I have specific information," she clipped. "I have more specific information than you would believe. The devices he acquired are just part of his plan; he is gathering an army, and when he is ready, he will unleash both on us. He means to wipe us out completely, Agent, and it doesn't matter to him who gets in the way. It doesn't matter to him if he has to destroy this entire city to get rid of us."

"Fawkes has an army of revivors?"

She nodded.

"Where? How?"

"We don't know how yet," she said. "We don't know where, either—not yet. We're closing in on their location, but what I said before about probabilities is true; stopping Fawkes is not a certainty. There is a very real possibility that this entire city and everything you see around you will cease to exist in a matter of days."

Her eyes stared at me evenly from across the table, while a bad feeling began to sink into my gut. Zoe's eyes were wide, and her mouth had parted slightly.

"The city gets destroyed?" she whispered.

"It will start here, but it won't end here," Ai said. "There will be almost no survivors."

I wasn't expecting that, but again, she was deadly serious.

"What do you mean 'It won't end here'?" I asked.

"Just what it sounds like," she said simply. "Fawkes will destroy this city, and then, one by one, the rest will begin to fall."

"That's impossible—"

"I've seen it too," Zoe said quietly. Her face was pale. She looked scared.

"When?" I asked her. "When does this supposedly happen?"

"Soon," Ai said.

"Fawkes has most likely been destroyed by now," I said. "If not, he will be soon. Haven't you seen to that?"

She raised her thin eyebrows a little, like she was surprised I was so dense.

"Fawkes doesn't get destroyed with the rest of his obsolete generation," she said. "You kill Fawkes. The cull will locate him, but you, the one who is immune to our control, will kill him. That's why you're here."

I wasn't sure how to respond. I looked to Zoe, wanting to ask her how accurate these visions really were, but doubted she knew herself. If there was any truth to it . . .

"How long before he attacks?" I asked.

"An exact time frame is difficult to pinpoint," she said, "but soon. We were unsuccessful in intercepting the weapons; he has them, or most of them."

"Do you have any leads as to where they went?"

"We're looking for them as hard as your agency is. We haven't located them yet."

"If Fawkes is operating out of the city, then give me something to go on," I said. "I can't just take your word for it."

Penny reached across the table and handed me a data spike.

"We recorded that less than six hours ago," Ai said.

I opened a connection to the spike and accessed the recording that was stored on it. It was a text message, repeated in a loop. The message used a revivor's transponder code.

Nico. This is Sean. I'm here. Help me.

"Several of our people have gone missing," Ai said, "and we recently tracked them to several locations. One is a facility called Rescue Mission. It is a nonprofit medical center for the homeless, which is run by the group known as Second Chance. Have you heard of them?"

"I've heard of them."

"I believe they've taken your friend, Agent."

Nico. This is Sean. I'm here— I stopped the loop.

"Sean told me this started with the Concrete Falls bombing," I said. "Do you know what he meant by that?" She shook her head.

"If Mr. Pu made that determination, he never got a chance to report it to me."

She looked over at Zoe then. She spoke again, but when she did her tone had changed, becoming softer.

"Someone has to stop it," she said. "You will be part of this too."

"How many of you are there?" Zoe asked. The nervousness was gone. She looked excited.

"Us," Penny said.

"How many of us are there?"

"More than you think," Ai said. "You are not alone."

The whole thing happened in the blink of an eye. Zoe opened her mouth to answer her when a wineglass on the table popped and something hissed loudly from directly in front of Ai's face. The air rippled, and there was a loud crack that made everyone in the dining area turn.

Outside the restaurant, a low boom echoed down the street.

A small object spun in the air in front of Ai, then dropped onto the tablecloth, trailing smoke. It was a piece of smooth, black metal, in the shape of a bullet.

"What the hell?" Zoe squawked.

She's wearing an inertial dampening field. It was the only thing that could stop a round cold like that. The slug looked like it came from a gauss rifle.

I turned to follow the trajectory. A thin trail of smoke led to a window out front where four inches of bullet-proof glass had a neat hole bored straight through. A waiter walked through the smoke trail, disrupting it without even noticing.

Back at the table, Penny recovered quickly. She used a cloth napkin to grab the bullet, then stowed it in her purse. As I stood, I saw her hand off the purse to a passing woman. The woman disappeared into the crowd with it.

This is Agent Wachalowski. We have an unknown weapon fired from the street at Suehiro 9, possibly a magnetic rail gun.

Roger that.

I stood up and as I turned, I saw Ai sag in her seat, just a little. She stared at the air in front of her, looking very tired.

"Go," Penny said.

I left the table and headed for the front entrance. When I got closer, I could just make out something through the window, a ripple in the air just past the glass. A gust of wind sprayed rain against the passersby, and for just a second there was a gap in the mist.

"Stop!" I yelled, drawing my weapon. The crowd was

in the way. I struggled through them, but the gap in the rain was gone.

"Stop!"

I shoved past the hostess and through the front entrance, onto the sidewalk. People were moving in every direction. I couldn't pinpoint him.

Damn it.

There was an alley alongside the restaurant and I ducked down it. Even if the shooter couldn't be seen, he'd need to get off the street and away from the crowd. People parted in front of me as they saw the gun; one man backed into a woman, who slipped off the curb and landed in the street. A car stopped short, and I heard the crunch of metal behind me as he got rear-ended.

Horns started blaring, people shouting, as I passed the valet. He followed me with his camera as I turned into the alley. Immediately, someone grabbed me.

Two hands gripped my lapels and spun me, shoving me back against the brick wall. I brought the gun around, but something I couldn't see blocked it.

"Wait!" a voice said from in front of me. "Nico, wait!"

The air in front of me rippled and Faye's face appeared, staring up at me from under the hood of an LW cloak. Her eyes glowed dimly in the darkness.

"It's me," she said. The rain drizzled off the cloak, and for a second a gust of wind whipped it around her. Her hair was gone, and her skin was the color of ash, but it was her.

I tried to move the gun, but she still had my arm. I let go of the grip, the weapon sliding free of my hand until it hung from my finger by the trigger guard. The pressure eased up on my wrist.

"Did you do this?" I asked her. She shook her head.

Her face was a few inches from mine, but I couldn't see her breath in the cold. No warmth came off of her.

"No," she said.

"Then why—"

"He sent me. I was following you."

She stood up on her toes and put her arms around my neck. She hugged me gently, the way she used to sometimes. Her cheek was cool against my neck as rain trickled down my collar.

"I'm glad you're alive," she said.

I could feel the low vibration in her chest through my coat. I meant to push her away, but I didn't.

Who sent you? I asked.

Fawkes. I stiffened, and she squeezed tighter, just a little, before stepping back. It was true. He was still out there. He was still out there, and she'd joined with him.

I've come to offer you a deal, she said. Her eyes glowed softly in the dark. I stood there, one hand on her waist, getting soaked by the rain.

What does he want? I asked.

He wants you to kill the woman Ai, and her main operatives.

Someone just took a shot at her with a rail gun and she walked away. What makes him think I'll be able to do it?

He knows you're immune to their influence. He knows she is bringing you in close. Someone like you could manage it.

I shook my head.

Whatever else she is, she's a private citizen who hasn't, as far as I know, broken any laws. I don't even have grounds to arrest her. I'm not going to assassinate her. Not for Fawkes, or you or anyone else. Understand?

She was telling the truth. Fawkes is building his forces, she said. *This is your only chance to stop it.*

No one would be able to smuggle hundreds of revivors into the country, especially after what happened. Fawkes's trick where he took control of the National Guard units wasn't going to work a second time either. The only other option was to manufacture them locally, but the procedure wasn't simple. In the current climate, gathering the hardware it would take for a large-scale operation like that would raise too many flags.

Where is he hiding them?

Just listen. The assault will begin soon.

Is that what his offer is? Kill Ai and he'll call off the attack?

No. He won't stop the attack.

Then what's he offering?

He's willing to take the nukes off the table.

That stopped me for a second. Rain rolled down her face as she stared up at me.

Faye, those weapons will kill hundreds of thousands of people—

We've learned a lot about Ai and her people, she said. *More than you have. They're strong, but not as strong as they'd have you think. They're a relatively new phenomenon, and they've organized only very recently, but already they control this whole city. Soon they'll control everything.*

I thought about that.

If they defeat Fawkes, she continued, *then their way will be clear. If this window closes, then nothing will stop them. Eventually, their control will be total.*

She paused, glancing down the alley toward the street. People were beginning to take notice of us. I moved my hands away as she went back on the soles of her feet.

If it's true, then show me what he knows, I said. *Give me something concrete.*

She slid her arms from around my neck and put her palms on my chest. When I looked in her eyes, for a second her expression seemed human. It seemed . . .

She reached into her cloak and the air warped around her. There was a flicker; then she was gone.

Connection closed.

"Faye?" I reached in front of me, but she wasn't there anymore.

I turned and started back through the fog and out of the alley. As I walked, I brought up the stats on the program to decommission the obsolete revivor stock; it was ninety-seven percent complete. There was only three percent to go, and the son of a bitch wasn't in there.

Somehow, he'd managed to avoid the ax. Fawkes was still out there, and he was coming.

Calliope Flax—Pleasantview Apartments, Apartment #613

If the address was right, the stick lived in a shit hole called Pleasantview. There was trash piled on the curb, and someone had used bolt cutters on the chain-link fence around the lot. I parked my bike on the street and killed the engine. The rain tapped on my helmet while I sat for a minute, watching; then the reminder to check my hidden file popped up in the dark in front of me.

She had me paranoid. Any time I did anything I wanted to remember, I wrote it in the file and I checked it twice a day. I knew the stick could make me forget, and I wasn't taking chances. A lot of people knew a JZI could record, but I kept the text file under my hat. No one could make me erase it if they didn't know it was there. There were four messages there:

Back from TSP. Wachalowski bailed early, but might help.

Scored Zombie Maker from Eddie.
Called Buckster. He said he'd drop by sometime.

I remembered all those—meeting Wachalowski, Eddie hooking me up with the drugs, then roping in Buckster, who the drugs were for. People had a way of blabbing when they were on Z, and that went double when they didn't know they were on it. If he had any inside intel Wachalowski could use, I'd get it out of him and he'd never be the wiser.

All that I remembered. The last message, though—that I didn't remember:

Found a door behind the flag. Checking it out.

A door behind the flag? The only flag I could think of was the one back at my place. I'd brought it back with me from my tour, and I hung it up across from the door to the toilet. There wasn't anything behind it but wall.

Checking it out.

Something made me write it. There was nothing after, and I had no memory of doing it. Someone fucked with my head. Keeping the list worked; I'd gotten my first hit.

"Son of a bitch."

I armed the bike's alarm and stowed my helmet, then went up to the front door and pulled. It didn't budge.

"ID please," it said. I flashed my card at it.

"Flax, Calliope. First class. Violations including . . ."

"Yeah, yeah."

"You are not a registered occupant of this residence. If a registered occupant of this residence is with you at this time, they should provide their ID now. If you are not with a reg—"

I leaned on the buttons next to the door until someone got sick of my shit and buzzed me in. The door was still talking when I slammed it behind me.

Inside, the elevator was out, so I headed up the stairs. The place smelled like piss.

When I shoved the stair door open, I almost ran into some woman with big lips, hips, and tits. She had a mean black eye.

"Excuse me," she said. She kept her eyes down and tried to go around me.

"Nice eye."

"Yo, get back here!" some guy yelled from around the corner. From the look on her face, he put the shiner there.

"A regular Romeo, huh?" I said. She stared at me.

"What?"

"You gonna take that?" I asked her.

"What, are you taking a poll?"

"Did you hear me, bitch?" the guy hollered. "I said get back here!"

She pushed past me and went down the stairs.

"Yeah, fuck you, then," I said as the door slammed shut behind me. I was there for a reason, and she wasn't it.

I turned the corner and went down the hall until I found 613. When I knocked, someone in there threw something; then footsteps stomped up to the door.

"Fucking bitch," a guy said under his breath from inside.

The door flew open and a big guy stood there. He had on a tank top to show off his big arms, but half his size was fat. I knew his type; they showed up at the arena all the time. They had big arms and big mouths, but they couldn't go three rounds.

"Who the fuck are you?" he asked, making a face. He was the same guy that yelled after the girl.

"I'm looking for Zoe Ott. She in?"

"Who?"

"Ott. Scrawny. Red hair. Big beak."

That made him mad. He knew who she was.

"Oh, that bitch."

"She here or not?"

"You got the wrong apartment," he said.

"Records say she lives here, asshole," I said. The guy was starting to piss me off.

"They're wrong, dyke."

I checked her last known address again to make sure. The number said 613. I looked past him to try to see in, but he moved to block me.

"I said she ain't here!"

"Did she used to live here?"

"You a cop?"

"No, asshole—"

"Then get the fuck out before I either call one or kick your ugly ass out of here."

"Like you kicked your lady's ass?"

He gave me the finger and went to shut the door.

"Yeah, I bet that's the only thing you ever get up you, limp dick," I said through the crack, and the door stopped. It opened back up, and the dude's face was red.

"What'd you just say to me?"

"I said fat pieces of shit who hit their lady can't make their dick get ha—"

He moved faster than I thought he would, and he caught me off guard. He put his hand on my left tit and shoved me hard. I went back on my ass, cracking my head on the wall behind me.

"Fuck you, bitch!"

That was it. I was pissed before, but that was it. He looked surprised when I got back up and came at him.

He even tried to shut the door, but he didn't make it. It slammed against my boot and I shoved it back open with my shoulder. I reached through with my dead hand and grabbed a fistful of tank top and skin, then pulled him out into the hallway.

"Ow! You fu—"

Still holding him with my left hand, I creamed him with my right fist, and he went down like a sack of sand. He wasn't out, though, just pissed.

"You want it like that?" he said, blood coming out of his nose as he got up. He came at me like a bull and got his big arms around me when he hit. My boots came up off the floor and he heaved me back with his fat gut. I went down on my back, and he came stomping toward me.

"You want it like that?" he said again. "Get up bit—"

From the floor I shot my leg out and put the heel of my boot right in his paunch. His eyes bugged and I thought he'd puke, but he just staggered back. His face went dark when I got up, and I saw death in his eyes. The guy was a straight-up psycho. He blew blood through his nose, down onto his shirt.

"You're dead, bitch ..."

He came at me, and I swung. I broke his jaw, but he kept coming. A door opened behind him and someone looked out, but went right back in. He slammed me into the wall by the stairs and I locked my wrists behind his fat back.

I squirmed under his sweaty arm, scooting behind him. With his gut hanging over my arms, I spun him, pulling him down until we hit the stairwell door and it banged open. He went down on the landing with me on top of him.

People get a look when they start to lose a fight, when they know the beat-down is coming. He got that look when he fell. He went nuts, trying to buck me off and get back up, but he didn't have the abs for it. I got one knee on his left shoulder, pinning him, and planted my other foot a couple steps down. I hit him with the dead fist, and his lip split open. I hit him with the right, and one of his teeth broke off.

I'd been put in the hospital twice in my life, both times by fuckers like him. I forgot about the skinny bitch with the weird eyes. I hit him again and his nose crunched under my fist. The door slammed open behind me.

"I'm calling the cops!" an old woman screamed. "You hear me?"

He tried to push himself away, but he slipped and started going down the stairs. The door slammed shut as he rolled, landing on his back on the next landing down. I followed him and put the toe of my boot in his ribs. I kicked him twice more, then knelt back over him. I hit him in the face until he shut up and quit moving.

I stood back up and wiped my nose. It was bleeding. He was in a heap in the corner, nose mashed and mouth full of blood. My knuckle was cut and blood was coming out fast, dripping off the ends of my fingers.

I could hear people out in the hall, and from up above. It was time to get out of there.

"Asshole."

The trip was a bust. The bitch was going to have to wait. I took the steps two at a time down to the ground floor and went out the way I came before the cops showed up.

Faye Dasalia—The Healing Hands Clinic

Deep within the shadows of a disused alley, I slipped between a trash bin and a brick wall, into a dark cul-de-sac. The ground was littered with trash, where pitted brown ice still lingered from winter. On the far side was a rusted metal door, near where a group of homeless men were huddled underneath a plastic tarp. A sign on the door read HEALING HANDS CLINIC.

Incoming call: Fawkes, Samuel.

I'd expected another contact from him. I'd been lucky at the restaurant. With the lip-reading software, I'd transcribed some interesting information. Motoko was trying to recruit Nico. They knew Fawkes had the weapons. Nico, at least, had drawn a connection to Concrete Falls.

The only thing I hadn't shared was one phrase, one that Motoko had repeated to Nico: *You kill Fawkes.* I wasn't sure yet why I hadn't told him.

Call Accepted.

I've reviewed your report, Faye.

And what have you decided?

That giving Wachalowski the information he wants would be extremely risky.

Fawkes had gathered a lot of concrete data. Over the years he had tracked down many names, and had verified connections between them. He had connected many secret accounts, and traced money trails to key politicians. He'd managed to peel back their many layers and identified their many different fronts. He tracked their holdings and their hidden assets. He knew where they'd based themselves, and the chain of their command. Outside a court of law, he could prove it all, but exposing them would accomplish nothing. Those told would simply forget, and all Fawkes would expose was how much he knew.

Still . . .

It is the only thing that will convince him, I said.

I agree, but I'll only authorize a small piece, and we must control it carefully. I'll draw something up to present to him. It will have to be enough.

He won't kill her anyway.

I've seen Wachalowski's war record, Faye; don't be so sure. He's made decisions that might surprise you.

He didn't offer up what those might have been. It didn't really matter.

Lev is waiting for you. He'll have your work detail.

I understand. May I ask you one question?

Yes.

Why attempt the shooting at the restaurant?

I'd not been told that the shot was coming. After, I saw him follow the trail of smoke, and spot the hole in the glass. I had to move quickly to get off the street, as the paparazzi swarmed. The slug had passed within six inches of me.

I didn't order that, Fawkes said. *If killing her was that easy, I'd have done it by now.*

Then who fired the rail gun?

Not a revivor. Maybe one of the Second Chance recruits acting on his own.

With a million-dollar high-tech weapon?

Maybe she staged the assassination.

You think the shooting was staged?

I don't know. Like you said; not many people have access to a weapon like that. I'm looking into it. Concentrate on Wachalowski for now.

Understood.

The call dropped, and I moved toward the metal door as the words faded away.

No direct sunlight could reach the area, but neither could rain or snow. It was cold, but I sensed warmth under the tarp. I sensed the low, staggered beats of the men's hearts, and one conspicuous pocket of silence. Two eyes opened in the dark, and cast a moonlit glow into the alley.

When the revivor moved, the living men stirred, but not much and not for long. Except for the eyes, it looked no different from them. In the cold, no one noticed its lack of warmth. Under layers of dirt, blankets, and plastic, it was ignored completely.

It thumped the metal door three times with its fist. A moment later, I heard a dead bolt turn and the door opened slowly.

Lev appeared in the dark space, his eyes staring down from under his thick brow. His expression didn't change, but he extended a private connection. I accepted it, and he began to stream. This assignment would be different from field work, but it would be simpler. One of the revivors who was stationed there was receiving the upgrade. He assured me the job was temporary, and understood why I cared; some of us liked the quiet, but I wasn't one of them. It left too much time to pick through memories and to contemplate the blackness beneath them.

You're in luck tonight, he said.

How is that?

Tonight will not be quiet.

He walked into the darkness, and I followed. The door creaked closed behind us.

He led me down a cinderblock corridor, to an old wooden door at the halfway point. At the far end was another heavy door, a slit of light underneath. In the hall, I could smell rubbing alcohol and human body odor. Lev pushed open the wooden door and stepped through.

Inside was a musty storage area. Boxes had been stacked up along the far wall, but had since been pushed aside. In the space between them was a heavy door, made of thick, shielded metal. A security scanner was mounted there, its lens glowing a soft red.

Lev stooped slightly and placed one eye to the lens, which flickered and turned to green. The door opened silently, and a huff of humid air blew over me. Through the metal door, I saw sheets of plastic. The eyes of revivors stared from along the walls there. I heard the hum of electronics inside, and heavy, scraping footsteps.

I'd heard groupings of revivors called nests and, on one occasion, hives. The terms were meant to be derogatory, but there was some truth to them. I found a certain comfort in these places, the stillness and the quiet. In life, I might have called the feeling cozy. The vibrations of their hearts and the faint smell of decomp inhibitor had become familiar and safe to me.

Lev and I found empty spots along the wall, and watched the figures move behind the plastic as we tuned to each other, out of the common communications pool, to share our thoughts in silence.

What do you think of the upgrade? Lev asked me.

I like the different voices, I said, *even if I can't understand them. It's hard for me to explain.*

I sense hundreds of them, Lev said.

Yes, me too.

Like tuning to a common pool, but larger.

Yes.

I like the sound, too, he said. *I think they're a promise of something greater.*

Across the room, his eyes jittered rapidly in tune, I knew, with my own. I thought that was a good way of putting it; the whispers were a promise. A new community about to wake.

Where do they come from? I asked.

You'll see for yourself tonight.

Fawkes said they might be dreaming.

He's being poetic. I think it's subconscious bleed-back from wired humans who are still alive.

Do you know that for a fact?

No, but it's what I think.

Before Lev was made into a revivor, I eventually learned, he had been an engineer. His knowledge was put to use by his captors, before he was turned and packaged with the rest. He'd fought in Orikhiv for close to two years, before its collapse, when he was impounded. Later, he would end up on the black market.

Can I ask you something about Orikhiv?

Orikhiv no longer exists.

But it did when you were there.

Yes.

When you were first brought here, you were refitted.

Yes.

You had a ghrelin inhibitor installed.

His eyes continued to move like moonlit blurs. We'd talked about many things over the years, but never talked about this.

Why do you ask now?

I've wondered for a long time.

But why now?

We won't see the end of Fawkes's assault plan. If we do, we'll be impounded and destroyed.

Lev didn't deny those things.

What do you want to know?

Did you feed on human flesh?

Yes.

Did you try to stop yourself?

No. At the time, I saw nothing wrong with it.

But you feel differently now?

It's easy to feel differently with the inhibitor installed.

Do you think it's wrong?

I think it's unnecessary. Tell me what your interest is in this.

These hundreds of new voices. Revivors created outside of Heinlein won't have the inhibitor.

Maybe not.

Will they feed?

I can't speak for them. Without the inhibitor, I would guess, that eventually, yes.

Fawkes is going to use nuclear weapons.

Yes. Across the room, I saw his eyes stop moving.

Won't that—

You're moving into dangerous territory, Faye.

Before I could answer him, a yellow light blinked on over the door frame. A broadcast message appeared:

Subject isolated and ready for transfer.

Forget that, Faye, Lev said. *That line of reasoning is dangerous. Just stick to the plan.*

The door opened silently, and two revivors stepped away from the wall. One was a female who wore contact lenses that doused the light in her eyes. She was dressed up like a nurse. The other was a big male. He picked up a long, thin aluminum rod from a hook on the ceiling. Lev moved in behind the two.

Come on, he said to me, and I tailed them back out into the hallway. *They're going to bring one in now. If he gets free, then stop him. Otherwise, stay clear of the path between the doors.*

The overhead lights came on. I turned left, toward the end of the corridor, and saw the door there open. A human doctor in a white coat stood there, his hands guiding a man who appeared homeless. He ushered him through and into the hallway where the revivor nurse was waiting for him. The homeless man looked unsure.

"The examination room is down the hall," he whispered to the patient. "Nurse Westgate will show you the way. I'll be in to see you shortly."

Some of the disquiet left the patient's eyes, but it didn't last for long. The nurse had moved between him and the way out, and then the door swung shut and he heard the latch click. He stared, not understanding, as the noise suppressors mounted there turned on and emitted a low hum.

"Who are you?" he asked the revivor with the metal rod. His eyes widened as he watched a loop of plastic cord extend from the end to form a noose. "What's going on?"

The nurse grabbed him from behind. He struggled, but the other one had reached them. It looped the noose over his head and pulled tight, choking off his scream.

The revivor heaved the rod, slamming the man into the cinderblock wall. It used it to guide him down the hall toward us, while the man pulled at the cord around his neck.

"Stay calm," the nurse revivor said, but the man was beyond that. Eyes bulging and teeth bared, he struggled harder. He fell to the floor and rolled, twisting the noose tighter around his neck.

"Careful," Lev called. The man was flopping madly on the floor now.

The revivor who held him loosened the cord and tried to untwist the leash. When he did, the man on the floor kicked forward and the rod slipped from the revivor's hands. The man stumbled down the hall, the leash jutting behind him. He'd spotted the exit sign, back behind me.

He closed the distance between us, then tacked left to try and shove his way past me. Before he could make it, I stuck out one leg, catching him at the ankle. The rod clipped my cheek as he crashed to the floor.

The others were moving down the hall toward us. The man had slipped his fingers under the cord and was struggling to his feet. Blood and adrenaline pulsed through his body, so that I could almost feel the heat of him. He was beyond any thought; he was being driven now by pure instinct, a hardwired imperative to survive. The energy of it was captivating.

Faye, stop him.

Before he could get back up, I stepped in close behind him and grabbed the rod. I heaved it forward, and his skull struck the floor. Blood dotted the dingy tile in a trail as I swung him back around.

"Please," the man grunted, trying to twist free. "Please, let me go."

I could have done that for him; it was within my power. I could have released the cord and let him make his mad dash toward the exit. I could have held up the others long enough to let him escape into the back alley. He might have gotten past the others outside. He might have disappeared into the city and gotten to keep his life. I could have done that for him, but the truth was, it never occurred to me. Not until the other revivors reached us and I gave the rod to Lev.

Good work, Faye. He said. The man's toes brushed the floor as he lifted him and began to carry him back down the hallway.

He dragged the man through the large, open doorway, and I followed them inside. The heavy steel door glided closed behind us, and the magnetic lock thumped. An overhead light flickered, then lit the room.

The tent of plastic sheeting was pulled open, and underneath it was an old, reclined chair with surgical arms affixed to either side. With the rod, Lev shoved the man down in the chair. He pinned him, while they strapped his wrists and ankles.

Lev removed the noose, and the man gasped in air. He coughed, spraying strings of spit, then rattled out a string of hoarse, shaky words.

"What the fuck is this? What the fuck is this? Who are you people? What do you want with me?"

His eyes darted frantically. He'd seen the eyes of the figures around him, and he'd realized what they were.

"Quiet," Lev said, but the man kept going, unable to stop. When he saw Lev hold up the plastic syringe, his whispers became incomprehensible.

As I watched, my calm had begun to waver. My memories stirred, evoking an old inner voice.

This isn't right.

I waited for that old drive to follow it, all the old passion and the old obsession . . . but they never came to me. I was distracted by the swirling embers and their hidden memories.

"This isn't right," I said to a man. He was propped over my body, which felt sore and used. Each time, he'd made me forget.

"It doesn't matter," a woman said, exhaling a sour breath through brown teeth. *"It's all going to burn. This whole city and everything in it—it's all going to burn. . . ."*

That one, there . . . what did that mean? I knew that face. We were in my old precinct. Why couldn't I remember?

I saw a chat portal as I sat alone:

She had something to say. Something you didn't hear.

Then another face, of a man I'd never seen.

"You never heard the name Samuel Fawkes . . ."

The man in the chair cried out, and the memories scattered.

"What are you doing?" I asked. Lev had uncapped the syringe. I saw it was filled with inky black fluid.

The glowing orange mass in the man's rib cage beat at a dangerous rate. I watched the heat throb up the side of his neck and branch across the weathered skin of his face. His bloodshot eyes bugged out, and stared up at Lev as he guided the needle. The tip pierced his skin, above the band of light, and he pushed the plunger down. As the fluid was injected, I scanned it, and caught the cold sparkle of nanomachines.

"What is that?" I asked.

"You'll see."

He injected the last of the black fluid, and the man began to sag back in the chair. His eyes swam and lost focus. Behind Lev, a timer appeared on a screen. It began to count down from ninety seconds. As it did, the man stopped struggling, and twitched. His heart rate began to fall. At thirty seconds, I thought it had stopped cold, but it maintained a slow beat. His body went into deep relaxation; then with fifteen seconds left, his pulse began to creep back up toward normal.

Since my death, life never had the same meaning. When I looked through my memories, it was clear I'd once valued human life. I'd seen lives ended or destroyed every day, and their suffering had begun to eat at me. I'd struggled hard to keep it at a distance, but over time, the barrier eroded. At the end I was worn raw, and even a revivor's death could touch me.

Death no longer bothered me, not in the way it once did. The loss of human life could affect big change, when some lives were exchanged for those of others. Maybe Nico had been right all those years back. Maybe I just should have gone away from the rule of civilian law and made my stand in the grind.

Maybe, but still the voice inside insisted. Without feeling, or passion, it insisted.

This isn't right. None of this is right.

The countdown dropped to zero. The man in the chair had regained consciousness. He no longer looked afraid, and instead he looked confused. He stared at the empty space in front of him.

"I can't read," he whispered. "What does it mean?"

The yellow light over the doorway turned red, and all of them turned at once.

Someone's here, Lev said. *We've been found.*

Outside, down the hall, there was a commotion. The other revivors began moving, packaging up equipment. Lev signaled that I should follow.

We have to go now, he said.

What about him? I asked, pointing at the chair.

Lev's left forearm snapped apart down the middle, and the blade inside shot out. It punched through the man's breastbone, and his eyes bugged open wide. He looked down at the thing that had impaled him, like he didn't understand.

I heard the bone split as Lev twisted the blade. The warm mass in the man's chest fluttered and stopped. The light went out of his eyes, and his chin lolled to his chest.

The others filed out toward the back exit. With a loud snap, the bayonet retracted. A map appeared in the air in front of me with a route traced across it. Two security feeds appeared next to it, showing police vehicles in the front lot, and armed men in the lobby.

We can't risk him being taken into custody, Lev said. *Come on.*

All but three of the revivors left the room. They kept their backs to the walls, the glow in their eyes becoming more intense. Energy was building up inside their chests.

They're going to blow, Lev said. *This entire facility will be destroyed. We don't have much time. Go with the others.*

I nodded and left the room. As we followed the others, I glanced back for one last look at the dead man. When I did, I saw him move.

He lifted his head an inch, and his eyes stared up to meet mine.

5

Atropos

Zoe Ott—Pleasantview Apartments, Apartment #613

I'd been standing across the street, staring at the neon sign in the window of a convenience store for a long time. People passed by me on the sidewalk, leaning into the rain as I watched the water trickle down, blurring the brightly colored light. I counted the bottles that were lined up there behind the glass, all different shapes and sizes. All filled with different colors, warm colors.

This is stupid.

I told Nico he'd leave me there. I knew it would happen. He acted like I was wrong and he wouldn't, and he meant it, but it didn't matter what he said he'd do or even what he meant to do. I knew it would happen, and it did.

I was useless anyway. Nico was hoping I was going to get something out of them, but it was obvious the minute we walked in that there was no way that was going to happen. When I tried to concentrate on her, I couldn't get anything. That halo was there, above her big head, but I couldn't see anything past it. When I pushed a little harder, I got pushed back. She looked over at me then, and she wasn't smiling. My head spun, and I got a cold feeling in the pit of my stomach. I didn't try it again.

After the shot went off, when Nico ran out of the restaurant and left me with the others, I started feeling like I couldn't breathe. It was too much. I had to get out of there. Ai offered to have Penny drive me home, but I didn't want that. I looked around for Nico, but he hadn't come back inside the restaurant. I said I had to use the bathroom, and ducked out.

I was still staring at the bottles through the window when a car turned onto the street in front of me, and when its headlights flashed on the brick wall, I saw two shadows there. They were in the shape of people, but there was no one there. The shadows were burned onto the bricks.

"Soon," a voice whispered.

I turned, and a woman was standing next to me. Her long coat and her clothes were burned black, and when the rain landed on her body, it hissed, throwing up smoke and ash. Her face was covered in soot, and her hair was scorched. When the wind blew, a cherry red glow swelled under the ash of her clothes. Embers scattered and flew up into the air around her.

I looked back toward the burned shadows, but the building was gone, along with everything around it. A big expanse of wet soot and sand sprawled out in front of me, sheets of rain coming down to form gray rivers and pools. Big shadows stood at angles in the distance, and I thought they were the remains of buildings.

I'd seen this before. I'd started seeing it back when I first met Nico. This city, the whole city, was gone.

"How soon?" I asked the burned woman. She turned to me, ash flaking away from her face.

"It had to be done," she said.

Lightning flashed behind the canopy of gray clouds overhead, and a few seconds later, thunder rolled across the empty field.

"How soon?" I asked again.

"Soon."

The wind blew, and more ash streamed off of her body until she just disappeared. When I looked back to the empty field, it was gone. The buildings and the neon were back. The lit store window and the rows of bottles behind it were back just like before.

I turned away from the window and the bottles, and headed down the street. At the corner, I turned and began making my way toward the sign for Pleasantview. Up ahead, flashing blues from a police car were lighting up the outside of the building.

Perfect.

As I got closer to my apartment building, I saw there were actually a couple squad cars out there, and an ambulance too.

Passing by the police cars and heading up the main steps, I wondered if I shouldn't have waited for Nico, but I had to get out of there. So far he hadn't even called to find out where I'd gone.

Jerk.

I went inside. The elevator was still out, so I had to walk up seven flights of stairs. When I got up to the landing between the fifth and sixth floors, I saw blood on the floor.

"Gross."

Drops of it were all over the place. In the corner of

the stairwell, it was smeared around and I could see part of a bloody handprint. Did someone get stabbed or something?

There were drops on the stairs leading up, and when I looked up the stairwell, I saw the door to the sixth floor was propped open.

What the hell?

I passed by on my way up to my floor when I heard a bunch of people talking down the hall on six. Through the doorway I could see shadows from around the corner, and someone was talking on a radio.

"We're bringing him down now," a voice said. Footsteps were coming down the hall. Something was wrong.

". . . for the EMT?" a man said over the radio.

"The elevator's out. They're coming down via the stairs."

"It's six flights," the voice on the radio said.

"You got a better idea?"

I was still standing there listening when three men came around the corner and almost ran into me. Two of them were cops in uniform. In between them was Ted, his hands behind his back.

"Coming through, ma'am," one cop said.

Ted had been beaten up bad—real bad. His whole face was covered in bruises, and there was a big cut over one eye. He was missing a tooth, and there was a bandage over his nose that had blood seeping through it. There was dried blood all down the front of his shirt.

When he saw me, I felt a big surge of anger from him.

"There she is, fucking bitch!" he snapped. The cops grabbed his arms.

"Keep moving, asshole!"

"You send that crazy bitch over to fuck with me?"

He got free from one of them and kicked at me. I fell back as his big foot stomped into the wall right next to me.

"This how you planned it, bi—"

He was cut off when one of the cops stuck a stun gun in his side and zapped him. He went down and flopped onto the floor.

"Piece of shit," the cop said. Ted looked out of it, but he managed to get back up on his hands and knees, glaring at me through his sweaty hair. I'd seen him mad before, but never like that. When I looked, the colors around him were all red, like a fire, a fire that was raging. He wanted to kill me. His eyes were so crazy. I just stood there. I didn't even try to push him.

"Get up, asshole," the clean-cut cop said. "You can add that to your list of charges."

Ted just stared at me from his hands and knees, panting.

"He said, get up!" the other cop yelled. "Now do it, or I swear I'll use this thing again and ride your sorry ass down to the ground fucking floor! Move it!"

"Happy now, bitch?" Ted muttered. He started to get up, and one of them grabbed him and hauled him up the rest of the way. The big guy shoved him through the door and followed him while the other one checked on me.

"You okay, ma'am?"

I nodded. My legs felt weak.

"What happened here?" I asked.

"Domestic dispute, ma'am. Do you live on this floor?"

"No, but—"

"If you don't live on this floor, then please move along while we—"

The room got bright as I pushed him, easing him back.

"What happened?" I asked again. This time his eyelids drooped a little and he answered.

"Best we can tell," he said, "someone beat the shit out of the perp. When his girlfriend came home, it looks like he took it out on her."

"Let me by," I said. He didn't move when I scooted around him.

Down the hall there were more people. They were all in uniform. One was a cop, but the others looked like medics. I started running toward them. They were all standing outside Karen's apartment.

"Ma'am!" one of them said, holding up one hand. "Ma'am you can't come down here!"

The medics were moving a stretcher through the door. The person lying on it had a face covered in bandages and blood.

"Karen?"

"Ma'am, step back please. We need to get through now!"

They were all around her. One pushed and one pulled while two stood on each side. One had a mask over her mouth and nose while the other started prepping a syringe. Her face was beaten to a pulp. Her body was totally limp. She looked dead. All the strength went out of my legs and I had to lean against the wall as they passed by.

"Try to keep her steady!" one of them yelled.

"Ma'am, do you know Karen Goncalves?" someone asked me. I watched them wheel her away. There was a light above her head, but it was faint.

"Ma'am, do you know her? Are you family, or do you know anyone we should contact?"

I stopped hearing him. I just stood there, frozen, and watched them wheel her away.

Nico Wachalowski—The Rescue Mission Clinic

The Rescue Mission Clinic sat on a small urban strip, just outside Bullrich. To the left of the place was an Indian grocery and a laundry. The small parking area was empty, and the storefronts were dark. I cruised to a stop in front of the main entrance, then cut the engine and waited, listening to the rain drum on the roof. A rusted chain-link fence ran along its right side, a coil of razor wire running along the top. The wall facing the narrow gap had been spray painted. The blacktop was littered with wet trash.

According to the records, it was a nonprofit provider for the homeless, run by the local Second Chance chapter. According to the records, they dispensed everything from flu shots to methadone. They did blood work, and provided cheap contraception. Everything was legitimate on paper.

Nico. This is Sean. I'm here. Help me. The message appeared in the dark in front of my eyes. It had repeated every thirty seconds since I came in range.

I pushed the car door open and stepped outside into the cold. Through the glass doors ahead I could see the alarm system was armed. I approached, aware of the security camera mounted on the wall.

I put in a call to Noakes, but got rerouted to ID Hsieh, A. It was picked up immediately.

Who is this? I asked.

Agent Alice Hsieh, she said. *I'll be filling Agent Pu's position. Can I help you, Agent Wachalowski?*

Yes. I need the alarm system deactivated at this address.

She didn't answer, but a few seconds later, I saw the display on the alarm system go dark.

Okay, you're clear, she said.

I put my badge to the scanner, and it overrode the security code. I pushed open the door and went inside.

The main entry opened into a small waiting area. Wooden chairs were arranged there, facing a wall with a sliding window and next to that, a door. Old magazines with curled edges were stacked on a wall-mounted shelf.

I pulled up a blueprint of the facility. The sliding window opened into a small office or reception area, and the door next to it led to a hallway that gave access to it, along with three small examination rooms. The hallway formed an L and led to a restroom, two large storage rooms, then continued to a fire exit that opened into the back alley.

The door was unlocked. I went through, then took a left into the office behind the sliding window. A desk faced out into the waiting area. I turned on the computer and set up a 'bot to break through security.

I gave the desk drawer a tug, but it was locked. Touching the phone's screen, I pulled up the address book and recorded the contacts there. One name jumped out at me.

BUCKSTER, LEON.

I knew that name. Calliope had mentioned him. He was her Second Chance contact. There was no other information except his contact number and work address.

Alice, pull the phone records, please. I need all calls placed to and from this location, starting at the date of the Concrete Falls attack.

She was fast. After a short pause, the data began streaming in. I filtered out anyone on the patient list or the employee directory. Only a handful of the numbers were unaccounted for. One in particular was tied to an organization called CCO: Charitable Contribution Organization. The number was leased under its name, maybe to hide the owner's identity. I saved it aside.

The 'bot continued to work on opening a connection to the computer, but something was blocking it. The security there was a lot tougher than it should have been.

Something's not right.

I backed out of the office and continued down the hallway. The examination rooms were open, and they were all empty. I continued on to the storage rooms. At the bend in the hall, I saw the storage room door in front of me. Down at the end of the corridor to my right was the metal fire door.

Nico. This is Sean. I'm here. Help me. I switched off the connection, cutting off the message.

The storage room was crowded with stacks of cardboard boxes containing medical equipment. To my right, a wooden door led to a closet. Inside there were shelves of sample drugs, along with a locked metal cabinet that covered the far wall. Peering through the side, I saw what looked like pill bottles and other pharmaceuticals.

Sweeping the main storage area with the backscatter, I noticed a metal door behind one of the stacks of boxes. There was a scanner mounted next to it.

Closing the door to the storage closet, I approached the metal door and pushed the boxes aside. Unlike the rest of the place, the door looked modern and new. The scanner next to it was fitted with a lens for performing retinal scans. A retinal scan wasn't even required to get into the FBI building.

Putting my forehead to the surface of the door, I turned the backscatter up to full intensity. The metal was thick, but I could make out images on the other side. The edges of the room were lined with what looked like computer equipment. The middle of the room was dominated by what I guessed was a large reclining chair, like you might see at a dentist's office. Several IV racks stood next to it.

Scanning along the edges of the door, I could see it was secured with magnetic bolts. I was trying to decide the best way to tap into it when the red light shining above the mechanism's lens flickered and turned green. The bolts retracted with a dull thump.

I stepped back into the shadows as the heavy door opened, revealing a dark room behind it. A revivor stepped through the doorway, and the faint smell of sweat and decomposition drifted out behind it. Inside, I saw several sets of glowing eyes.

Before it could spot me, I slipped toward the wall next to the doorway and took the EMP wand from my belt. The revivor was male, with a heavy frame. Its head turned as it scanned the dark in front of it, trying to pinpoint my heartbeat.

I touched the wand to the back of its neck and the metal filament slipped through the skin and up its spinal column. Its body went rigid, and I caught it under one arm as it fell back. Quietly, I eased it onto the floor.

Before it could send out an alarm, I recorded its signature, then triggered the EMP. The light faded from its eyes. Using an old war trick, I looped the recorded signature through a custom transponder I'd installed back in Bontang. Revivors didn't rely on signatures for identification purposes, and they would still detect my heartbeat, but it would keep them from attacking as long as I didn't attack first.

I stepped through the doorway and looked around. Three revivors stood inside, each with their backs to one wall. Their eyes shifted ceaselessly, moving rapidly, almost like they were dreaming. They didn't seem to see me or hear me as I moved into the room.

The light was low enough that even with the enhancements, it was hard to pick out details inside. I shined a flashlight beam, and swept it across the room. Shelving had been set up, stocked with towels. I saw several rolling trays that held surgical instruments, and empty vials for taking blood samples.

There was a faint thermal trace on the chair. There was no other indication that anyone else—anyone living, at any rate—had been inside.

A tent of plastic sheeting hung from the ceiling in the center of the room. I could see dark shapes inside, and a series of flashing red lights. There was a gap in the curtain near the middle, and I pushed through.

On the other side of the curtain were five gurneys, and each one had a nude male corpse on it. From behind each of their heads, a thick wire trailed across the floor. I followed them behind a bank of electronics where the red lights flashed. The skin on each body was rigid. Dark veins were visible underneath the surface from head to toe.

Revivors. A scan didn't produce a signature from any of them. They were dormant.

Back in the office, the 'bot broke through security and a connection opened to the main computer system. I accessed the link and began scanning the files. Most of them were innocuous—medical records of patients coming and going, payroll, ordering and inventory—but one section was isolated from the rest. A list of names and dates had been recorded there. The last four were displayed:

Subject: Harris, Erica. Female. 42. 23042091.
Subject: Janai, Ryu. Male. 30. 10052091.
Subject: Uris, Henry. Male. 32. 13052091.
Subject: Takanawa, Hiro. Male. 28. 14052091.
Subject: Pu, Sean. Male. 41. 15052091.

Sean.

The connection to the computer broke, and the stream of data stopped. When I tried to reconnect, I found it was completely offline. The power to the system had been cut.

"Gathering for iteration six-three-two," a metallic voice said softly from behind me. I turned suddenly, aiming the gun, and saw that the bank of red lights on the electronic equipment had turned amber. As I watched, they began to flicker and turn green.

A loud snap issued from the back of the room, loud enough to make me jump. One of the bodies moved on its gurney, then another. The toes arched back slightly, and I saw the fingers flex. Information began streaming by on one of the screens.

"Hold."

"Gathering for iteration six-three-two."

I felt a low hum through the floor. The gurneys creaked as the bodies arched their backs; then I picked up a signal on the JZI. It warbled and snapped into the waveform of a revivor's heart signature. Another one quickly followed, then another as the hum's pitch increased.

"Active," the computer said.

Back on the gurneys, several sets of eyes had cracked open, creating softly glowing slits in the dark.

Moving the flashlight beam, I caught the face of one of the revivors who had lifted its head off of its gurney. One of its eyes was missing, leaving only a dark slit between the collapsed lids.

"Sean."

He didn't answer. His eye stared up from the dark, not recognizing me.

He'd been turned, and there was no way he'd gotten wired for it willingly. Sean was like me on that score. If we hadn't decided when we joined up, then a few years of dealing with those things settled it for both of us. Sean turned out to have a secret, but I knew the man and I knew he was afraid of revivors. He never voiced it, but something he saw when he looked at them scared him. Whoever took him wired and then killed him.

I looked in his remaining eye for some trace of Sean, but it wasn't there. Unlike Faye, he hadn't been processed at Heinlein, and it looked like a hack job. As he worked at the restraints, I watched and I couldn't look away, even though it felt like a block of ice was sitting in my gut. I'd known Sean longer than anyone else in my life. He'd pulled me out of that hole back in the grind and saved my life. Even if he had lied, he'd . . .

"Sorry, Sean."

I moved next to the gurney and removed the probe from inside my coat. Turning his head away, I pushed it through the skin near the base of his skull.

The system tree came up, but only partially. For some reason it was having trouble reading the components. For the ones it could identify, none were tagged with manufacturing codes.

I managed to isolate his JZI. I found a socket and opened a connection.

Link established.

The connection triggered something; a routine executed, sending a text message across the link.

If you're reading this, they've taken me. I have verified; Fawkes will launch a major strike in the next twenty-four to forty-eight hours. I wasn't able to learn specific targets, but he will attack on two fronts; part of his army will come by sea, most likely by way of Palm Harbor. I intercepted the ID of a ship, ISO 10927718240, and I believe the bulk of his forces are there. Find the ship and you'll find them. The second part of his army is already here, inside the city. I have no idea where he's managed to hide so many, but there are already hund—

The message ended abruptly. I felt Sean's jaw clench underneath my palm. His skin was cold.

His heart signature drifted in the periphery of my vision. There was something different about it. It had an arc that was more elegant than the standard waveform.

Hundreds. It didn't seem possible, but I knew Sean. Something made him believe it. If Fawkes really had hundreds of revivors already inside the city, with potentially thousands more coming in by sea, it was going to be a bloodbath.

I managed to locate Sean's revivor communications array, and opened the spoke connection.

Link established.

Immediately, a rush of data came streaming in. Before I could react, half the JZI's buffers had filled up. It was as if hundreds of individual data streams were bleeding back over the connection. My systems weren't designed to handle an influx like that, and I struggled to abort the link before—

"And stop," the soft, synthesized voice said. The connection broke, and the flow stopped.

What the hell was that?

The bodies all relaxed on their trays. The light in their eyes began to fade. One by one, their signatures winked out.

"Checking signature . . ."

"Signature is gone."

"Commencing cool down."

I removed the probe. The revivors had gone dormant again.

They're being cycled over and over, between animate and inanimate. Why?

I checked the rest of the bodies. Besides Sean, there were four others. One looked well kept, a first or second tier. The other three showed signs of exposure and malnutrition. One had track marks in his forearm. One had a thick scar running along one side of its face, trailing from the chin, up over the cheek, all the way to the ear. It looked like a cut from a knife, maybe.

Wachalowski, head's up; we just got a report of an explosion across town. They think it's tied to your location.

What was it?

A free clinic was just bombed. Healing Hands, over in Dandridge. Second Chance runs that one too. They know we're on to them and they're covering their tracks. Get out of there now.

"Initiating download and purge," the metallic voice muttered from off to the side. I looked over and saw the counters had all reset to zero. The data was no longer being collected. The green lights had turned red again, and I was watching when they all went dark.

Hang on.

Wachalow—

I cut the connection as an electric snap came from the bank of electronics behind me, and the low hum began again. The metal gurneys creaked under the bodies. One by one, the heart signatures reappeared.

"Active," the computer said. Their toes began to arch, fingers curling into fists. The glow behind each set of eyes got brighter.

The lights on the equipment went dark, and the hum stopped suddenly. One of the revivors sat up on the tray, the electrode wires growing taut, then snapping. The one next to it sat up as well.

Keeping the flashlight trained on it, I fired a burst at the first one, and it crashed back onto the gurney. I managed to get the second one before it could get up, and caught a third as it placed its bare feet on the floor. It staggered, then fell into the rack of electronics before landing on a rolling tray and scattering surgical tools.

Sean and the remaining revivor were on their feet. They split up and moved toward me.

I backed through the plastic curtain, and Sean followed. The three revivors along the walls still weren't moving, but the jittering of their eyes had gotten more frantic.

Through the gap in the plastic tent, I saw white smoke billow up from the floor. The revivors I'd put down were dissolving.

Sean took another step toward me and I fired, putting a bullet into the middle of its chest. He didn't stop. There was no recognition in his eyes as he lunged, clamping one cold hand down between my neck and shoulder. With his other hand, he tried to grab my gun. Twisting the barrel down, I shot him in the kneecap. Revivors didn't feel pain, but the joint gave out and it started to fall to one side.

I lost my footing and came down on top of him. He tried to get up as the second revivor approached from my left.

I aimed and fired a burst. The first bullet caught it in one eye, and the next two tracked across its face, blowing out the back of its skull as it fell backward into a rack of equipment. Sean's hand reached up, pawing at my face.

My JZI flagged a warning as it picked up heat signatures from around the room. They were sourced from the three revivors along the walls. In each one, a ton of energy was being rerouted to a component inside the torso. I fired several more shots as warning codes began spilling by. Sean's hands slipped away as I staggered back from the body.

"Shit!"

The eyes of the three revivors began to glow brighter. Their faces turned dark, black veins standing out as pressure built up somewhere inside.

I stood up and scrambled past the chair, back out through the heavy door. Grabbing the handle, I pulled it shut as a set of fingers slipped through and the metal crunched down on them. Another hand wormed through the crack and began to pull it open. I stuck my gun barrel through the space and fired several rounds, then turned and ran for the fire exit.

At the end of the hall I hit the door and shoved it open. A gust of cold wind hit me, and my foot splashed down into a puddle. My heel slipped on a patch of ice and I fell back onto the blacktop, skidding toward a metal Dumpster.

I hit the rusted metal and rolled as a thud pounded through my chest and an explosion ripped through the wall behind me.

Calliope Flax — Wilamil Court, Apartment #516

I sat up on the couch and grabbed the pint bottle off the table next to it. I took a swig of hot whiskey and blew fumes out my nose. My right hand hurt like hell, and the left one kept ticking. I cut open the knuckles on both of them when I beat down that fat piece of shit the night before. The last thing I needed was another assault charge, but the cops never came.

The reminder to check my files popped up in the dark behind my eyelids. I pulled up the text from where I'd buried it. There were three notes:

Called Buckster. He's coming over.

I remembered that one. The other two, I didn't.

There's a padlocked door behind the flag. Wooden door, three locks. It was here the whole time.

Started a JZI record.

I opened my eyes and sat up. I checked the JZI buffer. It was empty.

Son of a bitch . . .

If I didn't remember it and the JZI record was wiped, then someone who knew I might be recording was fucking with me.

There's a door behind the flag.

I could see the flag from the couch—black and red with a green shield on it. I'd ripped it off the wall of a bomb-shelled office in Juba after we took out a pack of rebels inside. I used it to wrap the naked girl when I took her out of there. It hung ceiling to floor on the wall right across from the shitter. I knew for a fact there was no door behind it.

Didn't I?

I put down the bottle, then got up off the couch and

walked across the room to the wall with the flag. After a minute, I pulled up the file and made a note:

I'm taking down the flag. I'll move it somewhere else. I'm starting a JZI record. The next time you read this it should be moved, and if there is a door behind it you'll know.

The buzzer went off at the front and I jumped.

"Shit!"

I stood there for a minute. My hand was still out, hanging there like I was scared to look.

This is bullshit. I grabbed the edge and moved it out of the way. There was no door.

The buzzer went off again.

"Keep your pants on!" I yelled. It had to be Buckster.

I let the flag fall back into place and went to the front door. When I opened it, Leon was there, wearing a rain coat with the hood pulled back.

"Hey, Chief."

"Hey, yourself. Bad time?"

"No."

He looked past me and smiled.

"Looks like you're making yourself at home."

"Yeah."

The place they set me up had started to grow on me. The pipes worked and the heat and water stayed on. The people there weren't a bunch of drunks and bums. After Bullrich and the grind, it was actually not half bad.

"You gonna let an old man in?"

"Sorry," I said, opening the door. "You want a drink or something?"

"Don't mind if I do."

He shut the door behind him, then shook off his coat and threw it on the hook.

"I gotta piss first."

"Have at it."

I hit the can and left the door open a crack while I took a seat. I made one last note before I shut the file down:

Buckster showed up. I'm giving him the Zombie Maker, and we'll see if he knows anything that might help Wachalowski.

The flood gates let go and I cracked my back.

Incoming call.

Call accepted.

Cal, this is Nico. Have you seen Leon Buckster since we last met?

Yeah, the old fart's here now. Why?

Outside, I heard the old man's ass hit the chair.

"You on Second Chance time or your own time?" I called out.

"Mine."

Keep him there. I'm arresting him.

Arresting him? Why?

Because this investigation just turned ugly, and his name came up. He's officially a person of interest and I need to bring him in.

Well, don't bust down my door and do it here. He'll fucking know I was in on it.

Cal, don't start. I just tracked down a dead friend and almost got blown to hell myself.

What? Where?

Rescue Mission and two other Second Chance–funded clinics were bombed tonight, Cal. Buckster's name is connected to Rescue Mission. I'm bringing him in for questioning.

"Damn it . . ."

Right now you've got someone on the inside, I said. *You grab him now and that goes out the window. Let him have his little visit, and pick him up when he goes home.*

I finished up and flushed. When I came back out to the main room, I found him leaning back in my chair.

"Make yourself at home," I said. Wachalowski was still idling on the other end of the circuit.

Look, you know I'm right, I said. *Put him under watch in case he runs, but have your goons wait for him at his place so he doesn't link it to me.*

You're not part of this investigation, Cal—

I can take care of myself, asshole. If this goes back to what happened before I shipped out, then I'm involved. I'm not some street punk for hire anymore, I—

Okay.

Really?

The team will stake out your place and follow him when he leaves. We'll pick him up at home. Gain his trust and find out what you can, but don't tip him off.

Roger that.

Be careful, Cal.

He's an old man. I think I can handle him.

He might be associated with some very dangerous people. Even if he isn't, he might be a target. Be careful.

I will. I've got to go.

I closed the link. In the kitchen, the sink was full of dirty dishes, but I had two clean glasses on the counter. I headed back out and used the whiskey bottle to fill the bottom of the glass I'd dripped the Zombie Maker into. I gave it to the old man and he took a swig.

"Place looks nice," Buckster said.

"Thanks."

"Got everything you need?"

"Everything except a damn job."

"Anything pan out with your friend?" he asked.

"Not yet."

"Well, don't worry. We'll find something before the month's end. There's plenty of things you could do."

"I was thinking maybe Stillwell Corps."

"Not a bad option," he said, "but not if you want things to quiet down."

"You got any better ideas?"

"Maybe Heinlein. We've got contacts there too. They might be able to use someone like you."

"What is that, a fucking joke?"

"I don't mean in development," he said. "They use a lot of ex-military in the testing facilities for the next-gen stuff. Just think about it."

It was as good an in as any, I figured. Buckster was halfway though his drink and the Zombie had to be starting to kick in.

"What is it with you and revivors?" I asked, and for just a second, his eyes flashed. He got twitchy.

"What's that mean?"

"You send third tiers over to get wired up. You send first-tier vets to Heinlein . . . What, do they give you a kickback or something?"

He grinned at that, relaxing a little.

"I don't work for Heinlein, believe me. Second Chance is about just that: a second chance."

"So the bums you recruit end up second tier?"

"Homeless," he said, "and some of them do, yes. I get them as far as I can—clean them up, get them blood tested, and get them basic inoculations."

"You pay for that?"

"We run a series of free clinics throughout the city. It's paid for by donations and fund-raisers."

"How many clinics?"

"Three, on record."

"On record?"

He seemed to think maybe he said something he shouldn't have. "The point is, we don't make anyone get wired. That's a decision they have to make on their own."

"What about scar-face, the guy I saw you with at the train station when I came in?"

"He . . ." The old guy drifted off. His eyes had started to look a little dopey.

"He what?"

Buckster shook his head. "He didn't sign up."

"No second chance for him, then, huh?"

"He'll have his day," Buckster said. There was something weird about the way he said it.

"What?"

He drained his glass, and gave a big shrug. "Every dog has his day, right, Corporal?"

"Sure."

He got quiet for a minute. I grabbed the bottle from the table and filled his glass again.

"You worked with a lot of revivors over there, huh?" he asked.

"Yeah."

"You wired?"

"Fuck, no," I said. "Why, are you?"

He nodded.

"You did your time," I said. "You made first tier. Why the fuck would you go and do that?"

Buckster was looking at the flag hanging on the wall. He had a far-off look in his eye.

"Is that blood?" he asked.

"Yeah."

"Yours?"

"No," I said. "One of the girls from the Juba ghetto got grabbed as a hostage. Me and my team went in to take them out."

"Your team of revivors?"

"Yeah."

"How many?"

"Five."

"She live?"

"Yeah. After we took care of them, I found her in the cellar, naked and half starved. They'd . . . used her pretty rough, but she was in one piece."

"And her captors?"

That mission was the first time, and last time, I'd let them eat. I was mad enough to do it, and I wanted to send a message. I wanted the other fuckers who used that camp to burn it down, and cross themselves when they drove by the ashes after what they saw there.

"We took care of them."

He nodded, understanding. It actually felt good in a way to talk to the old man. He'd been there, so he knew.

He took another drink, and leaned back. He sucked in a deep breath and let it out, still looking at the flag.

"You don't like revivors much, do you?" he asked.

"Not much."

"But they were human once."

"Were."

"But they're conscious. They have memories."

"My TV has memory too."

"Your TV was never alive," he said.

"Look, Chief, lesson number one when dealing with those things is, don't get confused about what they are.

Trust me. Whatever they used to be isn't what they are now. They're weapons, and that's all they are."

"If you really believe what you say, then why not get wired for PS?"

"Because if someone gets their face chewed off, my dead ass ain't gonna be the last thing they see."

He drifted off for a minute. I hoped I didn't give him one drop too many. I didn't want him falling asleep on me.

"Revivors save lives sometimes," he said.

"When they slagged the Congo, they said that saved lives too."

He shrugged.

"They're weapons, Chief. That's what they are. They're not soldiers. They're weapons. Get it? They're good at killing, eating, and soaking up bullets."

"Say what you want about them. They can't be corrupted."

"Corrupted by who?"

"Anyone."

His eyelids got heavy again. His eyes went back to stupid.

"They can't be corrupted," he said. "Just remember that."

"I'll do that."

"They remember things."

That got my attention a little. Revivors did remember things, sometimes a lot of things. If it got quiet enough and you talked to them long enough, they'd tell you the story of their lives. Alone in the field with them for months on end, they were like TVs or radios.

"What kinds of things?" I asked.

"Things they forgot."

"Like what?"

"Things they were made to forget."

That got my attention, a lot.

"What does that mean? 'Made to forget'?"

He looked at me, his eyes trying to focus. They went from being out of it to being a little bit scared. Tears shone in those old eyes of his.

"They make us forget," he said, his voice quiet.

"Forget what?" I asked, but his eyelids were coming down. His eyes still looked scared as they closed, and he eased back in the chair.

"Old man?"

His mouth opened a little, and he started to breathe deep and slow. He was out.

Damn it.

I took the glass from his hand before it fell and threw a blanket on him. Zombie was short-lived; he'd wake up in an hour or two and I'd send him home.

I leaned back on the couch and took another hit from the whiskey bottle, listening to the old guy snore. Wachalowski said the shit that happened before I left never stopped, and I knew now that someone had been messing with my head. Someone had been making me forget. That's what Buckster meant. He knew something.

I called Wachalowski on the JZI, and he picked up like he was waiting for it.

I think I might have something for you, I said.

What?

I'll send you the recording I took, but long story short, I think he's mixed up in something just like you said. Don't hold him, though.

Why not?

Because he's looking for a friend, I said. *Someone he can bring in, and he just found one.*

What makes you think he'll trust you enough to do that?

I watched him sleep. He was relaxed now and the fear was gone from his face, but I knew what he'd been trying to say, and I knew what scared him.

I just found out we have something in common.

Zoe Ott—La Madre Emergency Ward

I made one of the policemen tell me where they were taking Karen, but I didn't know what to do. I froze up in the hallway. I stayed there until the sirens went away and people went back into their rooms. I never realized until then how attached to her I really was.

When I finally did move, I went out into the rain without even going back to my room. I got on the subway, soaked from head to toe, and sat there, numb, the whole way over. The emergency room was completely packed. Some looked sick, and some were bleeding. They looked like they'd been there a long time.

There was a big line to get to the front desk. I managed to make my way through the crowd and cut in front of the first person. He looked like a biker with big, tattooed arms.

"Hey!"

"I need to know where Karen Goncalves is," I said. The woman behind the desk looked at me over her glasses.

"Ma'am, please step to the end of the line."

"Yeah, end of the line, bitch," the biker said.

"I'm not checking in. I just need to know where—"

"Ma'am, I cannot help you until you step to the end of the line and wait your turn like everyone else."

I looked back at all the angry faces. The line went to

the door, and that didn't even count all the people in the waiting area. Half of them were standing because there was no place to sit.

"Bitch," the biker guy said, "get to the end of the line before I—"

I stared in his eyes and he trailed off as the room turned bright around me. All the color in the room faded away, until the only colors left were the ones rippling above everyone's heads. There were so many people that they all started to merge together, but his was red and orange. His was angry and violent. Usually I eased them back, turning them to a calm blue, but not that time. That time I contained them and forced them back.

"Before you what?" I asked. It was like someone else said it. He just stared at me, his face going slack.

"Before you what?" I asked again. He just stared, mouth hanging open a little.

There's no time for this. I need to find her.

I looked past him and pushed the next few people in line until they just stared too. I turned to the woman behind the desk.

"Tell me where she is."

The woman's eyelids drooped and she started tapping on her computer. She looked down at the screen, reading something there.

"She was admitted through the ER. She's currently awaiting emergency surgery."

"What does that mean?"

"It means the available ORs are full and she's being kept stable until—"

"Where is she now?"

"Third floor. East wing."

I walked away and took the elevator up to the third floor, where I followed signs to the east wing. It was crowded up there too. In the hallway there were gurneys parked in rows along the wall. There were people lying on them, but none of them was Karen.

I started trying the rooms along the hall one at a time. The first room had an old man in it, lying on a gurney and not moving. He looked dead. The next room had a fat, middle-aged woman with an afro.

"Are you a doctor?" she whispered. I shut the door.

One door down, a man in a dark blue jumpsuit was standing outside. He had a black case in one hand and was leaning against the wall, watching a little screen he had in his other hand. When he saw me heading toward the door next to him, he started to say something, but I cut him off.

"Are you a doctor or a nurse?"

"I'm a technician."

"Then leave me alone."

He went back to looking at his little screen. I opened the door and went in.

The room was dark. There was a gurney in there surrounded by a bunch of machines. One of the machines was beeping slowly.

"Karen?"

She didn't move, but one of her eyes opened a little and looked over at me. It was her.

"Karen, shit . . . shit . . ."

I turned the light on so I could see her. Her face was all purple, red, and black. Bandages covered one eye, and under a big piece of bloody gauze, her nose looked flat. The one eye that could still open had tears in it. The white part had turned red.

"Zoe," she said, her mouth barely moving. Her jaw was broken and some of her teeth were gone. I thought I was going to be sick.

"Don't cry," she said, but I couldn't get control of myself. My hands were shaking.

"Karen, I'm sorry. I'm so sorry," I said, wiping snot away.

"It's not your fault."

It was my fault, though. I knew it would happen. From the first time I saw her, watching me from behind him while I made him go to sleep, I knew. I saw the bloody eye. I knew this was coming.

"Come here," she whispered. I went up to the bed and stood next to her.

"Someone beat him . . ."

"What?"

". . . someone . . . beat him . . . up . . . he . . ."

I shook my head no. She groped with one hand, and I took it.

"Karen, you'll be okay. You'll be—"

"I'll never forget . . . the first time . . . you came down . . ."

"Me neither," I said, but I already had, a long time ago.

"I knew . . . you were special . . ."

Her one open eye fluttered and then looked around, confused. She looked like she didn't know where she was.

"I'm going to get somebody to help you," I said.

"This . . . is not because . . . of you. . . . It was my . . ."

She drifted off and a tear, pink with blood, rolled down over her swollen cheek. She coughed and something came up. She winced and swallowed.

"I'm sorry I kicked you out. . . ."

She coughed again and made a face. She was in pain. I stared at her until the room got brighter. Her colors were very dim. Little bright spots swirled here and there, like they didn't know where to go. Tiny orange spikes flaring up, like glowing coals. There was pain—physical pain, but more than that. I'd never realized how much there was, how much of it she kept covered up.

I smoothed the lights back, calming them. I focused on the hot-looking spikes and cracks until they dimmed, turning cooler. Karen's face relaxed and got a little dreamy. She managed a smile.

"... you ... do that ... ?"

"Yeah."

"Thanks ..."

There were a million things I wanted to tell her right then. I wanted to tell her how much she meant to me and how much she helped me. All the shit I put her through, I wanted to tell her I didn't mean it. There were so many things I thought I should say, but I didn't. I just stood there.

The floor felt like it moved for a second, and I grabbed the bed to get my balance. The room got darker.

Shit. Not now ...

Everything slowed down, and I felt cold. The tips of my fingers and toes started tingling. My head got heavy.

No ... not now ... I need to be here now ...

"Zoe?" I heard Karen say.

"Karen, I—"

The darkness moved in like black smoke. For a second, all that was left was Karen; then it covered her too. The floor moved again.

... how much longer?

Almost there ...

The words flashed in the dark. No sound, just words. The smoke cleared just a little, and I felt myself moving through the fog. I heard footsteps on metal, but it was muted and faint. I was running. The walls were sprayed red, and down on the floor I saw empty clothes, wet with blood.

Not now . . . I have to go back. . . .

I moved through a big, metal door and out onto a walkway. There was a railing to my right, and I could see a huge open space down below. There were coffins down there. They were stacked up high, arranged in rows. I slipped and saw a man's hand grab the rail. People were starting to move down below. They started yelling, but I could barely hear them, like I was underwater.

"Stop!"

I heard gunshots. I was moving again. There was another heavy metal door up ahead, with a wheel mounted on it. As I got closer, I glanced down to where the coffins were stacked and saw the dead woman, the one from the green room. She looked up at me. There were tears in her silvery eyes.

The doorway opened into a dark room. There was a single light overhead. It shone down on a bed where someone was lying. I ran up to the bed and saw that it was the mean-looking woman, the one with the black lipstick that cornered me in the elevator at the FBI. She was covered in sweat, big muscles standing out. She had on a hospital johnny. Her legs were spread apart and her ankles were locked in stirrups.

"You're too late!" she screamed.

Something black and wet, something living, something dangerous, shot out from between her legs. Cords and veins popped out of her neck. I lurched forward as the man's hand came hammering down on her heart, a blade held tightly in his fist.

"You're too l—"

Everything went black. The screaming stopped. All I could hear was a steady tone.

I opened my eyes. I was back in the hospital.

"Karen?"

She was still there, lying in the bed in front of me. I'd grabbed fistfuls of the sheets and was leaning over her.

I tried to focus again. While I looked at her, the room got bright again, but I couldn't see her colors.

"Karen?"

I realized then that the steady tone was coming from the heart monitor. I looked harder, until the room got so bright the color leached out of everything, but I could see her colors. I didn't know what to do.

The door opened behind me and someone came in. I thought it was the doctor, but when he came around to the other side of the bed, I saw it was the man in the blue jumpsuit from out in the hallway. He reached over and shut off the heart monitor. The beep stopped and the room got quiet.

He took something out of his pocket and shined it in her one open eye. Then he lifted one of her shoulders, until she was on her side. He put his black case on the bed and snapped it open. He reached in, and I saw him take out a black syringe.

He stuck the needle in the back of her neck and I got a clear look at the logo on his chest for the first time. He worked for Heinlein Industries.

I left. I went back the way I came, back down to the lobby, and back through the crowd in the waiting room. I walked back out into the rain and into the street. A car screeched to a stop, the bumper an inch from my leg. Horns blared while I crossed, rain blowing across headlight beams in front of me.

I walked past the subway stop, following the sidewalk and the water rushing beside the curb. It wasn't until I saw the neon sign to my right that I looked up.

When I first tried to quit, I'd break into a sweat every time I walked by that place. I started taking a different route so I didn't have to see it. I never took that route again, but that night, it appeared out of nowhere. Right when I needed it most.

I pushed open the door and went inside. Without thinking, I grabbed a bottle of ouzo, the biggest one they had. I walked up to the counter and put it down.

"Long time no see," the clerk said. After I stopped drinking, I realized the guy must have always known what a complete drunk I was. He might know what it meant, then, that I was back in his store. As stupid as it was, I think on some level, I was hoping he'd say something that would stop me, but he didn't. He took my money, and I left with the bottle.

The only time I hesitated was back in my apartment. I stopped for a second with the glass to my lips and breathed in through my nose, feeling the licorice burn of the fumes. It was a mistake. It was a bad mistake, but it was going to happen. Deep inside me, the pain was gathering. The only reason it hadn't hit me yet was because I was in shock, but it was coming, I could feel it. At any minute, I was going to realize what just happened. When I did, the reality of it was going to stick its hooks in me. It would be there for the rest of my life. In the end, I couldn't face it.

When I took the first swallow, it burned going down. Heat flooded all the way back up my neck to my face, until air from the fan chilled beads of sweat on my forehead. The feeling that went through me was mellow and giddy. For a second, I forgot everything else. For the first time in as long as I could remember, I felt happy and I even giggled as I sat on the floor and let it flow out through all my veins, all the way down to my fingers and toes. For the first time in a long time, I felt right. It was like waking up after a long sleep.

I'm sorry, Karen. I'm sorry, Nico. I'm sorry, but I can't do it. I just can't.

I lifted the glass again, and that time I didn't stop until my stomach turned over and threatened to puke it all back up. I sat down in the middle of the floor and broke out in a cold sweat as the numbness made its way through my body. I was crying, but some part of me felt such relief I didn't care about anything else.

I love this so much. Why did I ever stop?

Her being gone did come, just like I knew it would. Before the night was over, Karen being gone hit me for real, but by then I was numb and beyond feeling anything.

6

Huma

Zoe Ott — Pleasantview Apartments, Apartment #713

I woke to the smell of smoke. Wind was flapping at my clothes, and I could feel grit peppering my face. I was lying on the pavement, but the rain had stopped. It was hot and dry. I didn't hear any cars or any people. All I could hear was the wind.

I opened my eyes and saw the burned-out shell of a car lying on its side a little ways away, and scattered near that were big chunks of concrete with rebar sticking out. The road I was lying on was broken into big pieces, the cracks filled in with dust.

I got up on my hands and knees, my hair trailing down in the grime. There was rubble scattered all around me, crumbled concrete and sand along with something shiny, like powdered glass. Here and there I could pick out little pieces of metal peeking out of the dust. They looked like electronic components. Some were connected with little wires, and some had what looked like hairs or legs sticking out.

A few feet to my left, a long blade with no handle was stuck right through the blacktop. A tiny pink T-shirt, scorched and smudged with soot, had snagged on the top of it and waved there like a little flag.

I sat back on my heels and let the wind blow my hair out of my face. When I looked down at my hands, I saw there was a piece of broken glass stuck in one of them. I picked it out and dropped it on the ground in front of me. The sharp corner had blood on it. I closed my eyes, listening to the little girl's shirt snap in the wind.

A shadow fell over me as I heard footsteps crunch on the pavement. I opened my eyes again, and a woman was standing in front of me. She was burned, and smoke trailed from her hair and clothes. Behind her, there was nothing but open space. The buildings were gone. Nothing was left but jagged pieces sticking up. I held one hand up to shade my face so I could see. The woman's face was covered in soot, and cracked so that raw red showed through.

"Who are you?" I asked.

The wind blew again, fanning the embers that were buried in the ashes of her clothes. Black bits crumbled from her and were blown away.

"Why . . . ?" she asked.

"Why what? Who are you?"

She held out her hands, and I saw that her fingertips were burned down to the bones. The wind ruffled her coat, spraying cinders. Tears ran down her black face.

"You did this."

"What?"

"You did this . . ."

I gasped and opened my eyes. The wind stopped, and the woman was gone. I was staring at the ceiling of my apartment. Off to the side, I saw a cartoon playing on the TV.

My head hurt and my mouth was dry. My stomach was burning, and I felt like I was going to puke. I knew that feeling. It was how I was used to waking up, at least until . . .

A lot of times when I'd wake up from a binge, there would be this time where I blissfully forgot everything I did the night before. A lot of times it never came back, but sometimes it did, like a slap in the face. That morning, lying on my couch, I got two, one right after the other.

The first slap was that I fell off the wagon. After not having a single drink for so long, I'd blown it. It wasn't a small slip, either. I went all the way.

"Shit . . ."

If I'd had the strength, I think I would have cried. I'd been working so hard. I'd really tried. I'd woken up from dreams where I drank and felt guilty about it, then felt relieved when I realized it hadn't really happened. But that time it wasn't a dream. I'd really done it. My whole body ached.

He's going to be so disappointed. . . .

I wondered if I should even tell him. He didn't need to know. It was just one time. I could just get back on the program and forget the whole thing ever happened, right? It was just one slipup. What the hell was I think—

The second slap came then. My stomach rolled and I scrambled to my feet. I stumbled into the bathroom, just managing to get through the door before I fell down on my knees in front of the bowl. Everything came up; then I dry heaved on top of it to the sounds of cartoon music from the next room. I flushed and spit, leaning over the toilet while sweat rolled down over my stomach.

"Karen . . ."

I cried. I couldn't do anything else, so I just sat there, staring into the toilet, and cried until I couldn't anymore.

When I managed to get up, I walked on pins and needles, trying not to fall. Stumbling back to the living room, I accidentally kicked an empty bottle across the floor. It whacked against the coffee table. That's when I saw Penny.

She was sitting on the arm of the couch, watching the TV. She had a bowl in one hand and a big spoon in the other, and was laughing with a mouthful of cereal when I came back in. How long had she been there?

She turned and looked over at me and she stopped laughing. For a second, she looked sad. She put the bowl down on the end table and dropped the spoon into it.

"Sorry, I ate some of your cereal," she said. "Feel any better?"

"No."

She nodded.

"I heard what happened."

I didn't know what to say to that. My head was spinning and I couldn't think of where I would start. I didn't want her there. I wanted to be alone.

"Lie down," she said, pointing at the couch. "Come on, before you fall."

The last thing I wanted to do was talk about it, but I really did need to lie down. I limped over to the couch and flopped on my back while she looked down on me from her perch on the armrest.

"Drink this," she said, tossing me a bottle of vitamin water. She pulled a pair of pill tabs out of her pocket and tossed them to me too.

"Those will stop the nausea."

I pushed the pills through the foil and swallowed

them, washing them down with a gulp of water from the bottle. My stomach turned, but they stayed down.

"Look, I know you don't want to talk right now, so I'll keep it short," she said. "Ai doesn't want to see you like this anymore, and, honestly, neither do I. This, what happened here with your friend, it wasn't your fault and it wasn't fair. This kind of thing shouldn't be happening to you, so it's time."

"Time for what?"

"Some tough love, I guess. We look out for our own, Zoe. I know Heinlein took her, but if you want to have a service, then Ai will take care of it. You don't have to worry about a thing. None of it will cost you a dime. Anyone who wants to be there can be there, and we'll stay out of it. How does that sound?"

I couldn't think about Karen's funeral. I didn't want to think about Penny either, but Karen didn't have anyone else to deal with that stuff. If someone else didn't take care of it, I would have to do it, and I didn't think I could.

"Okay," I said.

"We're getting you out of here," she said, waving one hand at my living room.

"Out of here?"

"This place," she said. "Is there anything left here for you?"

"No."

"We're putting you up in a new place, a better one, away from all this."

"I—"

My phone rang in my pocket. When I fished it out, I saw the call was from Nico.

"That him?" she asked.

"I don't want to talk to him right now."

"I know, but you should answer it. Things are moving fast."

"What do you—"

"He's going to ask you to help him question a man named Leon Buckster. You should do it."

"How do you know what he's going to ask?"

"Just trust me. Quick, answer the phone."

The phone was on its fourth ring. I picked up.

"Hello."

"Hello, Zoe. This is Nico."

"Hi."

"Hi. Look, I'm wondering if you would be available to do me a favor today."

It was the last thing I wanted to do. I didn't want him to see me like I was. He was smart; he'd pick up on it right away. No matter what I did, he'd figure it out. It made me mad that he'd call wanting a favor after what happened. It wasn't fair because he didn't know, and he wouldn't have any way to know, but I didn't care.

I opened my mouth to say no. I was tired and dizzy. I didn't care what Penny said; I couldn't do it.

"Sure," I told him.

"Thanks," he said. "I know this is an imposition, especially after what happened at the restaurant, but things are heating up. Did you have a good time, at least, before the shooting started?"

"Yes." My voice sounded very small.

"Good."

Penny had gotten up and stepped back from the couch. She took a little blank business card out of her pocket and handed it to me.

"Hang on," I said, muting the phone. I took the card.

"Help him. Do whatever he wants," Penny said, "but make sure you ask Buckster that."

I turned the card over. On the back she'd written:
Where is Samuel Fawkes?

She smiled, and gave me a little wave as she headed back toward the door and opened it. I'd never seen the name before.

"Why?" I called.

"Because we're pretty sure he knows," she said over her shoulder. "Later."

She shut the door behind her. I turned my attention back to Nico, unmuting the phone.

"What do you want me to do?"

"I'm bringing someone in," he said. "He has information vital to—"

"I understand."

"Can you be here in an hour?"

"Sure."

"Is something wrong?"

"No."

"You're sure?"

"You're nice to me, Nico," I said. I don't know why I said it.

"I'm your friend, Zoe," he said, but he wasn't, not really.

"I know."

"Is an hour enough time?"

"One hour." I hung up. Afterward, I sat there, staring at the phone in my hand and not moving. Those were the only times he called anymore: when he wanted me to come and do my tricks for him.

"Zoe, these people, I don't think they are your friends."

He'd said that. He kept saying that, but he wasn't the one that showed up to see how I was after the night before. He wasn't the one who offered to help when I really needed it.

He just called up and wanted me to help him. He didn't care about me, not really. If I couldn't do what I did, he'd never call at all. But it didn't matter.

I wasn't doing this for him. I was doing it for them.

Nico Wachalowski—FBI Home Office

Through the glass door, I watched the streams of people pass by on the sidewalk. None of them was Zoe. A dark window hung against the gray, rainy background, displaying the strange examination chair and the equipment surrounding it. Sean must have been wired right there, in that chair. The site wasn't set up for full transfusion, which meant the revivors would have a very short shelf life. It also wasn't equipped to do any kind of major surgical procedures or cosmetic procedures. That meant no physical augmentations and no weapon upgrades.

The JZI recording Calliope had sent over from the night before wouldn't be admissible in any court, but it proved Leon Buckster knew more than he was saying. His statement about revivors remembering things they'd been made to forget implied he was familiar with Zhang's Syndrome, the condition that Fawkes himself had discovered. If he knew that, he might be sympathetic to Fawkes's cause. He might even have learned it through Fawkes.

A widespread, legitimate organization was possibly assisting terrorists. Revivors were being created with no shelf life, no weapons, and no cosmetics. Several had been rigged with bombs to strike soft targets and destroy evidence, and all indications were that Fawkes intended to detonate multiple nuclear weapons inside the city. It all spelled big trouble.

Hell of a night, Wachalowski. It was Alice Hsieh. She was sliding into Sean's role almost too easily.

Yeah.

Three clinics bombed on the same night. The streets had already been crawling with police, and now the National Guard was moving in, this time padding their ranks with Stillwell Corps soldiers rather than revivor units. So far nothing concrete had leaked, but the media was beginning to speculate and the tension level was rising out there. Fear and a lot of anger had begun to brew.

Any evidence of revivors at the second site? I asked.

They didn't find any, but they're still looking.

Footage piped over appeared in a new window. All three places had burned to the ground. At the remains of the Healing Hands clinic, a camera focused on the remains of a large dentist's chair with a twisted mechanical arm attached. It was the same as at Rescue Mission.

We got word back on that maritime ID you sent over. It was the KM Senopati Nusantara, *an Indonesian tanker.*

Was?

It disappeared close to a year ago on the open sea. The official report indicates it was likely pirated.

They never recovered it?

Never. The transponder went silent, and it was never picked up, even on a satellite sweep. It was presumed sunken. The shipyard put in an insurance claim, and six months ago they collected.

If Sean's last message had any truth to it, though, then the ship was still intact and somewhere in UAC waters. Somewhere close.

How long you going to let Buckster stew?

I'm waiting for my operative.

You hit your head pretty hard last night. You sure you're up to this?

I'm sure.

Outside the glass wall where I stood, people moved quickly past, heads ducked down against the rain. They moved behind the small window containing the JZI image, disappearing, then reemerging on the other side as they trudged by. I spotted Zoe in the crowd as she stepped out of the flow and started toward the front entrance.

She's here. We're on our way up.

I cut the connection. Zoe shuffled toward the entrance, looking half asleep.

Damn it, Zoe . . .

Even from a distance I could tell she'd been drinking. Her eyes were puffy and bloodshot. The dark circles were back. She trudged forward, staring out from under the rim of her umbrella like she was marching to the slaughter. When she saw me, she wouldn't look me in the eye.

"Zoe, this way," I said. Her eyes were shiny as she closed the distance between us.

"You okay?"

"Can we just get this over with?" she asked, wiping her eyes.

"Yes. His name is Leon Buckster. He's the head of one of the local Second Chance chapters."

She nodded.

"Just follow my lead, but work inside the reference I gave you."

"Fine," she said, "and before you say it, yes, I'm sure. I know what I look like and I know what you're thinking, but I can do this."

"That's good enough for me."

She followed me to the interrogation room where Buckster sat, looking down into a paper coffee cup. He wasn't happy.

"Mr. Buckster," I said, holding out my hand. "I'm sorry to keep you waiting like that. My name is Nico Wachalowski, and this is Zoe Ott."

He gave my hand a firm shake, then held it out to Zoe. When she didn't take it, he leaned back into his chair with his palms on the table. He noticed the lacerations on the left side of my face from the explosion, but he didn't ask about them.

"I'm here to help," he said. "Kind of like to know what this is about, though. Am I in some sort of trouble?"

"I want to talk to you about Second Chance."

He raised his eyebrows.

"Second Chance? What for?"

"You've heard of the Rescue Mission Clinic?"

"Yeah I've heard of it."

"Healing Hands? Mercy Medical?"

"Yeah, they're free clinics we run downtown. What is this about?"

"When was the last time you were in contact with any of these facilities?"

"I don't know. A few weeks ago?"

Galvanic skin response indicated curiosity and some stress, but it didn't look like he knew about the bombing.

"Do you know what sort of work goes on there?"

"Yeah, they offer quality medical care to third tier citizens who otherwise can't afford it," he said.

His GSR jumped while he talked. The topic of Rescue Mission had him tense.

"Anything else?"

"They're authorized to distribute methadone. They do basic blood work, mostly AIDS testing. Aside from that, it's mostly handing out antibiotics and the like.

Why is the FBI interested in a bunch of free clinics? The paperwork for the drug treatment program—"

"It's all in order, Mr. Buckster. That's not why you're here."

"Then if you don't mind Agent, why am I here?"

"The Rescue Mission, Healing Hands, and Mercy Medical clinics were all bombed late last night."

"What?"

"The facilities were completely destroyed."

His shock looked genuine, but there was something else underneath it. He was shocked but not completely surprised. He knew something about those places, something he was hiding.

"That's impossible," he said.

"Impossible?"

"I just mean . . . why would—"

"Do you recall the Concrete Falls bombing, Mr. Buckster?"

"Of course."

"The bomb that destroyed the Rescue Mission facility was of similar, if not identical, makeup. We have found links between the attack at Concrete Falls and your medical centers—"

"Hey, they're not my medical centers. I'm just—"

"You're the head of a local Second Chance chapter that covers Bullrich as well as Dandridge. We've combed security archives that put you coming and going from each of these facilities as early as three days ago. Are you sure you don't want to change your story, Mr. Buckster?"

His face fell a notch. I reached into my jacket and pulled out an envelope containing two photographs. One was the photo of Henry Uris alive, and the other was the image of Henry Uris's revivor lying on the gurney. I dropped them both on the desk in front of him.

He looked down at the gray face. Black fluid had pooled in the socket of its missing eye.

"You were caught on a surveillance camera at the Brockton–Stark train platform, talking to that man," I said. He didn't say anything, but he recognized the face.

"I want my lawyer."

I held up a card with the number I'd pulled from the phone system, the one with no name attached.

"Who does this number belong to?" I asked.

"Never seen it."

"It was registered to the SCO, run by the organization Second Chance. Who used it?"

"How the hell should I know? You want to search our records, get a court order."

"I will. You're lying, Mr. Buckster. Right now I have you tied to three separate acts of domestic terrorism; that's enough to put you in the ground."

"I had nothing to do with that! I said I want my lawyer!"

"No," Zoe said. When I turned to her, she was staring down at him, eyes filled with tears.

"What the hell do you mean, no?" he asked. She glared at him, and her pupils went wide. A moment later, Leon's eyelids got heavy, and he slumped in his chair.

"Enough bullshit," she said. She walked up to the table and stood in front of him. Before she could do anything else, I crossed behind her and pulled the plug on the surveillance camera.

"Zoe . . ."

"I'm going to ask you some questions and you're going to answer them. Do you understand?"

"Yeah."

"Tell me you understand."

"I understand."

"Did you talk to the revivor in the picture or not?"

"I did."

"When he was alive or dead?"

"Alive."

"Were you there when he died?"

"No."

"Do you know how he died?"

"No."

"Don't lie to me," she said.

I'd never seen her like that before. Her stare was intense and angry. She didn't let up after she put him under. If anything, she pushed harder. He seemed to drift further into whatever trance he was in. Saliva began to collect in one corner of his mouth.

"Zoe, take it easy," I told her.

"Who uses that phone number? The one he showed you?"

"We've got no connection to illegal—"

"I didn't ask that," Zoe snapped. "I asked who the number belongs to."

"Heinser. Michael Heinser."

"Who is he?"

"I don't know anything about—"

"Who is he? Who does he work for?"

"He works for . . . Heinlein . . . Industries . . ."

A heat spike appeared on the scanner monitoring his GSR. It started growing, causing his skin temperature to rise.

"Zoe, wait. Hold on."

I moved behind him and found the source of the heat on the back of his neck, near the base of his skull. A component there had gone active. Whatever it was, it was drawing a significant amount of power.

I accessed his JZI and brought up a schematic. The configuration was old, but some upgrades were fairly recent. Despite the fact that he was unconscious and not coupled to the implant, a lot of energy was moving around in there. It was building in a single component.

"Zoe, stop!"

"What was going on in those clinics?" she asked. "How many more of them are there?"

"They . . . have to wake up . . ." he said softly.

The device was a kill switch, and it was about to go off. It was monitoring him, ready to blow his brains out if he fell under the influence of hypnosis or mind control.

"Zoe, let him go!" I shouted, louder that time, but she wasn't listening.

"Where is Samuel Fawkes?" she snapped, but I didn't have time to ask her where she'd heard that name; the device was about to trip.

There wasn't any time to be delicate. I spun Zoe away from him and slapped her across the face.

Her eyes went back to normal, but the look on her face was one of pure shock. A blush began to swell in her pale cheeks. Off to the side, I sensed the energy surge from Buckster begin to ebb, easing back.

"Zoe, I . . ."

I reached forward and she slapped my hand away, backing up and knocking over her chair.

"Zoe, wait!"

She turned and shoved the door open, running down the hallway.

"Hey, G-man," Buckster said. When I turned back to look at him, he seemed a little confused, but there was a wary look in his eye. Anger was brewing on his face. "I want my fucking lawyer."

"You're free to go," I told him. "If we have any more questions—"

"You know where to shove them," he said, brushing by me on his way out the door.

I watched him leave. With what we had, I could hold him. With what we had, I could hold him indefinitely, but Leon Buckster was a drone. He wasn't behind this. I put a call through to Calliope. After a few seconds, she picked up.

Buckster's on his way out of here, I said. *I think he'll try to run. I want to know who, or where, he runs to.*

It's done.

Be careful. He's dangerous.

I still had the image of the scan in front of me. The kill switch wasn't the only surprise. Despite being a vet, Leon Buckster was also wired.

The connection closed. I thought about it for a minute, then called Noakes.

Wachalowski, what the hell's going on down there?

I got something. I need a meeting with. Heinlein Industries.

Faye Dasalia—Parking Garage, Roof Level

I lay in the car's backseat and listened to the raindrops drum on the roof. Electric signs had begun to flicker on. Nico still hadn't returned.

A persistent cluster of old memories kept coming to the forefront—memories of winter, when I had tracked Lev. I had crouched down on a snow-covered sidewalk and leaned into the car where he had waited. The woman behind the wheel was hours dead, her body covered in blood. Lev had waited in the backseat of that car, while the sun set and snow covered the windows. When she returned, he'd grabbed her and targeted the beating mass of her heart. While streams of shoppers passed by them, unaware, he'd stabbed her through the breastbone.

I couldn't identify the blade he'd used. That had really bothered me.

I would have been horrified to know, I think, that one day I would walk in that killer's shoes. It was that same killer who instructed me how to avoid the security cameras and access the vehicle.

The clinic, and three others, had been destroyed in response to police raids. That implied a coordinated attack. Motoko and her people were closing in. If they located the ship, then we might lose everything. When I died and realized the truth of my life, I knew I'd found my purpose—one more important than the law I'd upheld. That absolute control over so many could not go to so few; it would change human society forever.

I knew that we couldn't fail. Still, when I was alone and it was quiet, I imagined the attack that was to come. The more I learned, the clearer I pictured it. When I did, that academic doubt returned:

This isn't right.

The memory of the man at the clinic, the one that Lev injected, wouldn't seem to leave my mind. What was it that I had seen? Lev had killed him, there was no doubt about that, but near the end, I knew I'd seen him move. Somehow the man had been reanimated. Fawkes wouldn't respond to questions about it, nor would Lev, which meant he had been told not to. There were things in play I wasn't aware of, and I wondered exactly how far that went. At the restaurant, when I'd recorded them, some things were said that I couldn't reconcile:

"... it won't just be this city that is destroyed. Fawkes will destroy this city, and then, one by one, the rest will begin to fall...."

Was it just a ploy of theirs, a scare tactic? Or had they really seen it?

The rain picked up and began to fall harder. A message came in from Fawkes.

Call accepted.

Has he returned yet? he asked.

Not yet. Were all of the safe houses destroyed?

No. They missed one, but we'll have to step up the plan. The ship has begun its approach. When it arrives, the forces inside the city will be awakened, and will be joined by those on the shore. The devices will be distributed at that time, and carried into the targets during the assault. At that time, a pool of names and identifications will be accessible to all units. Eliminating them will be the top priority.

It's going to be chaos. How will we locate them all?

The new units will become active at that time, and you'll be connected through your secondary communications node. The new units will have an information-sharing array that will be very useful in tracking individuals. They will pinpoint them, and update the locations in real time.

I understand.

Do you?

I understand enough.

Good. When you're finished with Wachalowski, regardless of the outcome, there's one more thing I need you to do before the ship arrives.

An abduction?

An assassination.

Who?

An image appeared, floating above my face. A woman

with large eyes peered through long red hair. Her beaklike nose protruded over thin lips. I recognized her face immediately. She had been with Nico at the restaurant.

Zoe Ott, I said.

Yes. Do you remember her from the factory, two years ago?

I sifted through the field of my memories, isolating the specific time and place. I was inside the clean room, and Nico was there with me. He had removed my Leichenesser capsule, which had nearly destroyed me. He meant to save me, I think, like he hadn't yet realized it was too late. . . . The door he'd come through opened, and a woman stormed through, dragging another.

The first woman's name was Calliope Flax; I'd seen her with Nico too. The one being dragged was a redhaired woman, Fawkes's target Zoe Ott. I recognized the white smock she was wearing.

She was part of the original testing, I said. That meant two years ago, Lev had taken her.

Yes. She was designated Patient Nine. She exhibited some abilities that I'd honestly like to study further, but I won't have the luxury. We have to move soon.

Why bother to kill her now?

Wachalowski's using her, and she nearly got to at least one of our operatives. We can't take any chances at this stage. Make sure her body can't be found.

Understood.

Do it tonight.

He broke the link, and I stared at her image. She looked so pathetic, so innocuous. She didn't look powerful.

She tried to tell you something. Something you didn't hear, a voice seemed to whisper in my ear.

You never heard the name Samuel Fawkes. . . .

Her memory had stirred up others in its wake. Her face reminded me of someone else's, someone with that same look of desperation. The hair was different and the nose was different, but those haunted eyes wore the same expression. They looked like they saw too much. I'd seen eyes like that on another woman, years back, when I was a cop. The memories had been hidden, and I hadn't pieced them back together yet.

"He doesn't destroy everything . . . I do . . ."

I drew forth one of the broken memories, and looked into the place that had been altered. I was in my old precinct, where I sat in the interrogation room. The woman sat across the table from me, her body worn out and sick. She was emaciated, and her teeth were decaying. Bony little fingers picked at needle tracks. At that point, her mind should have been gone as well, but her eyes were like two suns. Like the woman Zoe Ott, she'd seen more than she'd wanted.

"You need to get to a shelter," I'd told her, but she'd just shaken her head.

"You can't help me," she said. *"I made a mistake. This is bigger than you."*

"If you're in some kind of trouble, I can help you." She seemed to find that funny.

"You're getting dragged into this just by talking to me," she said. *"They know I'm alive now."*

"Who knows?"

At the time I thought a dealer or a pimp. I'd honestly thought that I could keep her safe, but in the end I couldn't. We never found the body, but the blood was hers, and there was far too much.

She tried to tell you something . . . something you didn't hear . . .

I wasn't sure who'd said that. Was it that I hadn't heard? Or did I hear, but was forced to forget it?

I remembered a knock at my door at night. I took my gun from the drawer and answered it.

"Who is it?" I called, not opening the door.

"I'm sorry to disturb you so late, Miss Dasalia," a man's voice said from the other side. *"This is about that woman."*

"What woman?"

"You know the one I mean."

I opened it, but kept my weight on the door in case he tried to force it. There was a man standing there. At the time I'd never seen his face before, but I recognized it now. Years later, when I finally made detective, he would become my partner.

His eyes went wide, and I felt strangely dizzy.

"Put down the gun," he said, *"and let me in."*

... and knowing better, I let the stranger in.

"Forget everything that woman told you." I remember he'd said that.

"You never heard the name Samuel Fawkes. . . ."

My thoughts scattered as someone approached the car. The lock released, and the driver's-side door unlatched. I let the memories fade.

The door groaned open and Nico climbed inside, lowering himself into the driver's seat. He slammed it shut, shaking off rain from his coat, then gripped the wheel with one hand. He reached toward the ignition with his other, and stopped with his thumb over the starter pad. His heart rate jumped suddenly, and I saw his body tense.

I sat up as his pistol swung back around. I caught his wrist before he could target me, impressed by how fast he was.

"It's me," I said.

His eyes were wide, but when he saw me, they changed. They looked at me the way they had since that night, when I woke to find that he'd brought me back. It was hard for me to know what the look meant. I could see fear in his eyes, and something else there as well. It might have been pain or longing or sadness. Maybe it was just guilt over what he had done.

"Faye," he said. He blinked hard and then opened his eyes again. When he did, the flicker from his JZI had faded from his pupils. "You can't keep coming to me like this."

"Fawkes authorized me to bring you what you asked for," I said.

"Really," he said, like he didn't believe it.

"Yes."

"You could have sent it. You shouldn't be here."

"I'm here because of you, Nico."

He looked down for a moment and he nodded. The gun was still in his hand, but he'd moved his finger off the trigger. Smoky breath trailed from his nose in the cold air. His heart was beating quickly, but his face and eyes looked calm.

"Give me the information," he said.

I sent him the files Fawkes had given me, and although he held them over for scanning, he accepted the package.

"It goes deeper than you think," I said.

"You don't know what I think."

"You might be the only one who can stop her."

"I'm not going to kill anyone, Faye," he said. "You won't convince me to do that."

"I'm just here to give you the information."

"You didn't need to come here to do that."

"I wanted to see your face."

"That's it?"

"I wanted you to see mine."

That bothered him, I could tell. His fingers kept squeezing the grip of the gun.

"I remember every time I was with you," I said. "Before you left for the war, and after you got back too. Those memories all mean something to me, Nico, because all of them are real."

"Shut up."

"You understand it academically. I know you understand it. You realize what your friend, and her friends, can do. You must know, even, that they've done it to you, at least back when they still could. You know all these things, but you still don't get it. You can't, because you can't see how much you've lost. You can't see what was taken away from you, and you never will see it."

"I said, shut up," he said.

"But I can," I said, "and I know you loved me—"

He slipped his wrist from my grasp and stuck the gun in my face.

"Don't finish that sentence," he said. He glared at me down over the pistol's sight.

"Please do what Fawkes wants," I said. "If you don't do it, he's going to kill you—"

"Shut up!" he barked, knuckles white on the gun's grip. Blood had rushed into his face, lines of orange branching out underneath the skin. They glowed like electric light. The breath that blew out of his nostrils was warm. He seemed so alive right then.

"You're not Faye," he said in a low, even voice. His vitals spiked, but his eyelids had drooped. He looked the way he did when he first woke me, with calm murder in his eyes. "I shouldn't have done what I did. She wouldn't have wanted it."

"I didn't know what it meant," I said. "I couldn't know what I wanted."

"She would never have helped Fawkes."

"But I did help him, Nico."

"She never would have killed Sean. You aren't Faye. You're Faye's corpse."

"My memories are the same. My consciousness—"

"It's not the same," he said. "I thought it was. I hoped it was, but it's not the same. I don't want to hear anymore. Tell me where he's hiding them."

"I can't."

"I pulled the maritime ID for a tanker called the KM *Senopati Nusantara* off a revivor. Is that ship still out there? Is that where they are?"

"Please help us, Nico. Fawkes can still get to you."

"He's already done his worst."

"No, he hasn't."

"He has to me."

His body grew very still; then his eyelids drooped and the muscles in his trigger finger twitched. I almost didn't get my hand up in time. The muzzle flash lit the inside of the car, and I felt the heat of it against my face. Burned powder peppered my skin as the bullet punched through the seat behind me. Smoke drifted from the barrel as I swung my other hand and slapped him across the face.

I hadn't meant to do it, but it stopped him. He just stared, the gun forgotten in his hand.

"How could you?" I heard myself whisper to him. The words, like the slap, came from some unknown place, some old remnant of myself.

He didn't try to fire a second shot. He was still staring when I opened the door and slipped out into the dark.

7

Tokkotai

Nico Wachalowski—Heinlein Industries, Industrial Park

I cruised across the tarmac, and tried to push the encounter with Faye out of my head. For the second time I'd had her in my sights, and for the second time I'd let her go.

It wasn't the slap that stopped me, or what she said. It was the look in her eye, that look a revivor wasn't supposed to have. That same look that I saw, just for a second, in that girl revivor's eyes during the Goicoechea raid, when this all started. As if somehow what I'd done had wounded her.

"How could you?"

I shook my head and tried to focus. That look was imagined. It was only there because I put it there, because I wanted it to be there. Maybe she did carry around memories of our time together, but unlike the girl in Goicoechea, Faye was someone I'd known, and something didn't carry over. Faye could never have gone along with this. She would never have asked me to either. The thing that waited for me in the backseat of my car knew there would be a nuclear detonation inside the city, and didn't care at all. If its ghrelin inhibitor was switched off, it would . . .

A sheet of rain misted the windshield. Rather than go down that road, I sifted through the information she'd given me again. Fawkes had heavily redacted it, but even so, it was extensive. To prove any of it would take years of independent investigation, and since the FBI had been compromised, that would never happen. Still, if there was any truth to it, then the situation was even worse than I'd thought.

The names that appeared on his list were high-profile, powerful people, and not all of them were as secretive as Motoko Ai. Robin Raphael was a media mogul with an empire based out of the Central Media Communications Tower, one of the largest buildings in the city. He ran video and print news on at least fifty different fronts. Charles Osterhagen was a retired general whose name was known to anyone who'd served in the grind. He was the founder of Stillwell Corps. Two of the other names on the list were investors on the list of superwealthy.

They weren't people you just called out and accused, not even with proof. They weren't people you just approached on the street, or who quietly disappeared. They had teams of lawyers and professional security. If he thought I could get to any of these people, Fawkes was out of his mind.

A Chimera helicopter crossed the gray sky up ahead, and I picked up its scan as I approached. It had been two years since I'd been to Voodoo Proper, as the Heinlein facility was known. It hadn't gotten any friendlier. The half mile of open tarmac that circled the main facility was dotted with guard stations, and electronic eyes followed my vehicle as I made my way across it. A second helicopter appeared and moved across the sky in the distance, and off to the northwest, a jeep was patrolling the main campus.

Wachalowski, this is Noakes. Any word back from the Indonesians?

It's a dead end. The shipyard already collected the insurance on the lost ship. They don't want any talk that it might still be intact.

I don't know how long the DoD will let us sit on that satellite.

That ship is out there.

I'll do what I can, but right now the majority of our resources are tied up tracking the nukes. We can't afford to waste time.

The weapons are on that ship.

I'd like to believe that, Wachalowski, but we can't say for certain they're not still in the city, and that has to be our priority. Find something concrete.

Understood. I'm entering Heinlein's main facility. I'll have to switch off soon.

This would be easier if we just brought him in.

If we try that, Heinlein's lawyers will crush us.

There's no delicate way to do this, Wachalowski.

Maybe not, but Michael Heinser was one of their major players. The check I ran flagged him as a high-level revivor R & D man, but the specifics of his position were classified. There was no way to bring him in for questioning without some level of public exposure. No matter how else you looked at it, the one place no media would be able to follow was onto the grounds of Heinlein Industries.

You are entering a restricted area. No unauthorized communications are permitted in or out from this point forward. No unauthorized scans, visual, audio or data recordings are permitted beyond this point....

A red flag popped up in my visual display and warning data began streaming by as the JZI detected an orbital beam painting my vehicle. I'd just been targeted by a satellite capable of incinerating me right there on the tarmac. A second later, a pulse caused the information to warp in front of me, and my JZI powered down.

They were jumpy. I couldn't blame them.

I checked my cell phone, and it had powered down too. Not knowing exactly where we were supposed to meet, I continued straight toward the main compound. A full minute passed before I saw another vehicle come into view up ahead. It moved to intercept me.

The vehicle was a black military jeep. Without the JZI I couldn't make out who was in it, but he flashed his lights and I cruised to a stop. The jeep pulled up a few car lengths away, and a middle-aged man with dark skin got out. He was wearing a suit, and a badge fluttered in the wind from a clip on his belt.

Whoever he was, he wasn't alone. Two revivors in body armor climbed out of the back. I began to doubt I would be coming face-to-face with Michael Heinser, but whatever they had set up for me, it was going to have to do. I cut the engine and got out of my car, walking toward the man.

The revivors stepped in front of him and met me halfway. One of them looked me up and down until its scanner found the badge inside my jacket. It turned to the man.

"It's him," it said.

The man removed an electronic device from his jacket and held it up in front of me. After a few seconds, it emitted a sharp beep.

"You're bugged," he said.

"I know better than to try that. Anyway, you shut down the JZI."

"This is independent of the JZI," he said, moving closer. He held the device close to my left eye, and it beeped again.

He turned the device around so I could see the screen. A snapshot from a tissue scan was displayed there. I could make out the corner of my eye at the edge of the screen. There was a tiny speck there that stood out as a bright white dot.

"What is it?" I asked. He looked at me skeptically.

"You don't know?"

"No."

He looked at the screen again, then switched off the device.

"I believe you," he said. "The device is nearly microscopic. It could have been delivered through casual contact without your feeling it or knowing it. It piggybacks onto your JZI's systems, so as long as that's offline, the bug is cut off from its source."

The bar.

"What's the matter? Are you not used to a woman touching you?"

The blue-eyed woman with the wool hat who showed up at the restaurant; she planted it when she stopped me in the bar. It was a setup.

"Someone is spying on you, Agent Wachalowski."

Ai was hedging her bets, then. She'd been watching since that night. She knew what I found at the Rescue Mission clinic. She knew Heinser's name, and that I'd traced him to Heinlein Industries. She knew about the Buckster interview too.

"I used a magnetic pulse on it; it's destroyed," he said.

"When you leave the campus and your JZI reinitializes, it will not come back online. You should be more careful."

The man waved at the revivors, and they retreated. They moved back toward the jeep but didn't get in. They stood in front of the grill and waited.

"Sorry about all this," he said. He held out his hand, and I shook it. "As you can see, we must be careful. I'm Anan Bhadra. I represent Heinlein Industries."

"I thought I was meeting with Michael Heinser," I said. "Where is he?"

"Unfortunately, Mr. Heinser is out of the country on business at the moment."

"When is he due back?"

"It's hard to say, but in the meantime, I've been sent to make a statement and to answer any questions you might have."

"Out here?"

His face didn't change, keeping an even smile as the wind ruffled his suit jacket. I had expected them to hold back, but even so, it was a hostile reception. They had me at a big disadvantage; with no JZI and no line of communication to the outside, there was no way I could verify whether he was telling the truth about Heinser. By the time we were finished and I was back outside their perimeter, he could be in the air, if he wasn't already.

"We have become aware of several handheld nuclear devices whose whereabouts are currently unknown," he said. "Heinlein is a high-profile target."

"You're saying this is a security measure?"

Bhadra shrugged, without saying one way or the other. It didn't matter; he had his instructions. I wasn't getting inside.

"We were able to verify that someone at the Rescue

Mission facility attempted to contact Mr. Heinser several times," I told him.

"I don't believe Mr. Heinser would have received such a call on either his private or business lines."

"It was a wireless line, leased by a Second Chance arm called the SCO."

"I don't believe Mr. Heinser is a member of the Second Chance organization."

"He's not, but for whatever reason, he had the phone in his possession and the calls were made to him."

"Can you prove that?"

"I don't have to prove it. I know it's true. I also know that the bombs used to destroy the Rescue Mission Clinic, and the others, were almost identical to the one used to destroy the Concrete Falls recruitment center."

That ruffled Bhadra's feathers. His cool demeanor slipped a notch.

"There were Heinlein employees at the Concrete Falls site, Agent Wachalowski. Do you have any idea—"

"I'm not suggesting Heinlein was behind the attack. I think that whoever hit the recruitment center was there to hit Heinlein Industries. I think whoever did it then set themselves up at the Rescue Mission Clinic. What I don't understand is why. That's what I want you to explain to me."

The rain started up again, misting over the tarmac. Bhadra signaled to one of the revivors, who approached and handed him an umbrella before returning to its spot. He opened it as the rain picked up, then moved closer so that it covered both of us.

"This is off the record, Agent."

"Mr. Bhadra, I am conducting an ongoing investigation into—"

"I'm not asking, Agent Wachalowski. I am telling you.

This is off the record. Neither your JZI implant nor any other recording device you may be carrying will work here. If I or anyone from Heinlein Industries is asked about this later, it will be denied."

He stood there, waiting for my reaction. It was clear that if I didn't agree to his terms, the discussion was over.

"Go ahead," I told him.

"I can't comment on why Mr. Heinser's name was in the Rescue Mission directory, because I don't know," he said. "However, I can say that what you found there is connected to the incident at Concrete Falls."

"You knew about what was going on at the Rescue Mission Clinic?"

"No. We didn't know about the facility, but there have been concerns that someplace like it might turn up."

"Concerns?"

"A specific piece of technology was at the Concrete Falls center the day it was attacked."

"What kind of technology?"

"I can't disclose that—"

He stopped short as I stepped in and grabbed him by the shirt collar. His eyes went wide as I hauled him up onto his toes, and he dropped the umbrella.

Immediately, the two revivors at the jeep began to close in. I drew my gun, and Bhadra flinched as I fired a single shot. The pop echoed down the tarmac as the revivor on the left spun around, spraying an arc of black blood from the side of its neck.

"Stop!" Bhadra shouted, holding his hands near his face. The second revivor held its position while the one I'd shot collapsed face-first onto the ground, blood pooling around its head.

"There are eleven nukes somewhere in the city," I

said, putting my face close to Bhadra's. "Eleven nukes. Don't stonewall me, Bhadra. Do you understand?"

"What are you going to do?" he asked, his hands still near his face. "Shoot me?"

"I'll place you in Federal custody, and before I'm done, I promise you, you'll tell me what I want to know."

"You'll never get me to the perimeter, Agent."

"Answer me. What was Heinser involved in?"

"We don't know," he said. "I would tell you if I could. He was involved in something, but we don't know what. They've put him out of reach as a precaution. They don't have any specifics."

"I want to talk to him now."

"You can't, Agent. He's gone. You won't be able to reach him, not in time to help you. I'm sorry."

A gust of wind blew mist against the side of my face, and made the umbrella roll in a circle.

"They're monitoring us," Bhadra said. "Security will be here soon. Let me go, please. You don't have to do this."

He met my eye when he said that last part. He was trying to tell me something.

"No?"

"They wouldn't send someone out here that they thought knew any specifics about Heinser or Concrete Falls," he said. "If there was information that would be useful to you, it couldn't come from me."

I put the gun away and let go of him. He straightened his shirt and picked up the umbrella.

"I found several revivors at Rescue Mission," I said. "Their signatures were different. The components were different too."

"Technology changes, Agent."

"It was a new model of revivor, then?"

"I can't say for sure."

"Was that technology at the Concrete Falls facility for some reason? Was that their interest in it?"

"If it was," he said evenly, "it didn't turn up in the wreckage after the blast."

It was the closest to a confirmation I was going to get. Something of Heinlein's had been stolen, and the blast covered it up. It was taken to the Rescue Mission Clinic, and probably the others that had been raided as well.

"And Heinser?" I asked.

"If some new technology had been developed, it would be highly valuable. To obtain it, someone would need an inside contact."

"Why not turn him over to us, then?"

"This is a highly sensitive situation, Agent. In the end, Heinlein Industries is a military contractor. This isn't just a matter of industrial espionage. It's a matter of national security, and it goes far over your head."

"Then why see me at all?" I asked.

"To make an official statement. To stonewall you, as you said, and send you away."

"Then why not do that?"

"Honestly? I'm afraid. I've heard you are a man to be trusted. You were very helpful in uncovering the breach into our company two years ago. Thanks to you, the Zhang's Syndrome study has been designated classified, and we've been appropriately distanced from Samuel Fawkes."

"I wouldn't thank me for that."

"You are also known, by us at any rate, to have had a government-issue revivor illegally transported and revived from stasis. Since then, that revivor is also known to have fallen into the hands of established terrorists."

"Is that some kind of threat?"

"I'm just laying out the facts as I see them." He closed the umbrella and wrapped the tie around it. "A security force will be here very shortly, Agent. I'd advise you to be on your way out when that happens."

He held out his hand, and his eyes looked nervous.

"One last thing: I saw something at Rescue Mission I couldn't explain," I said. "You want to take a crack at it?"

"If I can."

"The revivors were being monitored while a machine cycled them between active and inactive. Why would someone do that?"

"For the same reason we do it here," he said. "To try to streamline the revival process."

"Why?"

"A time may come when you need them in a hurry."

He signaled to the remaining revivor, and it climbed back into the jeep. Behind it, two more vehicles were approaching.

He held out his hand again, and this time I shook it. When I did, I felt something against my palm. He looked me in the eye and held the handshake a few extra seconds.

"I'm sorry I'm not permitted to help you more," he said.

"Thank you for seeing me," I told him. "Sorry about the revivor."

He let my hand go and I palmed the object, slipping it into my pocket.

I got back into my car and watched him walk back to the jeep. The look in his eye as he turned away said he wasn't just worried about security breaches and lawsuits. He was worried that the thing he had implied was stolen had ended up in the wrong hands, and that the consequences of that might turn out to be dire.

Zoe Ott—Alto Do Mundo

After I left the Federal Building, I kind of lost track of what happened. I stopped at a bar and had a few drinks; then at some point I remembered stopping at a convenience store and getting a bottle. I was wet now, and the bottle was almost empty. The paper bag it was in was almost soaked through, and the sky had gotten dark.

I stepped off the curb and into a puddle as tires squealed and the grill of a car rocked to a stop a few inches from me. A horn blared, and I stumbled back the way I came while someone cursed out the window. I sat back against a fire hydrant and took a swig from the bottle while people trudged by behind me.

I was still sitting there when a slick black car with tinted windows pulled up next to me. I thought maybe it was Nico, tracking me down after what happened with the interrogation, and it made me mad that I caught myself really hoping it was him. It wasn't his car, though; it looked way too expensive. Its engine hummed, sounding like a jet plane over the rain.

The window on my side rolled down and I could hear music coming from inside, a loud, thumping bass. I started to walk away when I saw Penny lean across the passenger's seat and wave.

"Yo!"

"What?"

"What's up?" she asked.

I held out my hands, liquid sloshing in the bottle. "You're looking at it."

"You want a ride somewhere?"

I didn't really feel like dealing with her, but I was wet and cold. The rain had gotten worse, and I wasn't completely sure where I even was.

I shook my head, letting my wet hair fall in front of my face.

"Come on," she said. "You'll get pneumonia. Get in."

Warm air was coming out of the open window; I could feel it when I leaned in. The seats looked like real leather.

"I'll wreck your seats."

"Don't worry about the seats."

I opened the door and got into the car, feeling the bass vibrating through the seat under me. The windows slid back up as the engine hummed and she zipped out into traffic.

"Rough day?" she asked. I shrugged.

"I guess."

"That why you're walking in the rain?"

"I guess."

"What happened?"

"He slapped me." I meant to say more, but that's all that came out. It was the only thing that seemed relevant. She looked over at me out of the corner of her eye.

"Who?"

"Nico. He slapped me in the face."

"What the hell did he do that for?" she asked.

"I don't know why he did it," I said. "I had this guy under—I mean, way under. He was totally . . ."

I was going to say "at my mercy," but I didn't like the way that sounded.

"What guy?" she asked.

"I can't say."

"If it was going so good, why'd he hit you?"

"Well . . . he slapped me."

"Slapping is hitting."

"I . . ."

I was confused. I couldn't think straight. The first thing that came in my mind was that Nico wasn't like that. He wanted me to stop for some reason, but I was so mad, and it was hard to explain, but taking it out on that guy made me feel a little better. Nico was trying to get me to stop, and I didn't listen. I thought that might be what happened.

I wanted to tell Penny that, but the words didn't come out. Saying that it was really my fault I got hit sounded like the kind of thing Karen would have said.

"Don't worry about it," she said. "Just relax. We'll be there soon."

"Be where soon?"

"Your new place," she said. Not "your place," but "your new place."

"What are you talking about?" I asked.

"Remember this morning? I said we wanted to set you up in a new place, and you said okay? It's a done deal."

I did remember that, sort of. She was sitting on my couch when I woke up, and she did say something about that. She said something about getting me out of my place and into a new one. Did I agree to that?

"What do you mean, it's a done deal?"

"Hey, sorry, but you don't have much choice at this point; Ai paid off your old landlord and sent people over to move everything. They kept your security deposit, but to be fair, you kind of trashed the place, and anyway, you won't need it."

"Wait a minute. Are you saying my place is—"

"Gone."

"Wait," I said. "You can't just . . ."

Penny looked over at me, and all of a sudden I felt really tired. Something didn't feel right, but I didn't have any strength to argue anymore.

"Just relax," I heard her say, as I slumped back into the seat.

I felt like the whole thing should have freaked me out, but for some reason it didn't. The more I thought about it, the more okay it seemed. Penny made the whole thing sound so reasonable, and I really wanted to get dry and then get into bed. I could worry about the rest of it later.

"This is a good thing," Penny said as I started to drift off. "Relax."

I yawned, settling back into the seat. It was really comfortable and the low hum the car made, with that faint whistle over it, was kind of relaxing. I felt dizzy, and my eyes closed. I felt my head get heavy, and the next thing I knew, Penny was shaking my arm gently. The engine noise had stopped and I could hear the rain on the roof.

"Hey," she said. I cracked open one eye.

"How long was I asleep?"

"Not long. We're here."

It seemed more like a second, but I felt a little better. When I looked out the window, the people outside looked better dressed than they did when I closed my eyes. The sidewalks were clear and there wasn't any graffiti anywhere.

"Where are we?"

"Alto Do Mundo."

"Why?" Rich people lived there.

"Because this is where you live now. Come on."

She opened the door and got out. I followed her, kind of in a trance. We were in a little private lot in back of a huge, fancy building with shiny glass panels. Alto Do Mundo was one of the tallest buildings, and ritziest places, in the city.

"Wait. This is where you moved me to?" I asked.

"Yeah. Come on. You'll like it."

When I looked around, everyone looked rich and well dressed. They looked clean. One old guy across the street was looking at me like he thought I was a hobo or something.

"Don't worry about them," Penny said. "Trust me. You'll fit in fine. Follow me."

She took us inside, through a lobby that looked like it must have cost a million dollars, then up a fancy elevator to the sixty-first floor. She turned left in the hall, and then left again before stopping at a door with a bronze number 11 on it. She flashed a key badge at the scanner, and the lock snapped open.

"Here we are," she said as she walked through the door. She stood there, holding it open with one hand. "What do you think?"

I walked past her and looked inside as she turned the lights on. My mouth hung open.

"Nice, huh?" she said, shutting the door. I nodded.

Nice was kind of an understatement. It was amazing. It was too nice for me.

"This is for me?" I asked. It was all I could think to say.

"Yes."

"How much . . . I mean, how much does it cost? I—"

"Rent's taken care of. Don't worry about it. Ai's putting you up. All expenses go through her."

"But . . ."

"Oh, come on. You've got to admit it's great. Ai's richer than God. This is nothing to her. Believe me. It's not even on her radar. You lucked into something good. How often does that happen?"

"Not very often."

"So live a little."

I looked around. The apartment was five times the size of my old place, and every inch was spotless.

"My place is kind of a mess," I said, still staring.

"Your old place. I've seen it. I was in it."

"I . . . can't keep this place like this."

"So don't," she said. "I don't. It's your place. Keep it however you want."

"But why?"

"Is she giving you this? You're more important than you think, sister. Besides, she does stuff like this. I think she forgets sometimes the rest of us aren't like her. I know it seems like a huge deal, but it's just how she is."

"Do you live here too?"

"I'm your new downstairs neighbor," she said, kind of apologetically. "Come on, I'll give you the tour."

"Okay . . ."

The floors were hardwood, and the kitchen had stone countertops. The living room had a gas fireplace, and expensive-looking furniture set around a huge flat-screen TV. They'd installed surround sound and a big stereo rig, and someone even wired up the old switch-box I used to listen in on the psychic line calls. The bathroom was huge and had a giant hot tub in it. There was a TV on the wall in there too. It was incredible.

"Where's my other stuff?" I asked.

"In boxes. It's all in the spare room. You won't need any of it, but keep what you want. Same with your clothes; she set you up with some stuff in the closet you can wear. If you really want to, you can keep your old clothes, but you ought to think about giving it to the needy or something."

I walked down a short hallway and I could see a big queen-sized bed through a doorway at the far end. To my right was an open doorway leading to some kind of study with a big, wooden desk. There was an expensive-looking computer set up on it with a huge, flat screen.

"Your notebooks are here," Penny said, pointing to a stack of boxes against the far wall. "From now on, though, use the computer to write that kind of stuff down. Ai will want the handwritten stuff transcribed at some point, but she'll have someone else do that."

"You keep track of that stuff?"

"All of it. It all goes in the database."

"Why?"

"Probabilities," she said. "If one person sees something, it might not be a big deal. It might even just be a dream, or a hallucination . . . but if that person sees the same thing twenty times, then probably not. If twenty people see the same thing, and they all see it twenty times, then the probability it's a real event goes way up. You follow?"

"Sure."

"This way we'll know. Scratching stuff down in notepads won't cut it, there's way too much data."

She walked over to the computer and waved her hand in front of it, turning it on. When the screen lit up, a colorful shape appeared. It reminded me of a nebula, in the shape of a big, wavy ring. There were bright points sprinkled throughout it, and the inside of the loop was completely dark. One big bright point, like a big star, sat on the edge of the dark center.

"That's it," Penny said.

"That's what?"

"The future. Well, a mathematical model of it."

She touched a spot on the ring and it zoomed in. As the zoom got tighter and tighter, I saw that the shape was actually made up of millions of tiny lines that crisscrossed to connect millions of tiny icons.

"What is that?" I whispered.

"Entries, like in your notebooks," she said pulling a chair up next to her. "Come here."

I sat down, and she touched an icon on the screen. When she did, it zoomed in on it until the lines connecting to it filled the screen. She tapped it and a page of text came up next to it.

"This is a single entry," she said. "The circle means it has a connection to at least one more entry, meaning at least one other person saw something related to it. The green lines connect to related entries."

She zoomed back out, then back in on a square shape. That one had hundreds of lines connected to it.

"When enough entries reference the same thing, it's considered an 'event'; something that most likely will happen, but we don't know when or how. If the rate of recurrence gets high enough, meaning enough entries reference the same event over and over persistently, then you get something like this."

She zoomed out again then panned over to a spot where the lines were so dense they formed a white star around a little diamond shape.

"The diamond means an event is almost certain, and that the event will have a serious impact."

"What is it?" I asked.

"That's the wasteland," she said.

I stared at the diamond shape. It looked like thousands of lines were connected to it.

"That many people have seen it?" I whispered. Penny nodded.

"Now watch." She tapped the screen again and the whole thing zoomed out until the lines blurred together and became the nebula shape again. The diamond and all the connecting lines became that bright star that sat on the edge of the dark hole in the middle.

"What's in the middle?" I asked. "In the dark part?"

"We don't know," she said. "Ai's trying to close that gap, to find out. You can see that all around the rim there's nothing much, nothing conclusive, except right there. That one big event happens right on the edge there."

"Then what?"

"No verifiable entries. The model falls apart."

"But why no entries?"

"Maybe there's nothing left to see."

Nothing left. I remembered the wasteland and how everything was gone.

"But even in my dream, it's just the city," I said weakly.

Penny shrugged. "Ai calls it the void. It doesn't necessarily mean there isn't anything after the event, just that no one has seen anything after it."

"Why not?"

"No one knows for sure. Maybe it means no one will be left."

I stared at the image on the screen. The star sat on the edge of the dark like it was being sucked into a black hole.

"You get it now?" she asked.

"But what are the visions?" I asked. "How do they work?"

"We're not completely sure yet, but there are some things we know, some rules they all stick by."

She held up a finger.

"One: the people and places seen in the visions are real. If you see a person in a vision, they exist in the real world, somewhere. Same for places."

She held up a second finger to form a V shape.

"Two: visions modeled here have probabilities that can change, but once an event hits one hundred percent probability, it always occurs, with no exceptions. A vision modeled at one hundred percent can't be changed, as far as we know."

She held up a third finger, forming a W.

"Three: no one has ever seen something in a vision that couldn't feasibly happen in their lifetime. So no one has ever seen anything hundreds of years down the line or anything like that. We think that no one can see past their own death."

She tapped the dark center of the ring.

"We expect to see some emptiness then, here," she said. "No one lives forever, but the problem is that this bright star, this 'event,' is less than five years away. It could happen tomorrow. So this void is troubling. You follow?"

I nodded weakly.

"But what does it have to do with me?"

She tapped the screen and a tree of icons appeared. She tapped on, and it zoomed in to show my face.

OTT, ZOE. POTENTIAL E1.

"Potential what?" I asked, still staring at my name on the screen. Penny panned back, showing other faces in the tree. I saw Nico's go by, and some others I didn't recognize. It landed on an image of Penny.

BLOUNT, PENNY. POTENTIAL E1 (DISPROVEN). E10.

"Significant people are termed 'elements' and assigned numbers," she said. "Just like there are significant events that people report seeing, there are significant people. Based on the events people see and their probabilities, we can get a sense of who will be significant . . . who will be directly involved in what's to come."

"I don't get it," I said.

She pulled up one of her sleeves and held out the arm so I could see. There were pocked scars all down it from her wrist to her elbow, following the veins there. They were needle tracks.

"Ai pulled me out of the gutter," she said. "She saved my life. For me, though, when I got clean, I lost my precog ability. I can still do everything else, better than most, but I stopped having the visions."

"You don't see them anymore?" To me, that sounded great.

"I get the odd sighting, but not like I used to. Not like Ai. Not like you. We're not all the same. All of us can influence others, but not everyone can see. Even those that can, not everyone can see as well as Ai. It's what makes her special. You see that out there?"

She pointed out a window across the room. Through it I could see the lights of the city as it sprawled off into the distance. From that height I could see the two other major, huge towers, lit up like colored spikes.

"Ai doesn't run the show alone," Penny said. "She's got powerful friends. You'll meet them someday, for now just know we run everything. We've got our own organization, but it all comes back to Ai. She's the one with the vision. She's the one that sees and knows everything. It's all for nothing without her."

She pointed to the big star shape again.

"She's looking for someone, someone related to that event. Element zero begins it, but element one ends it. Ai's been looking for this missing element. She was wrong about me, and she's been wrong before, but she's been looking. She's been looking for you."

I looked at the star on the screen.

"Is everything really going to be destroyed?" I asked.

"Not if we can help it."

She put one hand on my shoulder and squeezed. Gently, not like she had before.

"Look, I'm sorry," she said. "In some ways, I don't envy you. I know it's hard. I was in your shoes once, but it is what it is. You might need to step up, and soon."

She stood up and walked to the doorway, turning back before she left.

"Enjoy your new digs," she said. "You're totally free to do whatever you want at any time, but don't cross Ai. Understand?"

"Yes." That part I got.

"Sorry about your friend," she said, and left. I heard her walk back out to the front door and close it behind her. I barely heard her, though, because I was still looking at the screen and trying to figure out what was going on.

"Yeah, me too," I said, but she was gone. I was alone.

It was too surreal. The night before, I was sitting at a table in a fancy restaurant with a bunch of people I didn't know, practically dying of embarrassment. Someone shot at us and all hell broke loose, and then my best friend died right in front of me. I fell off the wagon, and Nico hit me in the face. Just when I thought I was at rock bottom, I end up in a palace. I'm told I'm important, and that my dreams and crazy visions are not only not insane, but also that they could help stop a disaster.

"How much of this is real?"

Any minute now I'm going to wake up. I'll wake up on my couch in my apartment, and Karen will be alive.

I got up and walked around the apartment, trying to shake the feeling that I was trespassing. It didn't feel like home. It was too much. It was too nice. The bed in the bedroom looked really comfortable, though. The inside of the bathroom was all tiled, and along with the giant hot tub was a cascade shower the size of my old bathroom.

In the bedroom I opened a huge walk-in closet and saw what Penny meant when she said that Ai got me some stuff to wear; it was filled with expensive clothes for pretty much every occasion. There were more shoes in there than I had ever owned in my life. Hanging from the door on the inside was what at first looked like a bra, but turned out to be a shoulder holster, like the kind I'd seen Nico wear, but smaller. It had a gun in it too, a little silver one with a pearl handle. There was a note pinned to the holster: FOR EMERGENCIES ONLY. I closed the door.

Shrugging out of my wet coat, I let it fall on the carpet and walked back out to the living room with the big TV. There was a big wood cabinet there with a bunch of glasses arranged on top. I opened the doors and saw it was a liquor cabinet, stocked to the hilt. Right up front were four big bottles of ouzo. I grabbed one off the shelf and shut the door, walking with it across the room, toward the couch.

I was going to flop down on the couch and maybe try to figure out how to work the TV when I saw a set of doors on the far wall and I wondered what they went to. I walked past the couch and pulled them open. When I did, cold, damp air blew over me.

"Wow."

It was a balcony. I was looking out over the city. Still holding the bottle, I walked outside and up to the rail.

"Wow."

I'd never had a view like that from so high before. It was amazing. The city was all lit up like some giant machine with a billion flashing lights. Down below, traffic flowed like glowing veins. I was in one of the biggest towers in the city. To the left and right the city went off as far as I could see, and in front, a little ways in the distance, some even bigger buildings loomed. Way off in the distance, two of the largest towers in the world sat on the skyline. The wind blew through my hair and mist sprayed my face, but I didn't care. It was the most beautiful thing I'd ever seen.

Without even thinking, I cracked the bottle. When you do anything a lot, you get a comfortable sense of where you stand in that situation, and I'd been drinking my whole life. The year or so when I stopped was a footnote. It was an experiment, a mistake. I knew how drinking affected me at every stage, from the first shot to the inevitable blackout. The ouzo was warm going down, trickling down into my belly while I stood out there in the cold. It started to mellow me out, make me feel more comfortable. I knew it wouldn't be long before I started feeling more at home in my new place. Once I'd had enough to drink, I would begin to accept that what Penny said might be true.

"She's been searching for that missing element. She's been searching for you."

Before it was over, all of my nagging doubts would be erased. That included the offhand warning about not crossing Ai. It also included the fact that if these people were laying any kind of hope, any kind at all, on me, then we were all going to be in for a world of hurt.

Calliope Flax—Archstone Plaza, Room #103

I tromped down the hall and banged on Buckster's door. No one answered, but I heard a guy's voice.

The JZI picked him up. He was in there. I looked through the front door with the backscatter and saw a shape move past it. I banged on the door again.

"Open up, Chief. It's me," I called.

I heard the voice again. He was talking to someone. Either he wasn't alone or he was on the phone. A fan or something started blowing inside, and I went to bang again when I heard him coming. He opened the door, but not much. He looked out at me, then back over his shoulder.

"What's your fucking problem?" I asked him.

"Nothing," he said. "What do you want?"

"Nice."

"Sorry. It's not a good time."

"I came to give you a heads-up," I said. "I heard through my Fed friend, they're looking to pick you up."

"They already did," he said.

"You got their dicks in a twist, from the sound of it. What the hell did you do?"

He looked up and down the hall, then moved like he meant to grab my arm, but he stopped. He was freaked out.

"What did you hear?" he asked.

"Not out here."

"I'm sorry," he said. "Come on in."

He opened the door the rest of the way and stepped back. I took the opening and went in. The place was messed up a little. A desk drawer was still out. The old guy looked rattled.

"What did he tell you?" he asked.

"He didn't tell me anything; I heard your name and tapped his JZI communication."

"That's a federal off—"

"Hey, I was watching your back."

"Why?"

"Because you helped me out. Because you're a slummer from Bullrich, like me."

He thought about it, and it looked like he bought it.

"What did you hear?" he asked.

"Not much, sorry. Just that you stirred up a hornets' nest and they were looking to pick you up. They're still watching you, you know."

He nodded. His eyes darted around like he wasn't sure what to do. That's when I picked up the jack.

My JZI picked up the signal, and when I locked on, a revivor signature snapped on the scanner. It was somewhere close. Inside the apartment.

"Something wrong?" he asked.

"No." I scanned around. There was a closed door down the hall. It was where the fan noise was coming from. The signal was in there. I caught a whiff of something, a chemical smell that I knew from the grind.

That's Leichenesser.

"You sure you're okay, Chief?"

"I'm fine."

"You don't look fine. You look like you saw a damn ghost."

"I don't know," he said, and shook his head. "Maybe I did. The truth is, I've got to take off for a while."

"A while?"

"I might not be back."

I looked around, but I didn't see any bags or anything.

"Where you going?"

"It's not important. Just do me a favor."

"Shoot."

"If your friend asks, you never saw me today."

"They sicced that red-haired bitch on you, didn't they?"

That stopped him. I could see it was true. The look, like he saw a ghost, came back.

"What do you know about that?"

"I know her name. It's Zoe Ott."

"How do you know her?"

"I saw her when I went to look up Wachalowski at the FBI. Did she get in your head?"

The look on his face said yes. I chanced a look at the closed door and scanned through. The revivor was in there; I could just make it out. That's where the smell came from. A body had been cleaned up in there.

"You knew?" he asked. I turned the scan on him and saw the gun tucked under his shirt. "How much do you know?"

"I know what she does."

He nodded. I saw the JZI flicker behind his eyes, and he got quiet for a second.

"The Fed, he's an old soldier, like you," I told him. "He got me out of a bind. Whatever his beef with you is, it's got nothing to do with me. I just want some answers."

The orange light went out. He sighed.

"Cal, look. You need to get out of here, okay? I'm telling you this for your own good. You need to leave, and so do I. Just . . . you didn't see me."

"I can take you out of here. They won't be looking for me."

"Cal . . ."

"I'm not being tracked. I owe you."

He thought about that. His hands moved to his hips. His right one was close to the gun.

"What are you going to do?" I asked. "Shoot me?"

His hand didn't move. He stayed like that too long for my liking, though.

"Wait here," he said. "I got to make a call."

He went into the next room and shut the door partway. On the other side, I could hear him rooting around for something. I didn't hear him talking, but I picked him up on the JZI. I turned the backscatter onto the bathroom door up close and saw the revivor in there. It had a gun in its hand.

Through the walls I could see pipes and wiring. He paced in the next room, then went to a big safe. It was too thick to scan through. I lost him behind it.

I gave him a minute, but he stayed out of sight. The safe was big enough that he could have used it to cover his ass while he went out a window or something.

"Chief?" He didn't answer.

I stepped up to the door, ready to shove it when he opened it and came out.

"I said to wait," Buckster said. He had a metal briefcase in one hand.

"Sorry."

"You want answers?" he said. "Let's go."

"You sure?"

"Yeah."

"Grab what you need."

He held up the metal case.

"I got all I need," he said. "Let's go."

8

Fathom

I didn't doubt who planted the monitoring device, but as soon as I passed through the perimeter and my JZI came back online, a message was waiting that confirmed it.

Ai wants to see you.

I still couldn't reach Calliope; her JZI was showing a status of blocked, meaning it wasn't taking calls. There was any number of reasons she might do that, but the last time we spoke, she was with Buckster. I'd feel better when she responded.

You worry about me?

I did, a little.

The truth was, I'd worried about her more than I let on. I wasn't sure why. I hadn't known her well at all, but somehow she'd gotten under my skin. When we started writing back and forth, I caught myself getting concerned when she stayed quiet too long. It was my first experience being home and waiting for someone to finish their tour.

Was that how Faye had felt? If so, it must have been worse, because back then when I stopped writing, I never started again. I didn't even look her up when I came back. I never got a chance to make that right.

I shouldn't have sent her. Calliope was tough. She knew what she was getting into, and she could take care of herself, but sometimes things went outside your control. She didn't need to put herself in trouble to get me on her side. I didn't need her to get to Fawkes.

JZI Status: BLOCKED.

I shut the front door behind me and locked it. I hung my coat on the rack and moved into the living room, removing from my pocket the object Bhadra had slipped me. The small electronic device fit in my palm. It was the shape of a capsule, with a smooth outer shell and several built-in data ports.

I slipped a probe into the port and gave it a gentle twist. Right away a flood of messages scrolled by in front of me, before the HUD cleared and a set of indicators began to appear.

Init version 0.3

Detecting . . .

Initializing . . .

Property of Heinlein Industries, Inc.

A series of specs, nondisclosure statements, and legal warnings scrolled by, then cleared away as a connection opened to what I recognized as a revivor network. It was empty.

Interesting. It was some kind of freestanding revivor communications port. It provided a tunnel onto an existing revivor network band.

Searching . . .

A grid appeared, filling my field of vision, and one by one, nodes began to appear on it. It happened slowly at first, but they quickly filled the screen. I zoomed in until the points began to spread apart. They weren't connected in the traditional hub-and-spoke configuration; they were all separate, free-floating.

Searching . . .

Something's wrong . . .

The total node count kept increasing, but none of them was tagged as active. They were in some kind of standby state. When the count was finished, it numbered more than six hundred.

Six hundred. The number was like a weight on my chest. Once, during my tour, I saw close to 150 of them let loose on a suburb. Not a shantytown or slum, but a developed region with brick homes and locked doors. It took us two hours to reach them from the nearest base, and by the time we got there, the carnage was visible from the air. Bodies lay torn apart in the streets, where blood baked in the sun. The old, the young, children, and babies were all pulled to pieces, and the revivors were rooting through the remains. We airlifted out fifty or so people from two rooftops. Then command declared the site lost, and it was razed.

They had to be on the tanker. There was no way that many revivors could be stored inside the city limits and not attract attention. Not even Heinlein kept a stockpile like that.

I started to try to trace them, when another process took over and opened a window over the grid. The image of a man's face appeared in it, part of a digital recording, embedded in the unit's software. I recognized him; it was the man Heinlein had designated as their liaison back during the first crisis.

MacReady.

Bob MacReady had met me at the Heinlein labs to discuss the case initially. Later he contacted me after I'd secured Faye's body to provide information on Samuel Fawkes. I had never been able to determine whether he had done that with or without Heinlein's knowledge.

"Hello, Agent Wachalowski. Listen carefully; this message will not repeat itself and will decay after playback. You have just connected to an experimental component designed to interface with the technology code named Huma. It has all the basic capabilities of the new revivor model. The link you've established will place you directly onto any existing Huma network that exists. This version of the revivor communications band is not backwards-compatible with the old one, which is very similar to your JZ interface. Be prepared to gather your information quickly, as we believe the node count is growing and could overwhelm your JZI."

Huma. It sounded like a new revivor prototype. Was this what I'd seen in the clinic?

MacReady manipulated the computer terminal in front of him, and a second window appeared in a frame next to him. It displayed a schematic of the new node.

"The main reasons for the incompatibility are greater throughput, and a new layered mesh model. The hub-and-spoke configuration, where many revivors are controlled via a single command node, will still exist, but the revivors themselves use a full-mesh configuration. This makes them significantly more effective in the field. It allows large-scale, coordinated operations to remain fluid. Units quickly become aware if an existing directive has become undesirable or invalid. They can quickly relay that information back to the command node."

The schematic in the window disappeared and was

replaced by the Huma logo, followed by several bullet points:

- Field deployable
- Field revivification
- Enhanced control
- Enhanced intelligence network

"All of this is accomplished using the next generation of nanotechnology." The bullet "Field deployable" moved into the foreground.

"You may recall we discussed this possibility during our meeting two years ago. The traditional model of getting wired for revivification will be replaced with a simple injection. The nodes are constructed inside the body using the material contained in the injection payload. Long-term preservation will still require a blood transfusion, but this new model is extremely desirable in situations where longevity is not an issue."

That was most of them. At least half the revivors uncrated in the field didn't last a month. The bullet "Field revivification" moved to the foreground.

"The new revivor model can also be made field ready without a trip back to the Heinlein labs, another improvement that will greatly enhance their effectiveness."

It had been talked about for years. They'd finally managed it, then. If it was true, a soldier who was wired could theoretically revive right there on the battlefield.

"What I'm about to tell you is not something Heinlein wants getting out, but the situation is out of control and someone has to intervene. You're the only one I believe I can trust fully. Recently, Heinlein detected a network of these revivors coming online. Whoever took the prototypes has deployed them. I've sent out feelers, and learned that your agency is currently looking for a large revivor force; I believe this is the source of them."

I had no idea the technology was so far along, but it would explain a lot. Fawkes wouldn't have to smuggle in revivors from overseas. With something like this in his hands, he could create them on the fly.

"Heinlein Industries had reached the phase of human trials, Agent. That was never going to be officially sanctioned in the current climate. They conducted it in secret, at the Concrete Falls facility, where they processed the new recruits. They mixed the injections in among the standard inoculants battery given before deployment overseas. They monitored progress during routine checkups once the subjects were safely out of the country, with the military's cooperation. It works, Agent, and it's highly effective."

In the feed, MacReady shook his head.

"Officially, the company will deny any existence of the prototype," he finished. "This device was never given to you. A series of enzymes will destroy it in less than twenty hours. Any longer than that, and Heinlein will trace it back to you and me. Find them before then."

The recording cut out and, as promised, it immediately wiped itself from memory.

Link established.

A flood of data came pouring over the connection so quickly it actually managed to begin to fill the JZI's buffer, something that had never happened before. As it struggled to sort and distribute the information, it started grabbing chunks of memory from other applications. Modules I kept running, like the optical-filter array, translation software, and listening ports, started dropping off. I lost the interface to my internal chemical packs; then even the diagnostic packages shut down.

Shit . . .

MacReady had underestimated either the total node count or my implant's ability to field the circuits. The JZI tried to route the information, but it was having trouble classifying a lot of it. Routines began to thrash. The last time I'd felt anything remotely like it was when it had been deliberately hacked. I lost my balance and groped behind me for the sofa as my standard visuals began to fail. The lens in one eye widened to its maximum zoom capacity, causing the room to spin around me before both flickered and started losing frames. The light began to strobe as I fell back onto the couch.

I tried to shut down the connection, but nothing was responding. The conduits that dealt with text and audio filled up, causing a constant stream of unintelligible chatter to fill my head while a random character stream filled up the HUD. What little I could see was blotted out.

What the hell is this?

The streams were coming in from the remote nodes, but they weren't directed at me specifically. If I could get off the network, I thought it would stop the flow. . . .

The longer it came in, though, the more it began to take some kind of shape. I sensed it was legitimate information; it was just streaming in from too many sources. It was as though hundreds of people were streaming consciousness, rambling randomly, all about different things.

Where? I thought. I didn't care about the rest. *Where is the ship now?*

I began to get flashes, images from the remote nodes. Some were darkness, almost like thoughts or dreams, but some were of places and things. I caught a glimpse of a sink with running water, and another of characters appearing on a computer terminal. I saw hallways, rooms and doors from different places, but I couldn't identify them. I couldn't put together a complete picture, but a realization had begun to sink in.

That's not the interior of a ship. Was I wrong?

The input became a field of static. It felt like I was floating in a void. I could still feel the fabric of the couch underneath my fingers, but it was like the sensation was coming from far away.

If I could get the influx under control, I might be able to trace a single connection and find out where it was originating from. If I could—

Link broken.

The JZI shut down and recycled. The buffers were flushed, and, after a pause, it began to reinitialize. The white noise stopped. My vision cut out completely for a few seconds, then returned.

They're not on the ship, I thought. *Not all of them. They're already here.*

That's what MacReady was trying to tell me. Field deployment and field reanimation; they weren't dead. Maybe some, enough to do Fawkes's legwork, but the rest were just injected. That's why no one could find them. They wouldn't appear on the streets until Fawkes was ready.

My JZI systems finished initializing. Immediately, a connection opened.

Hello, Agent. Why do I keep finding you on my private network?

Who is this?

This is Samuel Fawkes.

I sat up, looking around. According to the JZI's chronometer, I'd lost a good ten minutes. The probe was still plugged into the strange device, but the signal had been cut off.

Where are you?

I don't know that for sure, Agent. I told you that last time we spoke.

Where's Calliope?

The one you had shadowing Buckster? Maybe he recruited her. Wasn't that the same woman that helped you storm my factory?

Where is she, Fawkes?

Lying in the bed you helped her make, I imagine.

I checked the status of the revivor scrub. Less than two percent of the remaining units were left to be decommissioned.

Whatever you're planning, it's not going to happen. They're closing in on you.

Then I guess we'd better hurry.

There is no 'we,' Fawkes.

The last of the diagnostics ran, the output scrolling by in the corner of my eye. Nothing was damaged.

That will be up to you. This is your last chance to accept the offer I've made you. Kill Motoko Ai. And her top people. Do this, and you have my word I won't use the nuclear devices that you know I have.

I can't just kill them, Fawkes.

You've killed many people, Agent Wachalowski. Many people. You can't convince me you don't have the stomach for it. Is it that you place more value on the lives of those three people than you do on the lives of thousands?

I made a fist. If it was in my power and I had to choose, he knew I'd have to save as many lives as I could. He'd seen my war records. He knew, or thought he knew, how I would react in a situation like this, but I wasn't a soldier anymore and I wasn't ready to concede. Not yet.

I can't easily verify the information you sent, Fawkes.

Even if it's true, this isn't the grind, it's the UAC. Robin Raphael is one of the richest men in the world, with a private security detail. Charles Osterhagen is a retired general who heads Stillwell Corps. He runs a privately contracted army. I couldn't get close to either one of them if I had to.

You are a trusted FBI agent, and, more importantly, you are trusted by them.

You're overestimating how far that trust goes. Your plan isn't going to work.

They've seen you kill me in their dreams, Agent, and they believe it. They believe that you will be the one to stop me. They don't think it's possible for you to betray them. Their arrogance could easily be their undoing.

I'd seen enough to make up my mind; Ai and her people were dangerous. They were a threat to the UAC and the world. There might even be some truth to what Fawkes implied, that the window to stop them might be closing. Still, I couldn't let the assault happen. The other threat was a possibility; Fawkes's attack was real.

Call off the attack altogether, I said.

No. Without the ground assault, someone else will eventually fill the empty seats and take control again. With their leaders dead, though, I'll hand over the nukes.

I only have your word on that.

It's all I can offer.

It's not enough.

Then I have my answer.

They've seen this. It doesn't play out the way you think, Fawkes. It will get out of your control.

They are manipulating you. They've seen their own destruction; that's why they're so scared.

They've seen the destruction of the whole city.

It's a lie. No matter what she's told you, she's far more

ruthless than I am. She has no intention of being stopped by me or you or anyone—but they have to be stopped.

You both do.

There was a pause before he answered.

That would be acceptable to me.

The connection closed.

I looked at the time remaining for the scrub. They could be finished any day, but Fawkes didn't seem concerned by that fact. They were going to miss him, and he wasn't worried because he already knew that.

It didn't matter. He was right about one thing: I was out of time. The rat's nest Sean had stirred up went deeper than anyone thought, and Calliope was in trouble. I called Alice Hsieh.

Alice, I know you're not Sean, but I need a favor.

Go ahead.

Buckster's on the run. I need a team covering his apartment.

Buckster's our only link to the nukes. Where the hell are you?

Following up on a lead.

Everything is secondary to finding that case, Wachalowski. Everything.

I know.

I'll get Vesco over there.

Thanks, but do it quick. We're running out of time.

Calliope Flax—Bullrich Heights

The route the old man gave me took us deep into Bullrich, and he was right; it had gotten worse since I left. No one lived down there. Even the dealers peeled off after a while. The streets were full of trash; the shops were shut up and spray painted one end to the other. It was fucking no-man's-land.

You sure this is right?

Yes.

There's nothing out here.

That's the point.

I cruised under an old rusted bridge where chunks of metal had flaked off into the street. Water ran through holes up there, coming down in streams. A tight path led through an alley. Piled near an old brick wall was a burned-out metal drum and some old shopping carts. There wasn't a streetlight for a mile, and it was getting dark.

The map marker showed the end point right nearby. I slowed down and cut the engine.

"What are you doing?" he asked. "We're almost there."

"Almost where, Chief? We're in the middle of fucking nowhere."

"The area's clear, trust me."

"Yeah, right."

I looked around. I didn't see anyone else down there. I couldn't hear shit over the sound of the water streaming down onto the blacktop.

"Down there," he said, pointing over my shoulder to the dark alley. I could see trash piled up back there that had been there for years. No sane cop would go near that place.

"What's the matter, you scared?" he asked. I held out my hand.

"Give me the gun."

"I don't think so."

"You want me on point, give me the gun."

He grumbled, but he dropped the piece in my hand. I checked it; it was fully loaded.

I fired the bike back up and took us in. When I got to the corner, I saw a path between two concrete walls. It was too tight for a car, but not for the bike. At the end was an alley in part of a used-up project.

"There," he said. There was an old metal door in the back of one of the buildings. I cut the engine and walked over. The metal squealed when I pulled it open, and rank air blew out.

"After you," I said. He went in. I kept the gun in my hand and went in after him. When I looked through the back of his jacket, I saw he had a knife tucked in his belt.

"This is the place." It looked like the guts of a bus terminal, rotted from the inside out. I kept the old man where I could see him.

"What'd you say her name was?" he asked. "The one who questioned me at the Feds?"

"Ott."

He reached in his coat, but not for the blade. He pulled out a pint of whiskey and took a swig.

"Tell me what you remember about her," he said, handing me the bottle.

"Not much."

"But some?"

I took a swallow.

"I got caught up in that shit two years back."

"How?"

"Some kid I met in jail. He got himself killed."

It was a long time since I thought about Luis. He'd gone down hard, that one.

"Who was he?"

"Some rich kid. They killed his whole family, then got him too."

"How?"

"I found him facedown in a public toilet. He almost took me with him."

I shrugged, and took another pull off the bottle before I gave it back.

"He was okay, though."

"That's when you met your friend the Fed?"

"He's okay too."

"He's working for them, Cal. Don't let him fool you."

"You're wrong."

Light moved past the open door, and a second later I saw a car pull up on the other side of the narrow concrete path. The headlights went out, and from across the way, I heard two doors slam.

"That woman Zoe Ott, she was part of an experiment back then," Buckster said.

"You don't say."

All I knew was I had to go down there. In the firefight, I took off and lost Wachalowski. Goons were torching the place, and I just ran, deeper and deeper in. I never met that crazy bitch before in my life. I didn't know who she was, and I still didn't know. I just knew I had to find her.

"He's been trying to stop them," Buckster said.

"Who's 'he'?"

"My contact."

"And how's he going to do that?"

"By finding out how it is they do what they do, and how to stop it."

"Yeah, I saw the little outfit he had going down there."

"Hey, you know as well as I do—sometimes the

things that need doing aren't pretty. Someone has to do them."

"Uh huh . . . and who put your 'contact' in charge?"

Buckster took a swig from the bottle and shook his head.

"People want freedom," he said, "but no one wants to get their hands dirty."

"Fuck you, asshole. My hands are plenty dirty."

"Your friend helped destroy that operation. He used you."

"You got it wrong. I dragged his ass down there, not the other way around. She did something to me."

Footsteps came up to the metal door. Outside I saw a couple of guys coming up in the dark.

"I'm giving you a chance to be on the right side," he said. "You want a chance to stop what happened to you from happening again? You want to stop them?"

"Them?"

"This goes way beyond that girl at the bureau," Buckster said. "They can make you do anything. They can make you think anything, they can make you forget anything, they can make you believe anything, and they're all around us. They do it all the time."

He got me there. I didn't want to believe it went that far, but if one person could do it, why not more?

"Just tell me this," I said. "When you met me coming off that train, did you do it so you could take me?"

"What?"

"I know about the jacks you had wired up at the clinic. I know that bum was one of them. Was I supposed to be next to him?"

He looked at the floor for a second.

"Yeah. Originally."

"You knew I was first tier."

"I got news for you, Cal. It doesn't matter what tier you are. A nobody is still a nobody. No ties, no job, no friends that we knew about... no one to miss you."

"Then what changed your mind?"

"Your connection to the Fed ... at least at first. I don't know. I guess I remembered where I came from. I guess I realized you weren't a nobody. I thought I'd give you a chance."

"To do what?"

"Be somebody."

A couple revivor sigs blinked on in the corner of my eye; then two big guys came in through the door. I could see their eyes glowing as they moved through the dark.

The reminder went off then. The text file popped up and displayed two messages:

There is no door behind the flag.

Leon Buckster is going to take you to the ship. You can trust him.

Right away, I knew it was wrong. I changed the name on the file when I saved it, and it was the same as last time. Whoever was fucking with my head found out about the text file. Someone else had written that note.

Leon Buckster is going to take you to the ship. You can trust him.

I didn't know anything about any ship. Whoever made me write it wanted me to go there. They wanted me to trust him. That was all the reason I needed not to.

I pointed the gun at the old man and cocked the hammer. Off to my right I saw the two jacks pull guns from their coats and level them at me.

"Cal, take it easy!" he said. "Don't!"

"Fuck you."

I kept the gun on him. The two thugs had their guns pointed at my chest.

"Cal, you can trust me. Lower your gun and they won't hurt you."

"I think you're the hub, Doc. I think if I take you out, they won't do shit."

I saw orange light behind the old man's eyes, and I the two jacks relaxed. They put the guns away.

"That girl, the redhead, she's not the only one, Cal. There are—"

"Shut up! You're full of shit!"

"I'm not, I'm telling you. . . . For me it started as far back as the service, and that was a long time ago. Please give me the gun and I'll show you."

I scanned the jacks. Besides the guns, they each had a bayonet tucked in their arms, and each one had a brick of explosive strapped to its belly.

"You'd never get all three of us, if it came to that," the old man said. "It doesn't have to come to that."

I aimed for his shoulder and pulled the trigger, but he was faster than he looked; his palm connected with my wrist and the bullet blew a chunk of brick from the wall. Before I could bring the gun around, something stung me in the side of the neck.

I turned and saw something whip back into the closest revivor's arm as it snapped shut. Before I could do anything else, my head got heavy and my legs went soft.

"Sorry," Buckster said.

I wanted to throw a punch, but my arms were like lead, hanging by my sides. I made it one step before I went down.

"Get her in the car," I heard him say. The revivor

standing over me nodded, and things started going blurry.

"Don't hurt her," he said. His voice sounded far off. "She'll come around. We can use someone like her. . . ."

It was the last thing I heard before the lights went out.

Zoe Ott—Alto Do Mundo

I'd been staring at the computer for hours, but I hadn't entered anything. In fact, I hadn't even unboxed my notebooks yet. I was too busy reading what was already in there. I stared at the screen with all the lights off, not totally believing what I saw.

I thought no one knew much about what happened two years ago. No one talked about it and Nico said it got covered up, but these people knew about it. They knew everything about it. People from their group were seeing the needle heads long before I ever was. More than thirty people saw it a year in advance. They reported in from all over the city, the state, and beyond. They knew about me and Nico. They knew about everything.

Ott, Zoe. Potential E1.

I stared at the icon that represented me, until the heart shape blurred. There were a lot of connections that led there, along with the two who came before me. Penny, and . . .

Hyde, Noelle. Potential E1 (Deceased).

Potential E1. Whatever E1 was, it was important to them. They'd been looking for it a long time. They thought it might be me, but I wasn't the first one they'd thought it about. At least one of them ended up dead.

I touched the heart with Noelle's name over it, and a red message box popped up.

Classified.

None of the references to her said how it happened, how she died. There were a few pictures of her; she reminded me a little of Penny, except her eyes were green like mine. In one picture she was dressed up in a suit, with her hair in a tight bun. She had the same tattoo as Penny, the snake around her neck, swallowing its tail.

In the next picture she looked like a bag lady. Her hair was a rat's nest, her teeth were yellow and brown, and her clothes were filthy. The last picture might have been taken with a cell phone. She lay on the sidewalk, covered in blood. I closed her file.

When I picked up the glass to take a drink, I realized it was empty. I grabbed the big bottle and tipped it until the neck clinked against the rim. I watched the clear liquid trickle in and the level rise until it got a half inch away from the top. I put the bottle down and the cap on.

Back at my old place, I'd had an old shot glass I liked to use, but on top of my new liquor cabinet I'd found a smoked-crystal glass that I really liked. It was twice the size of a regular shot glass, and had a fancy emblem carved into it. I picked it up and drained half of it in one gulp.

I didn't know where to start, so I just surfed around to try to get the hang of their system. I tried to follow single threads, but there were so many of them and they branched out so often, I didn't know how anyone could make any sense out of it all. There had to be some kind of data miner....

After some fiddling, I found it. I entered in my name and set it going, but right away parts of the nebula changed color as hundreds of little green points appeared.

Do all those reference me?

More kept coming. There were still too many. I tried again:

Nico W.

I didn't know how to spell his last name. What I punched in got a similar result . . . worse, actually.

I thought for a minute, then entered in the phrase:

Green room.

I set it going, but that time nothing popped up, at least not right away. I let it spin in the background while I brought up one of the dream entries at random:

. . . I'm sitting in the dark, in some kind of cage. I'm sitting in a couple inches of cold water, and there are wires connected to the base. I know he can electrocute all of us if he wants, from wherever he is. They did something to us, I can sense that, but I don't know what. Some of the people in the cages around me seem disconnected, almost lobotomized. . . .

Someone named Petra Loeb had made the entry. I opened another one:

. . . a flash that lights up the street as bright as day, and then the noise comes. The first boom is like a hammer in my chest, and I feel like my heart skips a beat. It keeps getting louder and louder, until it feels like my head is going to split apart and I'm screaming and staring as the tower begins to fall into the fire. I can see it's the CMC Tower. It's so big it doesn't seem possible, but it's falling, and everyone is screaming as that cloud of fire begins to expand through the streets, toward us.

That was by a Daniel Moser. I picked out one more:

. . . from the balcony of Alto Do Mundo, and watch as one by one the buildings turn to shadow and blow into ashes. It's nukes; I know that. It probably happens in seconds, but to me it seems slowed down, so I can see every

goddamned detail. Nuclear fire, cleansing it all, and wiping the slate clean . . .

The miner popped up. It was pretty quick, but nothing seemed to happen. I panned back until the grid took on the shape of that big ring, the nebula with the dark center, and the star sitting on its edge. At that distance, I saw three green points scattered across the map, and unlike the others, they were inside the dark part. I touched the first one.

> THE GREEN ROOM. Location of significance.
> Frequency: Extremely Rare.
> As of this time, location N1071 (the green room) has been seen by only Element One potentials and is the only known vision time-wise to breach the void after the Event takes place. The few existing reports all describe common dimensions and common fixtures.

A picture appeared, and my mouth parted slightly. It was the room—the green room where I first saw the dead woman. The table in the middle looked a little different, but it was the same rectangle shape and the same gray color. The folding chair was there in front of it. It faced the far wall, where three lights hung overhead against the cinderblock. The walls were all painted dark green.

> The image displayed here is a computer rendition modeled on verbal descriptions. So far, no attempt to locate this room in the real world has been successful, leading us to believe that it may not exist in our reality at this time.
> The common room elements are:
> The switchbox, observed to control the lights at the far end of the room.

The call box, on a swivel system set in the wall. It presents a blank metal panel when closed, and a single handset with no keypad when opened. The location of the remote connection is unknown.

The table and chair, which together form what appears to be an observation area, focused on the far wall beneath the lights.

The scanner, which appears to be concealed in the wall behind the observation area. It has been observed on one occasion to direct a laser reader of some sort toward the far wall. Its schematics and purpose are unknown.

The room has a single metal door with a glass pane affixed at eye level. It leads to a short corridor, but it is not known where that corridor leads.

As of this time, the location has been seen by only Element One potentials, and it seems often to overlap with visions of other key Elements; these human Elements may appear in the observation area, or on the other side of the room. Whether or not the others who appear there truly have, or will, appear inside the room itself is a subject of some debate. It may be the viewer's mind combining the jumbled information.

It is believed that the rarity of this vision is tied to the fact that it may exist only after the Event occurs. That would imply that potential Element One candidates may be among the few who will survive it.

This is also the only vision in which subject Vagott has appeared.

The purpose of the room has not been determined.

I just stared for a minute. It wasn't in my head; other people had seen it. Not many, but some. It was real.

. . . it may not exist in our reality at this time. What did that mean? And Vagott . . . was that a name?

There was a knock on the door, and I jumped in my chair. I screwed the cap on the bottle and stowed it under the desk, then headed over to the door, stumbling a little. I was drunker than I thought.

I got on my tiptoes and looked through the peephole. It was Penny. I opened the door.

"Hi," I said. She looked around. It hadn't taken me long to mess up the place. There were pizza boxes stacked up on the floor next to the door, and clothes draped over all the furniture. The boxes with my notes, still taped up, were stacked along one wall. The sink was filled with dishes, and I hadn't made the bed in days.

"Sorry about the mess," I said. She didn't look pissed or even surprised, though.

"It's homey." She nodded over at the computer. "Reading up?"

"Yeah."

She walked over to the computer and sat down. When she did, her foot clunked against the bottle I put underneath, but she didn't say anything. She just reached under and grabbed it, then took a swig before putting it back down on the desktop. She looked at the entries I had up.

"It's a head full, huh?" she said. I nodded.

"Did you ever see that room?"

"No. It ruled me out as a potential. I don't survive long enough. Almost no one does."

She tapped the screen and an image appeared of an intense-looking guy with stubble and thick black hair. He had on a white shirt and tie, but he looked like he hadn't slept or bathed in a couple days.

"That man is Element Zero," she said. "His name is Samuel Fawkes."

I'd never seen him before in my life. This was the man

I was supposed to stop? I looked at the screen, not quite sure I believed it.

"What am I supposed to do?" I asked.

"Look, I know it's hard for you to swallow right now," Penny said, "but believe it or not, you stop the event."

"How? I don't even know what it is."

"The amount of data they've been crunching would make your head explode," she said. "Most of it is still varying degrees of probability, but some things are pretty much certain. Element One stops the event. Ai's been looking for that person. She thinks you're it."

"Thinks?"

"It's not easy to pinpoint one person in a city this size when you don't know their exact identity, but like I said, we have a ton of data on this."

"She's been wrong before, though?" I said it kind of hopefully.

"Not this time," she said.

I looked at the strange man on the screen, and wondered what he was thinking when the picture was taken. His eyes looked wild, scared, and determined all at once, and they shone a little, like they had started to tear.

"What happened to the first Element One?" I asked. Penny frowned just a little.

"She did something she shouldn't have done," she said. "Just stick to the plan. You'll be fine."

Don't cross Ai.

"Right now, this is the important part," she said. She touched the screen and brought up an event that was close to the current date. I looked over her shoulder at the screen, and saw a big block of text written there. Something about a boat. My eyes jumped to the end:

This alignment may represent our best chance to circumvent the disaster.

"That looks like it's soon," I said.

"It is."

"Will I be part of it?"

"In a way," she said, "but that's not why I'm here tonight."

"Why are you here?" I asked. She snapped off the computer, and the screen went dark.

"Sorry to do this," she said, "but we've got to go out."

"Go? Go where?"

"It's a surprise," she said. "Come on, get your coat on."

I stretched and cracked my back. The room spun a little, and I stood there for a second until it passed and I could make my way to the closet. I really didn't feel like going out, but she had me curious. I grabbed my coat and shrugged it on.

"I don't usually go to bars or clubs or anything," I told her.

"That's not where we're going," she said. She reached into her purse and pulled out a smoked-glass flask in a leather case.

"Ouzo, right?" she asked, holding it out. I took it. "You can keep the flask. Come on, let's go."

She walked to the front door and opened it.

"Am I in trouble?" I asked.

"No. This is a good surprise."

On the way out, I saw two guys in suits. They were against the wall on either side of the door, where they'd been standing out of the range of the peephole. Penny started down the hall and I followed her, while the two men followed me. She took us down the elevator and outside, and one of the two men held an umbrella over my head as we walked over to a big car with tinted windows. He held the back door open, and I slid into the warm interior. Penny scooted in next to me; then the two men got in up front. The driver started the car and pulled out.

"When we get there, don't freak out," Penny said.

"Freak out why?"

"I can't say. Just don't."

"I won't." I opened the flask and took a swig. "I haven't seen you around here much."

"You miss your friend."

I didn't say anything. My ears got hot and I shrugged.

"Sorry," she said. "I didn't mean anything by that. I just meant to be there for you a little more, that's all. She's got me doing something, so I've been staying somewhere else for a while. I would have come by sooner."

"That's okay."

"No, it's not. You shouldn't be alone right now."

She was looking out the window while she talked. She actually looked a little upset.

"It's okay. I'm always alone."

"Not anymore."

She looked over at me then and smiled a little, which she didn't usually do.

"Believe me. I'll be glad when it's over," she said. "I'd much rather be getting loaded with you than doing the other thing."

I handed her the flask, and she took a big guzzle off of it.

"Thanks." She handed it back.

"Can't you tell me where we're going?"

"Sorry. I'm not trying to be a bitch. It'll make more sense once we're there. Just enjoy the ride."

I decided to go with the flow and just watch the city

go by out the window, until after a while, I lost track of where we were. We went through some really nice sections, filled with people, and I felt giddy as the neon trailed by over my head. The inside of the town car was big and comfortable, and talking with Penny was easier than I was afraid it might be. She was a lot like me. We even joked about the visions, and when the flask ran out, she had the driver stop at a corner store so we could pick up more.

It was almost an hour before the car finally slowed down, and by then the lights had tapered off. It got darker outside and the rain was starting up again when I saw a concrete train platform up ahead. It was lit with a single light, and there were three men—one big guy in the middle, and one to either side of him—standing at the edge of the tracks, facing us; there was a black limousine parked in the small area next to the platform.

"We're here," Penny said. The car stopped a little ways across from the limo, and the two men got out. One came around and opened the door for us again, and we both got out too.

"Where are we?" I asked. Penny waved to the limo, but the windows were dark and I couldn't see in.

"Somewhere where no one will bother us," she said, reaching into her coat and handing me a big white envelope. "Here. This is from her."

It had my name written in little black script on the front. I opened it, and found a card inside. A message was written on it:

I am sorry I couldn't be there in person, but know that I am with you in spirit. I have watched you for a long time. I know about what happened to your parents. I know that your ability has been

*a burden to you, and that while it has provided
you with some security, it has done nothing to ban-
ish the emptiness from your life. I know that your
life has been filled with disappointment and loss. I
say this not because I pity you, but because I also
know that you recently found a small light in that
darkness, and then that light was taken away from
you as well. I did not know your friend, but I have
an idea of what she meant to you, and words cannot express how sorry I am that this has happened.*

The words blurred in front of me. I wiped my eyes as
the wind blew against the umbrella the man held over
me.

*Nothing can ever make this right, but what I
can do is offer you a choice. You are not powerless.
What happens tonight will be entirely your choice,
and there is no wrong choice to make. No matter
what you decide, we will be here for you. I will be
here for you, and if you let me, I will try to be, as
she was, that light for you in the darkness.*

It wasn't signed, but I knew it was from her. It was
from the little one, Ai, their leader.
Our leader.
"Come on," Penny whispered, and started across the
blacktop. I followed behind her. No trains stopped there
after hours, and it was dark. The place looked kind of
sketchy. I could see broken glass and a lot of graffiti.
Wedged behind the corner of a chain-link fence was an
old, empty purse.
"Don't worry about security," she said. "No one will
bother us here."

I was confused, and so drunk I could barely walk in a straight line. All I wanted to do was go back home and go to bed. The train platform looked like the kind of place where bad things happened. I looked past Penny to where the single light was shining down on the platform. We were getting close to the three men.

It wasn't until we got right in front of them that I finally realized who the big guy in the middle was. It was Ted.

"You," I said, but he was too far away to hear over the rain. He was leaning forward, squinting to see who was coming. His face was puffy and bruised. I wished whoever did it had killed him.

When we got in front of him, he realized who I was. He shook his head, and tears actually came up in his eyes.

"You fucking bitch," he said. "You fucking bitch . . ."

I took a breath to yell something, anything, at him, but Penny spoke first, cutting me off.

"Quiet," she said, without raising her voice.

Ted's face went slack. The way his eyelids drooped and his thick bottom lip hung down reminded me of the way he used to look when I'd go downstairs to . . .

"What are you going to do to him?" I asked.

"I'm not going to do anything to him. He belongs to you now."

"For what?" She shrugged.

"For whatever you want," she said. "But I know what I would do."

She walked away and the others followed her, leaving me alone with him. His eyes cleared, and when he saw me, the anger came back right away. I focused on him, and I could see the spikes of red flaring up. He hated me. Just the sight of me was enough to make him crazy.

I thought I hated him before, but standing there on that platform, watching him stare at me like the whole thing was my fault, I hated him more than I think I'd ever hated anyone or anything before.

"These more of your goons?" he asked.

"You should shut up, Ted."

"Who are these guys—your FBI goons? Fuck you and them."

"She died," I said, tears coming up.

"Yeah, they told me." I could see sadness there. Not much, but a little. I saw guilt there too. Mostly, though, it was fear. Under the anger, it was mostly fear. He was afraid of jail, of punishment. He was afraid for himself.

"It wasn't my fault," he said.

"Wasn't your fault?" I yelled, but my voice cracked so it came out like a pathetic squeak. "You beat her to death! She died!"

"You're the ones that sent that fucking—"

He stopped before he said whatever he was going to say. He was still mad, still scared, but I saw something else then. It was shame. He was ashamed, but not because of what he did. It was because of something that happened to him.

"I didn't send any—"

"She was looking for you, bitch. She called you by name."

"She?" It took me a second to figure out what he was saying. It was that woman, the one that tried to trap me in the elevator. She came looking for me.

"She beat you up," I said.

"Fuck you!" he yelled. His eyes bugged out, and the light around him flared out. It swirled, with bright strings of hot red flicking through like they were out of control.

He wanted to wreck something. He wanted to tear me apart. I could see it in his eyes, and in the pattern that surrounded him. I'd thought before that by stopping him, I might be making him worse. That night, I thought it might be true. It was who he was. The longer he went without being able to feed his urge, the worse it got. He looked crazy.

"Shut up."

"Fuck you!"

"I said shut up!" I yelled. I'd started crying, but I didn't care. "All I have to do is say the word and those people will kill you. Do you get it?"

His fists started opening and closing, like he was going to have a seizure or something. His face was beet red and his sweaty jowls shook.

"You tell me you're sorry," I said. "I won't make you do it. Admit what you did and—"

"I didn't mean to kill her. She asked for that."

"I should have stopped you. She deserved better than you. She—"

"Karen was a fat-assed slut," he spat. "I warned her what would happen, and she didn't listen."

I didn't say anything. I wanted to be tough, but I was crying and I couldn't stop. I couldn't believe he could just stand there and say those things after what he'd done. He wasn't even sorry. He'd killed her, and he knew she was my best friend, and he still kept saying those things. . . .

"How many times did the bitch have to get slapped before she fucking figured it out? Did she fucking want to get hurt?"

The others were back there somewhere, watching me. They were watching me stand there and cry with my face in my hands while the man who killed my friend shit all over her. The wind picked up and blew my hair in front of my face, covering it up so no one could see me.

"Cry all you want, you fucking stupid, ugly bitch," I heard him say. "She was fine before she met you. You had to get her going. You weren't happy until she got put in her place. This happened because you—"

I didn't think about what I did before I did it. My eyes were covered by my hands and my hair covered my face, but I could see the part of him that mattered as clear as day. The storm of colors floated there in the dark like a ghost of him, and all at once they got clearer than I'd ever seen them before. I stopped crying, and while he spit and yelled, I reached past the reds and yellows and all of his violence and anger and hate. I reached in as deep as I could, until everything was gone except a single hot, white band. Everything else was connected to it. It was the source of everything he thought and everything he was. It was the source of everything he'd ever done and would ever do.

He was still ranting when I focused on the stream and turned it off. When I did, his voice stopped. The flow of light stopped and went dark. The reds and yellows scattered and faded until nothing was left behind.

I moved my hands away and opened my eyes. When I brushed my hair from my face, I saw Ted standing there, but his eyes were blank. His mouth hung open, and a string of drool dangled from his bottom lip, getting blown in the breeze. The smell of pee hit me, and I saw he'd gone to the bathroom in his pants.

"Ted?"

He went back on his heels and fell, completely limp, off the platform and down onto the tracks.

I heard him hit, and I was going to look when the

train blasted by. I screamed. It was all over before I could even move. The wind from the passing train blew my hair across my face and made my jacket whip and snap around me. The side of the train was a blur that filled up everything, and then just as fast, it was gone.

My heart thumped in my chest as I stared, unable to move for a minute. The wind died down, and the sound of the train faded into the distance. When I looked, I saw the red lights zoom off into the distance.

Finally, I moved to the edge of the platform and looked over. I wasn't sure I wanted to see what was down there, but it turned out that except for a spot of red that the rain was washing off the side of the concrete, there wasn't anything at all. Ted was gone.

9

Element

Nico Wachalowski—Wilamil Court, Apartment #516

Wachalowski, where are you?

I was stepping off the elevator when the call came in from Vesco.

I'm at Flax's apartment. What have you got?

Buckster's long gone. Looks like he cleaned out a safe and left in a hurry.

You find anything?

Yeah. There's something you need to see.

A window opened and live footage streamed in. Vesco moved through Buckster's apartment and into the bathroom. He looked down into the tub, where a set of women's clothes were sprawled. They were arranged in the shape of a person. The body that was in them was gone. One high-heeled shoe was lying on the floor next to the toilet.

Looks like he killed an unknown female and then used Leichenesser to dispose of the body. Trace particles indicate it happened recently. Could it have been your civilian?

The stream moved closer, looking over the shirt and pants. They looked expensive. A pin on the collar of the shirt looked like a diamond set in gold. The shoe had a three-inch heel.

No.

You sure?

Someone died in Buckster's place, but it wasn't Calliope. Whoever it was, she was wealthy and fashion conscious. She didn't leave any components behind.

Flax has a JZI.

Got it. Nothing like that here.

Any sign of the radiation signature?

Nothing. If he was hiding something here, it wasn't the nukes.

Understood.

What about your end?

I'll let you know.

When I knocked on Calliope's door, there was no answer. I listened, but didn't hear anything inside.

Alice, I need an override on a residence at my location.

No.

What?

I'm denying that request.

Do you want to find the case or not?

Yes, and tracking down those weapons is more important than tracking down your friend.

I hadn't told anyone at the bureau about getting Calliope involved. It was a safe bet Calliope never told them.

Are you watching me?

Yes. Your friend is fine. Get back in the field and—

Are you refusing to give me the override?

Yes. Don't go in—

I cut off the connection and aimed my gun at the lock housing. Using the backscatter, I found the bolt, then fired two bursts into the door.

It bent but didn't break. I stomped my heel down over the still-smoking hole as someone shouted from the floor below. With gunshots and a break-in reported, it was only a matter of time before the police showed up, but with everything else going on they'd be tied up for a while.

I threw my shoulder against the door and it finally gave, flying open and slamming into the wall as I stumbled in after it. I turned on the lights. The place looked okay. It was a mess, but it hadn't been tossed.

"Cal?"

The living area was set up with a couch, a TV, a weight bench, and a heavy bag that hung from a chain. According to the thermal scan, she'd been gone for a while.

I looked over the floor, turning up the filter's sensitivity until faint footprints appeared. I knelt down for a closer look.

There was more than one set of them. I counted maybe four in all, but it was hard to pick hers out of the mess. The freshest ones were small. They looked too small to belong to her. I followed them from the kitchen through the living area. They passed out of the room to a short hallway that led to a bathroom and a bedroom. Whoever it was had sat on the toilet.

I smelled the air. It smelled like sweat, but there was something else under it, something antiseptic.

Wachalowski, this is Noakes. I'm getting grief from Agent Hsieh. What are you doing?

Following a lead on Buckster.

Well, wrap it up there. It looked like the satellite just got a hit on your missing ship.

Where?

About fifteen miles offshore, and getting closer by the minute.

That was lucky; if it was the ship we were looking for, it was in UAC waters. We could seize it.

Are they sure it's the right one?

It has to be. It was practically invisible since it's running on minimal power, and the comms, transponder, and sat-nav are all dark. It's hiding.

We need to coordinate with the Coast Guard.

Already on it. They're putting a safety and security team together. You can go in by air.

Understood.

The team will be assembled and ready for launch within the hour. Be ready.

Zooming in, I followed the footsteps from the toilet back out the bathroom door. They didn't head left, for the bedroom, or right, back to the living room. They went right up to the wall across from the bathroom door. A large flag from one of the African republics was hung there from ceiling to floor.

I knelt down. The stride of the footsteps took them right into the wall. There was heat concentrated at the base of the flag, rippling out from underneath it.

I pushed the flag out of the way. There was a door hidden behind it. Whoever the footprints belonged to, that was where they'd gone. Another pair overlapped them, heading back out in the opposite direction. I knocked quietly.

"Cal?"

No one answered. I didn't hear any movement. Looking through the front of the door, I couldn't make out anyone inside.

I turned the knob—it was open. I pushed open the door. It was warmer inside than in the rest of the apartment, and dark. The air smelled like rubbing alcohol and body odor. I reached over and flipped on the lights.

Shit.

Clear plastic covered the floor and had been stapled up the length of every wall. A hospital gurney sat in the middle of the room, flanked by two surgical trays. An IV rack had two bags hanging from it, one of clear fluid and one of blood. Both were mostly empty, the tubes trailing to the floor. Blood spots dotted the mattress on the gurney, and I could see bloodstained gauze wadded up in a wastebasket underneath it.

What is this?

There were scalpels and a suture needle on one of the trays, along with a spent hypo. Impressions were left in the plastic that covered the floor where boxes had been removed. It looked like most of the equipment had been packed up. Whatever happened here, it was over.

I looked around for anything that might tell me where she'd gone. On the metal frame of the gurney, someone had stuck a small note:

Destroy everything. Report to me.

The room wasn't set up on the fly. From the look and smell of it, it had been occupied for days, maybe weeks. There was no way Calliope didn't know it was there....

Unless she'd been made to forget.

Someone else must have been there, right in the apartment with her. Ai had planted someone there, and kept Calliope from consciously knowing about it. I stared at the surgical tools and the bloody gauze. What had they done to her?

I picked up my phone and called the contact number Ai had given me. A woman's voice answered, but it didn't sound like the woman from the restaurant.

"Hello?"

"This is Agent Wachalowski. Who am I speaking to?"

"You are speaking to Penny. What's up, Agent?"

"I need to talk to Ai."

"Oh, now you need to talk to her?"

"Can you put me through to her or not?"

"I can, but I'm not going to."

"I—"

"Save the threats. I don't care who you are; you don't get to demand to talk to her. You'll talk to me."

"Put me through to Ai, or I'm hanging up."

"Fine, but if you do that, you'll never find out what happened to your friend."

"What?"

"Your friend Flax. I assume that's what this is about."

"Where is she?"

"You found the room, didn't you? Do you have any idea how many times I had to replant that memory so she'd remember seeing a wall instead of that door? She's got a stubborn streak, that one."

"If you know where she is, then tell me."

"Not on the phone. I want to see you."

"I don't have time for this—"

"Make time. I'm at Zoe's new place. You know where that is?"

"I . . ." it was the first I'd heard of it. I didn't even realize Zoe had moved. "No, I don't."

"Of course not."

"Look, just—"

"I'm sending the address. Decide what you want to do."

She hung up. I checked the time. The MSST would be in the air in less than an hour.

If I hurried, I could make it.

Faye Dasalia—112th Street Station

I knelt near a pile of plastic trash bags and looked out through the mouth of the alleyway. Through the LW field, the people who flowed by had a ghostly look. Facial recognition software scanned each one, matching it against my target.

While I waited there, hidden, I looked through the array of my memories for other references to the strange woman. I found one other instance, before Flax had hauled her into the clean room. I'd seen her shortly after I'd been brought back. As the crowds of people streamed by the alley, I brought up the memory and looked inside.

I was in the underground storage unit where Nico buried his past. He brought me there so that he could bring me back, and no one would ever know. The concrete room was cluttered with forgotten boxes and old furniture. He'd chained my ankle to a grate in the floor, and he told me to stay still when a knock came on the heavy metal door.

I watched from next to the bed we'd once lain on, while he crossed the unit and opened the door. A tiny woman stood on the other side. She was zipped up in a huge purple parka, red hair sticking out from under a wool cap. She stared up at him from over a beaklike nose, and I saw heat stream through the veins in her face. She was excited by him.

She'd stepped closer, then, and spoke softly to him. I saw her pupils expand.

"What happened?" she asked. *"Why are you so scared?"*

"Don't—"

She put one shaking hand on his. *"Shhh."*

"Stop doing that," he said.

"Why?"

She had put her other hand on his stomach and spread open her fingers.

"I know you miss it," she said, putting her forehead to his chest. *"I know you know how I feel. I wanted to thank you."*

"For what?"

"For caring about me, even a little bit."

She was placing Nico under her control. At the time I didn't realize what I'd seen, but I recognized it now. I saw the guilt in her eyes as she touched him, knowing his acceptance of it was coerced. I stepped out from the shadows, and she saw me.

"You're dead—you can't be here!"

She'd recognized me back then. We had never met, but still, she knew my face. She stared up at me, hands curled into tight fists, as heat coursed out from her chest. Even then there was something, some base instinct that told me she was trouble.

A small figure passed the mouth of the alley and toward the entrance to the convenience store. The computer took a snapshot of her face. It ran the comparison and got a match.

Target is spotted.

I stood and walked to the mouth of the alley. People streamed past me less than four feet away, but under the cloak, I was invisible. They'd see her, of course, and hear her if she screamed, but it would be over in a few seconds. By the time anyone realized she was dead, I would already be gone.

I watched her enter the store. Through the window, I watched her make her purchase. When she came out, she had a brown paper bag. Her red hair was draped around her sullen face, her lips drawn into a frown. She walked quickly, with her eyes on the sidewalk, and it looked like she'd been crying.

Now.

When she passed by me, I grabbed her by the wrist. I put my other arm around her thin waist and pulled her into the alley. She stumbled, but I held her as the brown paper bag slipped out of her hands. A bottle popped when it fell and hit the ground. An older man who passed by glanced down toward us, but didn't even slow down. He could not see me; just some staggering drunk.

"Hey!" she yelped, and I clamped my hand over her mouth. She stuck both her legs out straight, but her heels just scraped along the wet blacktop as I pulled her deeper into the alley.

"Quiet," I said in her ear.

I hauled her behind a trash bin, out of view. Running water ran down an open storm drain and helped cover the sound of her struggling. I forced her back and slammed her to the brick wall, then moved my right hand over her bony chest. I shut off the stealth cloak's field, and her face went white as she saw me appear.

"You," she whispered.

My open palm snapped apart, and my forearm split apart to my elbow. As the two halves splayed apart, she stared at the tip of the blade hidden there.

"Wait!" she said. "You're not supposed to kill me!"

The blood rushed under her skin, and I watched the

veins that pulsed along her neck. The blade was in position. One pneumatic blast would send it through her heart.

"You need me," she gasped.

"There's nothing I need you for."

"You said the fate of everything was in my hands."

"I never said—"

"In my visions. You said it."

I was about to kill her, but that stopped me. The exact nature of their abilities was something that we hadn't determined yet, but there was no disputing that they were real or at least based on reality, on possible outcomes. Imposing will or manipulating minds could be done by anyone, if not as well, but not the precognition. We didn't know what it was, but we knew what it wasn't, and it wasn't prediction. The data points to lead them to their visions simply never existed. Nothing led them to the conclusions they reached; they just saw the end result and they were usually, if not always, right.

Fawkes had warned me against listening to her, but still, I was curious.

"What is that supposed to mean?"

"I don't know," she said, "but that's what you told me. You come to me in my dreams, and sometimes when I'm awake. You keep trying to tell me something, something important."

"You saw me in a vision?"

"Yes."

"Where?"

"The green room," she said. "You come to me in the green room."

I didn't know what she was referring to. "And I spoke?"

"You were the one who told me to go to Nico two

years ago," she said. "The last time, you told me the city will burn."

I remembered her back at the restaurant. Motoko had said that too.

"What did I mean?"

"I don't know," she said. "I don't know why the messages come through you. Maybe I'm fixated on you . . ."

She stopped to think about that, curious, like she'd forgotten where she was. It wasn't until I moved, stepping in closer to her, that she snapped out of it.

"You know something," she said. "Or . . . some version of you does. You told me the fate of everything will be in my hands. You need me. . . ."

She was bargaining for her life, I knew that, but I believed she meant it. I didn't know what it meant, but I believed that she saw what she'd described. Part of me wanted to question her further, to extract the truths out of her ramblings, but there wasn't time for that.

"You're trying to tell me something," she stammered. "You need me for something, or else the whole city will—"

"I'm sorry," I said, "but I have my orders."

Her eyes were desperate for a few more seconds, and then she seemed to give up. She closed her eyes and let out a long, hoarse sigh.

"Can I at least have a drink first?" she asked. One of the bottles from her bag was intact. I reached down and picked it up.

"Here." I held it out by the neck.

She opened the bottle and then tipped it back. She drained nearly a quarter of the bottle before she choked and sprayed liquor from her nose. She bent over coughing and, I thought, laughing.

"I'm going to die in an alley," she said, smiling with

tears in her eyes. "I knew it was too good to be true.... I knew all this was too good to be true...."

"It usually is," I said.

"You want to know what I did last night?" she said, ignoring me. "I killed someone. I killed the guy that killed my friend.... I think I might have actually done it before. I actually killed somebody. Hey, didn't you used to be a cop?"

"Detective."

"Right . . . so doesn't it bother you, then? To kill people?"

"Did it bother you?"

"Hmm . . . not really. It felt . . . good, actually," she said, taking another drink. "It's weird. I thought it would freak me out, but it felt pretty good. It felt . . . right, like he deserved it. You know? Is that how it feels when you do it?"

"No."

"I saw you die, you know."

"What?"

"I saw it right before it happened. I called Nico, and he tried to save you." She frowned. "I actually tried to help you...."

"What do you know about that?"

"I know he went down there, down in the factory, for you, back then. I know he's been looking for you ever since."

I'd indulged her, and myself, for long enough. I positioned the blade back over her chest.

"He does it because he still loves you," she slurred.

I heard the shot before I knew what it was. It boomed through the small alley, and I pitched back suddenly as a collective gasp came from the sidewalk. I noticed several people on the street stop, and some looked over toward us. When I looked down, I saw black blood blooming there. I looked back at Zoe and I saw the gun. It was small, with silver plating and a pearl grip. Smoke drifted from the barrel as warning messages appeared in the air, flickering in between us. My signature wavered before snapping back.

The gun was small, but it had left a large hole. The armor plate under my skin had been pierced. Blood gushed as the nanos assembled a clot, then jetted in a stream as the pinhole closed. Zoe stared with her eyes wide.

I pushed myself off the brick wall behind me, the bayonet firing out as I did so. It whipped through the air as she stumbled backward, then slipped and began to fall. The blade's tip snagged on her coat, slashing it as she fell into a puddle.

She kicked back, away from me, pointing the gun in front of her. I reached to bat it aside and land the blow, but wasn't quite fast enough. She fired two more shots into my torso, and I staggered back from her. My signature warbled again, then came back, but not as strong as before. Back on the street, people had started to run.

The blood was coming out fast. My system couldn't work around the trauma.

I'm hurt. Requesting retrieval.

The confirmation came back as warning messages continued streaming. I tried to reach for Zoe, but she was too far away. When I tried to move, my leg didn't respond. I stumbled forward and went down on one knee.

I could still kill her if she came close enough. I held out my free hand, the blade by my side with its tip scraping the ground.

"I need to tell you something," I whispered.

"Why do I keep seeing you?" she asked, looking

down at me through the tangles of her hair. "Who are you?"

My heart signature flickered. She stood five feet away, not sure what to do.

"Come closer . . . and I'll tell you."

She stepped through a puddle toward me, and I lunged. My leg didn't perform as well as I'd hoped, but it held as I pushed off the blacktop. I grabbed her collar and pushed the gun aside as she went back on her heels. We fell into a pile of wet trash bags, her struggling beneath me as the blade came down.

She twisted away, and the blade grazed her cheek before it punched through the bag and hit the ground. Blood welled up inside the wound and began to run back into her wet hair as the gun barrel pressed into my rib cage. It fired off its last round, then just clicked as she kept pulling the trigger.

I tried to raise the blade back but I couldn't. It retracted on its own, and without its support I slipped to one side. I fell into the trash, face-to-face with her. I could smell the alcohol fumes on her breath.

She realized that she'd stopped me and let out a single, explosive laugh. Then the smile faded and her eyelids drooped. The way she flipped between relief and anger was almost mechanical.

"I remember now," she said. My blood sizzled on the end of the barrel as she pulled the gun away. "Thirty, one hundred, and zero. Respectively."

She shoved me over on my back as she stood. I didn't know what she meant.

"In my visions, you like to give percentages," she explained. "You said we meet three times. You said my chances of winning were thirty, one hundred, and zero. This is our second meeting. You can't win."

Her statement implied that she couldn't either, but that fact seemed lost on her. She reached into her jacket and pulled out a fresh magazine for the gun. She removed the spent one and tossed it away.

"I think this is all your fault," she said, reloading the gun. "You dragged me into this mess. I lost everything . . . I lost . . ."

She put her hands to her eyes, the pistol pressed against her face as she cried. For a second, she looked like a little girl who was lost and on her own. Then, like before, like a switch was thrown, she stopped. She looked down at me, and her face became calm.

I managed to reactivate the stealth cloak just as she aimed the pistol. The air rippled between us, and her face changed as I disappeared from view. She still held out the gun, but looked uncertain. I moved away as she prodded with one toe. When I wasn't there, she turned in a circle with the gun still pointed out in front of her.

"Were you real?" she asked.

"Hey!" a voice barked from the mouth of the alleyway. I looked and saw a uniformed policeman. Another stood behind him. Both of them had their guns pointed at Zoe.

"Did you see someone else here?" she asked them.

"Drop the gun," the one in front said. She touched the cut on her cheek, then saw blood come away on her fingertips.

"Someone else is here," she said.

"I said drop it," the policeman said.

She looked over at the men and realized then who they were. I watched her eyes turn a shiny, tear-filled black and the men's guns inched downward.

"You made a mistake," she said. "You heard a transformer blow or something."

The policemen both began to nod slowly, despite the fact that they could still see the gun. I managed to push back with my one good leg and roll off onto my side. Still leaking blood, I moved toward the open grate.

"You're not needed here," Zoe told the policemen. She'd noticed the black puddle on the pavement. "Go away."

I gripped the edge of the storm drain and slipped through. I fell down in a torrent of rainwater, then splashed down hard on my back.

Request emergency extraction. My vitals were wavering.

Rain poured through the grate above, the stream splashing over me. I saw the shadow of her head appear there, in that circle of gray light up above me. All she could see was darkness.

"Leave me alone!" she yelled from the opening, and her screech echoed down the concrete tunnel. My vision began to fade.

The swirling cloud of embers, that vast field of stars that were my memories, began to grow cold and dim. Beneath them the void waited, cold and black and without end. I felt myself begin to follow them down, and for the first time since my death, I felt fear.

Her silhouette moved away, before the last of the gray light disappeared.

Calliope Flax—KM *Senopati Nusantara*

A blast of ammonia went up my nose and I woke up to a cold floor. My head weighed a ton.

"Easy there," I heard Buckster say from somewhere in front of me. I cracked one eye open and saw him toss a smelling salt capsule to one side.

"Why did you bring her here?" someone asked.

"She's okay," the old man said.

"We don't need a repeat of the Takanawa incident. Fuel is limited, and we've already had to alter our course once."

"She's not bugged, goddamn it. I checked."

"What the fuck?" I was out of it, but I counted four of them. I put one palm on the floor and used the JZI to set off a stim. It hit me, but not as hard as it should have.

"You okay?"

I went for him, and I would have had him, but I was still fuzzy. Even with the stim, I was too slow. His pant leg slipped through my hand; then a big mitt grabbed my arm. It squeezed, and I was hauled up on my feet.

"Easy!" Buckster snapped. The hand let up, but not much. There were two jacks in front of me, plus the one in back that had my arm. It spoke, and I felt its cold breath on the back of my neck.

"They know we're taking them. Takanawa got them too close."

"She's not one of them, I told you. Take it easy."

"Where the fuck am I?" I asked.

"You're on the KM *Senopati Nusantara*."

"The what?"

"A cargo ship. We're off the UAC coast." If it was true, then I'd been out a long time.

"Why the fuck am I on a ship?"

"It was that or kill you under the bridge. Besides, in a few hours this is going to be the safest place to be—trust me."

I tried to call Wachalowski, but there was no link. I kept the channel open.

"He won't pick up," Buckster said. "Local communications only; nothing leaves the ship."

He gave a nod to the revivor behind me, and it shoved me toward a hatch on the far wall.

"Come on," Buckster said.

"Where?"

"To the brig. Look, this is how it has to be. If you stayed in the city, you'd get killed for sure. You helped me out, so I'm helping you, but I can't risk you causing any trouble. You'll cool it in the brig until this is over. Then you'll be free to go."

He went through, and I followed. The revivors pulled up the rear. Past the hatch, I saw dried blood on the deck—a lot of it. Balled up near one wall were a bloody shirt and a pair of pants. I kicked a shell case when I went by.

"What the hell are you mixed up in?" I asked him.

"Our country has an infection, Cal," he said. "It's not about politics. It's about freedom. It's about the freedom to make your choice, whatever that choice is. It's about the freedom to act according to what you believe in, not what someone else makes you believe. Someone has to stop them."

"How?"

"With fire."

"What are you going to do? Blow up the city?" I asked. He didn't answer. He just kept walking.

"Buckster, what the fuck are you guys going to do?"

"Can you be sure anything, or even everything, you've lived hasn't been a lie?" he asked. "Knowing even the little bit you know, can you say with complete certainty that everything you did while you were over in the grind happened the way you know in your heart that it did?"

I'm going to unstick the elevator now. When I do . . .
You don't know me. Tell me you understand.

"Are your actions truly your own?" he asked. "Or are

you a tool, a machine, used by someone else, the same way you used those revivors back in the grinder?"

"Answer me. What are you going to do?"

He pushed open a hatch and the jacks behind me pushed me through after him. I stumbled through a bunch of junk and shell casings that were scattered across the floor. A big table had been knocked over and used as cover, but it looked like the bullets had gone straight through. Blood spatter had dried on the walls and floor, but the bodies were gone.

Before we could reach the door on the other side of the room, it opened and three guys stepped through. That made Buckster stop short, and I almost bumped into him. Two of the guys had guns, and one had a metal case in his hand. They made right for us and stopped in front of the old man.

"This the one?" one of them asked.

"Yes. What is this?"

The one with the case opened it and took out a big needle. It was full of black shit.

"What the fuck is that?" I asked.

"Hold her," he said.

The jacks grabbed me from behind. One held my arms and another one held my head. I tried to move, but they had me pinned. It felt like my neck was going to break.

"What are you doing?" Buckster snapped.

"Don't struggle," a voice said in my ear.

"She's not one of them!" the old man said. "She doesn't want to be—"

One of the men bashed Buckster behind the ear with the grip of his gun, and he went down onto his knees. He leaned over, and dots of blood started to cover the floor in front of him.

"We don't need him anymore," someone said, and the guy that hit him aimed the gun at the back of his head.

"Wait!" I yelled, but never even got the word out before the shot went off. The old man jerked once and went facedown. Blood started to pool around his head.

"Hold her still," one of the other men said.

The guy jabbed the needle into my neck, and I saw him push the plunger.

"I said hold her still!"

I had only one shot. I brute-forced my way through one of the M8s behind me and dropped in a virus that shunted the command hooks over to me. One, two, and three, they all came up in my HUD. I pulled up their specs, vitals, and visual feeds, then took control of them.

The gun went off behind me, and the guy with the syringe jerked as the back of his head blew out. The case fell out of his hand, and the needle spun across the floor as his body fell in a heap. The other two raised their guns, but they were too late; the jacks shot them to pieces.

With the command spokes in place, I had full control of all three. In the feeds they streamed over, I could see what they saw and hear what they heard. It was like being back in the grind.

Orders?

"Get me off this b—" I started to say, when a sharp pain stabbed me in the gut. It hurt like hell, and my link to the revivors almost cut when the JZI's power dropped.

What the hell was that?

I pulled inventory from the jacks; they each had a sidearm, extra ammo, and three grenades. They were all strapped with enough C4 to sink the ship. I used another virus to turn off their inhibitors.

Orders?

"Get me the fuck off this boat now—"

The room spun, and I felt like I'd been drugged again. I set off a stim to cut through it as warnings flew past. My heart rate had dropped, but as the chemicals spread through my bloodstream, it spiked back up.

The pain hit again, worse this time. It felt like a hot coal in my gut.

"What the fuck did they stick me with?"

I ran a check on my systems and saw that something in there was drawing power. Whatever it was, it wasn't tied into the JZI's control system. There was something inside me that didn't belong there.

Orders?

Give me a layout of this place.

A map blinked on in front of me. There was a helicopter I couldn't fly up top, and a small ship-to-shore craft down below. I set a route to it.

There, I told them. *We're getting off this boat.*

10

Fate

Nico Wachalowski—Alto Do Mundo

The Alto Do Mundo was the second-largest skyscraper in the city, and its base covered almost an entire block. It had its own underground rail station beneath it, and contained shops and restaurants the likes of me could never afford. I had to flash my badge twice just to get through the gate and into the parking area, where a well-dressed valet quickly moved my car out of sight. I had to present it again to the automated security system at the main entrance, and wait for my identity to be verified before I was allowed in.

The foyer was like the inside of a palace, with enough wealth on display to spark a revolt. Just inside, two uniformed doormen stood at attention. They had a military stance, and each one had a gun under his coat. I flashed my badge at them as I passed, and I saw the orange flicker in their eyes as each one scanned it. One blew air through his nose, and followed me out of the corner of his eye, but neither one moved to stop me.

I headed through the huge foyer and up to the security desk, where another clean-cut, military type sat. Time in the grind had a way of bridging class gaps, but he still kept a close eye on me as I approached.

"Good evening, Agent Wachalowski. How can I help you?"

"I'm here to visit one of your residents, Zoe Ott."

"Are you here in an official capacity?"

"No."

"Sign here, please."

He swiveled an electronic tablet around, and I penned my signature. The tablet disappeared back behind the desk.

"Go on up."

The elevator was decked out in bronze, glass, and marble. I'd never actually been inside Alto Do Mundo before, and it was hard not to be impressed. Like Suehiro 9, it was the kind of place people associated with first tiers, but I was first tier and it was way out of my pay scale. Zoe may have had an ace in the hole, but her citizenship was third tier. Ai and her people were giving her the royal treatment. A deal that good was usually a devil's deal.

At her door, I rang the bell, but no one answered. I turned the knob and stuck my head in.

"Zoe?"

"Back here!" she called from down the hall.

I stepped inside and closed the door behind me. The place was a complete mess, but even so, it was incredible. The living area was huge, and full of top-of-the-line furniture and electronics. Hardwood flooring gave way to stone tile in a vast kitchen area. Looking around, I saw a gas fireplace, a huge flat-screen television, a half bar, and even a balcony. Next to the door, pizza boxes and other trash sat in a pile—Zoe's signature. Her clothes were lying on the furniture and the floor. It smelled like fast food and body odor.

Heading down the hallway, I heard a low, bubbling sound. Steam was drifting through an open door, and I heard a splash, then two women laughing.

"Zoe?" I moved into the doorway.

Zoe and Penny were sitting on opposite sides of a big hot tub, the surface bubbling around them. Penny wore a black bathing suit and Zoe wore a white one. Bottles were racked up along the edge of the tub, and they were both blind drunk. A huge flat-screen television was mounted on the wall across from them, and on it men in military gear were scrambling across a helipad toward a waiting chopper.

"Hey, look who decided to show up," Penny said, pointing. Zoe smiled.

"This thing is awesome," she said. It was the first time I'd seen her look that happy in a long time.

"Hop in. Join the party," Penny said, making Zoe blush.

"Cut the bullshit," I said. "We found the ship. Now where's Calliope?"

"No, *we* found the ship," she said, using the remote to shut off the TV. "The situation is under control. You can call off the MSST."

"That's not going to happen."

"You don't get to just decide that. It's not part of the deal."

"There is no deal."

"Sure there is. Ai still wants to see you, by the way."

"I know."

"You shouldn't keep her waiting."

"Did she hit the Healing Hands Clinic?"

"Hit it? Hey, they blew those clinics themselves."

"But she had them raided?"

"Sure, but no one made Fawkes blow them up. What is this, our fault now?"

"If she has the resources to track those sites down, then why get me involved?"

She shrugged. "Because you kill Fawkes. She told you that. You're part of it. Ai saw all this. All I know is that the destruction of the ship is tied to you, and that's what we really care about. You verified the location when you found your friend's message."

"You've known all of this?"

"We knew they bombed Concrete Falls to steal something from Heinlein; someone on the inside confirmed that. They ran a search on their own, but they never tracked it down. Whatever it was, it has them real nervous. Nervous enough to talk to you."

She took a pull off a long-necked bottle sitting on the edge of the hot tub. The clear liquid inside sloshed as she put it back down.

"You're going to meet with Ai and tell her what you talked about when you were over there. If you know anything about what was taken from Concrete Falls, you're going to tell her that too. Forget about your little trip to the boat."

"You—"

"Don't worry," she said. "You were totally right about Buckster. We knew he'd take Flax, but we didn't know what the connection to you was until near the end."

"Take her where? What do you mean, take her?"

"She gets taken," she said. "That was seen—not as a certainty, but a high probability. We were sure he'd hand her over to Fawkes like the other hobos. We just didn't know you'd hand her to him."

I started to say something, but stopped. I wanted say it wasn't true, but it was. Cal thought she knew what she was getting into, but she didn't.

"Why didn't you tell me?" I asked.

She raised her eyebrows. "Because we knew you'd pull her out of there."

"I could have gone in."

"That's not how it happens. She goes. She was the last of the five—that's why I got assigned to her. Thanks to you, she bumped back into Zoe here."

"I made her forget me back then. . . ." Zoe said.

". . . and I made her remember when she got back," Penny continued. "So you arrest Buckster and put Zoe on him. Zoe gets into Buckster's head. Calliope and Buckster compare notes. Buckster decides to take her right to ground zero, right to the ship. Game, set, match."

"How?"

"She doesn't know it, but she's been busy since she got back. She's going to take care of them for us."

The room in her apartment, the one hidden behind the hanging flag, it had nothing to do with Buckster. It had nothing to do with Fawkes.

"You were set up in her place," I said. "What did you do to her?"

"Forget about her, Nico. It's a done deal."

"No."

"Look, it's an honor," she said. "Destroying that ship will be the most significant thing a slum rat like her could ever do. She's going to change history."

"Destroy the . . ."

It hit me then. The case, with its twelve small payloads, each designed to be small enough to smuggle even inside the body of a revivor. Eleven had been stolen, but one of them had been taken away by Takanawa. Takanawa worked for Ai. Ai believed that Calliope would be taken by Buckster and processed along with the others. Her body would be taken and placed with the rest of the revivor army he was building. She was going to use Calliope to destroy the others.

"The nuke," I said. The medical equipment, the lingering radiation signature . . . they planted it inside her. Takanawa was a test run. Cal was going to carry the payload. Penny smiled.

"It's done," she said. "Come on, Ai's looking for you. She wants to know what you found out at Heinlein."

"Leave Calliope alone, and I'll tell her what she wants to know."

"You don't want to play that game with her. The ship goes down; that wasn't a certainty until just recently, but it is now. The ship goes down."

"I—"

"The ship goes down," she said again, raising her voice a little. "The ship goes down, and she is on it, and you are not, and that's how it happens. You don't make it to the ship."

"It's true," Zoe said.

"You knew about this?"

"Just what they told—"

"You knew about this and you didn't tell me?"

"Hey, I'm not your little lapdog, okay?" she slurred, glaring up through the steam.

"She's going to die, Zoe!"

"So she dies," she said. "She dies, Karen dies, Ted dies . . . everybody dies . . . I didn't know you knew her. You can't do anything about it anyway."

"Wait. Karen is dead?" I hadn't known that, but from the look on her face, I could tell it was true.

"Just never mind," she said. "It's not your problem."

Karen was a lifeline for Zoe. If she was dead . . .

"Zoe, something's not right here. These people want you for something."

"They accept me, Nico. They accept me and they like me, which is more than I can say for you. I don't need your help anymore or your little jobs at the FBI or any of it."

"People don't offer this kind of incentive unless they want something, Zoe. Ask yourself why they're doing it."

"They're doing it because I'm one of them! They're doing it because they like me!"

Penny hung back, one arm draped over the edge of the tub. She didn't chime in. She just looked at me smugly and smiled from behind Zoe's back.

"That boat is going down no matter who's on it," Penny said. "Fawkes's little army is going to the bottom of the ocean, and he'll be switched off any minute."

"If she's dead—"

"She is dead."

Alice, this is Wachalowski. How long until MSST can mobilize?

Twenty minutes.

Twenty minutes. I could still make it.

"I'm going," I said. "When I get back—"

Someone grabbed me from behind. His arms were like a vise around my rib cage, pinning my arms to my sides. Penny grinned.

"I told you. You don't make it to the ship."

There wasn't time to mess around. I fired one of the stims and the adrenaline surged through my body. I stomped my right heel down onto one of the boots behind me and a voice yelled out in my ear. When the arms loosened, I slipped down through and fired one elbow back into his crotch.

I turned to see a guy in uniform stagger back, his face dark and twisted in pain. There were two others with him.

Before the first one could recover, I smashed his nose under the heel of my shoe. Blood squirted out in a gob as he went down on his back and into the wall. Zoe screamed. By then one of the remaining two was on me. He ducked my punch and landed a mean hook into my ribs. Pain shot up my side and the breath went out of me.

If it hadn't been for the stim, it might have knocked me down for good. I fell into the side of the hot tub and grabbed the first bottle I could reach. I swung it by the neck, but he got his forearm up in time. The glass smashed against it, and blood began to bloom through the sleeve.

He attacked again, spraying drops of blood from the ends of his fingers. When he came in close, I grabbed his head and slammed my knee into the side of his face. Pain shot down my leg as a piece of tooth spun through the air. The other guy crashed into me and knocked me back. As we staggered, I grabbed his belt and swung him around, broken glass squealing on the hardwood floor under my shoes.

I slipped and went down with him on top of me. The other one was back up, moving toward us. Zoe was screaming, while Penny barked orders at the men. My window to get to the boat—and Calliope—was closing.

I put my hand in my jacket and pulled out my gun. I fired, and knocked the guy's leg out from under him. He went down as the one on top of me reached for his own weapon.

"No guns!" Penny yelled.

I lunged and hit the bridge of his nose with my forehead. Blood spattered down my cheek and into one eye as he pulled away. Before he could recover, I stuck the gun in his face.

"Don't," I said. He stood, bent over, with one hand still in his coat. Blood ran in steady drops from one of his nostrils.

"Let him go," Penny said. Zoe was staring, her face white and her eyes wide. She looked afraid but also excited.

"Throw it in the tub," I said to the guy. Penny smirked as he drew his pistol, then tossed it into the water. It disappeared with a splash beneath the bubbles.

"You won't make it," she said.

"We'll see."

"I could still fish that gun out and shoot you, you know."

"Then do it."

I wiped blood from my mouth and stepped over the man I'd shot. Blood was pooling around his leg.

"It's better this way," Penny called after me. "You know what happens if they make it to shore."

I left the two sitting in the hot tub, and as I headed down the hall I heard the television come back on. Soldiers chattered over a radio while helicopter rotors wound up for flight. In the hallway, I began to run.

Alice, change of plan with the MSST.

What do you mean?

The team can't go in. I need them to get me on the boat, then wait for the extraction.

Why?

Just do it.

Faye Dasalia—KM *Senopati Nusantara*

Primary systems initializing. It was the first thing I saw in the darkness. Information scrolled at my peripheries, and I watched as feeling began to return. They listed the fallout from the failure of my assassination attempt.

Bone repair/replacement.
Armored plating replacement.
Complete transfusion.
Spinal repair.
Organ replacement.

Any one of those items was expensive. I was surprised that Fawkes had ordered them done, when surely a new revivor was cheaper.

With consciousness, my field of memories returned. They coalesced into their well-known clusters, reforming the shield between me and the void. While not technically alive, I was not lost. I didn't really care why.

One of the memories, the one that kept coming back, rose from the field. I was back in the interrogation room before my death, before I'd made detective. The street woman was with me.

"Name?" I'd asked her.

"Noelle," she said. *"Noelle Hyde."*

"Look, if you want a lawyer—"

"I won't need one," she said, not looking up from the table. *"I won't go to jail."*

I remembered feeling pity for her then. She didn't know how much trouble she was in. The man would live, but the stabbing was brutal.

"What you did was attempted murder, Noelle," I said. *"You're going to jail."*

She shook her head.

"I wish I was. They might not be able to get to me there. That's why I'll never go."

I sighed, not sure what to do. Could she be schizophrenic?

"Who is 'they'?"

"I was supposed to stop him," she said, *"I just wanted to stop him."*

"Who told you to stop him?" I asked, but she wouldn't say. She just stared at the table.

"Samuel Fawkes is a dangerous man," she said.

"He's some engineer at Heinlein Industries. The man is not dangerous."

She looked up to meet my eye. *"Things change,"* she whispered.

The memory closed and fell back into the field. Had I just seen Samuel Fawkes's killer?

I willed my fingers to move, and each of them responded. I was able to wiggle my toes as well. Whatever damage was done, they'd repaired the worst of it.

Removal of invasive bone splintering into soft tissue.
Two node power cells replaced and rewired.
Dermal patching (Four percent).

As the checklist drifted by, I thought about what I'd seen. I remembered that woman. Someone had posted her bail, and just like she insisted, she never saw the inside of a jail cell. We turned up pints of her blood, but no body.

"Faye?" The voice came from near my ear. I opened my eyes and saw his face near mine.

"Lev."

"Can you move?" he asked.

"Yes."

I sat up on the steel tray, where blood had pooled and thickened like black jelly. A dermal graft ran the length of my torso, from my sternum to my crotch. Two revivors in white coats stood beside me, aprons spattered and soiled. Chrome surgical tools lay in pans of water, turned inky gray from the blood. Other pans contained fragments of yellowed bone and chunks of preserved, gelatinized tissue.

"I thought maybe you were gone for good," Lev said.

I looked around me to find out where I was. The metal tray was in some kind of large hold where flood lamps had been set up. Beyond them it was all shadows that danced within a soft, electric moonlight. It was sourced from thousands of tiny pinpricks that flickered all around the walls of the hold, where dark shapes stood motionless. I realized then what it was I was seeing: the points of light were the eyes of revivors. Thousands of them stood waiting inside the hold, their eyes jittering as if in some mass dream.

"I'm on the ship," I said.

"Yes."

Some were hairless; some were not. All of them were nude and desexed. Black veins bulged and squiggled under waxy skin; they had all been in stasis for a long time, and it had taken a toll.

They were of all different races and colors, male and female, young and old. They clutched pistols and rifles to their bare chests, eyes staring up at nothing. I'd never seen so many.

"Can you stand?" Lev asked.

My diagnostics hadn't finished running, but my central nervous system was intact. Needle-prick jolts went through my muscle tissue as I moved to the edge of the metal tray. My arms were slow to respond, especially the left one, but I managed to climb down onto the floor. The deck was cold and wet under my bare feet. A limbless torso lay a foot from Lev's feet, part of an old revivor. There was a cavity beneath the rib cage where parts had been harvested for my repair.

"Not all of them were fully functional," Lev said. "They were only good for parts."

"You could have stripped me and repaired them instead."

"I didn't."

Even though I was long dead, the sight in the hold triggered a certain dread. It was really happening. The whispering from the dormant revivors had become soft and distant since I was so far from shore, but I could already feel them growing stronger. The ship was getting closer.

"You said something as you woke," Lev said. "Did you remember something?" I nodded.

"I think I know who killed Fawkes," I said.

"They ordered it. He knows that."

"I don't think they did," I said. The flickering of their eyes was hypnotic. "I don't think that they meant for this to happen."

"*. . . they might not be able to get to me there. It's why I'll never go.*"

"*You never heard the name Samuel Fawkes.*"

I'd actually processed one of Ai's people. With no idea who she was, I had actually arrested the woman. I'd arrested her for trying to kill Fawkes, but it didn't sound like Ai had ordered it. It was just the opposite; she had actually been killed for what she'd done.

"They wanted to avoid this," I said. This wasn't just

about Fawkes or Zhang's Syndrome. There was something else that predated either. Something they were afraid of.

I thought back to the conversation I'd seen, watching from outside the restaurant that night.

"*. . . it will start here, but it won't end here . . . Fawkes will destroy this city and then, one by one, the rest will begin to fall. . . .*"

"They think he's going to end the world," I said.

Lev didn't say anything. He dismissed the other two, then touched my hand.

"He's going to end their world."

I looked out over the mass of revivors. Lev was right; he had to be. The forces in that hold, even with the nukes, couldn't destroy a country, much less the world. The localized horror that would play out soon was a necessary drop in the bucket.

"Come on," he said. "We'll be reaching the shore soon."

I looked down by the flood lamps, where hundreds of metal crates were stacked up high. Revivors moved in between the rows of them, guiding winches that moved the crates to the floor. The deck was wet with sticky, spent blisters and the thick residue of stasis fluid. They were waking up more of them, even now.

"Where did we get so many?" I asked.

"A military storage site overseas. They think these units have been decommissioned because of obsolescence."

These were older models, then, from Fawkes's generation. That policy had placed them in Fawkes's hands.

"Don't you think that's ironic?" he asked.

"Maybe," I said, but part of me wondered if it wasn't more than that.

Another crate was lowered into the hold. I watched as they opened the front panel and mist began to seep out.

Calliope Flax—KM *Senopati Nusantara*

I brought up the map and drew a path to the escape raft. It was a ways off, but if I was quick, I might make it. No one had tripped the alarm yet, but someone out there saw three M8s drop off their network. They knew something was up. I killed all the comms on each revivor so they couldn't track them, then set up a POV stream for each over the command link.

"Up there," a voice said from down in the hold, and I heard footsteps.

Go.

The three revivors made a run for the hatch at the far end of the walk. I stuck close as the first shot went off and a bullet sparked off the rail.

One opened the hatch and I sent two through while the last stayed to close it behind us. Gunshots boomed through the hold as the door clanged shut.

One, take point. Two and three, cover the rear.

The POV streams fixed along the top of my line of sight peeled off as they split up. The one in front picked up speed, giving me a view ahead. The other two kept pace, looking back and letting me see behind.

Those crates in the hold, are they full?

Most of them are still awaiting processing.

What was the node count on your network before I cut you off?

Two thousand three hundred and fifty-one.

Too many. Once they started moving they'd box me in for sure. If I got lucky, I could get to the launch bay before they found me. . . .

A sharp pain stabbed into my gut, and my leg buckled. I stumbled and slammed into the wall, trying not to fall as I ran. It felt like I got knifed. The revivor in front pulled away, and one of the two in the rear clipped me when it passed.

"Damnit!"

Keep me in the middle. I saw myself whip by the frame of one POV as they adjusted.

Acid came up my throat, burning it. I swallowed, making a face. Buckster was right about one thing: that pain wasn't nothing. Something was wrong. If I didn't get to the boat, though, it wasn't going to matter.

A hatch came up fast in one of the POV feeds, and the jack stomped to a stop up ahead. It grabbed the wheel and heaved, but it was stuck.

The door is secured.

I checked the map. The next-shortest path wasn't short enough.

Use your charge to blow it. Two and three, follow me.

I tacked right down a side hall and hugged the wall. In the feed's window, I watched the jack lock its arms through the wheel. It put its chest to the door and pushed the C4 bricks against it. I plugged my ears and hit the deck.

It set off the charge, and the floor bucked under me. The blast slammed down the hall, and I felt the shock in my bones. Fire lit up the dark, and I caught a blast of air hot enough to singe me. I smelled burned hair and smoke. My ears rang.

One in front, two behind. Go.

The one in front ran into the smoke, and I went in after it. I followed it, half blind, as it made it to the hatch. The door was warped, twisted on one hinge. It grabbed it, skin sizzling on the metal as it heaved it to one side and held it out of the way.

I jumped through, and they followed me in. Smoke burned my nose, and under it I smelled rot. One took point again as I ran through the room. Lying in the middle of the deck was a body on its back, bones sticking out. Four more lay near the wall, dead.

When I passed, the toe of my boot hit a jar with an inch of piss in the bottom, and it spun across the deck. The revivor on point gripped the wheel on the hatch across the room and turned. It squealed open.

The second hatch was open. Why didn't they . . .

The jack went through. I saw the carnage on the feed just before I went through after it. The smell hit me, and I gagged. The deck was splattered with dried blood. Ripped pieces of clothes were stuck in it, mixed with bones. Up ahead, three sets of eyes glowed in the dark. They were sitting against the wall, waiting.

My foot came down on a shell casing and I slipped. I wheeled one arm then went down into a pile of remains. They were cold. When I tried to get up, I put my hand down on something spiny and sticky. Half a rib cage lay on the deck in front of me.

"Fuck!"

A cold hand grabbed my elbow as one of my jacks pulled me up, dragging me down the hall after it. Another cramp, like a sharp stick, twisted in my gut as I stumbled, kicking up bones.

Cal? Cal, are you there?

The words popped up as I ran, sweat beading on my face. One of the jacks kept ahead. The other still had my arm. Down the hall, the three revivors saw fresh meat and hauled themselves up. Past them, the light at the end of the hall was tilting.

Take them out.

The jack in front opened fire and ripped open the fat

belly of the closest one. I heard shit spill out on the deck and then the stink hit me. My stomach turned. The pain dug in like a saw blade. Two more shots came, and the thing's head blew apart.

Cal? Cal, respond.

My legs wanted to quit. The acid was burning my throat. I checked my comm link. It was Wachalowski. He got through.

I'm here.

Cal, I'm tracking you. Where are you headed?

Ship-to-shore vessel. In the docking bay.

The medical bay is on the way. Meet me there first.

Where the fuck are you?

I'm in a helicopter, approaching the tanker. I'm coming in. You need to go to the medical bay first.

Why?

Do you trust me?

Up ahead, I heard boots on the deck. There were a lot of them. Even getting to medical was looking dicey. Did I trust him?

I trust you.

My foot got snagged on a belt, and bones scattered across the deck as we ran toward the men up ahead.

11

Ship

Nico Wachalowski — KM *Senopati Nusantara*

In the back of the helicopter, fifty miles offshore, the Coast Guard Maritime Safety and Security Team looked at ease in spite of the extreme turbulence. They stared straight ahead as their team leader addressed me.

We'll be touching down shortly. The helipad will put you close to the entrance here:

A map of the ship appeared in my HUD, where the location was marked.

You know where you're going after that?

My target came into communications range when we approached the ship. She's located a ship-to-shore vessel; that's how we'll leave if we can. Right now she's headed to the medical bay in case I need to physically remove the bomb.

Understood. The software package we provided should allow you to pull the specs from the device. The virus contained in the package will shut the device down once it has the specs.

Got it.

Connect to the device, pull the specs, drop the virus. You'll know if it worked in less than a minute.

Understood.

If it doesn't, you've got to leave her there. If you try and remove the bomb it could detonate.

The team leader stopped for a minute, orange light flickering in his pupils.

Satellite data confirms well over a thousand revivors active on board the ship, but they're grouped down in the hold. You're going to have to be fast. If you can't disarm the bomb, we have to leave it to blow. If you do, we have orders to sink the ship. Either way, it never gets to shore. Understand?

I understand.

The helicopter dipped suddenly as the wind sheared. The pilot adjusted while rain streaked across the windshield. The team leader signaled, pointing down at the deck.

The helipad's below us. We're going in.

Understood.

He heaved open the door. Cold mist sprayed in as we descended. A bright floodlight aimed down through the rain, lighting up the helipad on the deck. Something moved down there.

Hostiles on deck. Computer's picking up SAM targeting laser.

We banked sharply. A heavy grinding noise started, shaking the floor as a gun turret moved into view through the open door. It angled down toward the ship.

Hold on, Agent.

The chain gun let loose. The muzzle flared up as tracers spit down toward the deck of the ship.

"The laser's down! I'm coming around!" the pilot yelled.

"Okay, we're going down!" the team leader shouted, clapping my shoulder. "Don't get out until I say you're clear! Got it?"

"Got it!"

Another blast of wind hit, and my stomach flipped as we dropped down. I could barely see the deck until we were on top of it. A spray of foam crashed up along the side of the ship.

"Hold on!"

The radio crackled as we banked around. The chopper bucked hard enough to rattle my jaw.

Agent Wachalowski. The message wasn't from anyone on the team, and it wasn't from Cal. It originated back on shore.

Who is this?

I'm contacting you on Ai's behalf. Why are you approaching the tanker?

Whoever you are, I work for the FBI, not Motoko Ai. It's not safe to board the ship.

She made that clear before I left.

The deck was coming up fast. Down below, I saw it tilt as another wave crashed into the hull. The floodlight stayed on the helipad as we hovered sixty feet above it.

You're going to get killed. We need you alive.

I cut the connection as the pilot signaled to me.

"We're gonna go in fa—"

There was a huge explosion from the other side of the ship, and a cloud of fire lit up the water around it. Pieces of debris were silhouetted against the flames before spinning down into the water.

What the hell was that? I asked.

There goes your ship-to-shore vessel, the team leader said. *Looks like they don't want anyone getting off. We're sticking close in case we need to sink her. If you can find your civilian and make it back to the deck, we'll extract you. Got it?*

Got it.

The deck stabilized and the pilot brought us in. It was a rough landing, but he put us down on the pad. I felt the motion of the sea under me as the team leader signaled.

You're clear.

Roger that. Thanks.

Good luck.

I jumped out, and as soon as my boots clanged down on the metal plating, I felt it move underneath me. Sea spray crashed up the far side of the ship. Behind me, the helicopter lifted off and ascended into the rain.

I made my way across the deck, debris sliding past as the ship rocked. My foot slipped and I went down on one knee just as the head and torso of a revivor rolled by.

Zooming in on the blueprint of the ship, I laid it over my main field of vision.

Cal, I've touched down. Where are you?

I'm on my way to the med ward like you said. Where are you?

On deck. I'm coming in now.

I'm telling you, I can get to the ship—

They just blew the ship-to-shore boat, Cal, and you're rigged with a bomb. I can stop it and get you off the ship, but you have to do as I say.

The chain gun went off from up above. Off on the other side of the ship, it was chewing up the deck.

Cal?

She didn't answer. Through the wind and the rain, I could see the metal hatch up ahead that led inside. I drew my gun and made a run for it.

Zoe Ott—Alto Do Mundo

The whole thing had scared me, at least at first. One minute everyone was just talking; then the next three guys came in, one of them grabbed Nico, and everything just exploded. I'd never seen him do anything like that before; it was like he was some kind of crazed animal or something. Some other guys had come and helped the security men away, but the floor was still covered in blood and broken glass.

"Don't worry about the mess," Penny said. "We'll get the floor refinished."

My heart had been beating really fast until Penny put her hand on one of my shoulders. Then a weird calm came over me, and the fear just kind of drifted away.

"He won't make it," she said. She'd found the gun in the water and held it up before putting it on a towel. "That was a pretty good fight, huh?"

I nodded.

"He'll be fine," she said. "He won't get there in time."

I nodded again, then drained the smoked-crystal glass and eased back, letting the hot water bubble around me. Being in that tub was the most relaxing thing I'd ever done. I couldn't believe I'd waited half my life to try it. Penny sat on the other side of the tub with a bottle of something called grappa, which was clear, came in a tall bottle, and tasted horrible.

"I totally needed this," Penny said, cracking her neck and leaning back. "I've been cooped up in that hellhole for days."

"Hellhole?"

"Yeah, that man-girl they assigned me to," she said. "That's where I've been. I had to camp out there until we got her set up. I've been sleeping on a secondhand couch."

"She let you stay there?" Penny laughed.

"Hell no. She didn't know I was there. It was three days of babysitting and memory manipulation. It gets exhausting after a while."

"Oh." I wanted to ask her if she wasn't afraid of getting beaten up or worse, but it was obvious that she wasn't, and I was kind of embarrassed to admit that I would have been. I'd seen Calliope up close, and she scared me more than most guys.

"Fortunately, she's as stupid as they come," Penny said. "It's like using a sledgehammer on a nail, with her. Anyway, that's why I haven't been around much."

"It's okay."

"No, it isn't. You've been through some major stuff lately. I wanted to be here."

I didn't know what to say, so I just didn't say anything. The truth, though, was that I was really glad she showed up.

"That thing with Ted . . . is that what you meant to happen?" I asked.

"It was all you. Nothing was planned."

"What did happen?"

"You shut him off."

"Like a machine?"

"Kind of."

She took another drink and looked me in the eye through the steam.

"You've got a particular little talent there," she said.

"I killed him."

"Are you sorry you did?"

"No." In the back of my mind, I had this feeling that Karen would have been upset if she was alive to know what I'd done. But she wasn't, thanks to him. "I should have done it sooner."

Penny nodded and smiled. She took a swig off of her long-necked bottle.

"I'm really sorry it happened," she said, "but at least you get it. Not everyone does, but you get it."

"Get what?"

"That there are people like Karen and people like Ted. People like your friend; they want to make things better. It's good that they do, but the problem is that people like Ted won't ever change on their own. You saw it when you looked inside him. People like him get in the way. Someone's got to make the hard decisions. You get that."

"If I'd done it sooner . . ."

"You can't change it now. Next time you won't wait. You can honor her that way. I'm sorry, but it's the best you can do."

I was starting to like Penny a lot. I worried at first about hanging out with someone like me, but it turned out to be really great. I could actually talk about the things I did and saw, and she understood. She'd been through it too.

More than that, though, she made me feel included. I'd been on the outside my whole life. It was nice to be on the inside, for once.

"Nicely done with that revivor in the alley, by the way."

"Thanks." I was so drunk that the thing in the alley felt like a dream. Had I told her about that?

"Gun work out okay for you?"

"Yeah." I thought it would have a big kick, but it didn't. It was light and easy to use.

"I picked it myself. Top-of-the-line."

I thought it might be too small to do much good, but it stopped the dead woman cold. It made me think back to that time the revivor got into my apartment and grabbed me. It was so strong, I couldn't do anything to stop it. It killed my neighbor, almost killed Karen, and took me away. I was totally helpless. There was nothing I could do. It was different in the alley. It didn't matter that I couldn't control the revivor. The gun changed everything.

"Is it really okay to just kill that woman?"

"Who, Calliope?"

"Yeah."

"Let me tell you something about her," Penny said. "We looked into her background, and you know what we found? She was raised in a state-run orphanage, but her mother didn't drop her off there; she sold the fetus off to one of those church-run facilities, where they grew her to term in a jar. That name of hers was randomly generated by a computer. How do you like that?"

"Really?"

"Those places don't have the room for all the ones that come in. The computer runs a lotto to weed them out when space gets tight. It's all based on genetic profiles and all automatic, so no one has to feel guilty. You know how many times she got passed over while she was there?"

"No."

"Thirteen times. Thirteen! That's beyond luck. She shouldn't even be alive. She was born to do this."

I nodded, but I wasn't sure.

"Look, if it bothers you, think of it this way—she's going to save a lot of people. Doesn't that make it worth it?"

"Is she really going to stop it from happening?"

"That's the plan."

"Will it work?"

"There's a chance that it will."

"So it might not."

"It beats doing nothing," she said. "Anyway, it's not even just about this one incident. Even if the city survives, look around it. It's rotting from the inside. The people who live in it are sheep who sell themselves to their government, literally. Their votes haven't meant anything for years. We didn't make it that way; they were living under the illusion they had any say in what went on for as far back as anyone can remember. Things were never going to change, not until we came along, not until we got organized. All Fawkes and his people can think about is their precious freedom. It's ridiculous. They're not free. They never were."

"I guess."

"People like Fawkes, they need to be removed. With them out of the way, things will start to get better. We won't get credit for it and we'll never get thanked, but things will get better."

The bubbles and the heat had me sleepy and kind of giddy.

"Anyway, you'd be crazy not to love the perks," Penny said. "The living arrangements, the clothes, the cars, the food, booze—everything. It beats scraping by."

". . . and you really think I might be this person?" I asked. "You really think I might be the one Ai is looking for?"

"I really think so."

She grinned, nudging me with her foot under the water.

"You're like me," she said. "We're not just one of them. We've got something even a lot of our own kind doesn't have."

"We do?"

"It's like anything else; some people are better at things than others. Not everyone can do what you did to Ted. We're a cut above, you and me. We're elite."

Elite.

It sank in for the first time then. I wasn't sure if it was the heat or the booze, or if I was just finally coming to terms with it, but right then at that moment, I felt it. I could see it. That woman I saw in the green room all those years ago, the one that looked rich and strong and together . . . that woman was me. I could see it. It could be my life. I didn't have to be a pathetic shut-in, and I didn't have to be a lackey either, getting used while I waited and hoped for a scrap of approval. I could be something bigger.

. . . but what about the first one? A nagging voice said. *What about Noelle? What made her betray them? If Penny's right about everything, what made her leave?*

She messed up. Maybe she wasn't in her right mind. She was a junkie. I didn't have to end up like her.

Don't cross Ai. That was what Penny said. It was one simple rule. Even I could handle that.

Calliope Flax—KM *Senopati Nusantara*

Footsteps came from the right up ahead. As soon as we hit the bend, something grabbed my number one. A shot went off and it got pulled around the corner, while my second took the lead. Shots boomed down the hall.

They kept them busy to the right. I went left. In the feed, I saw number one facing off with four jacks. The view pitched as it took a few hits, but one of its targets went down.

Two, stay with me; cover the rear. One, keep them under fire. If they get past you, detonate.

I slipped past and kept my head low. A shot clipped my boot and another hit the wall next to me as I banked left and covered the ground to the hatch up ahead. I spun the wheel and opened it, then ducked through. As the jack followed me in, I watched over the feed while the one I left behind took a volley that put it down. One arm ripped free at the elbow and spun to the floor. When it hit, it snapped open and the blade shot out.

I shoved the hatch shut as I looked back and saw its head get blown open, painting the deck behind it black. The feed went out. I locked the door and made for the next one, across the room.

Through here.

I was already down to my last jack. There were more out there, but they were on to me. I was locked out of their network. It was going to have to be enough.

The hatch opened into a big room full of bunks. No one was in them.

Watch the door.

I checked the place out. It was empty. I saw a set of clothes on the deck, shirt still tucked in the pants. They were shot through with holes. Down the rows of bunks, there were more of them.

Some of the crew got caught sleeping, it looked like. There was dried blood on the bedding. One pillow still had the dent from a head in it. A fucking JZI sat in the dent like a big, fat bug.

The lockers hung open. If any of them had guns or ammo, it was gone now.

I checked my route to the med wing; I was close. Bomb or no bomb, I could use the backup. That's if Wachalowski made it there.

The pain hit again, and I grabbed the bunk frame to keep from going down.

They rigged you with a bomb.

I peeled up my shirt and looked at my belly. Tucked in the crease of my abs were four red dots. I ran my fingers over them. They were sore and scabbed over.

Shit . . .

I leaned in and used the backscatter. Inside I could see the bottom of my ribs. Lower, under the scabs, something stood out. It looked like wires under the skin.

I followed them under my belt line. There was something down there, down in the bones of my pelvis.

Cal, how long?

Almost there. I was still staring at it. It was just like we used to do with the jacks back in the grind. It was in me. The fucking thing was inside me.

You don't have much time. Hurry.

Someone knocked me out and wired me up. How long had it been there?

"Goddamn it . . ." I knew what those things could do. I'd seen them go off. I'd set them off myself.

There was no way for me to shut down a bomb like that, and I knew it. If Wachalowski had a plan, it was my best bet—maybe my only one.

I pushed myself off the bunk frame and ran for the hatch on the far side of the room.

Nico Wachalowski—KM *Senopati Nusantara*

The entry point into the ship put me in a stairwell where a major firefight had taken place; the walls were scarred with gunfire, and blood spatter that was equal parts red and black. Two sets of clothing were draped down the steps. Another set was crumpled on the landing. The revivors made their entry there. The crew made a stand, but from the look of it, they weren't successful.

I headed down the steps and passed two more sets of clothes on the landing. Shell casings littered the floor. The air in the stairwell smelled of decomposition, but it was faint. Whatever happened there happened a long time ago.

I found the med ward on the blueprint and sprinted down the hall alongside an old blood trail. At the junction, they'd piled up metal cabinets that were crimped and bored through with holes. More remains were piled behind them.

The route took me through a hatch, past the barricade, where I passed different sets of clothing bundled in rough rows. Tied plastic bands lay on the floor near each one.

Wrist ties. They lined them up here.

I saw shorts, tank tops, and brightly colored shirts. They probably didn't belong to the crew . . . pirates, maybe, or local mercenaries. If they used hired guns, then they must not have had the numbers to take the ship alone. Either way, no one got off the ship alive. The weapons and ammo were gathered up. The corpses were dissolved, eaten, or went over the side.

The deck drummed faintly under my boots. Over the sound of the engine, I could hear movement in the halls of the ship below me, a lot of movement. I couldn't pinpoint locations, but the number of signatures I was picking up was off the chart.

In the corridor past the hatchway, moving walkways hummed along in opposite directions.

They've diverted power. They're on the move.

Roger that. Wachalowski, we're picking up signatures approaching from belowdecks.

I checked the blueprint again. The signatures were jumbled, but it looked like most originated from the hold and were spreading out from there. I stepped onto the walkway to the right and crouched. As it sped me down a long corridor, I heard a burst of gunfire coming from another part of the ship.

A revivor signature came up suddenly on the display, with a second one right behind it. Up ahead, two sets of eyes flashed in the dark.

We've got contact, one of the team called in. *Surface-to-air missile teams spotted on deck at points B and C.*

Roger that. Locking on.

A big boom shook the floor underneath me, and the emergency lights flickered. One of the revivors up ahead fired, and a bullet glanced off the deck next to me. I targeted the first one and fired a burst. Its left knee exploded and as its leg went out from under it, it went facedown on the walk. The conveyor jerked it back and it bowled over the one behind it. I caught the second one in the forehead as it tried to get up, and its gun clattered across the deck.

The revivor with the ruptured knee pushed itself off the walk and took aim down the hall. I fired three shots. It squeezed off a round before my third shot took it down. The bullet caught me in my left shoulder, and

I staggered. Blood seeped into my shirt, and when I moved my arm, pain bored into my chest.

The floor shook again as the sound of explosions boomed through the corridors. They were firing missiles onto the deck of the tanker in response to the stingers.

Wachalowski, we're getting swarmed. What's your status down there?

I released a painkiller into my bloodstream, followed by one of the stim packs. Right away, the pain began to dull and the corridor seemed to get brighter. I moved close to the fallen revivor being carried on the belt along with me, and scanned for its signature. It was weak, but hadn't cut out yet. I used the modification I'd installed in the grind to sample the wave.

I'm getting close.

Is the bomb still in play?

Yes.

The bulk of the revivor signatures were coming in fast. They'd be on me any minute. I recorded a full loop of the revivor's signature and began to transmit it. Feedback spiked until I put a single round in the fallen revivor and the redundant signature cut out. It wouldn't be perfect, but in the dark and the confusion, it would keep them off me long enough.

The walkway carried me along as a trickle of sweat rolled down my back. Adrenaline and oxygen flooded my system, keeping me alert. I fumbled a dose of blood-clotting serum out of my pack. Pressing the end to the wound, I pushed the plunger, and pain shot down my arm. The spent cartridge dropped from my hand and rolled off, trailing smoke. The tissue around the wound puckered as the blood hardened into a plug.

The hatch I was looking for was up ahead. I jumped

off the walk and a wave of nausea hit. I clenched my throat, tasting vomit as I went through the opening and came out on a walkway above the cargo hold. I slipped, catching the railing, then made a sprint for the doorway on the opposite side.

Cal, where are you?

I made it. I'm in the med ward.

On the map, I saw several signatures headed her way. They'd picked up her heartbeat and her body heat.

Give me full access to your JZI. I'm going to try to connect to the device.

It's in me.

I know.

Down in the hold, I saw stacks of stasis crates. There were hundreds of them. They cast shadows that flickered in the light of thousands of revivor optical cells. They were moving, flowing in the dark like traffic through a city street at night. They sensed a warm body on the walk above them, but the signature I transmitted had confused them. Several looked up, not sure what they were seeing.

"Stop!"

At the end of the walkway, I caught a glimpse of Faye standing below. She was with three other revivors. Our eyes met for just a second; then I was through the hatch and into the dark corridor behind it.

Cal opened her JZI and I used the package the MSST gave me with to try to connect to the bomb. After a few seconds, it managed to establish a link.

I'm pulling the stats from the device. Hold on.

Information came streaming in. It was true; the payload was nuclear. It was wired to her, but the trigger itself was on a timer that started when she passed a certain distance from shore.

Hold on.

The corridor ahead was filled with debris, and soot had formed on the walls. The hatch at the end had been blown from its hinges and pushed out of the way. I squeezed through into a room where several bodies lay, dead from thirst.

I pulled the information for the timer from the device. She didn't have much time. Once the virus was injected, it could take up to several minutes for it to break through and disarm the device. That was assuming it could do it at all.

Cal, do you see a bed there?

Yeah.

The med facility has auxiliary power. Find a bed near a power source and get in it. We won't have much time.

Roger that.

I ran through the hatch on the opposite side of the room, down a hallway filled with human remains. She was close. There wasn't time to take in the bones and the bloated revivors lying among them. There was only time to run, and I could feel my strength fading.

Give me something . . . Give me anything . . . anything to buy me some time.

I planted the virus and it began to drill into the bomb's systems. As I ran, I saw warning lights flash up red as it tried one deactivation failsafe after the next, and failed.

Nico, it's not working. . . .

I ran through a set of quarters where the crew had slept, through the door on the other side and down the corridor. The medical ward was through the hatch just up ahead. I saw movement down the hall to my right, where at least twenty revivors were thundering toward us, their eyes bobbing in the dark as they ran.

Cal, hold on . . .

More warning lights turned red. The virus had nearly exhausted its options and still hadn't gotten through. Countermeasures added to the device had detected it and were shutting it out. It wasn't going to work.

There were less than ten minutes left on the timer. The virus was being dismantled and the bomb was still active. It would take hours to get her back to shore and to a facility where they might be able to shut it down. I wasn't going to make it. I needed more time.

Wachalowski.

Cal.

It's getting hot. I can feel it.

I shoved the door open and staggered inside. Calliope was lying on one of the hospital beds, waiting. When she looked up at me, her eyes were full of tears and her face was red. Veins stood out in her face and neck. I was too late. She knew it.

I need more time. . . .

"Nico," she said.

"I'm here. Hold on. We're about to get company. Do you have an Eckles Transponder? Can you spoof a revivor signature?"

She shook her head, but I'd already scanned her systems. She didn't; the transponder wasn't standard issue. I might sneak through that many revivors undetected, but she wouldn't. They'd tear her apart.

"It didn't work," she said.

"I know."

"You did what you could. Get the fuck—"

"Shut up."

There was only one thing I could think to do. I hauled the stasis emitter on its track until it was right over the bed. I turned it on and guided it down over her torso. I pointed the lens at the middle of her chest.

"We're going to die," she said.

I flipped the switch. The stasis field was focused in a six-inch beam. It radiated through her breastbone and engulfed her heart, stopping it instantly.

The timer ticked down as her muscles relaxed, then went still. The pulsing under her jaw stopped. The light went out of her eyes.

I heard movement behind me and glanced back to see many eyes staring back from the shadows. They'd lost the vitals they'd been tracking, and were scanning around the room, trying to relocate them.

I turned back to Cal and drew my field knife. Looking through the muscle wall of her abdomen, I could see the device nestled in there.

Wachalowski, there are too many of them. We have to sink it. Report for immediate extraction.

I was no surgeon, but it was the only chance she had. I eased the tip of the knife through the skin beneath her belly button and the hard muscle underneath.

Wachalowski, do you copy?

Blood was running out of the wound. I focused, keeping the knife clear of the dark artery that showed up on the backscatter. I felt the tip touch the shell of the device, and saw it move inside of her.

The virus failed, I said. *I can't stop the bomb. I'm coming up.*

How long before detonation?

Eight minutes.

Understood. We'll wait as long as we can.

The revivors had begun moving through the room, not sure what to do. Several focused on me, trying to resolve the signature with the body heat they detected. If one of them grabbed me, that might be all it would take to set them off.

How many to be extracted, Wachalowski?

I grabbed a set of glorified pliers from a rack of surgical tools and held the tip above the wound. As soon as I pulled the knife free, more blood pumped out, and I jammed the pliers into the hole. As the warmth rushed over my fist, I found the edge of the device and grabbed it.

It didn't want to come. I winced as I pulled it free anyway and dropped the small, sticky brick and its trailing wires into a bedside pan. I injected blood clotter into the wound and watched it harden. Calliope's face was gray, the color fading from her lips.

Wachalowski, come back. What about your civilian?

I cut the connection.

12

Resurrection

Faye Dasalia—KM *Senopati Nusantara*

"We've got him," a voice shouted. Revivors carrying backscatter scanners walked atop the stacks of crates. One of them waved to the others down below. A loud snap from above echoed through the hold, followed by the whine of electric motors. One of the winches moved to retrieve the crate.

"Probability?"

"Near one hundred percent."

The cable lowered, and they attached the hooks. Ice flaked away with a crunch as the crate was pulled from the rest of the stack. They began lowering it down toward the deck.

An explosion thudded from somewhere above, and the lights overhead swayed, throwing shadows. A metal groan came from the remaining stacks, and something clanged to the floor. The men below used poles to steady the crate as the cable brought it in.

Someone has boarded the ship. The words flashed in

front of me. It was a broadcast from Fawkes. The thousands of eyes in the hold stopped moving, all at once becoming fixed.

The scout teams were unsuccessful. Find them and stop them.

The sound of a thousand weapons readying cracked through the hold like thunder. The figures began to move.

Above them, the winch lowered the stasis crate. It met the deck with a thud as the revival team moved in. The metal surface was dull and spotted with corrosion. There was lettering stenciled on its surface in both English and Hebrew.

"Open it," one of them said.

Two revivors stepped closer. One released the magnetic restraining bolts while the other broke the seal. Air rushed in with a loud hiss as they pulled the cover free. Mist trailed from the door as it was thrown aside.

Secure the nukes, Fawkes broadcast. *Those responsible for carrying them, retreat to the engine room. The power core there will mask the radiation. Once they are confirmed below, seal off the engine room and keep it secure. A second team will secure the bridge and keep it locked down at any cost.*

An armed helicopter has approached the helipad, a report said. *Only one confirmed.*

Take that helicopter out. Get as many stingers up there as you can. They can't stop them all. Do not allow them back onto the helipad; whoever boarded does not get back on that helicopter.

A stasis blister bulged there inside the crate, and I saw a male figure inside it. A revivor deployed its bayonet and jabbed the tip through the blister. It slit the plastic open and the stasis fluid inside flooded out. Two others plunged their arms into the thick soup and grabbed the figure inside. They lifted it out, arms and legs dangling, and more approached as it was placed on the deck.

One sprayed the body with a jet of water, washing it clean while others scanned it. I got a look at its face under the lights, and realized that I knew it. He was bonier now than in his pictures, and black veins wormed beneath skin that was pale and thin, but I still recognized him. The man was Samuel Fawkes.

"It's him," one of the revivors near him said. "Confirmed. It's him. We've got him."

Samuel Fawkes had been murdered; we knew that. A C-shaped dermal patch stood out on his side, just underneath the right side of his rib cage; I remembered it now from the crime photos. That's where that strange street woman had stuck the knife. She'd meant to kill him then, and she almost did. She believed her own people would come for her when they found out what she did. She disobeyed an order. . . . After that, she disappeared.

The second skin patch had sealed a deeper wound, where flesh puckered around his left jugular. He had lived for three more years, before a second murder attempt was made. The second was successful.

If the memories of it hadn't been taken, it would have been clear as day; at least one person had wanted to kill him, and at least one person wanted him alive.

Are they not as organized as we first thought?

A revivor pulled the tube out of his throat. Another held a metal wand to his neck. With an electric snap, his body convulsed, muscle striations standing out in shadow. The sound crackled through the hold as the soldiers continued to file out. Smoke began to rise from the metal wand in thin threads, and then a new signature began to initialize. It coalesced, and snapped into its waveform.

The waveform contained his encoded ID—that same ID that had reached out from far off, from across the desert and across the sea. It was here in front of me. As I stood and stared, I could feel him reaching. As the others helped him up onto his feet, he extended a connection out to me. I accepted the circuit, while he stood up for the first time in ten years.

Faye.

Yes. It's me. I'm over here.

Samuel Fawkes opened his eyes. A faint silver light swelled, and began to grow brighter.

Nico Wachalowski—KM *Senopati Nusantara*

With Calliope's body hoisted on one shoulder, I pushed through the throng of revivors as fast as I could. They'd noticed the blood on the gurney and were nosing past us to get at it. I adjusted her weight and headed out into the main corridor. Something crashed in the med ward behind me as I stepped onto the moving walkway and eased her down. My vision blurred as I knelt over her body, gasping. Another crowd of revivors was moving through the corridor up ahead. I couldn't risk reviving her yet, but I couldn't wait much longer. Her JZI would keep her blood oxygenated for a short time, but not forever.

The eyes watched us impassively as the walkway took us past them. As they receded into the shadows, several of them began to take notice, but none followed.

An explosion drummed through the ship, and the emergency lights went out completely. A beat later, the walkway slowed to a stop.

Shit . . .

The revivors behind us still hadn't moved. The way ahead looked clear. I turned on a flashlight and lifted Cal up again, pain shooting through my legs.

Something darted across the beam ahead, but whatever it was, it didn't stop for us. I staggered down the corridor, then shouldered open a door to my right, taking us into a stairwell. Up above, I could hear wind whistling through the open hatch. Gunfire cracked above the sound of waves.

She's unconscious and we're coming up. Can you clear a path?

Can do. Hold position.

A whine rose in pitch, then the sound of the helicopter's chain gun blared. A torrent of rounds crashed off the deck as the racket drowned out everything else, then stopped ten seconds later.

Okay, you're clear. Move now.

I hung on to the rail and hauled her up as cold, wet air blew down the stairwell. Over the ringing in my ears I could hear the wind howling on the deck, and the thump of helicopter rotors on the helipad outside.

Make straight for the airlift.

Got it.

Open flames blew in the wind as rain and smoke sheared across the deck in front of me. The ship tilted as a wave swelled, its nose rising in front of us. Ahead I could see the helipad. Most of the MSST who were left were inside, but two were moving toward us, carrying a stretcher between them. One of the men stopped to fire at something off to his left. I waved to one of the soldiers on the pad.

We're here.

We see you.

An explosion went off, and fire climbed into the night sky as the surface of the water lit up. Soldiers on the helipad began firing at something off to their left. The two soldiers on deck reached us and helped me get Cal strapped in.

Now. Go now.

They ran, Cal's body swaying on the stretcher between them as they made their way back. I stayed behind and covered them as more revivors appeared on the deck behind us. The rain was driving now, making it hard to see them, let alone target them.

Nico.

I turned toward the spot where the soldiers had fired. A small group of figures gathered on the deck, eyes glowing softly in the dark. As the spotlight swept over them, I saw a tarp come free, taken by the wind. It cracked like a whip and blew off into the darkness, revealing a small aircraft underneath.

Nico, wait.

As the floodlight focused on them, I saw Faye standing near the aircraft. Her coat whipped in the wind as she met my eye. Behind me, the MSST leader had spotted them.

We've got more hostiles on deck. Take them out.
Wait. Hold your fire.

There was another revivor next to Faye, a male. It had a coat draped over its shoulders, but was naked underneath. Its skin was waxy, and even at that distance I could see the network of dark veins underneath it.

As gruesome as it looked, though, I recognized that face. I zoomed in on it to be sure.

Fawkes.

He looked past Faye and met my eye. It was definitely him. Fawkes was out of stasis.

I took aim across the deck and fired. With the weather and the movement of the ship, the shot went wild and clipped his shoulder, dotting Faye's face with black spots.

Nico, wait.

I moved toward him and slipped on the deck. I went down hard on one knee and pulled the trigger again as pain shot up my thigh. By then, the others were crowding him. I caught one of them in the back of the head as it moved to shield him. Faye stepped into the line of fire.

My finger tightened on the trigger. From behind Faye, Fawkes was still staring at me.

You kill Fawkes.

Ai had said that. She said it at the restaurant where she first dragged me into the case. To her, it was a given. To her, it was something that couldn't be changed.

I might be able to shoot past Faye and hit him. The dark spot that floated in front of my eyes darted back and forth over his face as he watched me.

You kill Fawkes.

They were starting to move him, with Faye between us. My finger tightened on the trigger.

Wachalowski, what are you doing? Take him.

Faye broke from her position and ran across the deck toward me. Fawkes looked back over his shoulder and watched as she stopped in front of me. She stood there, like she wasn't sure what to do.

I began to move the gun toward her when she grabbed my lapels and, before I could stop her, she kissed me on the mouth.

I began to move back, but she wrapped one arm around the back of my neck, pulling me closer, and I felt her fingers move through my hair. It had been years since we'd kissed, and even in the middle of the chaos, it struck me how familiar it felt, how that one, small, human part of her hadn't changed. Her kiss was exactly the same as it had been before. Her lips were cold now, but still soft, and just like she had all those years ago, she still had the power to disarm me. As crazy as it was, there was still some small part of me that surrendered in her arms. There was still some part of me that remembered when my duty was to her and her alone. I'd meant to push her away, but when my hands found her waist, I didn't.

She broke the kiss and hugged me, pressing her cheek to mine as she extended a connection and I accepted.

This is for the best, she said. I felt the shot before I heard it.

I staggered back, slipping out of her arms as she aimed the pistol and fired a second shot. It struck the body armor above my solar plexus, an inch from the first shot. It didn't penetrate, but for a second I couldn't breathe as I fell back onto the deck.

Faye turned, smoke drifting from the barrel, and ran back to Fawkes and the others. Gasping, I raised my gun and fired after her, but between the rain and the motion of the ship, I couldn't get a clear shot. Fawkes climbed onto the escape aircraft as Faye reached them, and I saw her grab the rail and climb in after him.

"Wachalowski!" a voice shouted from behind me. I turned and grabbed the hand that was waiting, and climbed in as the helicopter began to lift off. As it pulled away, I saw the other craft below rise quickly, then the rotors turned and it banked quickly in the other direction as another explosion shook the ship. By the time the smoke began to clear, we were far overhead and moving away. One of the soldiers heaved the door shut.

"Three minutes, people! Get us clear now!"

"Cal!"

I pushed my way in next to her as the helicopter bucked in the wind. Leaning over her body, I released the stop I put on her JZI systems. It saw her vitals had tanked, and sent a jolt of electricity to her heart.

Come on . . .

Energy was building in the musculature around her spine and neck. The JZI detected it, but couldn't identify what it was. Her heart was still stopped. It sent another jolt.

Come on, Cal . . .

Emergency systems were feeding oxygen into her bloodstream and had begun a regular pulse to keep the heart beating artificially. That would work for only so long. I watched her face in the dark.

Cal, are you there?

The energy collecting at the base of her neck had me worried. I focused on it, looking through the muscle tissue. There was movement in there. Something was forming. As I watched, small nodes began to grow.

Huma. She'd been injected. She was already carrying the serum. The mechanisms inside had realized she was dead. The nodes began to branch out, connections forming between them.

I overrode her JZI and forced a payload of adrenaline into her bloodstream. There was a chance it would kill her outright, but she was out of time. Her heart seized. For a second her vitals pegged into the red, but through the stream of warning data I saw her heart catch; it beat on its own.

"Cal, wake up!"

The components had stopped forming. Her heart began to beat regularly. She opened her eyes.

"Cal!"

"Shit . . . you're here," she said.

"I'm here." I went to touch her shoulder, but she batted my hand away.

"What happened?"

"We're off the ship. We're going home."

She grimaced as she sat up and looked back out toward the ocean. The ship began to fade in the rain and the dark, and all I could see was the faint flicker of a fire on the deck.

"This is MSST. We have secured the civilians and are on our way back. We need an EMT at the landing site."

"Roger that, MSST."

"Detonation in three . . . two . . . one . . ."

The timer was still displayed on my JZI. I watched it trickle down to zero.

The flash was so bright I had to close my eyes and turn away.

13

Eddish

Calliope Flax—Mercy Greaves Medical Center

My left hand tingled. It tingled all the time, and it was cold, like the blood was cut off. I woke up to it every day. I stared in the dark and listened to the whispering.

It was still dark. I was still in the med unit, and I was still on dope. Nico managed not to kill me getting the bomb out, but he left a hell of a hole.

When I was out, I dreamed I was back in Juba. My left arm was a stump, and I grabbed my hand off the floor and threw it. The mob went for it. They fought over it and ate it. The crunching sound was burned into my brain, but in the dream, all I heard was a hiss. It was like static. When I woke up, I could still hear it. It was like a sound from deep in my head. Quiet, but steady. It made me think of voices, all whispering.

I thought it was the drugs at first. It wasn't the drugs. *What the fuck did you do to me, Buckster?*

Someone knocked on the door. I figured it was the nurse on duty, but when the door cracked, it was Wachalowski's ugly mug I saw. He had one arm in a sling and stitches over one eye. There was stubble on his face, and he looked older than usual.

"You're awake," he said.

"That your FBI training?" He smiled, even though I could see it hurt.

"Can I come in?"

"Knock yourself out."

He came in and closed the door behind him. He pulled up a chair next to my bed and sat down.

"How are you feeling?"

"How do you think?"

The whole thing got messed up. It was supposed to be easy. It was cakewalk; he was an old man. I thought I'd get in good with the Feds. I thought I'd get in good with him.

"I'm sorry, Cal."

"Sorry for what?"

"I should never have—"

"Oh, shut the hell up," I said. "Is that why you're here? Because you think this is your fault? Because you feel bad?"

"No."

"Because I swear I will fucking pop you—"

"That's not why I came. I wanted to see how you were."

"What are you, my dad?" I didn't really know what I was talking about, though. I never had a dad. He didn't answer anyway. He just smiled again, and I thought he looked relieved. It hit me, then, how tired he looked.

"I'm just glad you're still here."

"Yeah," I said. "I get it."

He was quiet for a minute, and I added, "I like you too. Fucker."

"Can I get you anything?"

"You can get me the hell out of here."

"You're going to be here a little while. Sorry."

I shrugged.

"It beats being dead. Thanks for coming to get me."

"You're welcome."

"So, is it over?"

"No."

"It never is."

I looked up at him, and watched the orange light flicker in his pupils. In my head, those voices whispered. It was like wind.

"I hear things," I told him. "In my head. I don't think it's from the JZI."

He made a cutting motion across his throat, shutting me up. His face got serious.

It's not from the JZI.

Then what? What do you know?

Something happened back on the boat.

What?

We were about to get mobbed. The revivors were homing in on you, and I needed you out to make the cut. I stopped your heart.

You stopped my heart?

I was counting on the JZI to revive you. It did—

How long was I out?

Not long. Your heart began to beat again, obviously, but for a few minutes your vitals were flat.

Are you saying I was dead?

For a few minutes, yes.

"A few minutes?" I snapped. He made the cutting motion again. "No, don't fucking shush me—"

Cal, be quiet. It was that or they'd have torn you apart. I didn't know you'd been injected.

Injected. I remembered Buckster and the case. I remembered the needle they stuck in my neck.

Injected with what?

Fawkes got his hands on an experimental revivor prototype developed at Heinlein Industries. It's introduced through the injection of a serum. Buckster and his followers were distributing it. You must have been injected with it before I got there.

So what are you saying? What does this mean?

It means you're wired, Cal. When your heart stopped, it activated. Some kind of connection was formed to a revivor network.

I can't be wired.

I'm sorry. You are. If you die now, you'll come back.

My teeth went on edge. My dead hand made a fist.

They can't do that.

They did do it.

Well, fucking undo it.

I'm working on that.

Working on it?

I don't know for sure what we're dealing with yet. Just keep it quiet for now.

I can't keep it quiet. It's talking in my fucking head. Get it the fuck out.

"Cal, calm down," he said. He put his hand on my shoulder and eased me back. "Calm down. I will. Understand?"

My heart was pounding, but my gut hurt and I felt dizzy. I nodded.

"I'll come get you in the morning," he said. "We'll figure it out from there."

I nodded again.

I don't want to come back.

I won't let that happen.

Promise me.

"I promise," he said. It was easy for him to say, but I believed him. I felt a little better, knowing he had my back.

"You've got a few hours left before sunup," he said. "Try to get some sleep."

I sighed and settled back. I think the drip was kicking in again. I watched him get up and walk back to the door. My brain still buzzed, even through the morphine. When I was sure he was down the hall, I cracked the bed frame with my fist.

Sleep.

I didn't scare easy. I wasn't so dumb I never got scared, but I didn't scare easy. I never was scared to die, not in Bullrich and not in Juba, but lying in that bed, I was scared. I was scared to die.

I won't let that happen.

My heart was beating fast. I tried to slow it down, but I couldn't.

You better not, Nico.

You better not let me come back.

Zoe Ott—Alto Do Mundo

"Zoe," a voice said.

It was dark, and I felt weightless. My arms and legs floated in the warmth that surrounded me. For the first time in as long as I could remember, I felt totally relaxed. I felt totally content.

"Zoe..."

I opened my eyes just a little. Nico was there. He wore slacks and a white undershirt. His clothes and his shoelaces kind of floated around him like he was underwater. His arms were out by his sides and his body was limp, like he was suspended in space. One of his arms was normal, but the other one, the one with the tattoo, was a totally different color. The skin was gray, and I could see black veins bulging underneath.

"What do you want?" I asked.

"It's not too late," he said.

"Too late for what?"

He didn't answer; he just stared at me. His shirt moved, and I could see where the gray arm joined the rest of his body. There was a clean seam there, but the black veins had started to cross it and branch under his regular skin. When he opened his mouth, I could see blood on his teeth. It began to slowly drift out from between his lips, forming a cloud. I was floating too. We were both underwater, but we could both still breathe.

"What's wrong with you?" I asked him.

"It's not too late to save them," he said.

"They're already saved," I told him. "The ship blew up. We fixed it."

Nico shook his head slowly.

The blood coming out of his mouth was turning everything pink. It started to get darker, until he seemed to turn red in front of me.

"You can still save them."

I opened my mouth to ask who, when his face changed. His eyes bugged out and his mouth opened wide like he was trying to scream. His body convulsed in the water, muscles standing out under the skin.

"Nico?"

Black dots appeared in the whites of his eyes and began to bleed like ink blots.

"Nico!"

All at once his face collapsed, the skin pulling tight against the skull underneath until I couldn't recognize him anymore. I screamed as his lips peeled back to show teeth and bloody gums. His eyes bulged as the skin around them sank back into the sockets. The skin around his neck wrinkled, and the whole base of his skull melted away underneath the skin.

He reached out for me, his misshapen head bobbing on the end of what was left of his shriveled neck, as black clouds began to bleed into the water around us.

I tried to scream again, but I couldn't breathe. When I tried to take a breath I choked, and panic pricked in my chest.

I can't breathe....

Thrashing, I began to hear a low rumbling sound. Above me, I could hear water splashing. I opened my eyes all the way and he was gone. The blood was gone and the darkness was gone too. There was light up over my head, rippling like it was on the surface of the water. There was smooth plastic under the palms of my hands, and when I kicked, my heel thumped against something hard.

Pushing off the floor, my face broke the surface of the water and I gasped. I was sitting in a tub full of warm water. It was bubbling around me. I started coughing until water dribbled out of my mouth and nose. Where the hell was I?

Looking around, I saw I was still sitting in the hot tub where Penny and I were hanging out the night before. There were empty bottles and glasses sitting on the marble edge of it. I held up my hands and saw that they were wrinkled like prunes.

I must have passed out. I'd passed out and slid underwater. How long had I been down there? I could have drowned.

"What was that?" I gasped. "What the hell was that?"

I tried to stand, but the heat had me woozy. It took a minute for me to get myself up onto the edge. The marble was cold on my butt as I swiveled my legs out and put my feet down on the floor.

I slipped and almost fell, but I managed to grab the sink in time. My body felt like it weighed a ton. In the mirror, I saw that my face was dark red.

When I got my balance back, I let go of the sink and peeled off my bathing suit. I tossed it on the floor and took one of the big, white robes off the hook on the bathroom door. It was cool and soft when I wrapped it around myself.

I opened the door and stepped out into the hallway. In the living room, I could hear Penny snoring on the couch. My stomach turned when the cool air hit me, and my hands started to shake a little. I ducked back into the bathroom and found an open flask that sloshed when I shook it. I tipped it back and swallowed until no more came out. It burned going down, and my stomach rolled, but it didn't reject it. After a minute, it calmed down and I started to feel a little better, but I couldn't get the image of Nico's deformed head out of my mind.

What was that? We fixed this. We won.

The TV in the living room was on, but Penny was passed out, still in her bathing suit. I tossed a blanket over her and plodded off to the computer room, where the database was still up on the computer. The shades were drawn, and the lines of light around them were gray. I pulled up the chair and fell into it.

I brought up the database model and stared at it. Nothing looked any different, but it was hard to tell. The huge fractal shape looked the same, and the big dark spot in the middle was still there. The bright star still sat on the rim. Did it not work?

I tried to remember everything Penny had said the night before, but it was fuzzy. From what I could piece together, the ship they kept talking about blew up before it got to shore. Stopping the people on the ship was important. It was so important, they'd sacrificed that woman, the mean one from the elevator ... element two, they called her. But that's what she was for, wasn't it? Hadn't Penny said that?

There was a bottle sitting on the desktop, and I grabbed it. I took a swig from it and sighed. My throat ached and my eyes watered.

I brought up the data miner and punched in NICO and REVIVOR. That got a bunch of hits. My hand shook as I called some out on the screen at random and skimmed the passages:

Element Three will be immune to phasing, similar to a revivor, though still alive. . . .

Most likely candidate is Wachalowski, Nico . . .

. . . I was not able to successfully influence him, although he could still be read . . .

. . . aspects of a revivor, in both mind and body . . .

One entry included a scan of a charcoal drawing someone had done. It didn't look exactly like Nico, but it was close. His right arm was joined to his body with stitches, and there were black veins branching under the skin.

. . . will destroy Element Zero.

There was nothing about what I'd just seen; the arm was the same, but there was nothing about his face changing like it did. I tried again, typing in "black" and "eyes," but that brought up too many references. The ones I bothered to look at talked about bruises, shiners. I typed "face," and then got stuck. My hands shook as I held them over the keypad.

"Bad dream?" I heard Penny say. I turned and saw her in the doorway, the blanket around her shoulders like a cape.

"Sorry," I said. "Did I wake you up?"

"No."

She crossed the room and stood beside me, looking at the screen. She looked at my search history for a minute, then reached over my shoulder and typed with one hand. She erased "face," and entered something else in:

VAGOTT DEFORMATION

The miner spun around for a few seconds, and then three green points appeared. Like the hits I'd gotten on the green room, all three were inside the dark center of the cloud.

My heart thumped in my chest as I touched one of the entries. The image that popped up made me jump in my chair.

"That's it," I whispered. It was just a drawing, but the face was the same as Nico's had been in the vision; head collapsed like a rotten fruit, on the end of a bent-stick neck. The whites of the eyes were dotted with black spots, and the lips were peeled back over long, crowded teeth. He was dressed in some kind of military uniform, with a name patch on it that read VAGOTT.

"I guess it was a bad dream," Penny said, pulling up a chair and sitting down next to me.

"What does it mean?"

"No one knows," she said. "Almost no one's ever seen it. That's the best lead we've had, and it's not much."

"Lead for what?"

"Stuff that happens in the void happens after what Ai calls the Event," she said, pointing. "It's empty because no one ever reports seeing anything from that point on."

"Because they're dead," I said.

"Worse than that," she said. "Nothing phases past that point, which means, if Ai is right, that of all the possible outcomes, almost nothing ever gets through. That's a pretty big hole."

"So it's the end of everything? Forever?"

Penny shrugged. "Probably not," she said. "But for us, and everyone walking parallel . . . maybe we're doomed to make the same mistakes."

I stared back at the screen. The dots stood out, very close to where the entries for the green room were stored. So far, nothing on the other side of the rim looked worth surviving for, but if I'd seen it . . .

"I thought we stopped it," I said. Penny squeezed my shoulder.

"Hey, the nukes didn't go off," she said. "That seems to trigger the rest, so who knows? Things don't change overnight. Give it time."

I nodded, but a bad feeling had wormed its way inside of me, and I couldn't shake it. Even when I drank most of the rest of the bottle, it didn't budge. I recognized the uniform Vagott was wearing; I'd seen it before in one of my visions. I'd seen it the last time I was in the green room.

A group of uniformed men came down the hall toward the door, shoving a man in handcuffs ahead of them. Behind them I'd seen a woman, partly in shadow . . . a small, skinny woman with her hair in a bun, and a beaklike nose. I never got a good look at her face, but it was me.

I was sure it was me.

Nico Wachalowski—FBI Home Office

Four hours after the *Senopati Nusantara* was destroyed, and two hours after I left Calliope in the hospital, I sat behind a locked door in the Federal Building. Alice Hsieh stood against the wall next to me, her arms crossed in front of her as we watched a display monitor mounted on the wall. In the corner of the ceiling to the left of it, the interrogation room's camera hung from its wire, unplugged.

On the screen, a recording of one of the many JZI feeds taken from the MSST helicopter showed a clear shot of me standing on the deck while Faye ran through the rain toward me. I watched as Faye grabbed my jacket then tiptoed up to kiss me on the mouth. With the revivor's black lips pressed against mine, Alice froze the frame.

"You want to explain that?" she asked.

"Believe me, I wish I could."

I'd thought a lot about that incident since we'd lifted off and the boat sank below us. If I was dosed with truth serum, which could happen before the debriefing was over, I might admit that I couldn't stop thinking about it. Faye's lips were smooth and dry. When she flicked her tongue between my teeth for that one second, it felt cool against mine. The body armor saved me from the shots she'd fired, but I still wasn't sure if she'd intended to kill me or not. When she'd said 'this is for the best,' did she mean my death, or Fawkes's escape?

"That revivor has been identified as Faye Dasalia. Do you know that name?"

"You know I do."

"Then you also remember going through illegal channels to have her body delivered to a secret location inside the city where you personally revived her."

I nodded.

"You stated at that time that this revivor was destroyed in the factory fire."

"I said it was most likely destroyed in the fire."

"When, in fact, you knew damn well it had not been."

"I didn't know that." If she decided to take the gloves off, it would come out that I'd tried to find her since she'd disappeared. That wouldn't look good.

Alice took a seat next to me and leaned close. She stared into my eyes, and I watched that dark blind spot drift across her face.

"Don't wait for me to try it," she said in a low voice. "I know it won't work."

"Cards right on the table, huh?"

"Look," she said. "Sean is dead. I know you'd learned his little secret, and I know that, in spite of that, you still trusted him, and even liked him. I'm taking over his responsibilities, and you're going to be working with me now. How that goes is going to be partly up to you."

"Sean had my back. He wasn't my shadow."

"He watched out for you," she said. "That's all he ever tried to do. I can do the same thing."

"I don't need a chaperone." She smiled.

"Think of me as your wingman," she said. "The partner you're inevitably going to get assigned? Think of him as your shadow."

"I won't partner with someone I know is reporting on me."

"Then you're free to quit," she said. "Leave the bureau. But I'll promise you this—certain people think you're significant, and we'll be keeping an eye on you, if we have to lock you away somewhere to do it."

I stared at the screen and the image of Faye with her lips on mine. Alice was serious. I had no doubts about that.

"This is bigger than you," she continued. "You can't

hide from us. We already know what you eat for breakfast, so it's a safe bet we know about your old girlfriend, and that secret deal Fawkes tried to make with you."

"I never considered that offer."

"The way I see it, you've got three options: you can trust that we know what we're doing and that stopping Fawkes is the right thing, you can trust that Fawkes is right and team up with him, or you can try to just check out—leave the bureau and walk away. Only one of those options is going to result in you walking around a free man."

She wasn't bluffing. If she wanted to, she could have me detained and held indefinitely. But I didn't think that was her plan.

"What's it going to be?" she asked. "You know how Fawkes wanted this to play out. If you won't trust us, can we at least agree that his way can't happen?"

"We can agree on that, yes."

"Are you sure?"

I nodded.

"We didn't stop him," I said.

"I know."

"The rest of the nukes and his army might have been destroyed along with that ship, but he still has one card left to play."

"Project Huma," she said. "I know."

When I'd used the device MacReady had Bhadra smuggle to me, I'd picked up hundreds of nodes. They hadn't been activated yet, but for them to be useful to Fawkes, he must have some way to kill them and bring them back quickly.

"The attack on Concrete Falls was two months ago, and already he's injected close to six hundred people," I said. "If it works the way it's supposed to, that's six hundred revivors he could have inside the city, under his command, at any time."

She nodded.

"He won't use Second Chance as a front again, but he'll set up his operation somewhere else," I said. "Every day that goes by, he'll add more to his ranks."

"You're with us, then?"

"Yes."

She tossed the remote down on the table between us, then sat on the edge. She looked down at me.

"This footage is going to go away," she said. "It's going away, because if it doesn't, you could have fresh charges brought against you and be placed under an internal investigation. We need you free to act."

She looked a little bit relieved. They needed me, or thought they did. I saw it on Ai's face in the restaurant when she tried to control me and couldn't. Even before she told me she'd seen me kill Fawkes, there was something in her eye. I didn't get what it was at the time, but now I thought maybe it was hope.

You kill Fawkes.

"I'm an agent of the FBI," I said. "I work for them, not her."

"Agreed," she said, "but we're pulling out the stops on this one. You'll get everything you need to help track them, and Fawkes, down. We have a long reach, Agent, and we plan to use it. That means control of the city, including local law enforcement and the media. We'll bring on Stillwell Corps to help cover the ground we need to cover."

She was expecting an argument, but she didn't get one. The truth was that even with those steps, finding the people who'd been injected was going to be difficult at best. They were third-tier citizens, and most of them were homeless, transient, or undocumented. Even for those who had a valid identification or address, the clinics that processed them had been destroyed along with their records. They were scattered over a huge area, and six hundred, even six thousand, was a drop in a very big bucket.

"I'll help you," I said. "You find the carriers, and I'll track down Fawkes. This won't end until he's stopped."

Alice nodded. I stood up, and she stood to face me. She held out her hand, and there was a look in her eye, a blind certainty that bothered me. Fanaticism was dangerous. With Fawkes creating new soldiers at a rate of six hundred a month, though, things could get out of hand quickly. There were literally millions of third-tier citizens scattered throughout the city. If he was allowed the resources and the time to make all of those millions rise, there would be no way for anyone to stop them.

I shook her hand, and she smiled faintly.

"You're doing the right thing," she said, and all I could think of was the way Motoko had looked at me from across the table the night we met. I remembered how sure she was when she said I would join them, like it was beyond anyone's control.

Even mine.

ABOUT THE AUTHOR

James Knapp grew up in New England and currently lives in Massachusetts with his wife, Kim. He is at work on the next revivors novel. Visit him at www.zombie0.com.